CH01022278

Fredric Brown (1906-1972) began se
During a career that lasted nearly thi
lished 150 short stories and thirty suspense, mystery, and
science fiction novels. *The Fabulous Clipjoint* (1947)
received a Mystery Writers of America Best First Novel
Edgar, and was followed by such other successes as *The
Screaming Mimi* and *Night of the Jabberwock*. His fresh plot
concepts and narrative techniques made him one of the
most innovative storytellers of his generation.

A full-time professional writer since 1969, Bill Pronzini
has published sixty-six novels, including three in collaboration with his wife, novelist Marcia Muller, and 30 in
his popular "Nameless Detective" series. He is also the
author of four nonfiction books, nineteen collections of
short stories, and scores of uncollected stories, articles,
essays, and book reviews; and he has edited or coedited
numerous anthologies.

Here Comes a Candle

FREDRIC BROWN

Here Comes a Candle

INTRODUCTION BY BILL PRONZINI

MILLIPEDE PRESS

LAKEWOOD, COLORADO

This is a Millipede Press Book
Published by Millipede Press
2565 Teller Court, Lakewood, Colorado 80214

Copyright © 1950 by Fredric Brown
Copyright renewed 1978 by the Estate of Fredric Brown
First published in 1950 by E.P. Dutton.

"The Joke" copyright © 1961 by Fredric Brown
Copyright renewed 1989 by the Estate of Fredric Brown
"The Joke" originally published as "If Looks Could Kill,"
in Detective Tales, October 1948.

"It's Only Everything" © 1989 by the Estate of Fredric Brown
"It's Only Everything" first published in Galiard, 836, April, 1965.

Introduction copyright © 2006 by Bill Pronzini
All rights reserved.

ISBN 1-933618-04-3 (pbk.: alk. paper)
ISBN 1-933618-05-1 (hc.: alk. paper)

Printed in Canada on acid-free paper.
10 9 8 7 6 5 4 3 2 1

September 2006
www.millipedepress.com

Contents

Introduction by Bill Pronzini 3

Here Comes a Candle 17

The Joke 281

It's Only Everything 293

Here Comes Fredric Brown

Fredric Brown's view of the world, of the entire universe, is paradoxical and slightly cockeyed. In his eyes, things are not always what they seem; elements of the bizarre and the commonplace intermix and are often in a state of flux. Madness and sanity, malevolence and benignity, tragedy and comedy, rationality and irrationality are all intertwined, so that it is often difficult to tell which is which.

He seems to have felt that the forces, cosmic or otherwise, which control our lives are at best mischievous and at worst malign; that man has little to say about his own destiny, and that free will is a fallacy. The joke is on us, he seems to be saying, and it is a joke that all too frequently turns nasty.

The characters that populate Brown's crime and science fiction reflect this paradoxical vision. Many are misfits of one type or another — madmen, dipsomaniacs, socially

3

and mentally retarded individuals, oddball writers and artists, sideshow performers, people with physical handicaps, people with phobias. Some prefer to live in fantasy worlds, as did Brown himself with his fiction, because the real world is too painful to endure. Perhaps the underlying source of his worldview is his "ardent atheism." In his brief essay, "It's Only Everything," first published in a fan magazine in 1965 and included in these pages, he wrote that he was "unable to understand... people, my contemporaries and predecessors, who give or gave lip service to the special divinity of Christ and the worship of God and who do or did spend less than their full time and effort and thought in carrying his gospel to the ends of the Earth – and to the rest of the universe, whenever we get there." Yet he admired St Francis of Assisi and Jesus of Nazareth "and whirling dervishes and anybody else who goeth whole hog with the courage of his convictions. I may not like him, but I understand him. I cannot and never will understand, and hereby spit in the eye of, any passive believer in a revealed religion who gives less than his whole life and thought to what, if it be true, is a matter of such personal and cosmic import that nothing else is worth a thinker's damn."

Fredric Brown had the courage of his convictions. Those convictions are evident in each and every one of his works of fiction. For he was much more than an atheist and a cynical idealist who dwelt in paradox; he was a dreamer, a visionary, and a writer of consummate skill – one of the most innovative genre writers of his time.

In most of his work he utilized a deceptively simple and offhand style that allows his fiction to be enjoyed by those interested only in entertainment and also pondered by those interested in the complex themes at its heart. He

4

invented several ingenious new ways to tell his stories, several of which he used in *Here Comes a Candle*. He introduced dazzling, sometimes outrageous, sometimes delightfully preposterous plot devices, apparently for the artistic satisfaction of developing them into salable stories. He was a master of the mordant short-short, having written dozens over the span of his career. His interest in psychology, particularly abnormal psychology, and his understanding of human behavior and motivations, imbues his characters with a reality not often found in the genre fiction of his day. None of Brown's villains is totally evil; many, in fact, are pathetically tragic figures. None of his protagonists is a superhero — or, for that matter, an antihero. All have weaknesses of one sort or another, a few have serious character flaws. Most are tipplers, as Brown himself was — men who require a mild alcoholic haze in order to function under the chaotic pressures of everyday society. (Brown's fiction is saturated with alcohol: characters spend pages upon pages consuming it, sometimes in staggering quantities. In *Night of the Jabberwock*, the middle-aged narrator, newspaperman Doc Stoeger, consumes enough liquor over the course of a single night to land the average person in the hospital with alcohol poisoning; yet Stoeger suffers no ill effects beyond a mild hangover.)

He was a man who saw the humorous side of things, who loved outrageous puns and often used them as the bases for his short-shorts. Humor plays an important role in much of his fiction, tempering its grimmer aspects; but seldom is it contrived or pointless. Comic relief was never Brown's intention. His humor is wry, caustic even at its most ribald — laughter with plenty of teeth in it, and with tragedy lurking darkly at its perimeters.

Personally, he was a garrulous sort who enjoyed the

5

company of people in general and other writers in particular; but he was also a loner who, in addition to his writing, spent considerable time painting in watercolors and playing the flute. He often worked out the plots for his stories and novels by taking long, solitary bus trips "to nowhere and back." Despite being "diminutive in stature, fine-boned, with delicate features partially obscured by horn-rimmed glasses and a wispy mustache" – a description provided by his friend and fellow writer Robert Bloch in an introduction to *Paradox Lost*, a posthumous collection of Brown's best science fiction and fantasy stories – Brown had a legendary capacity for alcohol, and a fondness for chess and all-night poker games. He was "impelled by intellectual curiosity...an omnivorous and discerning reader whose interests embraced music, the theater, and the developments of science...Words were his natural weapons, and his pun mightier than the word... Wordplay was more than a pastime, for he was a grammatical purist. The *mot juste* and the double entendre were grist for his mill, but he was equally fascinated by the peculiarities of ordinary speech and could reproduce it in his work with reportorial accuracy."

Fredric Brown was a man of many parts, those we know about and others about which we can only guess. Like his fiction, he was a paradox – a paradox, *un*like his fiction, now forever lost.

Here Comes a Candle is Brown at his most experimental and audacious – a novel that, in many respects, was well ahead of its time. It was first published in 1950, the second of three Brown titles to appear from E.P. Dutton & Company that year. (The other two were an Ed and Am Hunter mystery, *Compliments of a Fiend,* and the wildly frenetic *Night of the Jabberwock.*) Internal evidence suggests that it was begun by Brown two years earlier, at or near the date – August 26, 1948 – that the narrative commences. Reviews were mixed. Some critics of the day seemed bemused by its unconventional novelistic approach; others applauded it as unique and daring. One point on which all agreed: no other novel quite like it, in or out of the crime fiction field, had been written before. Nor has any quite like it been done since.

Set in Milwaukee, where Brown had lived for many years, it is the story of Joe Bailey, age nineteen – who grew up in poverty in Chicago and who has vowed to make something of himself no matter what it takes. There are two sides to Bailey in constant conflict. One is a well-intentioned young man with a passion for science fiction and a need for love and stability; the other is a numbers runner for a tough racketeer named Mitch who is drawn to the potential gains of a life of crime. His best friend, Ray Lorgan, a gloomy but well-meaning Marxist and fellow s-f fan, continually urges him to think and act as a rational adult rather than a wannabe "two-bit gangster." Mitch, meanwhile, in concert with a Chicago hoodlum named Dixie, the owner of "a harem of guns," works to turn Bailey into a full-fledged, gun-toting thug.

Although Bailey doesn't know it at the time, his life reaches a crossroads on August 26, 1948. On that day he meets two women who will play vital roles in determining which direction he takes – Ellie, a waitress, the embodiment of all that is good and wholesome, and Francy, Mitch's current girlfriend, who represents excitement, danger, all the fruits of a criminal life, and with whom he becomes sexually obsessed. The conflict between Bailey's feelings for the two women, and between the warring halves of his nature, form the basic plotline.

The story is familiar enough, if neatly handled. It is two other factors that lift *Here Comes a Candle* above the average suspense novel of its day.

One is its psychological complexity. Joe Bailey is a haunted young man, beset by fears, nightmares, childhood traumas. He is afraid of many things: Mitch, Dixie, poverty, tying himself down to marriage and a time clock, not getting anywhere, atom bombs, needing a gun to get a crust of bread, the belief that he caused the death of his father when he was six years old. His greatest terror of all is of candles and axes—a phobia that stems from a couplet in a nursery rhyme read to him by an uncle when he was three and a half:

Here comes a candle to light you to bed
And here comes a chopper to chop off your head

That couplet, with its dark and fearful images, is the core cause of his childhood traumas and his nightmares, and forms a chilling leitmotif that runs throughout the novel.

It is the second factor that makes *Here Comes a Candle* a tour de force: the array of narrative techniques Brown employs to tell Joe Bailey's story. There is the chatty, author omniscient, semi-documentary style of the opening pages. There is straightforward third-person narration. There are italicized scenes told in the second-person, present tense. And there are six chapters portraying defining moments in Bailey's life, past and present, written as a radio play, a film, a sportscast, an early TV video, a stage play, and a newspaper article. Not all of these stylistic pyrotechnics work well—the sportscast seems particularly labored in its attempt to achieve the desired effect—and

8

the sheer number of them give the novel a fragmentary quality rather than providing a well-integrated whole. Nonetheless, Brown's inventive virtuosity is redoubtable, and the pacing and character development are such that the reader is carried swiftly along to the savagely ironic ending.

Born in Cincinnati on October 29, 1906, Fredric Brown was an only child whose mother and father died within a year of each other in 1920-21. During that decade he worked as an office boy for a firm of jobbers of machine tool supplies, and later attended both Hanover College in Indiana and Cincinnati University, where he nurtured an interest in classic literature – in particular the works of Lewis Carroll, which figure prominently in his fiction.

After his first marriage in 1929, he moved to Milwaukee and worked as a proofreader for a printer of trade papers and subsequently for the *Milwaukee Journal*. Although he had begun writing in college, and had privately published two small editions of poetry in 1932, it was not until the middle of that decade that he turned his hand to popular fiction and not until 1938 that he sold his first short story, "The Moon for a Nickel," to *Street & Smith's Detective Story Magazine*.

This first taste of success encouraged Brown to increase his output and he was soon selling regularly to a wide variety of pulp magazine markets – crime stories to *Clues, Detective Fiction Weekly, Detective Tales, Dime Mystery, Phantom Detective, The Shadow, Strange Detective Mysteries, Ten Detective Aces, Thrilling Mystery*; science fiction and fantasy tales to *Astounding, Captain Future, Planet Stories, Thrilling Wonder, Unknown, Weird Tales*; even a pair of westerns to *Western Short Stories*. By 1948, his success in

9

the pulp marketplace—coupled with that of the novels he began to publish in 1947—enabled him to devote his full time to writing.

He continued to sell to the pulps until their demise in the early fifties, in all publishing more than 150 stories in that voracious medium. His professed first loves were fantasy and science fiction, yet the bulk of his output was in the mystery and detective field: upwards of 100 stories. Almost thirty of these were reprinted in his two hardcover mystery collections, *Mostly Murder* (1953) and *The Shaggy Dog and Other Stories* (1963). (From 1984 to 1991, Dennis McMillan published 19 limited edition Fredric Brown collections which include all of his criminous tales and several obscure stories originally published in science fiction and "little" magazines and in fan publications. These bear such evocative titles as *Homicide Sanitarium, Red Is the Hue of Hell,* and *Sex Life on the Planet Mars.*)

Brown's first novel, *The Fabulous Clipjoint* (1947), introduced the Chicago-based detective team of Ed and Am Hunter. Ed, the series narrator, is young and idealistic; Ambrose, his uncle and a retired circus performer, is both pragmatic and somewhat jaded—the voice of experience, the loudest of Brown's own voices. This novel, the first of seven featuring the Hunter team, was the author's personal favorite and is a forerunner in its complex plot and theme of much of his later work. Some critics were put off by its grimness, its sleazy carnival background; even Anthony Boucher, the gentlest of all mystery critics and an admirer of Brown's work, found it "sordidly compelling." Brown's peers, the members of the (then newly formed) Mystery Writers of America, had a much more favorable reaction, voting it an Edgar as Best First Mystery Novel of its year. Whatever one feels about the material, the novel's power is undeniable.

Arguably, the most accomplished of Brown's 22 criminous novels are *The Screaming Mimi* (1949), *The Far Cry* (1951), and *Knock Three-One-Two* (1959) – all stand-alones. *Mimi* is the story of an alcoholic Chicago reporter named Sweeney and his search for both a beautiful woman and a ripper-style killer; it is also an allegorical retelling of "The Beauty and the Beast," in which both beauty and beast succumb to evil. Its climactic chapter is one of the most harrowing in all of suspense fiction, rivaling Cornell Woolrich at his most intense. Set in New Mexico, *The Far Cry,* like *Here Comes a Candle,* is a tour de force. Its theme of a love/hate obsession is uniquely handled and its denouement is horrific and surprisingly bleak for its time. *Knock Three-One-Two* concerns, among other individuals, a salesman addicted to gambling, a Greek restaurateur, a mentally retarded news vendor, and a maniacal killer. From the novel's opening sentence – "He had a name, but it doesn't matter; call him the *psycho*" – to its shocking climax, this is Brown at his most controlled, dealing with material at its most chaotic.

Divorced in 1947, Brown moved to New York the following year to work for a pulp magazine chain, a job that failed to materialize because of a misunderstanding about the salary he was to be paid. He stayed on to write full time, and late in 1948 met and married his second wife, Elizabeth Charlier. The couple moved to Taos, New Mexico, in 1949, then to Venice, California, three years later, and finally to Tucson, Arizona in 1954. It was during this period, and throughout the 1950s, that Brown was at his most productive. Between 1947 and 1960 he wrote 24 of his 28 novels and scores of short stories published in the pulps, in the digest category magazines of the period, and in such slick men's magazines as *Playboy, Dude,* and *Gent.*

The Browns lived in Tucson for eighteen years, until his death from emphysema on March 12, 1972, at the age of 65. He did little creative work during the last dozen years of his life, and none at all for the final eight. His last novel, *Mrs Murphy's Underpants,* one of the weaker Ed and Am Hunter mysteries, was published in 1963. His last original fiction, a fantasy story in collaboration with Carl Onspaugh, "Eine Kleine Nachtmusik," appeared in *The Magazine of Fantasy & Science Fiction* in 1965.

During his lifetime, Brown received considerable approbation from aficionados and knowledgable critics of mystery and science fiction. And no less a personage than novelist Ayn Rand called him "one of today's Romanticists" in her 1969 book, *The Romantic Manifesto.* General readers and reviewers, however, were not always so approving; as was the case with *Here Comes a Candle,* many seemed to find his work bewildering, oddball, unsettling because it would not fit into comfortable category niches. His novels did not sell very well in hardcover, and with a few exceptions, fared but adequately in their various paperback editions.

No major films were adapted from his work. Indeed, only one of his novels was brought to the screen during his lifetime – *The Screaming Mimi,* a pallid 1957 B-grade adaptation starring Anita Ekberg and Philip Carey. One other novel, *Martians, Go Home* (1955), a sardonic science fiction fable, was filmed in 1990 starring Randy Quaid; instead of remaining faithful to the novel, it was played for cheap laughs and was widely panned. Brown's pulp story, "Madman's Holiday," provided the basis for part of one other feature film, the 1946 Pat O'Brien vehicle, *Crack Up.* Several Brown novels were posthumously adapted to the screen in Italy, France, and Hungary. The best of these was a second, much superior version of *The Screaming Mimi* co-written and directed by the noted Italian filmmaker, Dario Argento, and featuring Tony Musante and Suzy Kendall. Released in 1970, *L'uccello dalle piume di cristallo*, (*The Bird with the Crystal Plummage*) was a critical success but unfortunately had little exposure in this country.

Television has been a steady medium for the adaptation of Brown's short fiction, both before and after his death. More than a dozen of his stories were made into episodes of such shows as *Four Star Playhouse, Studio 57, Alfred Hitchcock Presents, The G.E. Theater, Outer Limits,* and *Star Trek.*

Only in recent years has Brown received the widespread critical attention his work deserves, and it is only in recent years that his popularity, owing in part to Dennis McMillan's limited editions set and reissues such as this one, has increased among collectors and general readers. It is as if the world of the forties, fifties, even sixties was not quite ready for Brown's wry, cockeyed, often dark paradoxes, whereas the world of the new millenium is perfectly suited to his views. In many ways Fredric Brown is the perfect writer for our times — a cynical idealist who always gave a thinker's damn.

Bill Pronzini

Here Comes a Candle

The Story

1

His name was Joe Bailey and the start of what happened to him was on a midsummer night in 1929 in a flat on Dearborn Street in Chicago, when he was pushed and pulled, head-first, from a snug, warm, moist place where he had been quite content. He did not ask, you must understand, to be removed from that happy haven. For that matter, he had not asked to be put there, nor would he have been had not two people named Alvin and Florence Bailey become a bit too drunk, one October night of the year before, to remember rudimentary precautions.

Anyway, you can't blame Joe Bailey for either of those events. He was not consulted, either upon the night of his birth or upon the night nine months before when the seed was so inadvertently planted.

He was six when Al Bailey died, killed in the holdup of a theater. He was seven when his mother moved with him to Milwaukee, Wisconsin, and took a job as a waitress there.

He was eighteen, just starting his fourth year of high

school, when his mother died. Joe had already been working on the side, for a man named Mitch, so he quit school and worked for Mitch full time instead. Did pretty well, until the heat went on.

And that, in a general sort of way, is everything that had happened to Joe Bailey, up to August 26, 1948. That's as good a starting place as any. It's the day Joe met the girl he was going to kill.

Let's take it from there.

2

Maybe it would be well for us to meet the day itself, first. Do you remember August 26, 1948? Were you, by any chance, in Milwaukee on that day?

It was a Thursday. It was hot. The temperature reached 94 degrees at 3:00 p.m., the same high as the day before, but Thursday was worse for it was more humid. Two more deaths from the heat brought the total to seven.

But some must have liked it hotter. A man named Lander was fined ten dollars by Civil Judge Wedemeyer for having set fire to a mattress by smoking in bed. Smoking in bed is illegal in Milwaukee. And fatalities mounted to four as the result of a flash fire in a bowling alley at Okauchee.

It was the day German Communists seized the Berlin city hall and set up a rump administration, but most of Milwaukee was more interested in the weather, which was closer.

The heat was still on in the numbers racket, too. That heat had started thirty-seven days before and still showed no sign of letting up. It had started on July 18th when the *Milwaukee Journal* blew the lid off the policy racket in the

Sixth Ward—the Negro district—and had started a sensational exposé of unduly intimate relations between the police and one Smoky Gooden, alleged to be payoff man for the policy wheels. Brought to light, in print, was the embarrassing fact that, in the neighborhood thereof, the little tobacco shop run by Smoky was known familiarly as the Sixth Ward Detective Bureau. Apparently with reason. The *Journal*, in preparing for the exposé, had parked a truck containing a camera across the street from Smoky's, and had taken pictures—a series of photographs of policemen and detectives entering and leaving the shop. Leaving, in most cases, with happy smiles on their faces.

And the *Journal* had facts and figures; they told exactly how many policy wheels were operating in the ward—there were eleven—and who operated them and where. They printed facsimiles of state income tax returns.

The police wriggled, with outraged innocence, upon the hook, and a John Doe investigation was instigated.

All good clean fun, of course, and in the long run no one was hurt very badly—such things nearly always end, eventually, in a whitewash—but the heat went on all over town and stayed on. The Negro district policy wheels were peanuts compared to the doings of the big operators like Mitch, but the heat covered all. No one knew what the *Journal* was going to expose next.

Yes, the heat was still on in more ways than one on August 26, 1948. Despite it, the Boston Store was advertising all-wool fur-trimmed coats at only $48, tax free, in claret wine, gray, green and black, sizes 10 to 20 — 38 to 44. And presenting a marionette show of *Alice in Wonderland* at no admission charge four times daily.

At the Alhambra Theater, cooled by air conditioning, *Life With Father*—Now! At Regular Prices!—was playing;

co-feature, *Police Reporter.* You could have *A Date with Judy* at the Towne, or at the Telenews you could see: BABE RUTH DIES! RED TEACHER LEAPS FROM CONSULATE! MATADOR GORED IN BULL FIGHT! Surely you remember August 26, 1948. It was the day Li'l Abner was thrown bodily from a high cliff to land (fortunately, on his head) in the Valley of the Shmoo. *Now* do you remember?

3

All right, that's the date; you've got it now. And it's ten o'clock, early in the morning. Early for Joe Bailey, anyway, because he didn't get to sleep until half past two last night. Oh, he got home a little before twelve—if you can call a furnished room on Wells Street home—but he wasn't sleepy and he got started reading a science fiction magazine, the September issue of *Startling Stories.* He got interested in the lead novel and finished it before he turned in. He went to sleep thinking of bug-eyed monsters from far Arcturus and unbelievably beautiful Earth-girls riding spaceships and wearing unbelievably abbreviated costumes.

He'd even dreamed about them for a while, but before dawn the old dream—the *bad* one—had come back. Nothing like as fearfully as it had used to come, making him sit up in bed and scream until someone shook him awake and said soothingly, "Now, Joey." And that was lucky because for a long time now, ten months, there hadn't been anyone to shake him awake and to say, "Now, Joey," to help him back to a real world that wasn't candle-lighted, ax-infested, nightmare-horrible. Yes, it was well, very well, that his mother, while she was still living, had taken him to a psychiatrist — a psychologist, really, because psychiatrists are too few and too expensive — and got him straightened out on that nightmare business. He hadn't had a nightmare since, not a real one.

Dreams, occasionally, but they didn't wake him up and he seldom remembered them. And what you don't know doesn't hurt you. Or does it? A dentist puts you under gas and pulls a tooth; you come out of anesthesia and you have no memory of pain. But can you be sure you didn't feel it at the time? Somewhere? Somehow? Did the gas kill the pain or only the memory of the pain? *Can* things you don't know hurt you? But we digress.

His name is Joe Bailey, and he's waking up now.

It's a good time to meet him, because his defenses are down. For one thing, he's naked. He's been sleeping that way since he's been rooming alone, and why not? It's more comfortable and it saves laundry bills. As a kid, of course, they'd made him wear pajamas. More lately, but before his mother died, he'd compromised on sleeping in shorts. Now there's no reason even for that. True, he has to put on a bathrobe to go down the hall to the bathroom, but he'd have to do that anyway, even if he wore pajamas or shorts. There are female roomers here as well as male.

No, there's no reason now why he shouldn't sleep raw if he wants to. Just last evening the matter had come up, in connection with talking about how hellish it was to sleep in a heat wave like this one, and he'd told his friend Ray Lorgan "There are two times I don't like to wear pajamas — when I'm sleeping alone or when I'm sleeping *with* somebody." Joe was bragging, though; he hadn't slept with anyone yet. Oh, I don't mean that, at nineteen, he hadn't had girls. But the few affairs he'd had had been consummated under less favorable circumstances. Twice, to be specific, in a parked car and once in Washington Park. He didn't yet know—although he thought, erroneously, that he could guess—how wonderful it can be with one's shoes off. But again we digress, and farther.

He's waking now, in a hot room in which no air stirs. At two-thirty o'clock he had pulled a single sheet up over him but it's gone now, on the floor. By nine o'clock, an hour ago, the sheet had become unbearable. The under sheet between him and the mattress pad is damp in spots and beaded perspiration glistens on his naked body. He lies, at the moment, upon his side and doubled up, his knees within a foot of his chest.

His body, well formed and moderately hairy, looks a bit older than the nineteen years we know it to be. Seeing him so, you'd guess twenty-one at least, perhaps as high as twenty-three or -four. And when he dresses, as he shortly will, you'll still take him for at least that, possibly a year or two more if you are not a good judge of ages. Partly because, since he has been on his own, he has made it a point to dress like a man rather than like a youth. But more because he has made it a point to cultivate a certain hardness in his eyes. Like Mitch's. Someday, he has decided, he's going to have as much money and as much power as Mitch has. The way to do that, obviously, is to *be* like Mitch. It's difficult, sometimes, but he tries.

If you step to the side of the bed now, though, and look at his face as it is relaxed in sleep or in waking, you'll know that he's nineteen, despite the faint blue beard that has sprouted overnight and that he'll shave off shortly after he gets up. His hair is dark brown, almost black, and it's stringy now with perspiration and strands of it cling damply to his forehead. It would be more comfortable worn shorter, but he has learned that a crew cut makes him look his age, not a good thing in the work he's doing – or *was* doing until a month ago – for Mitch. Right now he didn't know exactly *what* he was doing, but Mitch kept him going.

His face is moderately handsome – surprisingly, considering his ambitions at the moment, in a sensitive sort of way. His eyes – he's opening them now – are dark. They'll be intelligent eyes when he gets awake enough to have intelligence behind them.

He reaches up and pushes the damp hair back from his forehead and then, eyes open now, rolls over onto his back and stares up at the ceiling. Don't let what you notice now startle you. It is natural for men, especially young men, to awaken so.

But realization made him sit up quickly and swing his legs over the side of the bed away from the window. The shade wasn't all the way down and while he was not unduly modest he had a normal quota of self-consciousness. He sat on the side of the bed for a moment and tried to rub his eyes with the backs of his hands. But they were wet with perspiration and he picked up a corner of the loosened sheet instead. He might as well get up now, he knew; he'd never manage to get back to sleep in heat like this.

After a moment he stood up and went for his bathrobe. He gathered his shaving equipment and a towel and went out into the hallway to the bathroom. A nice thing about keeping irregular hours was that he didn't run into the usual early morning competition for the bath. Most of the other roomers had regular jobs, got up early, and would be gone by now.

But when he tried the door it was locked. Either that or

stuck; it stuck sometimes. Jamming his shoulder against it would push it open if it was stuck but he didn't want to try that unless he was sure no one was inside. Maybe one of the other roomers was sick and had stayed home, or it could be that the landlady, Mrs Gettleman, had gone in there while she was upstairs straightening rooms.

So he tapped lightly on the door and called out, "Anyone in there?"

It was a woman's voice, and not Mrs Gettleman's, that called back, "Be out in just a minute."

Joe couldn't place the voice. He leaned back against the wall opposite the door and waited. It was less than a minute, really. The door opened and, for the first time, he saw Ellie. He didn't know, naturally, that her name was Ellie. He merely knew that a girl he'd never seen before was coming out of the bathroom and that, since she was wearing a housecoat, obviously she was a new roomer. Must be in the room on the second floor that Rebecca Wilson had had; Miss Wilson, a quiet, shy woman with prematurely gray hair, who worked for the telephone company, had left the day before; she and another woman who worked with her had found, finally, a furnished apartment that they could share.

Joe Bailey said "Hello" in a friendly way. Not *too* friendly. She said "Hello" back in about the same tone of voice and walked past him and Joe went on in. His impression of her was as a rather plain girl, in fact not pretty at all, and rather thin for his liking. She had rather mousy colored hair and moderately noticeable freckles.

He locked the door and started drawing water in the tub, wishing, as he wished every hot day, that there was a shower he could use instead.

His room felt like an oven again when he got back to

it. It had hardly been worthwhile to dry himself after the bath; now he was all wet again. But he dressed carefully in a cream-colored linen suit, two-tone sport shoes and a lightweight panama hat he'd paid fifteen bucks for only six weeks ago—just a few days before the heat had gone on in the numbers game. He wished now that he'd bought a five dollar hat instead. Not that it really mattered; the ten bucks difference would have vanished weeks ago. And at least he had a fairly good wardrobe. Maybe he lived in a dump, but he could keep up a good front as far as clothes went. That was important, just like it was important to wear a hat; most fellows his age went hatless in summer, some of them even in winter. For that very reason wearing a hat kept you from looking like a kid, and wearing a good hat made you look like you were somebody and not just a punk.

He adjusted the hat carefully in front of the cracked mirror and then went downstairs and out onto the street. It was plenty hot outside but, except directly in the sun, it wasn't as hot as it had been in his room. There wasn't exactly a breeze, but at least the air moved, however slightly.

He wondered if he was hungry enough for breakfast yet and decided he could wait a while; if he waited a while it would be a combination breakfast and lunch and he wouldn't have to eat again until evening, not an unimportant consideration when he had only three bucks cash to last him two days.

It was too early to do anything. He strolled a couple of blocks toward town along Wells Street and dropped in at Shorty's poolroom. As he'd expected, there wasn't anybody there yet except Shorty himself. He said, "Hi, Shorty," and made a pretense of looking around as though he expected to see one of his friends. Shorty nodded.

It was cool there, much cooler than outside, with three big overhead fans going. Good place to kill a little time, especially since it would be for free. He strolled over to the cigar counter behind which Shorty sat and bought himself a pack of Chesterfields; that wasn't exactly an expenditure because he needed them anyway, or he would before the day was over. A *Milwaukee Sentinel,* the morning paper, was lying on the counter and he glanced at the headlines and then asked Shorty, "Mind if I look at this?" That was all right because the paper wasn't on sale; it was Shorty's own copy, mussed from his reading it, and obviously Shorty was through with it; he hadn't been looking at it when Joe had come in.

Shorty nodded and Joe took the paper over to one of the chairs beside the first pool table and sat down. He read the funny page first, especially Blondie and Dagwood, and then turned to the sports page. Cleveland, he learned, had walloped the Red Sox nine to one to regain the lead in the American League. He looked to see how the Chicago teams had done, and they'd lost in both leagues; both teams were still in last place and it had begun to look as though they'd both have to fight to stay even there. Joe frowned; he felt a slight proprietary interest in the Chicago teams, Cubs and White Sox both, on the slender ground that he, Joe, was *from* Chicago, even though he hadn't actually lived there for a dozen years, since he was seven. But he'd seen both the Cubs and the Sox play, one game each, during a week he'd spent with his mother visiting his uncle in Chicago, three summers ago. It gave him a sort of interest.

Milwaukee had beaten the Kansas City Blues and was in second place in the American Association, but that didn't interest him much. There were only two *big* leagues, the

26

American League and the National League; aside from them you might as well play in a sandlot with a softball.

He thought for a moment about turning to the want ad page, but he'd have a talk with Mitch about it before he decided definitely that he was going to look for a job. And the *Sentinel* didn't have as many want ads as the evening paper anyway.

He folded the paper back as it had been folded and returned it to the cigar counter. He went outside again, into the hot sunshine, and stood a minute deciding where he'd eat. Probably he'd get the most for his money at the Dinner Gong, a block back the way he'd just come. He walked there.

Now, at eleven-thirty, he had the counter to himself. A waitress, one he hadn't seen there before, came along behind the counter with a menu, but he wouldn't need that. He said, "Ham and eggs, potatoes, toast, coffee."

The girl said, "Yes, sir," and went back to give the order. He watched her, wondering why she was slightly familiar to him. He'd seen her somewhere and recently. By the time she came back with silverware and a glass of water, he had it.

He grinned at her and said, "Hello. Haven't we met somewhere?"

He could tell by her puzzled frown that she didn't place him and that she was wondering whether he was on the level or just trying to be fresh.

He helped her out. "An hour or two ago," he said. "Don't blame you for not recognizing me. My hair was mussed, I needed a shave, and my eyes were hardly open yet. Besides. you hardly glanced at me."

She smiled now, and he could see that she was relieved that he'd been on the level after all. She looked like the kind of girl who'd be embarrassed if someone got fresh with her.

She looked prettier now, with lipstick – not much of it – on her lips and with her hair combed and a little powder on her face. Not a raving beauty, but not hard on the eyes, either. And in her waitress uniform she didn't look as thin as she'd looked in that straight, severe housecoat.

She said, "Sure. I thought you looked familiar, but I didn't see how I could have met you. I just got in last night."

"From where?"

"Chicago."

"The hell," Joe said. "I'm from Chicago too." But then before she could ask any question it might be embarrassing to answer, he added quickly, "Born there, that is. Haven't been back much recently. You must be in the room Miss Wilson had."

"I don't know. The back room on the second floor."

"That's it. She moved out yesterday. Say, you sure found a job and started working quick, if you just got in from Chi last night."

"I came up to take the job. So I didn't have to look for one. Mr Dravich – Do you know him?"

Joe shook his head.

"He owns the restaurant here. He's my uncle and –"

"Oh, you mean Mike. I know him to say hello to; didn't know his last name."

"Well, he's my uncle. I'm Ellie Dravich. I didn't like Chicago – too much – and kind of wanted to get away. So I wrote and asked him if he could give me a job here and he wrote back to come right away."

"That's fine," Joe said. "Who steered you around to Mrs Gettleman's? Mike? I mean, Mr Dravich?"

"No, I just found it because there was a Furnished Room sign on the door. I came right here from the North Shore

28

Station and decided it would be handy if I could find a room right near here, and I did. My uncle's a bachelor, you see, and stays at a hotel downtown—the Tower—so I couldn't stay with him and had to find one right away."

"Well," Joe said, "I'm glad you picked Mrs G's. Maybe you won't like *her* too well, but the place is all right. For the money, anyway."

"My room's better than the one I had in Chicago. On Halsted. Say, I shouldn't, I guess, have used the bathroom up on your floor this morning, but someone was in the one on the second, the one I'm supposed to use, and I thought maybe it would be all right if I looked around for another one."

"Sure," Joe said. "Oh, and the reason I knocked wasn't to hurry you up; it's because the door sometimes sticks and I wasn't sure whether it was just stuck or if someone was in there. And I didn't want to try shoving against it if someone was."

A bell rang down at the window that opened from the restaurant into the kitchen and Ellie Dravich said, "'Scuse me," and went to the window. She came back with Joe's breakfast. From the way she carried the dishes he could see that this wasn't her first waitress job.

He said, "Forgot to introduce myself when you told me your name. It's Joe. Joe Bailey."

She smiled at him and it must have been the smile that made him say, without thinking about it, "Say, if you just got in town you must not know anybody here and you'll be getting lonesome. How'd you like to take in a movie with me tonight?"

"Why—" She hesitated, looking at him, and he could see that the hesitation was genuine; she wasn't putting on an act. "Why, I *would* like to, Joe. If you really mean it."

29

"Sure, of course I mean it. Why'd I ask you, if I didn't mean it?" That was just what he was wondering himself; now he'd have to hit Mitch for some more money and he already owed Mitch so much he was getting worried about it. "What time you get through?"

"Eight. I start at eleven and get through at eight. And I'll have eaten by that time; I get my meals here, in with the job. Say about five after eight; I'll have to change out of uniform back into a dress. But I won't have to go back to the rooming house for that; we change in and out of uniform in a room back there."

"Fine," Joe said. "Five after eight it is."

Two other customers had just come in, and now two more were coming through the door. The noon rush was starting and he knew he wouldn't be able to talk to her anymore. Well, he thought, he'd said too much already. Now he'd have to hit Mitch for at least another fin.

4

That was the morning. Call it an adagio movement. This afternoon he's going to meet another girl. Girl quite different, circumstances quite different. That's why—aside from the fact that you've got to start *somewhere*—we started with August 26, 1948. It's not too unusual to meet two girls on the same day. But when, between them, they're going to tear you apart, when you're going to kill one of them, well, it makes that day a good starting point.

Afternoon now. Except for the heat, an afternoon like any afternoon. Joe Bailey dropped into the tavern about two o'clock. Mitch wasn't in yet, but then Joe had hardly expected him to be in, that early.

The old geezer, Krasno, was behind the bar, and there weren't any customers in the place. No paying customers, that is.

The beat cop was there, talking to Krasno. The cop looked up as Joe came in, and frowned a little. Joe knew that was because of the shot of whiskey standing on the bar between Krasno and the cop; it could have been in front of either of them, except that Joe knew Krasno never drank whiskey. And the cop wasn't supposed to drink in uniform and he was probably wishing he'd downed the drink before someone came in the place. Of course if he'd known Joe worked for Mitch it would have been all right, but he didn't know that.

Joe didn't like cops; he'd have liked to sit down at the bar and turn around to face the cop and watch him until the cop either drank the whiskey openly or walked out without drinking it. But Mitch wouldn't like that; Mitch liked to keep in with the cops, even the beat coppers, although he had enough moxey to get any cop fired, or at least shifted off Clybourn Street out into the wilds of North Milwaukee if the cop got too much in his hair. And if Joe heckled the cop by watching him, old Krasno would probably tell Mitch.

So Joe walked on through the barroom and went into the can for a minute. When he came out, both the cop and the whiskey were gone. Joe sat down on a barstool and put his elbows on the bar. Krasno kept on polishing glasses but asked, "How goes it, Joe?"

"Okay, I guess. If only it'd cool off a little."

"Yeah. Ninety-two by the radio a few minutes ago. But they say it ought to break by tomorrow night. Want a beer?"

Joe shook his head. A cold beer would taste good, but

Krasno would put it down on the tab, and he had enough of a tab now. Besides what he owed Mitch otherwise.

Krasno must have read his thoughts. When he'd finished the glasses, he drew a beer and put it on the bar in front of Joe. He said, "On the house, Joe."

He studied Joe's face as Joe took a long draft of the cold beer and put it down. Joe said "Thanks" and Krasno, somewhat ambiguously, said "Sure," and then turned to stare out the window at Clybourn Street sweltering in the heat.

Then it was Joe's turn to study Krasno, and he did. He'd often, in the year or so he'd been coming into Mitch's, studied Krasno and wondered what made the old geezer tick. Krasno must be pushing seventy and at that age, Joe wondered, what did a guy want out of life, what did he live for, what did he do with his time off? Krasno had told him he didn't read, except newspapers, and he worked only eight hours a day; what did he do with the rest of his time? He'd been married once, Joe knew, but his wife had died a great many years ago; now he lived in a tiny room downtown at the Antlers Hotel. What did he do there? Wait to die? He didn't drink much — a short beer occasionally — and he didn't play cards or like movies.

There was only one thing about Krasno that was outstanding — his hair. He had a truly beautiful head of wavy pure white hair, thicker than Joe's. Had the rest of him matched that beautiful hair, he would have been distinguished looking. But the rest of him didn't match. His face was sallow; his eyes were watery and looked weak, although he didn't wear glasses; he dressed sloppily. His teeth, obviously still his own, were bad.

Joe wondered: What did Krasno live for? What made him tick? It was something to wonder about, but you can't ask something like that.

32

His gaze happened to follow Krasno's, and he saw a snazzy convertible, light blue, pull into the curb in front of the tavern. Mitch and another man, someone Joe didn't know, got out of the car and came in. Mitch first, his hat in one hand and mopping his forehead with a handkerchief held in the other. He said, "Christ, what lousy weather," and tossed his hat carelessly on the bar, as though it hadn't cost him thirty-five or forty bucks. He pushed his handkerchief back into a pocket of a white tropical worsted suit that had cost at least a hundred, plus the upkeep of a dry cleaning every time or two he wore it. He sat down on one of the stools in front of the bar, loosening the knot in his necktie as he did so.

He said, "Hi, Joe. Krazzy, make us a drink, huh? A cold one. Rye and water, lots of ice, for me. How about you, Dixie?" He glanced back over his shoulder at the man who had come in with him, and got "Sounds okay to me" for an answer.

Joe looked at the man who'd spoken. He was small, not over five feet six and couldn't weigh much over a hundred thirty-five, about half as much as Mitch weighed; Mitch was big. The small man was well, but not conspicuously, dressed and his age was anywhere around thirty. That's all Joe noticed at a casual glance.

He looked back at Mitch as Mitch said, "You, Joe?"

Joe had half his beer left and said, "Thanks, Mitch. I'll work on this."

"It's hogwash," Mitch said, "but okay if you want to drink it. Joe, this is Dixie. Dixie Ehlers. He's going to be around town a while."

Joe turned around a little more on the stool and stuck out his hand. He filled in Mitch's omission by saying, "Bailey. Joe Bailey."

He caught the small man's eyes as they shook hands, and saw what he'd missed before. Before, he'd noticed only size, age, dress. Now he saw face and eyes, both utterly expressionless, and the way the man held himself. A little wave of excitement went through Joe as he thought to himself, "Jeez, a *torpedo*. A real gunman." How he knew for sure, he didn't know, but he knew all right; the guy might as well have worn a sign.

Joe let go of Dixie's hand and turned back to the bar and to his beer. Somehow it had frightened him just a little to look into Dixie Ehlers' eyes. There was nothing there in those eyes, nothing at all. It was like looking into a pair of glass marbles—but you didn't expect marbles to look back at you with any expression, if at all.

Mitch was asking Krasno, "Any business?" Not that Mitch was really interested or even asked as though he was really interested. The tavern on Clybourn Street was a front and if it made a few bucks or lost a few bucks it didn't matter to Mitch.

Krasno was putting drinks in front of Mitch and of Dixie, who had taken the stool on the other side of Mitch. Krasno said, "Not much so far. Anybody with any sense is staying home."

Mitch drank and then nodded as he put down the glass. "Me, especially. It ain't exactly cold out at Fox Point, by the lake, but it's sure cooler than down here. If I'd had any sense I'd of stayed there. Why didn't you have sense enough to stay home, Joe?"

"Hotter in my room than here," Joe said. "Besides, I wanted to talk to you about something, Mitch."

"Need some money? How much?"

"Well—" Joe said. It embarrassed him, a little, to have Mitch ask him like that, in front of Krasno and the man

34

he'd just been introduced to. "Yeah, that. But something else, too. Could we talk a few minutes, back there?" He jerked his head toward the rear of the tavern where, off the hallway that led back to the toilets, there was a room sometimes used for card games, sometimes used as an office by Mitch, although he kept no desk or office equipment there. In fact, he kept no desk anywhere; Mitch's books were kept entirely in his head. Only suckers put figures on paper.

Mitch nodded and said, "Okay, Joe. In a minute when I finish this drink. Not in any rush, are you?"

That was a nice thing about Mitch. He didn't order you around; from the way he talked to you you'd never know that he was boss and in the bucks and you were just a punk. He treated you as though you were working with him, not for him.

Joe caught Krasno looking at him sardonically. He stared back at Krasno, trying—just for the hell of it—to put the same utterly expressionless look in his eyes that was in Dixie Ehlers'. He didn't know whether it worked or not; Krasno's expression didn't change and he didn't look away. He merely said, mildly, "Another beer, Joe?"

Joe nodded. He reached for money but Mitch said, "Forget it, Joe. On me."

Which was just as well, Joe thought, watching Krasno draw the beer. If he was going to make a break with Mitch now, a dime would be a dime until he got lined up somewhere or took a job and got a paycheck. He'd figured it out, though, and he could make it. He had only a couple of dollars and some change left, in cash, but there was quite a bit of stuff, including two watches and a ring, that he'd bought himself when the going was good, up to the time six weeks ago when the heat had gone on and Mitch had pulled in his

35

horns on the numbers. He could hock that stuff for enough to run on for a week or two, if the worst happened. And a job would be easy to get if he took anything that came along, first, and later worried about getting a good one that led somewhere.

Mitch asked him, "You free this afternoon, Joe?"

"Sure," Joe said.

"Okay. It's just to take the car out front out to my place—the Fox Point shack. Guess you'll have to come back by bus. That all right?"

"Sure," Joe said. Hell, he'd do that much for Mitch even if he was quitting. In fact, the only reason he even thought of quitting was that he wasn't earning the dough Mitch had been giving him. It had been one thing to make fifty bucks or so a week in commissions on selling baseball and football pool tickets; that was all right. But now that the heat was on, Mitch still told him to hang around. He'd been giving him enough money to keep going and a few little errands and things to do and a sales talk every once in a while about sticking around till things opened up again.

And that would have been all right if things had opened up after a few weeks, but they hadn't. The John Doe investigation of gambling in the Sixth Ward was just getting well under way, and nobody knew how long it would last.

Mitch put down his glass empty and started toward the back. He said, "Come on, Joe."

Joe followed him into the card room and Mitch sat down and put his feet up on the table. Joe sat down across from him and was thinking how to start when Mitch beat him to the punch.

Mitch said, "Joe, I know what's eating you. You think I'm stringing you along, giving you peanuts, lunch money. And you're getting tired of it. That right?"

"Not exactly, Mitch. It's—well, I can get along for a while; it's not the amount of money. But hell, I hate to take it when I'm not doing anything for it. And it looks like maybe a long time before things open up again. Why can't I take a job or something somewhere else and when you go back to operating, I can come back with you again? Without sponging on you meanwhile."

"Look, Joe, I been wanting to talk to you, to tell you something. Might as well now. But it's under your hat. Understand?"

"Sure, Mitch."

"Numbers is shot in this town, for a long time. And, Joe, I'm not going to sit on my fanny till the racket comes back. Instead, I'm going to shoot for even bigger dough. I'm going to open up a gambling joint, just outside the county. A big one, a fancy one. People are going to gamble anyway, and the tighter they close down in Milwaukee and Milwaukee County, the more of 'em are going to drive out of the county to get rid of their money. And that's where the big dough is, Joe. Not from the people that spend a quarter or a buck for a football pool ticket. The people who can afford to drop a few hundred or a few grand over a roulette wheel or a black-jack table. How does that sound to you, Joe?"

"Good. It sounds good. Have you got a place lined up?"

"Not for sure yet. I'm dickering on one. And there's a lot of stuff to arrange, protection and stuff. It might be weeks or it might be months before we're actually operating. Things like that take time and I'm going to be sure before I go ahead. But I want you in with me, Joe, and I want you to stick around till I get going."

"But gosh, Mitch—That sounds swell, but weeks or months! I hate to take money from you all that time till I start earning it again. Why can't I—"

"Joe, shut up, and listen to me. In that racket, the most important thing in the world is a guy you can trust. Someone that's loyal to you, that won't chisel on you or sell you out. What's a few bucks a week for a few months, if I can get a guy like that to go in with me? And you're a guy like that, Joe. You been with me only about a year, but long enough for me to find that out. And for sure. You're still kind of a kid, but you're ambitious—but not too ambitious. You're not going to try to cut my throat to take over—not till enough years from now that I'll have my pile and step out. And if you've stuck with me, Joe, you'll be in the chips by then."

"Gosh, Mitch—"

"Besides, Joe, you've got guts. I can tell that. I can tell by looking at a guy whether he's got guts or not. And that's the next most important thing to not chiseling or selling out. Now listen, Joe, I got money invested in you already and it's worth a few hundred more for me to have you around when I'm going to want you. So here it is on the line. I'll give you forty bucks a week till I get operating; you ought to be able to string along on that for a while. When the wheels start turning, you'll get sixty till I start showing a profit. After that—well, it'll be more. Maybe plenty more. And the forty you'll be getting for a while ain't all charity, either. I'll have some things to do even before we get rolling. Is it a deal?"

Joe said, "Hell, yes, Mitch. And thanks."

Mitch took out a thick wallet and managed to find two twenties among the bigger bills. He handed them over and said, "Okay, then, Joe. It's a deal. I'll tell you more about it later; got to run along now. Got a date to sink a floating crap game. Oh, and about the car. Here are the keys. Want you to take it out to my shack at Fox Point and leave it there."

38

"Sure. Where'll I put the keys?"

"There's a friend of mine out there. Francy. Francine. I had to use the heap to come in, but I promised I'd get it back to her before evening. So there's no rush, anytime this afternoon."

Mitch stood up and started for the door. Then he turned and was looking at Joe. Almost as though he was seeing him for the first time. He said, "Listen, Joe. No passes."

For a second Joe didn't even get him. He said, "Huh?" and then, "Hell, Mitch, what do you think I am?"

Mitch grinned. "A pretty good-looking kid. It just dawned on me. You might even make the grade. But don't try."

He turned back and went on out and Joe followed him. Mitch said, "Come on, Dixie," to the man waiting at the bar and the two of them went on out.

Since there wasn't any hurry, Joe sat back down to finish his beer. He felt swell now, after the things Mitch had told him. Even Mitch's warning about the girl was, in a way, a compliment. Not that he'd touch any woman of Mitch's with a hundred-foot pole, after all Mitch had done for him and all Mitch was doing.

Anyway, there were plenty of other women. Including—What was her name?—Ellie Dravich. Now, with forty bucks in his pocket, he was glad he'd dated her for tonight. Be handy as hell having a girl who roomed right in the same rooming house. And while she wasn't any raving beauty, still—

Old Krasno had said something, it just came to him, and he hadn't heard. He said, "Huh?"

"What'd he feed you, kid?"

He stared at Krasno, trying to figure out what the old guy was talking about. He said, "What do you mean?"

"Mitch. He's a smooth talker, kid. I'm wondering if he leveled with you. I don't think he did."

He kept staring at Krasno, wondering what he was supposed to answer to that. Sure, Mitch had leveled with him, but Mitch had told him to keep it under his hat about the gambling house, the big time. He couldn't crack to Krasno about it unless he found out that Krasno knew already.

Hell of it was that he wanted to talk about it, and Krasno—if Krasno knew already—was the only person he could talk it over with. He asked, "What do you mean you don't think he leveled?"

"Maybe I'm wrong, kid," Krasno said, "but I don't think you'd be here if he did."

There wasn't any answer in that. He still didn't know what old Krazzy was driving at, except that it sounded like he wanted to talk about Mitch behind his back, and had a wrong idea somewhere.

Anyway he'd finished his beer and what was he waiting for? He got off the stool and went to the door. Over his shoulder, he said, "Looks like you were wrong then; I'm still around. Be seeing you."

The direct sunshine outside was almost like a blow. It was three o'clock now, the hottest time of that particular day. Ninety-four was the official temperature, but it was hotter than that on Clybourn Street.

But before he got into the convertible, Joe walked once around it, admiring it. It was a beauty, in robin's-egg blue. Someday he was going to have a car like that.

He started the engine and found he could hardly hear it turning over. Before he pulled out from the curb he looked for and found the gadget that controlled the top. He worked the gadget and let the top fold itself back.

He had a momentary inclination to head east by way of

Wells Street, past the Dinner Gong; maybe the waitress he'd just dated would be looking out and see him drive by in a snazzy car. But that would be silly. Chance in a thousand she'd be looking out and see him, and if she did see him, he'd have to explain, when he showed up without it for their date, that it wasn't his car. So he cut north to Kilbourn and over Kilbourn to the drive along the lake.

Despite the sun it was cool and pleasant whizzing along the lake drive in an open-top car. A cooling breeze was beginning to come in off Lake Michigan. And the car handled like a dream; he had to keep an eye on the speedometer so he wouldn't go too fast and get a ticket. Fifty, in a car like that, seemed like twenty or thirty.

It was a good eight miles or more from Mitch's tavern on Clybourn to Mitch's summer cottage on the lake at Fox Point, and coming back by bus it would seem at least that far. It was so nice driving the convertible that he seemed to get there in nothing flat.

He turned in the driveway off North Beach Drive that led back to Mitch's place and parked the car alongside the neat four-room cottage of glazed yellow brick that Mitch called his shack and in which he spent part of his time during the summer months. A nice place, but not a patch on Mitch's apartment on Prospect Avenue.

Joe got out of the car regretfully and took the keys around to the front of the house. No one answered his ring and after a few minutes he began to wonder what he could do with the keys if Francine—whoever Francine was—wasn't there. He hated to take a chance on leaving them in the car, but he didn't know where else to leave them where she'd be sure to find them.

Then it occurred to him that quite possibly she was down at the beach. Mitch's property ran from the road back to the lake and was about a hundred and fifty feet wide, giving him a stretch of private beach at the lake end of it. It was a narrow strip along the bottom of a twenty-foot slope that ran down to the water, but part of it had the advantage of being private—a tiny cove that cut in from the lake and couldn't be seen from the beach on either side outside the borders of the property.

He strolled around the house and back to the top of the rather steep slope that descended to the cove and the beach and looked down.

At first glimpse he thought that a girl in a white bathing suit was lying on her back, sunning herself, on a spread-out terry cloth robe of dark blue. And then—it took his eyes and his mind all of a tenth of a second to readjust themselves—he saw she wasn't wearing a white bathing suit; she wore nothing at all. For a fraction of a second he'd been fooled by the contrast—a pleasing rather than a striking contrast—between the white untanned skin that would normally be covered by a bathing suit and the light golden tan of her legs and arms and shoulders. She was breathtakingly beautiful.

Joe Bailey caught his breath a little. But it must not have been audible, for she didn't move. He knew that she couldn't see him for one arm was thrown over her face to shield her eyes from the sun.

Slowly, carefully, he walked backward, his footsteps making no sound in the soft sandy soil, until he was well back from the edge of the slope. He wouldn't want her to look up and catch him standing there staring—and then tell Mitch about it.

He wished now that Mitch had mentioned the rest of her name; it seemed rude to call out a woman's first name when he'd never even met her, but there wasn't any alternative. He called, "Francine!"

Her voice sounded as he would have thought it would sound – had he thought about it. "Yes, who is it? Stay back where you are."

"Mitch sent me to bring the car and told me to give you the keys."

"Oh. Just a minute, please. I'm coming up anyway."

He waited where he was and in about two minutes she came up the slope and into his range of vision. She was carrying the blue terry cloth robe over one arm and for a breathtaking but frightening instant he thought she was naked. But this time it *was* a white bathing suit. It must have been lying beside the robe down there on the beach, but he hadn't noticed it. You can't blame him for that.

He went forward to meet her with the keys and, at the top of the slope, she took them and said, "Thanks."

"Left the car by the house," Joe said. "You can't see it from here, but I left it there." It sounded inane, even while he was saying it, but he had to say something, mostly to keep himself from staring at her. Even in a bathing suit, she was hard not to stare at. Her face, small and heart-shaped, was as beautiful as her body. Her hair was golden blonde, shoulder length, and softly wavy. She was small, only about five feet two, and her age could have been anything over eighteen, but not too many years over. Her eyes, surprisingly considering the lightness of her hair and complexion, were dark brown, almost black.

They were looking at Joe with what he thought, uncomfortably, was amusement. Then she looked down at something on the ground, looked up again at Joe, and laughed. A pleasant laugh, genuinely amused. Joe felt himself starting to redden a little, without knowing why, and then she looked down again. His eyes followed hers and he saw a neat unmistakable set of his own footprints leading up to the edge of the slope and then away from it, backwards.

He felt sudden heat in his face and neck and knew he was turning redder. He said, "I'm sorry. I didn't guess you'd be—uh—"

She managed to stop laughing. "At least you were a gentleman," she said. "You backed away before you called out. You're Joe?"

He nodded and fell in beside her as she started toward the house. She said, "Stan told me someone named Joe would bring the car back. Do you have a second name?"

He almost muffed the question because it had taken him a second to place who *Stan* was. Mitch's name was, improbably, Stanislaus Mitchell, but as far as Joe could remember he'd never heard him called by his first name.

"Bailey," he told her. "And what's yours? I felt funny calling out Francine, when I didn't even know you. But Mitch just mentioned that much of your name, so I didn't have any choice."

"Francine will do, Joe. Or better, Francy. Oh, not that the last name's any secret; it's Scott. Guess I haven't any secrets from you now, have I, Joe?"

That was dangerous territory. He said, "Francine Scott—that's a nice combination. Real?"

"The Francine is; my parents really named me that. They were French and my real last name was too fancy to use. Savigne. When I started dancing I thought *nobody'd* believe Francine Savigne was a real name, so I toned it down instead of fancying it up like most dancers have to do."

Joe said, "I guess I like Scott better. In combination with Francine, anyway." They were almost at the backdoor of the cottage. "Well, I'm glad to have met you."

"Any hurry, Joe? Drop in and have a drink. I'm going to make a cool one for myself; it's no more trouble to make two. How'd a Tom Collins go?"

"Well—" said Joe. But she was already going in and expecting him to follow. Which left him little choice if he didn't want to be rude about it. And besides, if he could lead up to it properly, it might be an idea, a damn good idea, to ask her not to mention to Mitch how he'd first seen her. Obviously it had amused Francine rather than embarrassed her—and she'd recognized that it was no fault of his. But if she told it to Mitch as a good joke, maybe Mitch wouldn't like it at all.

In the kitchen, she said, "Know how to make Toms? You could do it while I put something on."

"Afraid I can't," he admitted.

"All right. I'll be back in a minute. You can break out a tray of ice cubes meanwhile. And squeeze the juice out of a lemon and put it in two tall glasses, half in each glass."

She went into the next room, leaving the door open an inch or two. Joe went to the refrigerator and got a tray and a lemon and while he was at it—he did know that much about a Tom Collins—a bottle of soda. By the time he had the lemon squeezed into the glasses, Francine was back. She wore a white linen playsuit that covered very little more territory than the bathing suit had covered, and a pair of sandals. She'd run a comb through her blonde hair, making it even softer and wavier.

Arms akimbo, she watched what he was doing. "Fine," she told him. "Might as well complete your education, Joe Bailey, by letting you do it. Now put a teaspoon of sugar in each glass and dissolve it in the lemon. Then two ice cubes in each, and a jigger of gin—a jigger plus, if you want to do a good job of it. Then stir each one while you're pouring in

45

the soda. And then you'll know how to make a Tom Collins and you're one step nearer being grown up. How old are you, Joe?"

He grinned at her over his shoulder and said, "I don't know. My mother never told me."

He was deciding that he liked Francine, even with her clothes on. Damn it, why did she have to be Mitch's? Hell, not that a girl like her would give him a tumble. A kid like him with only forty bucks a week, if for no other reason. Take out a girl like Francine and you'd have to spend more than that in one evening, probably. But maybe in a few years, if he stuck with Mitch, he'd be making enough money to do things like that. After what Mitch had told him this afternoon—

As he finished making the drinks, Francine came over and picked one of them up for an experimental sip. "Good boy," she said. "You bring that one and come on in the living room. I hate kitchens."

He followed her into the front room and she curled up in a corner of the sofa, tucking her feet under her. Maybe he was expected to sit on the sofa too, but he didn't take a chance on that. He took a chair facing her, instead, and tried to keep his eyes and his mind off her legs. They were very beautiful legs, with just the faintest golden down that made them, somehow, much more sensually appealing than if it hadn't been there.

He asked, "What kind of dancing do you do? Chorus or—?"

"No, solo. But night club, not stage. I've never been on the stage." Her face was suddenly serious. "Not very good at it, I'm afraid, or—or I guess I wouldn't be here."

That was dangerous territory, too; there wasn't much you could answer, safely, to something like that. He took a

46

sip of his drink, rather wishing it was straight shot instead of a long drink, so he could down it quickly and make an excuse to get back.

Her face had done a quick change again; now she was smiling at him impishly. "What's the matter, Joe? You act like you were sitting on a thumbtack. Afraid of me?"

He laughed, and wondered if the laugh rang quite true. "No. Should I be?"

"Afraid of Stan — Mitch?" The quick change again; her face was serious, and the question had been serious.

It jolted him a little. Oh, it was easy to answer and, in a way he was glad she'd asked it; it gave him a chance to say, "I work for Mitch, Francy. Not only that, but I like him. I wouldn't cross him for a million bucks."

But the jolt had been there, in the question. He was afraid of Mitch. Implicit in the question had been a picture of Mitch angry at him, taking a poke at him. And Mitch was six feet tall and weighed at least two hundred, all of it as hard as nails, against Joe's moderately built five feet nine. Not only that, but Mitch had been in the ring for a while, way back when, maybe ten years ago. He was well over thirty now, but he still had the strength of a bull. Joe had seen him work on a guy once, a guy who wanted to get tough about a beef that he had a payoff coming on a ticket he'd obviously doctored up himself. Mitch had slapped him silly, just using the palms of his hands so as not to mark the guy, and then had picked him up bodily and carried him twenty feet to the door and tossed him out. And now Joe remembered the look on Mitch's face as Mitch had done it.

No, it had never occurred to him before that he could be afraid of Mitch — because he was loyal to Mitch and a situation where Mitch would want to do anything to him hadn't seemed possible.

But this was different. Mitch had warned him about Francine—and now, on top of the bad luck of his having discovered Francine raw, to her considerable amusement, here he was sitting drinking with her, alone in Mitch's house. And the whole situation was like walking on eggs, because it would be as dangerous to rush out as to stay. If he was too obvious about being in a hurry to get away, she might, out of pique, say something to Mitch that would give him entirely the wrong idea. Women sometimes did things like that just for the hell of it.

Worse, her question and his answer had made it completely impossible for him, now, to lead up to telling her to be careful what she said to Mitch. He couldn't say now, "Yeah, I *am* afraid of Mitch. Please don't tell him, as a joke, about how I happened to come across you." To say that now would make a complete sap out of him; it would seem like crawling.

Her glass was at her lips now and she was looking at him across the top of it. She said, seriously (or mock-seriously?), "All right, Joe, I won't worry you anymore. Relax and take your time finishing your drink and—How are you going to get back to town? Phone for a cab?"

The first part of what she'd said made him feel as transparent as a window. He averted his mind from it and concentrated on the last. He said, "No, I'll go back by bus." He started to add that he was in no hurry—to make it seem natural that he wouldn't take a cab—and then stopped in time.

She said, "I'll drive you over to the bus stop, then. Whenever you're ready."

He said, "Thanks," and then managed to keep the conversation, and his eyes and his thoughts, in safe places until he'd taken decent time to finish the drink.

He turned down an offer, not too pressing a one, of

another drink, and then she drove him in the convertible to the nearest bus stop on Lake Drive; it would have been a fairish walk otherwise, as there is no bus line on Beach Drive. She pulled in near the stop but far enough back to take advantage of the shade of a big tree, as the top of the convertible was still open. Joe stretched to look back and saw that a bus was coming, several blocks away.

He looked at Francine, her hair now badly windblown by the drive in the open car, but somehow even prettier than when it had been neatly combed. The impish look was back in her eyes again.

She said, "I *like* you, Joe. Going to kiss me goodbye?"

She saw his hesitation and laughed a little. "If you don't," she said, "I'll tell Stan that you *did.*"

Worried as he was, even Joe saw the humor in that and he laughed a little, too. He said, "In that case—"

He leaned toward her, putting a hand across to rest on the door on her side and touched her lips lightly—or he had intended it to be lightly. As one might intend to touch a pile of gunpowder lightly with a burning match. Without his even knowing how it happened, her arms were tightly around him and his around her; their bodies pressed together, their mouths together in a kiss that wasn't like any kiss he'd ever had before. He felt it all the way down to his toes.

And then the bus was coming and he was getting out of the car. He said, "Goodbye," and it sounded foolish, inadequate and utterly asinine.

She said, " 'Bye, Joey," quite seriously, and then, "Better wipe off the lipstick before you see Stan again."

The bus was swinging in at the stop and he had to run for it. He *had* to catch it, knowing he'd made a fool out of himself already and would make himself into a thousand

49

times worse one—one way or the other—if he missed that bus.

He caught it and sat down in a seat at the back, carefully not looking out either window lest he see a robin's-egg blue convertible and its occupant. He knew she'd be laughing at him. He sat there sweating, only partially because of the heat and the exertion of his short but hard run to catch the bus.

He thought, damn her, damn her, damn her. He'd never hated a woman as much in his life as he hated Francine. Or wanted a woman as badly as he wanted her.

5

The date with Ellie should have been anticlimax, but, surprisingly, it was fun. It got off to a good start by his getting to the restaurant at five after eight exactly, just as Ellie came out of the back room, having completed the change from waitress costume to street dress. Neither of them had had to wait even a second for the other.

And it was the third time he'd seen Ellie and she was a little prettier each time. Still no raving beauty, but she was much more attractive in a simple beige dress—almost a perfect match for her mousy hair—than she had been in the waitress costume. Just as the waitress getup had been an improvement over the severely tailored housecoat in which he'd first seen her.

Joe had brought a *Journal* with him so she could look at the theater ads and pick out what show she wanted to see. He'd looked them over himself and rather wanted to see an exciting jungle picture, *Man Eaters of Kumoan*, at the Warner. They sat down in a booth to look over the ads together and he had no difficulty at all in selling her on the jungle picture. Just casual mention of a slight preference did it; she said she hadn't seen a good jungle picture in a long time and she'd like it.

She vetoed the suggestion of a taxi to the theater and Joe vetoed walking – slightly over a dozen blocks – so they compromised on going by streetcar.

After the picture, which they both enjoyed, Joe took her around the corner to the Violina Room at the Kilbourn where they heard some good music and had a sandwich and a bottle of beer apiece; Ellie turned down a second bottle, but Joe had one.

They talked and he learned quite a bit about Ellie. She was eighteen and she'd been born and raised in Indianapolis. Her parents had both been killed in an auto accident when she was fifteen. She'd gone to live with an uncle and aunt in Chicago, but she hadn't liked them too well and apparently they hadn't liked her too well, either. She'd managed to stick it out with them a little over a year and she'd been on her own since then, for about two years. She'd worked as a maid in a private family for a while and then had become a waitress. She was working in a restaurant on South State Street and hadn't liked it very well; it wasn't a good neighborhood.

And since she had an uncle, Mike Dravich, who ran a restaurant in Milwaukee, she figured she might as well write him to see if he had a job open, and, as it happened, he had.

She didn't expect to be a waitress all her life; she had a little money, not much, saved up, and as soon as it got to be a little more she was going to take a business course, evenings, so she could do some kind of office work. A stenographer if possible, at least a file clerk or some sort of clerk.

51

She knew she'd have to study grammar and spelling quite a bit to be a stenographer; she'd had only two years of high school as against Joe's three. But if she once got into office work of any kind she could keep on studying evenings.

He learned that she read quite a bit, mostly novels, but that she hadn't read any science fiction, which was Joe's favorite reading. That she smoked occasionally, drank a little beer or wine occasionally, but not too much. That she liked "good" music, although she didn't really know anything about it, and liked good swing like Stan Kenton or Benny Goodman, but wasn't too crazy about most popular music and didn't swoon over Frank Sinatra. That she liked to dance once in a while, but not almost every night like a lot of girls do.

That was Ellie, what she told of herself that evening to Joe. Doesn't sound like much, but then the exterior, obvious things about most people seem pretty ordinary. Nor can you expect a girl of eighteen to have the background of a Mata Hari.

There was more, too, that Joe read between the lines and in the way they were spoken. Ellie didn't say so, but she was a nice girl. Definitely not a pushover. Long before the evening was over Joe knew that any faint idea he may have had about the two of them spending the rest of the night in one room at Mrs Gettleman's instead of two was so improbable an idea that it wouldn't be worth while suggesting it.

But he liked Ellie, and he could tell that she liked him.

For his share of the talking he told her as much as he could about Milwaukee—since she had been there only a day and knew little about it—and as little about himself as was reasonably possible. He had a pretty well founded hunch that she wouldn't like the idea of his having sold tickets in the numbers racket nor the idea of his intention of working — in just what capacity he himself didn't know as yet — in a gambling joint.

But he split the difference with her as far as telling the truth about those two things was concerned. He admitted that the only full-time job he'd held since leaving high school and up to a short while ago had been selling tickets on baseball and football pools. He explained that the heat was on in Milwaukee as far as numbers was concerned and that it would probably stay on a long time, and that he had no intention of going back to that way of making a living.

But he also told her, which was more or less true, that he wasn't doing anything at all at the moment. And he told her, which wasn't true at all, that he hadn't any serious idea what kind of work he wanted or expected to find.

Because he didn't want to worry her about the money he was spending on her — not that it was much; the whole evening was costing him only about five dollars — he managed to give the impression that he had money in the bank, saved up, and wasn't worrying about finding a job in a hurry; rather, that he was deliberately taking his time because he wanted to be sure he was getting into a kind of job that would lead him somewhere worth going.

All that, of course, added up to quite a bit of talking; it was almost one o'clock when they got back to Mrs Gettleman's. Not that that mattered, because Ellie's shift didn't start until eleven the next day, and his didn't start at anytime, although he usually dropped into the tavern by mid-afternoon to see if Mitch had anything for him to do.

At the door of Ellie's room on the second floor, she hesitated only a second before letting him kiss her good night. It occurred to him to suggest that they see another show—or dance, if she preferred—Saturday evening.

She made the countersuggestion that they make it

Sunday instead, if he had no other plans for then. Sunday was her day off; the Dinner Gong was closed on Sunday. Possibly they could go to the beach or to a park in the afternoon. That sounded good to Joe, so they set the date for two o'clock in the afternoon Sunday and decided not to decide, until then, just what they'd do.

Since there'd been that much conversation since the good night kiss and since he really was going now, Joe put his arms around her and kissed her again. And this time got a slight surprise. Oh, nothing like the amperage of that kiss Francine Scott had given him that afternoon, but then this kiss didn't have the buildup that one had had. And definitely Ellie's lips moved under his, and responded, and it was a very pleasant kiss.

Then she pushed herself away from him but stood looking at him a full second, her eyes wide and not smiling at all, before she said, "Good night, Joe," and went quickly inside and closed the door.

He almost raised his hand to knock lightly, and then thought better of it and went on upstairs to his own room.

For some reason he didn't feel like reading, as he generally did after getting to his room and before going to sleep. He got into bed and lay there thinking. He liked Ellie, but she was going to be a complication if he kept on seeing her. Rather, the lies and half-truths he'd told her would be a complication. If, within a month or so, he was working for Mitch at a gambling joint, he couldn't very well keep kidding Ellie indefinitely about what he was doing. Maybe he should have leveled with her in the first place; then, if she didn't like it and didn't want to keep on seeing him, that was that and neither of them would be hurt. Maybe he'd tell her Sunday.

He liked Ellie a lot. She was a swell kid, and that

second kiss had surprised him. He went to sleep thinking about Ellie.

But he dreamed of Francy Scott.

6

Nothing much happened on Friday. It was still hot and the humidity had gone even higher. Joe Bailey woke a little earlier than usual because of the heat but held off having breakfast until eleven so he could eat at the Dinner Gong after Ellie went on duty. He found himself a bit puzzled about her this morning and wanted to have a look at her again, even across a restaurant counter.

The look didn't tell him very much and this time there were other customers and they didn't have much time to talk. Mike was there today, behind the cash register. When Joe came up with the check, Mike said, "Hi, Joe. What you doing these days?"

Joe said, "Nothing much," and managed to let it go at that. But he felt uneasy, somehow. He had a hunch Ellie must have mentioned him to her uncle and he wondered what Mike would have said about him to Ellie. Mike Dravich knew that he'd been selling pool tickets for Mitch, but then he'd told Ellie that part of it.

Maybe, he thought as he went out, he'd better level with Ellie—a little more than he had, anyway—on their next date. If he was going to keep on seeing her, it would get harder and harder to explain why he wasn't working at some job or other unless he told her at least part of the truth. And if, after that, she didn't want to go out with him any more, the hell with her. There were plenty of other girls.

He dropped into the tavern at about the usual time and

55

found out from Krasno that Mitch had gone to Chicago and wouldn't be back till the next day. And he hadn't left any word for Joe.

It was too hot to do anything else, so he went down to the beach for a swim. He thought maybe he'd run into someone he knew, but he didn't. The beach was fairly crowded for a Friday afternoon. Seeing so many girls and women in bathing suits reminded him of Francine, although no one he saw came within forty miles of having as beautiful a body as Francine's.

After dinner, which he did not eat at the Dinner Gong, he called up Ray Lorgan and got talked into dropping around to Ray's little two room and kitchenette flat on Cass Street.

It was funny, really, that Joe liked Ray Lorgan and that Ray liked Joe. Outside of a liking for science fiction stories they had almost nothing in common. Ray was only two years older than Joe, but he was married and had a year-old kid. He had a job as a timekeeper at A.O. Smith and he was pinko, definitely pinko, although he was not a member of the Communist Party. Joe had met him two years ago when he had attended a meeting or two of a science fiction fan club. Most of the members had turned out to be creeps, in Joe's opinion, and he hadn't gone often. By the same criterion he applied to the others, Ray Lorgan was a creep, too. But for some reason he'd never been able to put his finger on, he liked Ray and was liked in return. In fact, if he'd had to pick out any one person as being, currently, his closest friend, it would probably be Ray.

When he got off the Wells Street car at Cass, he stopped in a liquor store and picked up a bottle of wine to take along.

He handed it to Ray as he came in and Ray took it to

the kitchenette to open it. Jeannie, Mrs Lorgan, wasn't there; she was attending a night class at the University of Wisconsin Extension; the baby, Karl, was asleep in the other room but the door was shut and they wouldn't have to worry about talking quietly.

Ray peeled the wrapping off the bottle and frowned at it. "A Goddam capitalist," he said. "You paid a buck and a quarter for this and you could have got just as good for sixty-nine cents. Just as good as far as we're concerned, anyway; we wouldn't be able to tell the difference."

Joe grinned at him. "Maybe I did it just to hear you squawk. Want to put it in the icebox to cool off a while?"

"That proves damn well you wouldn't be able to tell the difference between a cheap and an expensive kind. You don't chill sherry; you drink it room temperature. A man who'd chill sherry would put catchup on apple pie."

He came out of the kitchenette with two glasses and the opened bottle and sat down at the table before he did the pouring.

"Doing anything yet, Joe?"

"No, but something's coming up," Joe said. He wished he could tell Ray about Mitch's plans, but he'd promised to keep them under his hat. "Meanwhile, I guess I'm just being a Goddam capitalist. Without capital."

Ray sipped his wine. He said, "In a well organized society, Joe, there wouldn't be anyplace for a guy like you. But maybe you'll get along. This is a hell of a ways from being a well ordered society."

Joe chuckled a little. "If you don't like it here —"

"Why don't I go back where I came from, huh? Here's a thought for you, Joe, that I'll bet you never thought of. Where *does* a man come from? From the body of a woman. And he spends a good share of the rest of his life trying

57

to get back in, but he never succeeds. Not with all of himself, anyway. You know, Joe, I'm not completely kidding; there's a symbolic significance in that. What's the moment of greatest ecstasy in a man's life? The culmination of intercourse, the orgasm. The moment when a *part* of him *is* returning to the body of woman. That's the closest he ever gets to going back where he came from. His one moment of pure ecstasy."

"And besides, it's fun," Joe said. He thought of Francine.

"Don't you ever take anything seriously, Joe? Except making money, being a big-shot gambler? No, I guess I'm wrong; you do think some, or you wouldn't read the kind of stuff you read. It takes imagination, abstract imagination, to like science fiction and fantasy. Know what I think, Joe? That you're afraid to think, afraid to *let* yourself think.

"Look, I'm no psychiatrist, but I've read quite a bit on psychiatry. I can be wrong, but I'd say you've got a keener mind than you let show on the surface. But for some reason it's afraid of itself and keeps itself under wraps. It just could be that something happened to you when you were a kid—all deeply underlying psychoses date back to early childhood—that makes you literally afraid to think for yourself. Ever taken an I.Q. test, Joe?"

Joe shook his head.

"Bet you'd rate a hundred and twenty, at least. And that's good. Maybe you'd rate more. But I guess that only because a flash of it shows once in a while. Your intelligence is afraid of itself. You act—Look, Joe, we're pretty good friends. Can you take this?"

Joe wasn't looking at him. Joe said, "Go ahead," and realized that his voice had sounded sullen and that he hadn't meant it to be. "Sure, Ray."

"Okay. You act like a child afraid of the dark—no, that's not right. Let's see, just what *do* I mean? I mean that because you won't let yourself think straight, you think like a child. Children pass through a stage of wanting to be gangsters or Billy the Kids; when they play cops and robbers which of the two do they want to be? That's natural, for kids. But they grow up, most of them, mentally and get over it. Those that don't, *do* become criminals—or anyway asocial, people who don't contribute to society or who make a living pandering to its weaknesses, like selling numbers racket tickets, for instance—

"Hell, Joe, maybe I'm stepping on your toes too hard, but now I've got started on this, I've got to finish, unless you stop me. Grown-up people who act and think that way do it either because they're stupid or because they're warped by something—or a series of somethings—that's happened to them. And you're not stupid. If you could ever dig out of your mind what happened to you—"

Joe picked up the bottle and poured himself another drink, very carefully and deliberately.

He said, "You're off the beam, Ray. Am I a psycho to want money without having to work like a dog all my life for it? If you're smart you can get it—and lots of it. Look at Mitch—you haven't met him, no, but I've talked enough about him—he's probably worth at least a couple of hundred thousand bucks. More money than you'll ever have. Everything he wants."

He thought again of Francine and for the first time he felt more envy of Mitch than admiration for him.

Ray said, "But how did he get it? By taking quarters and dollars away from people who could have used them for something better than gambling."

"That's their fault; he never *made* anyone buy numbers.

59

And maybe it's illegal, but there's nothing dishonest about it. He pays off if they hit. And if he didn't sell tickets, somebody else would."

Ray grinned. "The sheep are there. Why not fleece them before somebody else does. I guess at that, Joe, your Mitch isn't much worse than other capitalists."

"Better than some, I'd say. At least he doesn't advertise to create an artificial demand—convince people they need something they don't even want—and then make them pay for the advertising that convinced them. By letting them gamble, he's just filling a demand that's already there."

"My God, Joe, you're *thinking*. That's one of the flashes I spoke of. Even granting it's for the purpose of rationalizing something wrong that you want to do, it *is* thinking. Yes, you're right in that it isn't especially your Mitch that's wrong, it's the whole damned system we live under, right down to its rotten core.

"Which reminds me, I happened to read a little poem of D.H. Lawrence the other day about a mosquito. Not that I like most of his stuff, but this one had a swell tag line. I forget the exact wording, but after a dozen or so not too hot lines about the mosquito he ends up 'But at least he takes only what he needs; he doesn't put my blood into the bank.' Neatest sideswipe at capitalism I've ever seen in a poem on some other subject."

Joe grinned appreciatively and, now that capitalism was the subject of discussion, he managed to keep the conversation in safe channels—away from himself—until Jeannie came home from her class and he could make his escape. Ordinarily he'd have stayed another hour but he didn't want to tonight.

Outside, he thought: *Goddam him, how did he know all that?*

It wasn't right, of course, but that had been some uncomfortably close guessing.

Only he wasn't warped; he was the sensible one of the two of them, intellectually brilliant as Ray might be. Wasn't Ray working hard everyday – and under a system he didn't even *believe in* – and for not much more money a week than he, Joe, was getting right now for doing nothing at all? And when Mitch's new place got going, he'd be making more, probably, than Ray was. And ten years from now, he'd be in the chips and Ray would still be a timekeeper or something not much better. Ten years from now Ray might have a little house of his own and a five-year-old car and a mortgage on both of them and he, Joe, would have a swell flat on, say, Prospect Avenue, and a place like Mitch's just out of town and a couple of snazzy cars, one of them a robin's-egg blue convertible.

And women like Francy. Maybe even – if somehow he could get into fairly big money within a year or two or three – Francy herself. She wouldn't stay with Mitch forever. He thought of Mitch with Francy, and his mind flinched away from it.

To think about something else, he thought about Ellie Dravich. Ellie was a swell kid. He liked Ellie. Ellie was, in some ways, a lot like Jeannie, Ray's wife. Not quite as clever, maybe, or as well educated, but at least as pretty and with the same sort of honesty and niceness.

Riding back on the streetcar, he let himself wonder for just a moment how it would be to be married to Ellie, to be living as Ray lived, sleeping every night with a woman who loved you. Nice.

But that cut out your freedom, it tied you down and made you a slave instead of a free man, and it killed just about all your chances of ever really getting anywhere, getting into the big money. Mitch had never married, and Mitch had got into the big money and now Mitch had anything and everything he wanted. Including –

He pulled his mind away from that again.

He wondered just where he was going. It was too damn early to go home, only a little after ten o'clock. But here he was riding west on Wells Street, toward home. Should he get off downtown and try to find something to do? Or he could ride on past home and then walk down to Clybourn to the tavern. But Mitch wouldn't be there; he was in Chicago. And somehow he didn't want to drink anymore tonight. Not that he felt, even slightly, the little sherry he'd drunk at Ray's. They hadn't even finished the bottle – a fifth – between them. And there'd been so much of it left that Ray had wanted him to take it along with him, but he'd insisted, naturally, on leaving it for Ray and Jeannie to finish.

He pictured them sitting there finishing it and then going to bed together, loving one another.

Which of them was crazy, at that, he or Ray? Yes, it would be wonderful to be married to a girl like Jeannie. To Ellie. But that was silly, even to think about. If he married a girl like Ellie, he could never go through with his plans with Mitch. And he was committed to that, now. Look at all the money Mitch had given him already, to keep him going. He couldn't turn Mitch down now; it wouldn't be fair. Because of that money Mitch had been giving him, he didn't have any choice.

Over six weeks – and the forty he'd got today – it amounted to quite a bit. Take him the rest of his life to pay it off a few dollars a week out of what he could make at any legitimate job he was qualified for. When he'd considered, yesterday, telling Mitch he was going to look for a job

62

to tide him over until Mitch was operating numbers again, until the heat was off, he hadn't considered the matter of paying Mitch back anything, because he'd figured he'd be going back to work for Mitch again anyway, as soon as it was possible.

But quitting Mitch permanently would be something else again. Then he would owe Mitch all that money and have to pay it back. And Mitch always managed to collect anything that anybody owed him. If they didn't pay –

But that was ridiculous, anyway. After what Mitch had told him yesterday, about how far and how fast he'd be going up, it was ridiculous or worse to think of becoming sucker enough, for whatever reason, to turn down a chance like that. The big chance he'd been waiting for and hoping for.

He suddenly realized that the car was passing Fourteenth Street. He pressed the buzzer quickly and got off at the next stop. He walked back to Mrs Gettleman's. Home, if you didn't mind what you called it. His room would be a Dutch oven tonight. He hated to go to it.

He looked at his watch and saw that it still wasn't half past ten. Maybe Ellie would still be up. No reason why she'd turn in early when she didn't go to work till eleven in the morning. Maybe she'd be willing to go out with him for a sandwich and a beer and he'd have someone to talk to. Not that he'd be able to talk to anyone, especially to Ellie, about what he'd been thinking about. But even talking about the weather might get his mind off things and put him in a better mood.

He went up to the second floor and back to Ellie's room. He made sure there was a crack of light under the door and then he knocked lightly.

He heard the tap of her footsteps coming to the door and

then it opened and she was standing there. Wearing, as she had worn the first time he had seen her, the housecoat. But, housecoat or no, she looked a little prettier this time than the last. This time, despite the fact that she had no makeup on, her face scrubbed and shiny.

She looked at him and suddenly there was concern on her face; she frowned a little. "Joe," she said, "is something wrong?"

He managed to smile at her. "No, nothing. I'm sorry for bothering you. Saw your light was on and hoped you'd still be dressed and maybe in the mood to drop downstairs with me for a drink or a sandwich. But unless you're hungry enough to want to slip on a dress again—"

"Gee, I'm sorry, Joe. I wish I could. But I'm late getting to bed now—early as it is. I mean, one of the girls at the restaurant is sick and Uncle Mike asked me to take the early shift tomorrow, when the restaurant opens at six. I'll have to get up at five o'clock, and I should have gone to bed before this."

"Oh, sure. I'm sorry I bothered you, Ellie."

"You didn't, Joe. And thanks for asking me, thanks a lot."

"Better turn right in then, Ellie. Good night."

"Good night, Joe."

He stepped back and she closed the door gently, smiling at him.

He went on up to his room, feeling a little more cheerful; even that casual bit of conversation had managed to change his mood somewhat. But what had she meant by looking concerned when she'd first seen him, by frowning, by asking whether something was wrong? Did he look like a psycho or something?

It was as unpleasant in his room as he'd feared it would

be; not a breath of air, despite the fact that the window was open wide. He almost decided to go out again for a while, but there wasn't anywhere he wanted to go or anything he wanted to do.

He probably wouldn't be able to go to sleep for a while, but he might as well stay here and read until he got sleepy. He stripped down to a pair of shorts, propped up a pillow on the bed, and did his best to read the shorter stories in the science fiction magazine in which, two nights ago, he'd read the lead novel.

But tonight his mind wasn't geared for reading, somehow; it kept wandering away from the stories he tried to read. Damn it, he thought, how had Ray Lorgan made so many uncomfortably close guesses? He'd never told Ray about anything that had happened to him when he had been a kid. He thought he may possibly have mentioned that he had had pretty bad nightmares when he was young, but that they'd gone away gradually. But probably Ray had forgotten that or he'd have mentioned it to bolster one of his close guesses.

Anyway, damn it all, he was over it now. Things like nightmares wore off as you got older. His mother had been silly in insisting on his seeing a psychologist that time, when he was fifteen. Even then it had been wearing off, not nearly as bad as it had been. And psychologists and psychiatrists are witch doctors anyway. They don't know what the score is, any more than you do, but they like to tinker around and ask you questions, thousands of questions, and get you talking.

And he'd done his best to answer straight; he'd told the truth, or most of it. All of it that mattered, as far as what the psychologist had been trying to find out. After all, it was costing his mother money, and she didn't have much of it.

65

And all that he'd got out of it had been that—what was his name?—Doctor Janes, a silly name, and he wasn't really a doctor anyway, except a Doctor of Divinity, an ex-minister who'd set himself up as a consulting psychologist, had told him, first, that he'd been wrong about his father. And he'd convinced him of that, almost. At least his arguments were reasonable. And second that he was suffering from a phobia and that a phobia wasn't anything to worry about once you understood what caused it. And after Joe had explained to Dr Janes what had caused the phobia, Dr Janes had explained it back to him, a little less clearly.

So that was that, and the phobia was cured, and what is a phobia anyway?—most people have a more than normal fear of something or other. Of heights, of confined spaces, of cats, of germs.

It didn't mean you were crazy, just because you had a phobia. Especially if it was wearing off, surely if slowly.

Why, by now he could look at a candle, even a lighted one, without his insides shriveling up into a tight little knot. Certainly without screaming, as he'd use to at seven or eight years old.

And he could pass the window of a hardware store where axes and hatchets were on display and manage to glance at them without averting his eyes. He could even clench his fists and make himself stop and *look* at them.

So maybe old Dr Janes really had helped him. At any rate, he hadn't been able to do these things when, four years ago...

The Radio

MUSIC: *Series theme (motif from Rachmaninoff's Isle of the Dead).*

ANNOUNCER: Hold tightly to your chairs, folks. Today we bring you another thrilling episode in —

MUSIC: *Eerie sting.*

ANNOUNCER: THE ADVENTURES OF JOE BAILEY!

MUSIC: *Up on program theme into*

ANNOUNCER: Yesterday we left Joe entering the office of Dr Janes, consulting psychologist. Dr Janes is a retired minister who has taken a small office in the Warner Building in Milwaukee. He is a kindly man with a deep understanding of human nature who scales his fees to fit the purses of those who come to him for help. Yesterday we heard Florence Bailey, Joe's mother, explaining about Joe's trouble to Dr Janes. We heard him explain to her that quite possibly Joe was in need of the help of a psychiatrist but he admitted that a complete psychoanalysis by a qualified psychiatrist might take months and run to a considerable expenditure of money. Florence Bailey told him that she has only her income as a waitress to support them and could not possibly afford such a service. Dr Janes expressed his willingness to try to help her son and told her that his fee, whether one consultation sufficed or several proved necessary, would be only ten dollars. She has now returned with Joe and is waiting in the outer office. Joe Bailey, age fifteen, is now entering the inner sanctum of Dr Janes. He closes the door.

SOUND: *Door closing quietly.*

DOCTOR: Hello, Joe. Sit down.

JOE: Yes, Doctor.

DOCTOR: I'd like to explain one thing, Joe, before we talk. It's something I make a point of explaining to anyone who consults me. It's about my being a doctor; I want you to understand that I am not an M.D., a doctor of medicine, although I have a pretty good lay knowledge in that field. You may call me *Doctor* if you wish—in fact, I like it—but I want you to understand that the degree that entitles me to be called that is the degree of Doctor of Divinity. But I believe myself to be qualified as a consulting psychologist, which is what I call myself. Both through the study of psychology as a science and the considerable experience I have had in helping people, individually as well as collectively, in forty-one years in the ministry. By the way, Joe, do you understand the difference between a psychologist and a psychiatrist?

JOE: Well—I think so. A psychiatrist deals with insane people, doesn't he?

DOCTOR: That's putting it a bit strongly. Most people who go to psychiatrists are sane; they merely have some slight abnormality that disturbs them. What we call a phobia, perhaps. Most people have slight phobias of one kind or another. They're afraid of heights, for instance. That's a very common type of phobia; we call it acrophobia. And some people are afraid of being closed in, of confined spaces; that's claustrophobia. (Smilingly) Or am I using too many big words for you?

JOE: No, I've read something about phobias myself, at the library. I guess that's what I've got, so naturally I was interested. And as far as I can find out, if you know and remember what causes one, you ought to get over it. Well, I know what caused mine, but still it isn't completely gone, although it isn't as bad as it used to be.

DOCTOR: And you dream about it, your mother told me. Is that right?

JOE: Yes. I used to have awful nightmares: Mom would have an awful time getting me waked up from one. But that's what I mean about it going away gradually; I don't often have them anymore, and they're not so bad, even when I do.

DOCTOR: That's fine, Joe. I'm glad to hear it. Probably you didn't need to come to me at all; it's something that will wear off as you grow older. But your mother worries about it, and—even if it doesn't do any good otherwise, and I hope it will—it will relieve her mind to have you talk things over with me. So for her sake as well as your own, I hope you'll be completely frank with me.

JOE: Sure.

DOCTOR: She told me quite a bit about it, and the incident that started it. A very unfortunate thing. But I think it will be better if we just pretend, between us, that she told me nothing at all and start from the beginning. You don't mind talking about it, do you, Joe?

JOE: Well, ordinarily I don't like to talk about it, no. But when Mom talked me into coming to see you, I made up my mind that I would.

DOCTOR: That's fine, Joe. Now would you rather tell it in your own way, or have me ask questions and you answer them?

JOE: I don't care, Doctor. Whichever you say.

DOCTOR: Well, then you tell it, but let me interrupt

anytime I want to ask a question, so I'm sure I understand each point perfectly as we go along.

JOE: Sure. Well, it started, *really* started, that night when I woke up and saw the – the candle and the ax. But I guess it began before that when Uncle Ernie taught me that verse, that nursery rhyme. That would have been not more than a week before though, because he was just visiting us for a week, the week up to Christmas.

DOCTOR: And you were three and a half years old then?

JOE: Yes, I was born in July and that was the Christmas after my third birthday.

DOCTOR: How much of this, Joe, do you actually remember? And how much do you know from your mother having explained it to you?

JOE: Well, I remember waking up and seeing – what I saw, all right. And I remember my Uncle Ernie – maybe not from having seen him that time, because I was pretty young then – but I've seen him since a few times. About the date it happened and the details and everything, it's just that I learned from Mom. I was asleep, of course, while they were trimming the Christmas tree and all that and just woke up when I did, so I can't remember that part of it; I mean, how it happened up to then.

DOCTOR: Do you remember your uncle teaching you the verse?

JOE: I guess I do at that, but not clearly. It was something about bells in London, something about "to ring the bells of London town" and then a lot of rhymes, one about each bell, and there was some kind of a game connected with it, I think. I remember one or two of the rhymes but there were a lot of them. I remember, "Kettles and pans, Say the bells at Saint Ann's," and – let's see – "When will you pay me? Say the bells at Old Bailey." And maybe

70

I could remember one or two more if I tried. Shall I try?

DOCTOR: I don't believe it matters. It was the final couplet that impressed you, wasn't it? Can you say it to me, Joe?

JOE: I can, now. There are all the rhymes about the bells and then it suddenly changes and ends up—(*His voice tightens a little.*) "Here comes a candle to light you to bed, And here comes a chopper to chop off your head."

DOCTOR: And did it frighten you when you first heard it?

JOE: I don't remember for sure. A little, I guess. I've often wondered why they put something like that in nursery rhymes for kids. It's silly, isn't it?

DOCTOR: Yes. Definitely.

JOE: But I guess it didn't scare me any more than it would have scared any other kid my age. And, come to think of it, I guess kids like to be scared a little. They must, or there wouldn't be nursery rhymes like that. But, even so, I must have been remembering it or thinking about it, in my sleep—dreaming about it, that is—just before I woke up. Otherwise seeing what I saw wouldn't have—have done what it did to me. I mean, I *must* have been dreaming about—about a candle coming to light me to bed and a chopper coming to—to chop off my head. I *must* have been dreaming about it, or it wouldn't have been so horrible. Don't you think so?

DOCTOR: Quite probably. Was your uncle English, Joe? That's an old English nursery rhyme or game and it's not too well known in this country; that's why I ask.

JOE: Yes, Uncle Ernie was born in England. He was my father's older brother, and my father was born in this country. They were ten years or so apart, and I guess

Uncle Ernie was about five when my grandfather and grandmother moved here; my father was born after they'd been here five years.

DOCTOR: Is your uncle still living?

JOE: Not that one; I have one uncle in Chicago, but he's my mother's brother, and he's the only relative I've got left, I guess, besides Mom. But Uncle Ernie was visiting us that week leading up to Christmas; he lived in Pittsburgh, and I think it was the first time he'd ever got to Chicago to visit us, at least the first time after I was born.

DOCTOR: And during that week he taught you that rhyme. And I agree that you were quite probably dreaming about it when your father came into the room that night and — Well, you tell me about it, Joe.

JOE: Well, it was Christmas Eve. We lived in a flat on North Dearborn Street, three rooms. I guess I was probably up a little later than usual, it being Christmas Eve, but I was asleep by then, alone in the bedroom. And Mom and Pop were trimming the Christmas tree in the living room; I guess they'd finished trimming it.

DOCTOR: Your uncle was there, too?

JOE: Not *just* then. I mean, he'd gone around to his hotel room — he was staying at a hotel nearby because with three of *us* in three rooms, and just one double bed and the bed I slept in, he couldn't stay right with us — anyway, he'd gone around to his room to get some presents. And a bottle, probably. Anyway, Mom and Pop were finishing trimming the tree, and they'd used the old-fashioned candles in holders that clip onto the tree branches. I guess they don't use them at all anymore, anybody, and most people didn't use them then, but a few did. And Pop liked them better than electric lights on a tree and said if everybody was careful there wasn't any danger of fire. Anyway — (*His voice has been fading, as*)

MUSIC: *Up and under. Silent Night, Holy Night.*

ANNOUNCER: It's a pretty tree, not a big one, but a pretty one. And those old-fashioned candles on it are really beautiful. Alvin and Florence Bailey have just lighted the candles and stepped back to admire their handiwork. Flo walks to the light switch on the wall beside the closed door that leads to the bedroom and turns off the light. The tree shows up really beautifully now. She sighs a little.

MUSIC: *Up and under briefly. Same melody.*

FLORENCE: Gee but it's pretty, Al.

ALVIN: Yeah. Well, maybe we better put out the candles and not waste 'em. We've seen how it looks now.

FLORENCE: Your brother ought to be back any minute; let's wait a few minutes to see if he gets here by then, huh?

ALVIN: Okay. Gawd, I can use a drink. Hope he brings that bottle and I wish I'd had sense enough to remember to bring one home myself.

FLORENCE: We're not going to stay up very late, though, are we? You know how kids are on Christmas morning and we want to be awake too, to see Joey's fun.

ALVIN: Sure, Flo, sure. I didn't mean I want to hang one on. Just that I can sure use a drink or two.

FLORENCE: Wish Joe could see that tree now, with the candles going and the lights off in here otherwise. In the morning, it won't be near as pretty as it is right now.

ALVIN: Why not, if he's awake. We ain't put the presents out yet. He can see the tree if he happens to be still awake.

FLORENCE: I'll see.

SOUND: *Two or three soft footsteps. A door opening very quietly.*

FLORENCE: (*Not much above a whisper.*) Joey...Joey...

SOUND: *Quiet closing of door.*

FLORENCE: (*Normal voice.*) He's sound asleep. Say, Al, it's really cold in there, in the bedroom. Felt like icicles coming out of the door at me when I opened it. I think we ought to get that window the rest of the way shut.

ALVIN: It's stuck. I pushed it down as far as it would go.

FLORENCE: I tried to push it farther, too, when I put Joe to bed. It's stuck because there's some ice on the sill. I thought it would be all right, but I didn't know it would be *that* cold. We'd better get it the rest of the way shut.

ALVIN: All right, I'll try to chip off the ice. But it'll probably wake the kid. Turning the light on, if nothing else.

FLORENCE: You can do it without the light on. Take one of those candles. And just noise doesn't wake Joey, if it isn't too loud. You can be careful, and the ice isn't frozen very tight. Maybe you can just pry it off with a knife.

ALVIN: Knife won't do it. I'll get the hatchet; I can chip it off quiet, I guess.

SOUND: *Footsteps. Drawer being opened and closed. Footsteps again.*

ALVIN: Good thing you thought of a candle. But remember tomorrow to get batteries for that damn flashlight, will you?

FLORENCE: Sure, Al. Be as quiet as you can now.

ALVIN: (*We hear him walking again as he speaks.*) Sure. I'll take a white candle; we got too many of them anyway and I'll probably use some of it up. Maybe you better put the others out. Ernie might be half an hour yet.

FLORENCE: I'll wait till you're through in there. Try not

74

to wake Joey, but if he wakes up anyway, we might as well let him see the tree.

ALVIN: Sure.

SOUND: *Click of latch as door opens, then closes again quietly.*

MUSIC: *Soft but menacing. Deep chords in bass.*

ANNOUNCER: (*Mysterious.*) It's dark in the bedroom, dark despite the single candle which Al Bailey carries carefully as he tiptoes past Joe's bed and then past the big double bed to the window. He carries the hatchet in his other hand. When he reaches the window he pushes the curtain aside with the hand that holds the hatchet and then puts the hatchet down on the sill while he looks around for a place to put down the candle so he'll have both hands free to work. He reaches to put the candle on the sill, too, and then realizes that the candle, in the clip, won't stand upright. He looks around and sees that the projecting edge of the top of a chest of drawers standing about two feet from the window is the answer. He opens the clip wide enough to put it over the edge, and the candle is firmly clipped there; he has both hands free. Holding the curtain back with one hand, he begins, as quietly as he can, to chip at the ice on the lower edge of the window sash. He pulls the window open a little higher to get at the ice better. The candle flame sways, but does not go out. Now he can get at the ice, and he chips away at it gently...Now let's go back over to the child's bed in which little Joe Bailey, age three and a half, is sleeping. We can see him dimly in the light of the candle and we can see on the wall behind him the monstrous flickering shadow that the candlelight casts there. And what's this we hear? A voice? Yes, but it's a voice that's inside Joe's head, a voice in a dream; no one but Joe—and you and me—can hear it. It's the voice of his Uncle Ernie reciting a delicious little jingle that puts pleasant little shivers up and down Joe's back. Listen carefully and you can hear the voice in Joe's dream — listen carefully —

VOICE: (*It is the voice of Joe's Uncle Ernie, but distorted in echo chamber. It is speaking with what would be mock menace normally, but sounds truly mysterious and menacing through the echo chamber.*) Here comes a candle to light you to bed, And here come a chopper to chop off your head.

ANNOUNCER: (*Softer, more mysterious*) And back at the window —

SOUND: *Window going shut, suddenly.*

ANNOUNCER: Joe Bailey's eyes jerk open. He sits up in bed, frightened, not by the sound that woke him but by the memory of what he was just dreaming. There is a strange dim light in the room but he hasn't turned toward it yet. He rubs his eyes with little fists trying to drive away the dream. But from the dream, he is still thinking to himself —

VOICE: (*It is Joe's own voice this time, a child's voice, but again through the echo chamber to indicate that it is thought rather than actual speaking.*) Here comes a candle to light you to bed, And here comes a chopper to chop off your — (*Voice fades out*) —

ANNOUNCER: And at the window, Alvin Bailey is turning to come away. But he has become entangled in the curtain. Finding it continually in his way as he tried to work, he had thrown it over him, standing, as it were, between the curtain and the window. Now he's tangled in it, just for a moment...Just for the exact moment that Joe takes his little fists away from his eyes and finds that the mysterious light is still there in the room, and he's now nearly enough awake to turn to see where it comes from. It comes from a candle that no hand holds. And beside the candle but not holding it is a robed headless figure whose raised hand holds a shining —

JOE: Screams. *Screams. SCREAMS.*

ALVIN: Joe! Joe, what's wrong?

SOUND: *Door being thrown open. Joe is continuing to scream at the top of his voice.*

FLORENCE: Joey! What is it, Joey? Are you having a nightmare? Wake up, Joey. Nothing's wrong, Joey! *Al, what—*

MUSIC: *Up and under on theme. Through a few bars of it we hear Joe's screams, then they fade.*

DOCTOR: Yes, Joe, that's the way your mother told it to me. Was she able to get you fully awake right away?

JOE: Well, Doctor, I guess the worst of it was that I was awake. She — and Pop — didn't figure out right away what had happened or what had scared me. And they thought I was having a nightmare and tried to get me out of it. But I was awake already; it was a nightmare all right, but not the way they thought at first. Finally when I got calmed down a little, I guess they put together what I told them and what Pop had been doing and where the candle had been and about the hatchet and everything and figured out what had happened and what had scared me.

DOCTOR: Were you able to go to sleep again that night? Or do you remember that part of it?

JOE: I'm not sure. I guess maybe I did after a while, but it would have been a pretty long while, probably.

DOCTOR: Did you have a nightmare — a real one — when you did?

JOE: Mom says I didn't, that first night. I had plenty of them from then on, though. And there was another thing; after that I stuttered pretty bad for a few years. Until I was six. The stuttering went away when I was six years old. Oh, one other thing I remember. I guess the first time it came out I had a phobia was the next morning, Christmas morning. You want to hear about that?

DOCTOR: Please.

JOE: It was when I went out and saw the Christmas tree and there were candles on it. I screamed and ran through the kitchen and downstairs and outside. Mom caught me about half a block away and brought me back; I mean, talked me into coming back. And when she found out what scared me, she came in the flat first and took all the candles off the tree and hid them somewhere. And then I wasn't afraid of the tree anymore. It was all right then.

DOCTOR: And you've been afraid of candles — and hatchets — ever since?

JOE: Yes, only like I told you it's going away. I can even look at one now. Either one, I mean. And while I still have a nightmare once in a while, it isn't as bad as it used to be. I guess I'm getting over it all right. Only Mom worries about it that by the time I'm as old as I am now I'm not completely over it.

DOCTOR: Did she get medical advice while you were still a child, concerning the nightmares?

JOE: I think she took me to doctors a few times, but what they told her I don't know or don't remember. I guess most of them said it would probably wear off or something. And we've — well, we've been pretty poor, I guess, most of the time, so when it didn't seem to do much good, I guess she quit taking me.

DOCTOR: Has there been any recurrence lately that caused her to bring you to me now, Joe? Anything at all?

78

JOE: No, it's been wearing off. I guess what gave her the idea this time was that she just learned about you from someone. She hadn't known that there was anything like a consulting psychologist that didn't charge money up in the hundreds of dollars for a long course of treatment, like a psychiatrist would, or she'd have taken me to see you—or somebody—a long time ago.

DOCTOR: I see. Tell me, Joe, does your feeling of fear towards candles specialize on any particular kind or size, or is it just any candle?

JOE: Any one, I guess. I mean, it doesn't matter if it's big or little or what color it is. But if it's lighted, it's worse. Even a candle that isn't lighted gives me the willies, but not so bad. And it's not any particular kind of a—a chopper, either. An ax or a hatchet, either one, is about the same. Unless maybe an ax, one with a long handle, is worse. I don't know why that would be, because it was a hatchet Pop was carrying that night—only of course I didn't know it was Pop—but anyway one kind of a chopper is as bad as another. Even a cleaver, like a butcher's cleaver.

DOCTOR: Do you happen to recall the first time—after that night—when you saw an ax or a hatchet?

JOE: No, I don't. I remember being scared as the devil everytime I saw one while I was a kid, but I don't remember the first time. It wasn't that same night, anyway. Pop must have dropped the hatchet or put it down somewhere getting to me after I yelled, and I think he knocked the candle, clip and all, off the edge of the bureau and put it out. Anyway, I don't remember seeing either of them again that same night; probably Pop carried them out while Mom was still working on me, trying to get me calmed down and back to sleep.

DOCTOR: It must have been a terrible experience. Tell me this, Joe, did you ever have a tendency – then or now – to blame anyone for it? Your father?

JOE: How was it his fault? It was just an accident.

DOCTOR: Of course it was. But that isn't a full answer to what I asked. Sometimes we blame people for things even when strict reason tells us they are not to blame. And a child of three or four isn't very adept at strict reasoning. Joe, did you love your father very much?

JOE: (*Hesitantly.*) I – don't know. He died when I was six, and it's hard to remember much about him that far back.

DOCTOR: Tell me something about him, Joe. What did he do, for example?

JOE: (*Hesitates again.*) Well – he was a bartender.

DOCTOR: Not at that time, was he, Joe? Prohibition would have been in effect in – Let's see, you're fifteen now? I believe your mother said that was your age.

JOE: Yes, I was fifteen two months ago.

DOCTOR: You look older. I'd have guessed you as seventeen. But let's see – this is forty-four and that was the Christmas you were three. That would have been nineteen thirty-two. Yes, there was still Prohibition then, and for a year or two after.

JOE: (*There is a touch of defiance in his voice.*) He was a bartender. In a speakeasy. After Prohibition did go out, he was out of work because he'd been arrested a few times and he couldn't get a license as a regular bartender.

DOCTOR: And what did he do after Prohibition ended?

JOE: Nothing much, I guess. That would have been in the Depression and he couldn't get a job, except part-time once in a while. Mom got a job as a waitress, and I guess we lived mostly on what she made.

80

DOCTOR: Do you hold against him, Joe, the way he made a living—before Repeal, I mean?

JOE: No.

DOCTOR: But you didn't love him very much, did you?

JOE: Sure, I did. What's that got to do with it? Sure, I loved him.

DOCTOR: As much after that Christmas Eve as you did before?

JOE: Sure.

DOCTOR: He lived only until you were six? Two and a half years after that Christmas Eve?

JOE: Yes.

DOCTOR: How did he die, Joe?

(*Pause.*)

DOCTOR: If it's unpleasant for you to remember, Joe, I'm sorry. But if I'm to help you—

JOE: He was shot. He was shot while he was on a holdup job, a box office at a movie theater. I guess he couldn't take being broke anymore. (*Even more defiantly; Joe's voice sounds as though he is on the verge of tears.*) And I don't blame him for that, either. I'd do the same thing myself, under the same circumstances!

DOCTOR: (*Very mildly.*) I see. I hope you don't really mean that, Joe. The part about doing the same thing yourself. And I don't think you do mean it, really. You said it, probably, just to prove that you really did love your father and that you don't blame him for his—mistake. And it's well that you don't try to judge him.

JOE: He was a swell guy.

DOCTOR: I'm sure he was. Tell me, Joe, how did you react to the news of his death? Do you remember how you felt when you heard that your father was dead? (*Pause.*)

DOCTOR: I'm sorry I have to ask you that, Joe. But can't you see that the very fact that you hesitate to answer shows that the answer might be important.

JOE: (*Sullenly.*) I didn't hear it. I was *there*.

MUSIC: *Eerie sting.*

JOE: I was there. I saw him get killed.

DOCTOR: (*Startled.*) You mean he took you along, on a holdup?

JOE: No. All right, if you've got to know! I took the cops there! It was my fault he got killed!

MUSIC: *Up and under on theme, the motif from Rachmaninoff's* Isle of the Dead.

ANNOUNCER: Does Joe Bailey mean that he deliberately got his father killed? Or, although he obviously blames himself, was it accidental? What really happened that night when Joe was six? Does he really remember it now as it actually happened or is it something in his imagination, something of a piece with the other hideous nightmares that stalked his childhood after that Christmas Eve in nineteen thirty-two when he saw, as he awakened from a dream, *the candle and the chopper*? The two things that thereafter became symbols to him, forever associated with nameless horror in his subconscious mind. Does Joe think that he really loved his father after that Christmas Eve—or does he protest too much? Was his father thereafter a symbol to him, also—a symbol of terror? We know now that not one, but two, very unfortunate things happened to Joe during his early childhood. Will he remain sane? *Or will the chopper get him?* Tune in again tomorrow for another thrilling episode in—

MUSIC: *Eerie sting.*

ANNOUNCER: THE ADVENTURES OF JOE BAILEY!

MUSIC: *Up to close.*

The Story

7

Sunday afternoon was nice. The weather was nice and the beach was nice. Ellie in a bathing suit was nice, too, although seeing any woman in a bathing suit made him think of Francine. Ellie hadn't any tan; you could see she didn't have a chance to go swimming often. Nicely shaped, though, with clean smooth lines that were nice to look at, although nothing like Francine's voluptuousness. Damn Francine, he thought; were all other women going to be spoiled for him just because he'd seen Francine?

Ellie had brought a blanket; they were both lying on it. Joe was face up with a forearm thrown across his eyes to shield them from the sun; Ellie was lying face down beside him.

She said, "We'd better not stay much longer. I don't want to sunburn. Should have started early in the season."

"Why didn't you?"

"I don't like the Chicago beaches, on Sunday. And that

was my day off there, too. In hot weather, like this, they're so crowded you almost have to stand up. And I lived quite a way west; it was a long trip."

"West. Cicero, maybe?"

"Near there. Where did you live in Chicago, Joe?"

"Near North Side. Dearborn Street, near Bughouse Square. But I was just a kid then. Cicero must have been something in the old days, during Prohibition. Where all the gangsters hung out; somebody told me they used to call it Little Mexico. But you'd be too young to remember any of that, if you lived there then."

"I didn't. I was raised in Indianapolis."

"Oh, sure, you told me. I forgot."

"But my uncle and aunt, the ones I lived with in Chicago, used to talk once in a while about the way Cicero used to be. I'm glad it wasn't like that when I was there. I don't like gangsters and shooting."

"Not even gangster pictures? Humphrey Bogart stuff?"

"Well, sometimes. In a movie."

"But you wouldn't want to be a gun moll?"

She laughed and sat up. "Is that a proposition, Mister Bailey?"

"If you're going to accept it, you'll have to call me Joe. Think you're baked enough? Let's see." He raised himself on one elbow and looked at her back and shoulders. "Nope, hasn't even started to turn pinkish yet. You aren't even half-baked." He bent forward and kissed her shoulder lightly. "And there's an anesthetic, if you do burn."

He lay back down, this time not covering his eyes completely but merely shielding them with his flat hand. She turned and looked down at him and he tried to tell from her face whether she'd thought he'd been too fresh. He couldn't tell.

84

She asked, almost lightly, "Doing anything yet, Joe? I mean, have you lined up a job?"

He shook his head. "No hurry. I'm taking my time."

"But, Joe, you must have *some*— You aren't a gangster, are you, Joe? A gunman or something?"

He grinned at her. "I hope I'm *something*. But I'm not a gunman. Never fired a gun in my life except a twenty-two rifle. And I never even owned one of them. But I had a popgun when I was a kid. It shot corks."

"I'm glad of that, Joe. I hate the very idea of—killing. Or crime of any kind. I guess I wouldn't make a good gun moll."

"Do you think gambling is a crime?"

"Well, not—Joe, I think we had better get out of the sun. Me, anyway. Let's get dressed and sit on the grass under the trees up there. And I'll let you buy me an ice cream cone if there's a place around where we can get them."

He said, "Sure, Ellie," and got up. They arranged where to meet outside the bathhouse and, miraculously, Ellie was there waiting when Joe got there. He'd expected her to take twice as long.

Shadows were lengthening as they strolled up the hill from the beach. Under a tree near the top of the slope they stopped and Ellie partly unfolded the blanket so they could sit on the grass and look out over the bright blue of the lake, dotted with little white sails.

"Getting hungry?" Joe asked. "Maybe instead of hunting cones we should eat pretty soon. I had a late breakfast, but nothing since."

"You shouldn't buy me dinner, Joe. Our date was just for the afternoon."

"You mean you've got one for the evening?"

"Yes."

Joe laughed. "You didn't say that fast enough. You're lying and you know it."

"All right, I'm lying and I know it. But, Joe, if you're not working, I'm not going to let you spend a lot of money on me. If we eat together, we're going Dutch."

"I'll let you think so till the check comes. Damn it, Ellie, quit talking and thinking as though I'm broke. I've got money. Do I have to show it to you?"

"All right, Joe. I won't argue this time, if we don't go to an expensive place. Anyway, I'm starting to look for another room tomorrow. A light housekeeping one."

"Don't you get your meals at the restaurant?"

"Well, yes. Except Sundays, of course. But I hate eating in restaurants, especially one I work in. I want to be able to get my own breakfasts at least. Or make coffee whenever I want it or a sandwich before I go to bed if I'm hungry. And be able to have someone in for a meal once in a while. I'm fairly good at cooking, Joe. Not fancy stuff, but I make good Italian spaghetti—and I like to bake cakes if I find a place that has a real stove and not just a hot plate."

"Huh," said Joe. "Trying to find your way to my heart through my stomach."

"Wouldn't it work?"

"It might."

"It should. How long has it been since you've eaten real home cooking, Joe?"

"Well—not very often since my mother died, a little less than a year ago. Even then, we didn't have regular meals at home except on her day off. She happened to have a shift about like yours, only an hour longer, eleven in the morning to nine at night. So she got breakfast for us and other meals I'd either have to rustle myself or eat in the restaurant she worked in. Except, like I said, on her day off."

86

"And you haven't eaten outside of restaurants since then, Joe?"

"Once in a while at the Lorgans'; they're friends of mine. Like you to meet them; I think you'd like Ray and Jeannie." He was thinking that if he took Ellie along the next time he went to Ray's, then Ray wouldn't get as embarrassingly psychoanalytical as he'd got night before last. "But the housekeeping room does sound like a good idea, Ellie."

"I'm paid through Wednesday at Mrs Gettleman's. I hope I can find one by then, so I won't have to pay another week. If I do find one, I'll have things – the kitchenette – in working order by next Sunday. And will you eat with me then?"

"Sure. Glad to. But I won't guarantee that that's the way to my heart."

"I'm not sure that I want to find the way, Joe."

She had sounded serious. He looked at her. "Bet I know why," he said. He didn't know whether he was being serious or not. "Because you still think I'm a gangster or a gunman. Because I'm not working. Or that I'm maybe an embezzler living on stolen bank money or something."

She shook her head slowly. "I don't think that, Joe. Not any of those things. Especially about the gunman. You were telling the truth when you said you'd never even owned a gun. I can tell."

"Can you tell when I'm *not* telling the truth?"

"I – I think I can, Joe."

It startled him a little. But he passed it off by pretending to shudder and saying, "What an awful wife you'd make, Ellie."

And then he wished he hadn't said it. Even talking about wives or getting married was dangerous territory when you didn't expect to get married at all, and certainly not now and still more certainly not to Ellie. Marrying Ellie would be good-bye to the big money; he knew that instinctively.

He decided he'd better break it up, and stood up. "Dunno about you, Ellie, but I'm getting hungry. Where shall we eat?"

"Anywhere you say, Joe. You know Milwaukee and I don't."

"There's a pretty nice place at Eleventh and Wells. If we eat there, we're near enough home we can get rid of this damn blanket and won't have to take it to the restaurant with us."

"Fine, Joe. I'd like to fresh up a little bit anyway."

They strolled south to Wells Street and took the streetcar. At the rooming house, Joe didn't bother to go up to his room. Ellie decided she wouldn't have to change clothes, except her shoes, and to put on a pair of stockings, so he waited in her room, noticing that she carefully left the door ajar. He picked up a magazine so he could politely not watch while she put on the stockings, thinking how silly it was that convention expected him to do so. He'd been seeing her legs all afternoon at the beach; now he was supposed to look away, just because she was more dressed now than she'd been then. But he knew that she'd have been embarrassed if he watched, however casually.

So he leafed through the magazine – a *Collier's* – casually, instead, glancing at the illustrations and story titles. He said, "You ought to read science fiction, Ellie. Some of it's really good and this is all junk. Nicely written, but it doesn't mean anything; stories are all the same. Boy chases girl, girl gets boy."

Ellie was putting on shoes now, higher-heeled ones than she'd worn to the beach. She said, "Sometimes girl does get boy. Anyway, it happens oftener than spaceships landing on Mars."

88

"Not to me, it doesn't. I don't expect to get married. Not for a long time, anyway."

She finished fastening the strap of the second shoe and then stood up and looked at him. "Joe Bailey," she said, and he couldn't tell whether she was really angry or not, "quit talking and acting as though I'm a mantrap. Or at least be a little more subtle about it. And if you're thinking I'm trying to get at your heart through your stomach, you can consider your invitation to a home-cooked meal next Sunday evening called off. For your information, I'm *not* hunting for a husband and if I was—"

He laughed. "If you were, you wouldn't have me if I was the last man on earth. Okay, Ellie, I apologize. Maybe what I said did sound that way. Let's go eat, huh; I'm starving." He stood up. "Like Wiener schnitzel?"

"What's that?"

"What we're going to eat, if you let me order. It's breaded veal cutlet, German style. It's the best thing Milwaukee German restaurants have. It's wonderful. You ready?"

"Okay, and if it's good enough, I'll still feed you next Sunday evening. If I find a light housekeeping room by then, that is. And if you quit warning me, subtly or otherwise, that you don't want to marry me."

He laughed again and said, "Okay, Ellie." And just before they reached the door that was still ajar he put his arms around her and kissed her lightly. Only, as it had happened Thursday evening, it didn't end quite as lightly as it had started.

Ellie pushed him away finally. She was laughing at him as she reached for the knob of the door, but he could see that she was just a bit shaken by the kiss. She said, "If you think I'm a trap, Joe Bailey, you'd better stop doing that. You'll get caught yet."

He grinned back at her as they went out the door. "Maybe there'd be worse things at that," he told her.

And he was surprised to find out how near he came to meaning it. It *would* be wonderful to be married to Ellie. Except that it would mean the end of all his ambitions, all of his chances to do the big things he wanted to do. It would mean taking a piddling little job somewhere and working like a dog the rest of his life.

Nuts to that, he thought. Then he managed to quit thinking about it, one way or the other. They had Wiener schnitzel and saw a movie, but Ellie wouldn't have anything to eat or drink after the show, explaining that she wanted to get up early in the morning to start looking for another place. She'd have to do her room hunting mornings because it was too late after she got off work in the evening.

After he left her at eleven, he was surprised to realize that he hadn't thought about Francine once, all evening.

8

He thought about Francine the next afternoon, though, because Mitch mentioned her. Mitch, back from Chicago, was already there when Joe dropped in at the tavern early in the afternoon.

Mitch and Dixie Ehlers were sitting in one of the booths along the side and Joe walked in and started toward the bar without even seeing them until Mitch called to him. There were two or three customers at the bar, which was probably why Mitch had decided to sit in a booth.

Mitch said, "Hiya, Joe," as Joe walked over. "Sit down and— Or how about getting us some drinks first? And one for yourself."

Joe said, "Sure, Mitch," and picked up the glasses already

in front of them. He took them over to Krasno at the bar, knowing Krasno would know what they'd been drinking. He said, "Fill 'em up, Krazzy. And just a beer for me."

Krasno made the drinks and drew a beer for Joe without saying a word. Joe took them over and sat down next to Dixie Ehlers and facing Mitch. He knew that Mitch liked to spread himself out and hated to sit next to anyone in a booth.

"How was Chicago?" Joe asked.

"Pretty good. Getting some things lined up." Mitch stared at the beer Joe had brought for himself. "That damn hogwash. Why don't you drink something worth drinking, Joe?"

Dixie said, "Let the kid alone, Mitch. He's smart. Get a taste for alky too early and you end up a stew bum."

"Hell," Mitch said, "I was weaned on whiskey. If you could call it whiskey in those days. I'd say just the opposite, Dixie; if you learn how to handle it when you're young enough, it *don't* get you. You know when to stop. I always know when to stop. Well, ninety-nine percent of the time, anyway."

Dixie said, "The other one percent can get you down, if it happens at the wrong time. I got me a straight rule, never more than three drinks at one time. One afternoon or evening or whatever it is. This is my second. I'll have one more if I want it, but none after that. Unless this evening after I've eaten. Then three more, if I want 'em."

"How about a party?"

"Depends on the party," Dixie said. "If I know everybody there, if I know there's going to be no trouble — and nothing in the way of business — then maybe that's different, once in a while. I may decide to get drunk, but I never let it sneak up on me."

Mitch said, "You sound like a Goddam cash register, Dixie."

"Out of nine guys in Joliet or Sandstone, eight of them wouldn't be there if they figured it that way."

Mitch laughed. "How the hell did we get on this? But speaking of parties, I'm going to throw a little one next Saturday night. Just a few people. Out at Fox Point. Fact, I decided it just now. Either of you got anything in the way?"

Joe shook his head. Once before he'd been on a party Mitch had thrown, last winter in Mitch's apartment in town. It had been something to remember. There hadn't been just a few people there, though; it had seemed as though half of Milwaukee had been there.

Dixie said, "Count me in, Mitch. Furnishing the dames or shall I bring one?"

"Hell, bring your own. You too, Joe." He grinned at Joe. "In fact, *especially* you. Francy seems to like you."

Joe grinned back, because from the way Mitch was grinning he could tell that it was all right, that Mitch was just kidding and didn't really mean anything. But he suddenly wished that he didn't have to go to the party, since Francine would be there. He'd decided he'd never see Francine again if he could help it—not while she was living with Mitch, anyway. But now he wouldn't be able to help it.

He said, "Then I better bring a dame, huh, to help me fight off Francine."

Mitch laughed. "Maybe you better, Joe. But listen, don't bring any Sunday School teachers. The party just might get a little rough."

"Yeah," Joe said, "I remember the last one. In February."

"You ain't seen nothing yet. That was practically a public party; this is a private one. And that was in town and this is out far enough we can raise all the hell we want. Say, Joe, how near can you come to using a gun?"

Joe asked, "Is the party going to be *that* rough?"

Mitch laughed again. "Maybe it will, but that's not what

I meant. I'm serious, Joe. How much do you know about handling guns?"

Joe shook his head. "Practically nothing, Mitch."

"I want you to learn, Joe. In a spot like I'm going to open, you got to know how to use one. There's a lot of cash around, and you always got to be ready for trouble. Sometimes you run into tough customers."

"Sure," Joe said. "But where can I get one?"

"Dixie here's going to take you under his wing, Joe. We talked it over. He can get you whatever you need and show you how to use it. Meanwhile, he'll lend you something of his to practice up with. And I want you to learn right and get good. Understand?"

"Sure, Mitch."

"I'm serious on this, Joe. Knowing how to use a gun – and use it right – can be damn important. Okay, Dix, you tell the kid where and when."

Dixie said, "I think the best idea's just to go out in the woods somewhere. There ain't any range around Milwaukee we can use without advertising, if you get what I mean. I know places in Chicago, but hell, it's just as easy to use the woods. Don't you think so, Mitch?"

"Sure. I can show you a place on the map where you can drive to in less than an hour. You could try out machine guns there and nobody'd know the difference. Not right now, anyway. 'Bout a month and a half from now when hunting seasons begin to open, it'll be jammed."

Dixie nodded. "Wednesday okay for you, Joe? Day after tomorrow."

"Sure," Joe said.

"Let's get an early start, then. How does six o'clock sound to you?"

It sounded awful, but Joe said it sounded fine.

"Okay, kid, I'll pick you up. Mitch gave me your address. Is there a room number on your door?"

"No, but it's the room at the end of the hall on the third floor. All right, Dixie, I'll be ready."

"Getting out that early we can get in a lot of shooting before it gets hot. Mitch, want me to buy a gun for the kid next time I go to Chi?"

"If he's sure what he wants by then. Let him try out some of yours meanwhile and see how he likes them."

Dixie nodded and turned back to Joe. He said, "Look, kid, I might as well show you some stuff before we go out. I can get you used to guns and let you do a little dry shooting, give you some pointers. How about tomorrow afternoon for that? Then we won't have to waste time on it after we're out where we can do some real shooting."

"Sure," Joe said.

"I'm staying at the Wyandotte, on Cass. Room thirty-five. Suppose you drop around a little after one o'clock tomorrow. We can pick out what gun you like. Say, Mitch, could we combine it with some real hunting maybe? Open season on anything here in Wisconsin?"

Mitch shook his head. "Foxes, but you can't hunt them without dogs, and you don't want to make an expedition out of it. I think there's open season on jackrabbits in some counties, but not where I'm sending you. Wait till fall and get yourself a deer."

He grinned at Joe. "Maybe come fall the three of us will go deer hunting, huh? Meanwhile, Joe, we'll make a gunman out of you."

Joe grinned back at Mitch and tried to look calm and unexcited, and to act as though getting lessons in shooting from a real gunman wasn't something to get excited about.

94

Mitch and Dixie left a few minutes after that and Joe discovered that, in the excitement of learning about the lessons in shooting he was going to get, he'd completely forgotten his beer. He didn't like sitting alone in the booth so he wandered back to the bar with it and took a stool.

The party worried him, though, for two reasons. One was that Francine would be there and he'd have to see her again. And if there was a lot of drinking, she might do some damn fool thing like talking about how he'd come across her Thursday afternoon—or some still more damn fool thing like sitting on his lap or making passes at him or razzing him for not making passes at her, or— Hell, you couldn't tell what a woman might do when she got too many drinks in her. And Mitch would be there. And the other reason was that Mitch had told him to bring a woman of his own, and he couldn't think of one who'd fit in at a party like that.

Ellie was completely out, naturally. Too nice a kid to take to a party where anything could happen. She'd like as not never speak to him again. He knew other girls, sure, and one or two who were tough enough not to be shocked by a wild party—but they weren't girls he'd want to show off in front of Mitch—and Francine. They were too obviously cheap little broads and next to Francine they'd look like something he'd picked up out of the gutter on his way there. They didn't have class, like Francine had.

Well, maybe he could get out of going by not having a girl to bring. He could let Mitch think he was fixed up and then Saturday evening he could phone Mitch just before the party and say the girl he'd lined up was sick and he didn't want to come alone.

Only, damn it, he *did* want to go. He didn't want to see Francine, but then again he did want to see her. What was the matter with him, he wondered? Was he afraid of Francine? Of Mitch? Of himself? He decided ruefully that he was a little afraid of all three of them.

"Another beer, kid?"

Krasno was standing in front of him and his beer glass was empty. He saw with surprise that he and Krasno were alone in the place; he hadn't noticed when the other customers who'd been sitting at the bar had left.

He didn't really want one, but he was startled into saying, "Sure, Krazzy," and then modified it by saying, "Make it a short one, though. Better get going pretty soon."

Krazzy drew it and cut off the foam with his white celluloid stick. Joe reached for a coin but Krasno said, "On me, Joe."

He leaned against the back bar and tamped tobacco into his pipe, staring at Joe.

Finally he said, "Joe, what's Mitch up to?"

"What do you mean?" Joe asked.

"Are you getting dragged into anything? You're a good kid, Joe; I don't like to see Mitch drag you down with him."

What the hell was Krazzy talking about?

"Joe, did he feed you the line that he's going to open a gambling joint?" Krasno looked around him as though to make sure that there wasn't anybody else in the place. "Listen, kid, it takes *money* to do that, big money. Mitch hasn't got it. Mitch is broke, kid."

That was so funny that Joe laughed. Mitch broke!

Krasno said, "I don't mean he's down to cigarette money, but I mean he's down to his last ten thousand bucks or so. And, Joe, that's broke—for Mitch. He's used to having it and throwing it away. And he's been going broke ever since his racket folded on him over a month ago. This place doesn't make money; it's a front. You know that. He hasn't had any source of income since numbers dried up. Some capital, yeah, but he's been gambling heavy, kid, and the way I heard it, he's been losing his shirt. He's got as much chance opening a swank joint in Waukesha County as I have of starting a department store."

Joe stared at him, wondering what to say, how to shut him up. The old guy was cracked. Mitch broke! Mitch owned half of Milwaukee.

Krasno did it for him. He shrugged. "Oh, hell, what difference does it make? Joe, you might as well have a good time while you got a chance. It's not going to last long. Maybe you're smart at that. How long do you expect to live, Joe?"

Krasno *must* be cracked.

He asked, "What do you mean, how long do I expect to live?"

"Don't you read the papers, Joe? Don't you know what's going on? I mean, we're heading for the blowup to end all blowups. And not many years more."

"You mean war with Russia? Hell, we can lick them."

Krasno shrugged. "Joe, every war up to now has been a *war,* but the next one won't be; it'll be something you can't picture. It'll end up with the few of you who are left living in caves and fighting wild dogs—if all the dogs aren't eaten before it gets that far. And it's going to happen, Joe. It could happen next week. Just read the papers."

It made Joe uncomfortable, Krasno talking that way. But it was better than having him talk against Mitch, when they were both working for Mitch. That was disloyalty, and he didn't like it a damn bit.

He said, "Maybe it won't be that bad."

"Worse than you can imagine it, Joe. Don't you realize how our civilization is centralized? Ten or twelve atom

97

bombs on our ten or twelve biggest cities and the whole thing falls apart like a house of cards. Our whole economy goes up in smoke. The only ones that have a chance to keep eating are the farmers and they'll be too busy shooting starving people heading out from the cities—or getting shot themselves. It's going to be a mess, Joe."

Krasno's pipe had gone out; he put it down without trying to relight it. He said, "I'm glad I'm old, Joe. I've had a life. But damn if I don't feel sorry for people that haven't had. That's why I say I guess it doesn't matter a damn what you do. You haven't got long to do it anyway."

"My God but you sound cheerful, Krazzy."

"It's inevitable, Joe. We and Russia—we're just too different to live side by side. I don't know which of us will start it first; maybe us because we're afraid of them. We know they want the whole world or nothing. They got a lot of Europe already. They're going to get China. And then they're stymied until they lick us."

"That's easier said than done. We got A-bombs."

"Oh, sure. They'll lose, too. Everybody'll lose. Who won the San Francisco earthquake? But they're going to try. And don't think they haven't got A-bombs, too. And maybe radioactive dust and God knows what else. Bacteriological warfare, too. Joe, can you shoot a gun?"

Joe looked at him, wondering whether Krasno could have overheard any of the conversation back in the booth. But he couldn't have.

"If I was young and wanted to have a chance of keeping on living, I'd get myself one and learn how to shoot it. And have a big stock of bullets for it, too; you won't be able to get any more after it starts. Everybody isn't going to get killed off—or, hell, maybe everybody will be killed

98

off if they start using bacteria. But if any come through, they're going to be ones who have guns when things start. You'll need a gun to get a loaf of bread. Money won't mean anything. And if you got a gun you might be able to make it a little easier for yourself if you get too bad radiation burns – or maybe the plagues will be something you'd just as soon not die from after you get it. Not that you'll need to be an expert marksman for that."

Joe gave a mock shudder. "Anything else you can think of to cheer me up?"

Krasno's yellow teeth showed as he grinned. Then he was serious again. He said, "Only this, Joe. It just might not be quite as bad as I drew it for you. But don't kid yourself about one thing – it *is* going to happen. Maybe next week – maybe it'll start from the Berlin Blockade and the air lift. They shoot down one of our planes on that air lift, and there it is. Or maybe it'll be a few years. But God help me, Joe, it's *going* to happen. You might as well face it. And it's the end of civilization as we know it."

Joe slid himself off the stool. He said, "Thanks, Krazzy, for both the beer and the sunshine to brighten my life. I better go and lay myself in a stock of hand grenades."

But as he strolled into town he couldn't get what Krasno had been telling him off his mind; he couldn't think of anything else, in fact. He decided, finally, that he was getting hungry enough to eat and he'd go around to the Dinner Gong. He didn't realize that he wanted to talk to Ellie to get his mind on other things, but there it was.

He sat down at Ellie's section of the counter; she came over to him right away.

"Good news, Joe," she said. "I found a room. A light housekeeping room, I mean."

99

"Fine. Where?"

"On State Street, near Seventeenth. Just a few blocks from here. Are you going to be busy tomorrow morning?"

"No. Why? Want me to help you move your stuff over?"

"If you wouldn't mind. I've got two suitcases and a small trunk, so I'll have to take a cab anyway. But the trunk isn't heavy, just clothes, and the two of us could carry it down the stairs one place and up the stairs at the other. It's second floor at the new place too. I'm paid at Mrs Gettleman's through Wednesday, but I had to pay for the housekeeping room starting right away in order to get it, so I might as well move tomorrow."

"Sure, Ellie. What time?"

"Oh, about nine o'clock, if that isn't too early for you."

"That's okay," he said. He'd have to get up at half past five Wednesday morning anyway; if he got up a little earlier than usual tomorrow morning he'd have a better chance of getting to sleep early Tuesday evening. "Even earlier than that, if you want."

"No, that'll be early enough, Joe. And thanks a lot."

"Good thing you decided on tomorrow morning and not Wednesday. I'm going hunting early Wednesday morning." He remembered he'd told her, truthfully, that he didn't have a gun and added, "Friend of mine's lending me an extra gun of his."

"Oh. What are you hunting?"

He had to think fast. Ellie might know that not much was in season now. She probably wouldn't know much about hunting foxes and anyway she wouldn't know they didn't have dogs. "Foxes," he said.

"Oh, Joe, don't shoot foxes. They're cute. I like them."

He laughed. "I probably won't get one. But, look, if I *do*, I'll have it made into a fox scarf for you. How's that?"

She laughed, too. "Don't bother, Joe; I've got a fox scarf, red fox. And that's what struck me as funny; my telling you not to shoot a poor little fox, and when I got that neckpiece—and I saved up for months to get it—I never thought that somebody had to shoot a fox for it. Two foxes, in fact. All right, I'll shut up and let you look at the menu."

The next morning he helped her move. The room on State Street wasn't much bigger than the one on Wells, but it did have a kitchenette with a few dishes and cooking utensils.

Ellie was checking possibilities of the kitchenette before she even thought of unpacking her belongings. She called back over her shoulder, "Joe, have you had any breakfast yet? Did you eat before you knocked on my door this morning?"

He said, "No, Ellie. Shall I cut some strips from the curtain here, so you can fry them?"

"I don't have to get to work till twelve, Joe; I fixed it with Uncle Mike so I could get in an hour late. And I'm going to have to stock this kitchenette and it's going to be a lot to carry, the first time. If you'll go shopping with me and help carry it back, I can make us a brunch."

"Brunch?"

"Cross between breakfast and lunch."

Joe grinned at her. "Been eating 'em all my life and never knew what they were. Sure, Ellie. Why not?"

There was a grocery only a block and a half away. Having to start from scratch with everything from salt and sugar on up the list, Ellie did quite a bit of buying and they both had plenty to carry on the way back. And when they got back, Ellie insisted on washing all the dishes and utensils before she'd use any of them. Also she looked back under the sink and stove and said, "Knew I'd forget *something*. Roach powder."

"We could try radioactive dust," Joe suggested.

"What's that, Joe? Something new?"

"According to a friend of mine, Capitalists use it on Communists and vice versa."

"Oh. You think it would work on roaches?"

He looked at her to see if she was serious and saw that she wasn't. He rather wished he could tell her about that horrible guff old Krasno had fed him yesterday. She'd laugh at it and he'd feel better. And yet he knew that, underneath, it would be as unpleasant to her as it had been to him. And the horrible part of it was that Krasno might be completely right—probably was at least partly right. Why worry Ellie talking about it?

He watched Ellie getting brunch for them, but his mind wasn't on eating; it kept going back to the things Krasno had said. Not that any of them—except the silly things Krasno had said about Mitch which had led up to the other things—had been new to him. He'd been reading science fiction stories for years—stories about the coming blowup, about the human race being obliterated or reverting to some form or other of savagery. Science fiction had been doing that even before the atom bomb had really been invented. Nuclear fission was old stuff in science fiction long before Los Alamos. But those were stories, fiction.

Krasno had been talking casual fact. That was the horrible thing; Krasno had probably never read a science fiction story in his life. And yet he was as sure of what was coming as he was sure that the sun was going to come up tomorrow.

It was one thing to think of something as fiction or as an

102

abstraction, something else to think of it as something that was going to happen to *him*, maybe next week, maybe next year.

He saw himself in ragged clothes walking along the side of a road, hungry; there was no one in sight. Behind him—

"Will you bring the chairs, Joe?" Ellie said. "Guess it's ready—such as it is. I'm afraid I kind of botched it."

She had, a little. She'd cooked bacon and eggs and the bacon was a little overdone, not quite burned but close to it. And the eggs had started out to be sunny-side up, but the yolks had broken and they were more nearly scrambled.

Ellie apologized and blamed the fact that one had to get used to a new stove and new cooking equipment. Joe insisted that it tasted swell, and found he wasn't exaggerating too much at that. It was quite different and quite pleasant to be eating home cooking for a change from restaurants. There was a difference somehow, somewhere, that you couldn't quite put your finger on. Like when he was a kid and he and other kids had built a fire in a vacant lot down near the canal and had baked potatoes. The potatoes had been underdone in the middle and overdone near the outside and they'd had only salt, no butter, to put on them, but they'd tasted wonderful. This was like that, somehow.

He said, "This is swell, Ellie. Honestly."

"You're lying, Joe Bailey. It's awful. But give me time to get used to that darned stove—"

"That damn stove."

"All right, that *damn* stove. And wait till Sunday evening. I'll have things ready by then and I'll cook you some spaghetti that's out of this world. And *not* because I'm trying to get at your heart through your stomach, either.

103

Just that I'm so ashamed of this that I've got to show you I can cook to save my own pride."

"It's wonderful, Ellie."

And it was.

She tried not to let him help with the dishes but he insisted on it. And by the time they'd finished with the dishes Ellie had to rush to get to the Dinner Gong by twelve o'clock. She still hadn't had time to unpack her clothes.

There wasn't time to do anything else because of his appointment at Dixie's room on Cass Street at one or a little after, so Joe dropped in at Shorty's and played a game of pool. For some reason he couldn't get his mind on it and got badly licked.

9

Dixie Ehlers was in love. Not with a woman or women, but with guns. He had a harem of them.

They – or most of them – were in a gladstone bag in the closet of his room. He got it out and opened it as soon as Joe got there, and the bed sagged under its weight. Each gun was in a fine leather holster of its own and was wrapped carefully and separately in a piece of cloth. Each one was loaded.

"Don't go pulling triggers, kid," he told Joe. "I wouldn't have an unloaded gun around me, unless I unloaded it to do some dry shooting. You have an unloaded gun around and you get to count on it being unloaded and someday it isn't; you've loaded it and forgotten about it and that's how accidents happen. Remember that, kid; not only about these guns but about any you have yourself. Keep 'em loaded, always *know* they're loaded. Besides, then you know they're ready to use."

He was unwrapping one gun after another and laying them in a neat row in the middle of the bed, sitting on one side of it himself. Joe noticed that he put them all down pointing one way, away from himself and Joe.

He said, "Sit down, Joe. Now look, here's the gun I'm going to start you on, first few times we go out. Want you to do a lot of shooting and twenty-two cartridges are for free compared with what thirty-eights cost. Twenty-twos are less than a cent apiece, even for the long rifles, and that's the kind you want to use. Thirty-eight costs you nearer a nickel a shot, even for shorts. Shoot off a few hundred rounds and that's a difference of three bucks, say, to fifteen bucks. Mitch is paying for the cartridges, but we don't want to stick him too bad.

"Now this gun's a twenty-two thirty-two target revolver, six shots. Come only with a six-inch barrel, but I had this one cut down to three. You can't carry a six-inch barrel in a shoulder holster—not and get it out quick when you want it, anyway—and you want to get used to carrying a gun in a shoulder holster. Know what I mean by a twenty-two thirty-two?"

"No," Joe said.

"Shoots twenty-twos, but it's built on a thirty-two frame. It weighs about twenty-two ounces. Nice accurate little gun, and cheap to shoot. But strictly not for business; you want a thirty-eight for that. And you can get a thirty-eight even lighter than this. Here. Try the trigger pull."

He swung the cylinder and ejected the cartridges and then handed the gun to Joe. "Not often; you're not supposed to snap guns when they're empty. Not good for them. But once or twice won't hurt."

Joe took the gun. He started to sight it at a picture across the room and then, before snapping it, put it down and swung out the cylinder himself to make sure Dixie had got all the bullets out of it.

Dixie nodded approvingly. "Attaboy," he said. "I was waiting to see if you'd have sense enough to do that. If a man hands you a gun that's not loaded, even if you *saw* him take the bullets out, make sure yourself. Especially with an automatic. One thing to remember about an automatic is that even after you take out the clip there's a bullet in the chamber. Now go ahead and snap it."

Joe snapped the gun a few times, first pulling the trigger all the way for double action and then trying the trigger pull with the gun cocked.

He said, "You said we should do some dry shooting. That's shooting this way without bullets, isn't it? But if it's hard on the gun—"

"It isn't hard on the gun if you've got empty cartridges in the chamber. Then the firing pin's got something to hit on, to cushion it. I don't happen to have any empty shells for a twenty-two, but I have some thirty-eights. I'll let you dry shoot with one of them. This one, in fact; this is the gun I'll graduate you to after a few days with the twenty-two."

He handed Joe a small, light revolver with a two-inch barrel.

"That's a honey," he said. "An S. & W. Terrier. Weighs only seventeen ounces and handles like a toy gun, but it's got plenty of shocking power at close range. Nice gun to carry, too. In a shoulder holster you hardly know you're wearing it, and it's good for carrying in a topcoat or overcoat pocket, too. I sometimes carry it in an overcoat pocket even if I'm carrying Maggie in a shoulder holster. Here's Maggie."

Maggie, it turned out, was the favorite of his harem. He

showed her to Joe with all the pride and care of a Sultan exhibiting a Circassian beauty. Maggie was a three-five-seven Magnum.

"The most gun there is," he told Joe. "She weighs forty-one ounces, damn near two and a half times what that Terrier weighs, but hell, kid, she shoots through bullet-proof glass, bulletproof vests, auto bodies, anything but the side of a battleship. And still she'll mush to fifty caliber going through eight inches of soft paraffin. It's got more shock power than an army forty-five and the range—by God, you could put telescopic sights on one of these things and use it at several hundred yards. Even with this three-and-a-half-inch barrel."

Joe was fascinated by the guns. Dixie showed them one at a time, explaining how each of them worked and its advantages and disadvantages. He let Joe handle them, all but Maggie the Magnum. There was a Luger, a forty-five Colt automatic, a little vest pocket twenty-five automatic that weighed only thirteen ounces—but that Dixie said was quite deadly at close range if you shot it straight—and a thirty-eight Banker's Special that was similar to the Terrier except that it weighed two ounces more, held six instead of five cartridges, and had a slightly larger butt. That was the lot, seven of them.

"Which one do you like, kid?" Dixie asked.

"The Terrier." Joe didn't have to hesitate.

"Okay. Take your coat off and strap this holster on. I'll put in some empties so you can dry shoot it. Then I'll show you something about drawing."

Joe had an hour of it and learned quite a bit. His reactions, Dixie told him, were naturally fast. Not a hell of a lot of practice, Dixie said, and he'd be really good. Shooting straight, once the gun was out of the holster, was something else again. Tomorrow they'd find out how straight he could shoot. It was better to be slow, Dixie told him, and shoot straight, than to be a fireball on the draw but not to hit anything when you started shooting.

When Dixie said he'd had about all he could take for one afternoon, Joe started to take off his coat to get at the shoulder holster. His first practice had been with his coat off, then with it on so he would learn to slide his hand across his chest toward the holster instead of having his hand out where he might get on the wrong side of the lapel or tangle with it.

Dixie stopped him. "Leave it on, kid."

"Huh?"

"Get used to wearing it. Leave it on. If you wear a gun only when you think you might have to use it, you're not used to the weight and feel of it on you, see? And leave those empty shells in it so you can dry shoot a little in your room this evening. And remember what I told you about how to squeeze and not pull."

"Okay, Dixie. Thanks."

"Now turn around and walk a little. Yeah, that's okay. It doesn't show at all. But don't hold your left arm out a little like you got a stiff shoulder or something. Hold it natural. That's it."

"Makes me feel lopsided," Joe said.

"Huh. That's seventeen ounces. Try wearing a Magnum, forty-one ounces, sometime if you really want to feel lopsided. That light little Terrier is a good one to start off with. That suit you got is cut okay. A single-breasted's better than a double-breasted for when you wear a holster, only you got to remember to keep one button buttoned. Otherwise you lean over and the coat falls away and somebody gets a flash of the holster or the gun butt. A single-breasted, cut loose."

Joe wore the gun the rest of the day, feeling as

conspicuous as though it was outside his coat instead of inside. When, twice, he walked past a policeman he walked very straight and stiff, but that, he realized, just proved Dixie Ehler's point; it would take a lot of wearing just to get used to doing it so it felt natural and let you act natural.

Early in the evening he dropped into Shorty's for a game of pool and then, after he'd lined up a game and was about to start, he remembered that he'd never yet shot a game without taking off his suit coat. It would look funny if he did it now, so he had to get out of the game by getting himself into an argument on the amount and odds of the bet. It occurred to him too late, after he'd left Shorty's, that maybe he could have gone back to the washroom and got the gun and holster in his coat pocket and then come back and he could have taken off his coat. But if anyone bumped his coat on the rack they'd have felt the weight of the gun there.

He happened to be in the neighborhood at the time and remembered Ellie had started late and was getting off at nine. So he dropped around to walk home with her. In the downstairs hallway of her new place on State Street she stopped before starting up the stairs.

"Maybe you better not come up, Joe," she said. "It's late already and I want to unpack all my clothes before I turn in. They'll get too wrinkled if I don't."

"Okay," Joe said. If it hadn't been for the gun, he'd have argued that he'd like to sit a few minutes and watch her unpack and they could talk while she put things away. But he'd discovered already that wearing the gun was particularly uncomfortable when he was with Ellie. He'd almost rather explain to a policeman what he was doing with a gun than explain it to Ellie. And no matter how careful he was, she might put up a hand to take a raveling or something off the lapel of his coat—girls did things like that—and feel the gun and ask him about it.

Right now she was saying "Good night, Joe," and from the way she said it he knew she expected, even wanted, him to kiss her good night. But she'd surely feel the gun if he put his arms around her and it would seem stranger just to lean forward and peck her lips without using his arms than if he didn't kiss her at all. So he said, "Good night, Ellie," and took a step back and she turned and started up the stairs. And because he didn't want her to think he was mad, he waited until she had gone up a few steps, a safe distance, and then said, "Ellie, how about tomorrow night? Like to see a show or something?"

She turned back. "Would the next night, Thursday, be all right, Joe? I'll still be straightening things up here tomorrow evening."

"Sure, Ellie. See you Thursday evening. 'Night."

He went out, still feeling foolish—and disappointed, too—because he hadn't been able to kiss her good night.

Hereafter, no matter how much he practiced wearing a holster to get used to it, times he would or might be with Ellie he'd leave it home. There was a limit. Funny, he thought, how different women are from one another; if he ever put his arms around Francine, he'd be proud to let her feel that he was wearing a pistol. Probably, now, she thought he was just a punk running errands for Mitch.

But he pulled his mind away from the thought of putting his arms around Francy. Francy was Mitch's girl and that was that.

He went right home after leaving Ellie, partly because he had to get up so early in the morning and partly because he was damned tired of wearing the gun and wanted to get it off. Maybe it would seem romantic to be wearing a loaded gun, when there was even a remote chance that you might have to use it, but wearing one loaded with empty shells had all of the inconveniences and disadvantages of the real thing, and none of the thrill and excitement. Dixie had told him one should never have an unloaded gun around; maybe he should have loaded it to carry it and he could have brought along separately, in his pocket, the empty shells to use for dry shooting.

In his room he took off the suit coat and the holster first thing. He pulled down the shade and tried sighting the gun at a picture on the wall. One picture was a shepherd leading a flock of sheep and he tried picking off the sheep one at a time, but without actually clicking the gun. If he clicked it in here, probably someone would hear and wonder what he was doing. But the sheep weren't very good; they were so small he couldn't really draw a bead on any one of them.

He tried sighting at the shepherd in the picture and suddenly lowered the gun, embarrassed. He'd remembered that the picture was a religious allegory and that the figure of the shepherd was a figure of Christ. He didn't really believe in religion; that was a lot of superstition, silly stuff they taught you about things that had happened so long ago they couldn't matter now if they ever had. And that picture—the metaphor of Jesus as a shepherd—had annoyed him ever since he'd had this room; he'd almost got around to asking Mrs Gettleman if she'd change it. The whole idea was wrong. A shepherd and his sheep! A shepherd raised sheep to sell, to butcher and eat, to fleece. If he worried about a lost sheep it was because it was costing him mutton and wool. A hell of a comparison for religious people to draw; if their Christ wasn't any better to them than a shepherd to his sheep, they'd better forget about him. Still, it had embarrassed him a little to have been drawing a bead on Christ with a revolver.

He tried the picture on the other wall, but it wasn't so good; it was a picture of a building, an ordinary small store with LEIBER AND HENNIG lettered on the windows in large letters and DRY GOODS below in smaller letters. Someone, sometime—probably either Mr Leiber or Mr Hennig, whoever they were—had thought enough of that store to have a photograph of it enlarged and framed. By now, probably, Mr Leiber, Mr Hennig and the store were all dead, but the picture still hung and would probably hang there irrelevantly as long as the building it hung in stood.

He tried sighting the gun at a window of the store but that wasn't any fun and he put the gun back in the holster and put it on the dresser. And just for the fun of it, to make it look like an arsenal, he took his hunting knife out of the bottom drawer and put it, sheath and all, beside the holstered gun. It was a hunting knife he'd won on a punchboard a long time ago and he'd never used it for anything more romantic than sharpening pencils, but it was a beautiful knife with a bone handle and a wide five-inch blade in a tooled leather sheath. He'd been proud of it ever since he had it and almost wished he could go in for hunting or fishing just for an excuse to use and carry it.

He set the alarm for five-thirty and turned in. An auto horn blatted outside and then it was quiet, so quiet that he could hear the clock ticking, and it got louder and louder as he lay there. Louder and louder and louder. For some reason it made him remember and think about that night when he was six, the night his father had died. He wondered why. The ticking of a clock had had nothing to do with that night. Or had it? Somehow it seemed that it *had*, but he couldn't remember how.

The Screen

1. *Dearborn Street, Chicago. It is early evening. During this scene* MUSIC *is playing "Chicago, That Toddlin' Town" in style of a jazz band of 1935. Camera mounted on southeast corner of roof of Newberry Library Building (corner of North Dearborn and West Walton streets) pans south along Dearborn Street past Bughouse Square toward the Loop. We pass Delaware Place and Chestnut Street and camera focuses on an old brownstone front building halfway between Chestnut Street and Chicago Avenue.*

DISSOLVE TO

2. *Closer view of front of same building. Camera focuses on a third floor window and moves toward it.* MUSIC *(same) continues but fades slowly until it vanishes coincident with first spoken line. Camera (on boom) moves through window into a small bedroom, furnished inexpensively and without taste. Camera proceeds without pause through doorway into next room, a living room, equivalently furnished. Camera proceeds through this room, again without pause, to doorway of kitchen. There are three people in kitchen.* FLORENCE BAILEY, *a light coat over her arm, is seen walking toward a closed door that leads to the outer hallway.* ALVIN BAILEY, *a big man with an unkempt*

mustache and somewhat in need of a shave, is sitting at the kitchen table engrossed in a game of solitaire with a pack of dog-eared cards. He is in shirtsleeves and wears carpet slippers. JOSEPH BAILEY, *age 6, is sitting on the floor in a corner busily making something unidentifiable out of an old Tinkertoy set. He is a thin, nervous-looking boy, physically small for his age. He is very intent on what he is doing. Florence Bailey opens the door and pauses.*

FLORENCE: 'Bye, Joey.

Joe does not look up.

FLORENCE: 'Bye, Al. Got to hurry; I'm late now.

ALVIN: Okay, Flo. So long.

He continues playing solitaire without looking up or turning.

FLORENCE: Don't forget, Al, half-past eight he goes to bed. You watch that clock and don't forget.

ALVIN: Sure. 'Bye, Flo.

FLORENCE: And you're staying right here with him, remember. You know how he is about being left alone. You know what I mean. You know what happened last time.

ALVIN: He's got to get over that sometime, don't he?

FLORENCE: Al! You're *not* figuring on going out, are you? If you are, I'm not going to work! I don't care whether we eat or not, and if you can't get out and earn some money, why should I?

ALVIN: Now don't get your bowels in an uproar, Flo. I'm not going out. I got twelve cents. Where the hell would I go on twelve cents? The Blackstone?

He sounds good-naturedly amused, not angry. Apparently he is stuck in his solitaire game; he gathers the cards and starts to shuffle them. His back is still toward his wife, but he glances over the edge of the table at Joe.

FLORENCE: And remember that r-h-y-m-e you're not supposed to mention. Don't even use the word c-a-n-d-l-e or the other one, especially just before he goes to bed. *Joe has looked up from his play, eyes wide, when the second word is spelled by his mother, but neither of his parents notices him or the expression on his face.*

ALVIN: Okay, okay, okay. If you've told me that once...

FLORENCE: And you're *not* going out?

ALVIN: Christ, no. I told you once. Thought you said you was late.

FLORENCE: All right, but don't forget. *She closes door.*

FADE OUT

FADE IN

3. *Close view of Joe Bailey sitting in corner working with his Tinkertoys. We see that a little time has passed for the object he has been making has grown. We see now that it is probably intended to be a power shovel. On the floor in front of him there chances to lie one of the cylindrical pieces of the Tinkertoy set and from the center hole projects upward a short straight piece; in miniature, an imaginative mind could visualize the inadvertent construction as a candle in a candleholder. Joe's eyes come toward it and slowly a look of horror comes into them. Then his eyes close suddenly and he averts his head as his hand reaches out for the two joined Tinkertoy pieces. His eyes open, looking this time at his father and away from the thing he holds in his hand and now pulls apart into two separate Tinkertoy parts.*

JOE: P-P-Pop!

ALVIN: Yeah, Joey?

There is a sound of knocking on a door. Camera pans past Al Bailey, looking up from his solitaire game, and focuses on door.

ALVIN: Just a minute, Joey.

He comes into view of camera again as we see him walking toward door. He opens door, revealing DUTCH ANDERS *and* TONY MONTOYA *standing outside doorway. Anders is short, stocky, coarse-featured, wears a cap. Montoya is sleek, dapper;*

his eyes are not quite right somehow. You wouldn't trust Dutch Anders in an alley; you wouldn't trust Tony Montoya anywhere.

ALVIN: Hi, boys. Long time no see. Come in.

They enter. Montoya has a package under his arm and puts it on the kitchen table. He takes off his hat and, after looking around, puts it on the icebox. Anders keeps his cap on but shoves it back.

MONTOYA: How you doing, Al?

ALVIN: Not so hot, I guess.

MONTOYA: Not like the old days when you used to work for me, huh, Al? Well, maybe those days'll come back. Good old Prohibition, huh, Al? They knocked off the big money when they knocked it out.

He sits down in the chair Al Bailey has just left. Anders pulls up another chair. Obviously, they intend to stay a while.

MONTOYA: Where's the wife? Gone to work?

From the way he asks, you get the impression that he already knew. Al Bailey merely nods. He starts to pull up another chair, the only one left in the kitchen, but Montoya stops him.

MONTOYA: Get some glasses, Al, huh? That's a quart in the package. Thought you might like a drink. For old lang syne. Heard you've been down on your luck and we thought we might cheer you up a little. Didn't we, Dutch?

ANDERS: Sure.

Al Bailey has already been eyeing the package, which is obviously a bottle.

ALVIN: Swell of you, Tony. God, can I use a drink.

He moves out of range of camera. Anders picks up the bottle and unwraps it, wadding the paper and throwing it in the general direction of the sink. Montoya picks up the deck of cards with which Bailey has been playing solitaire and starts to riffle them. Anders works the cork out of the bottle as Al Bailey, carrying three tumblers, comes back into the scene. He puts the glasses down on the table and gets the other chair as Anders pours three drinks.

ALVIN (*again*): God, can I use a drink.

MONTOYA: To you, Al.

ANDERS: Yeah.

They drink.

MONTOYA: Hell of a shame, Al. You, the best bartender in Chi—under Andy Volstead. And now that it's *legal* to tend bar they won't give you a license. Just because of a couple of little spots on your record. Just because you—

ALVIN (*quickly, warningly, moving his head slightly in the direction of Joe, playing in the corner*): Little pitchers!

MONTOYA: Sure, Al. Well, I'm in the same spot. Can't get a license to *run* a bar. The good old days. Gone forever, I guess. Look, how about a little stud, just to fill in some time. Small stakes.

ALVIN: With what, Tony? By me, I mean. I got twelve cents. Twelve Goddam cents to my name. If Flo gets any tips at the restaurant tonight we eat tomorrow. Honest, boys, I'm strapped. Do you think this Goddam Depression will ever end?

He leans forward, suddenly serious; you see that he's seriously interested in Montoya's opinion.

MONTOYA (*equally serious*): Damn if I know, Al. Way things are going, I don't know. Maybe we're going to have a revolution or something. Or else we got to get a guy in here like Italy's got—Mussolini.

ALVIN (*thoughtfully*): I don't know, Tony. This Mussolini—

He glances at the bottle and pretty obviously decides that he'd better not look a gift horse in the mouth—or argue with its giver.

MONTOYA: Oh, the hell with politics. Let's be cheerful. Me, I'm going to get by, whatever happens. Let's play a little stud anyway, to kill time. We won't play for much and if you lose, you can owe me.

ALVIN: I owe you twenty already, and for a hell of a long time.

Montoya shrugs.

MONTOYA: So what? Maybe you'll win it back and won't owe me anything. Don't worry about *me,* Al. I still got a little, and I know how to get more. Maybe I might even let you in on it if you get to owing me enough so that I get worried about it. Got any chips?

ALVIN: Christ, Tony. No.

MONTOYA: No, what? You mean you ain't got any chips?

Al's face is interesting. At the word "chips" he reaches into his pocket and pulls out change, two nickels and two pennies. He looks at them and laughs, but not with amusement.

ALVIN: Sure. I got lots of chips.

MONTOYA: Get 'em. Let's play some stud.

ALVIN: What's the racket?

Montoya grins and imitates Alvin's motion of head toward the boy playing in the corner of the room.

MONTOYA: Little pitchers. It's nothing much, Al. I just thought the three of us might take in a movie tonight—the Walton, over on Walton Street.

Camera has panned across to Joe Bailey, playing in corner, as Montoya speaks. There is a change of tone of voice after "Little pitchers" that makes Joe look up toward the men seated at the table. But there is nothing in Joe's face that tells you whether or not he understands the significance of what is being said. As he looks down again—

FADE OUT

FADE IN

4. *Same three men seated around table, a little later. They are now playing stud poker. Montoya and Anders have taken off their suit coats and hung them over the backs of their chairs. Alvin Bailey is cautiously lifting the corner of his hole card.*

MONTOYA: Costs you a quarter, Al.

ALVIN: I'll stay. I'm out fifteen bucks now; what's another two bits?

MONTOYA: Forget it, Al. I'll take it out of your cut of—tonight. It's all cased, Al. A lead pipe cinch.

ALVIN: What time? What's the score? Talk so that— *He jerks his head toward the corner.*

MONTOYA: Ten-thirty the B.O. closes. They take the—the stuff to the manager's office and start counting it. We're inside, last row, watching the show. All we need is some rope to tie up—you know what. And three—uh—

ALVIN: Got an extra one? I *had* one, but it's in hock.

MONTOYA: Everything we need's in the car. I figure we get there about ten. Leave here half past nine. Okay?

Camera has been moving around table until it faces Alvin Bailey over Montoya's shoulder.

ALVIN (*a little louder than he has been speaking previously*): No, Tony. I can't. (*He winks elaborately.*) I promised Flo that I'd stay home with Joe, so I'd better. I'll go to a movie with you some other time.

MONTOYA: (*winking back*): Sure, Al. Some other time.

ALVIN: Joey, it's time you started to bed.

JOE: Can't I f-finish this, P-Pop?

He holds up object he has been making with the Tinkertoys.

ALVIN: Look, Joey, you be a real good boy tonight and go right to bed and to sleep—and without any stalling—and I'll give you a dime.

MONTOYA: Make it two bits, if he really shows some

speed.

He shoves a quarter across the table to Alvin.

ALVIN: Sure, Joey. I'll make it a quarter. Now really get a wiggle on, huh?

Joe's eyes widen at the mention of so much money. He starts quickly to pick up the unused pieces of Tinkertoy and to return them to the box.

FADE OUT

FADE IN

5. *Close-up of cheap tin clock on top of kitchen cabinet. Hands stand at half-past nine. We hear it ticking loudly.*

CUT TO

6. *The three men at the kitchen table. The cards have been pushed aside. Montoya getting up, very quietly, and putting his coat on. All of ensuing conversation in very low tones of voice.*

MONTOYA: Come on, Al. Get your coat. And be quiet about it.

ALVIN: I'll have to make sure he's asleep.

MONTOYA: Hell, he's asleep. He's been in bed over an hour.

ALVIN: Yeah, but—

MONTOYA: Call him and you'll wake him up. Let's just sneak out.

ALVIN: But if he *is* awake—

MONTOYA: Leave the light on in here; that's all you gotta do. If he wakes up and sees there's a light, he'll go back to sleep. Hell, Al, you'll be back here in two hours. What can happen in two hours? And you'll be back with a couple hundred bucks in your kick.

DISSOLVE TO

7. *Close-up of Alvin's face. It shows indecision, concern. As one emotion struggles with another we hear echo chamber effect*

repeat last seven words that Montoya has spoken in previous scene.

ECHO CHAMBER VOICE: A couple hundred bucks in your kick.

VOICE OF MONTOYA (*normal*): Sure, go on and wake up the kid by asking him if he's asleep. Dutch and I can get by without you. Two's enough for that job; we were just cutting you in.

ALVIN: Okay, okay.

FADE OUT

FADE IN

8. *Door of kitchen (the one leading to the hallway) closing very quietly. But the click of the latch is audible.*

SLOW DISSOLVE TO

9. *Bedroom. Joe in child's size bed. Background music, very soft: Rachmaninoff's* Isle of the Dead. *Joe is sitting up in bed; his eyes are wide and he is obviously listening hard. Light comes from a dim bulb in a lamp near the head of the bed, left on as a night light. There is a look of near panic on Joe's face as he throws back the covers and, in one-piece cotton flannel pajamas a bit small for him, gets out of bed and runs to the lamp. He pulls a chain and the scene brightens as a bright bulb goes on beside the dim one. Camera follows him as he goes to door of bedroom (closed) and opens it. Living room is dark but through it we can see open door to kitchen and the fact that the kitchen is lighted. Camera stays still as, through bedroom doorway, we see Joe's back as he runs across dark living room into kitchen. He stands just inside kitchen doorway and we see his head turn as he looks around. We see his face as he comes back and there is more than a hint of panic in it now. But instead of running, he walks very straight and deliberately now, holding himself under control. As he walks through living room he flips a switch, turning on the*

lights in that room also. He leaves bedroom door open, walking straight toward the camera, walking into a close-up.

DISSOLVE TO

10. *Joe back in bed, this time half sitting, half lying; he has two pillows on end against the head of the bed. His knees are bent and he has a child's picture book resting against them. Music has stopped at change of scene. However, we now hear the sound effect of Scene No. 5, the ticking of a clock. Joe's eyes are sleepy he is obviously trying to keep awake by looking at the pictures.*

FADE OUT

FADE IN

11. *Same scene. Joe has fallen asleep. Book is on floor beside the bed. The lights seem dimmer; the camera has moved back so most of the room is visible, including door to living room. Again there is a sound effect instead of music; a kettledrum, tuned low, is being thumped to the exact rhythm of the ticking clock in the previous scene. Kettledrum continues at exactly same tempo and volume throughout this scene. Camera lens should be slightly out of focus to give a blurred, unreal effect.*

Joe slowly sits up in bed and his eyes open, although he is obviously, from the glazed stare in them, not awake.

On one side of the bed, in midair about four feet from the floor, appears a candle (lighted) in an old-fashioned candleholder with a curved handle. Its outlines, especially that of its flame, are wavy and distorted. It starts to grow larger in size and, simultaneously, the other lights gradually go out and the only source of light is the growing candle. It grows rapidly and by the time it is four feet tall (the candleholder now two feet from the floor and the flame six feet from the floor) it is throwing a very bright light on Joe's terrified face, but the corner of the room on the opposite side of Joe's bed from the monstrous candle gets darker, as though all the darkness dispelled by the light of the candle is gathering there. Something stirs in the darkness there; we see it only as a vaguely apelike shadow, darker than the darkness around it; it holds an ax.

The throbbing of the kettledrum continues. Joe sits in bed, staring unseeingly straight into the lens of the camera. He looks neither toward the candle — now six feet high — on one side of him nor toward the vague shadowy figure with the ax on the other side, yet obviously he is horribly aware of both.

The candle, now resting on the floor and eight feet tall, starts to bend over toward him, bending in a curve toward his head. On the other side of him, the shadow with the ax takes a shuffling step toward him. Joe suddenly comes out of the almost cataleptic state in which he has been sitting. He screams, almost falls over the foot of the bed, and runs toward the door.

CUT TO

12. *Kitchen door. Same as Scene No. 8 but wavy, distorted. We see Joe's back as he runs to the kitchen door, throws it open and runs out, leaving it open behind him. Silence— no sound effects for padding of his feet, opening of door, etc.*

Camera pans rapidly forward through kitchen door after Joe and goes to edge of stairwell in hallway, tilting down over banister. Looking downward, we see Joe running madly down the stairs.

CUT TO

13. *Exterior of front door and stone steps leading down to sidewalk. Camera just beyond curb, tilted upward at front door. Photography and sound effects (street noises) normal. Night. Door bursts open and Joe comes running out, barefooted and in his pajamas. He runs down the steps toward the camera, turns right (north). Camera swivels so we see him running away from us, north on the east side of Dearborn Street toward Chestnut Street. As he recedes into distance*

CUT TO

14. *Camera is in backseat of squad car cruising north on*

123

Dearborn Street. We see the heads of two policemen (BENZ *and* FOGARTY) *in the front seat, and between their heads we see through the windshield. Far ahead, on the sidewalk we catch sight of the running figure of Joe Bailey.*

BENZ (*who is driving car*): Hey, lookit that kid in pajamas up ahead. Looks like the devil's after him.

FOGARTY: Yeah. Maybe we better—

Benz has already stepped on the gas; the car speeds up to overtake Joe.

BENZ: I'll pull in ahead of him. You step out and scoop him up.

Car speeds up faster and camera swivels so we see Joe from the side as car passes him. Then it becomes a front view of him running toward us.

CUT TO

15. *Squad car stopping at curb. We hear brakes applied. Door opens and Fogarty steps out, just in time to catch Joe as Joe runs into scene past camera.*

FOGARTY: What's the matter, kid?

Joe doesn't struggle, now that he's caught and firmly held.

BENZ: Looks to me like he was walkin' in his sleep, Foggy.

FOGARTY: Hell of a fast walk. Come on, kid, wake up. Having a nightmare, huh?

He shakes Joe a little, gently, to help him awaken. Joe starts to cry.

BENZ: Let's get him in the car. It'll take him a minute or two to snap out of it. Come on, kid.

He takes Joe's other arm. Camera swings around to show them getting in car.

CUT TO

16. *Front seat of squad car, as though through windshield. Joe, looking reasonably awake and over the worst of his fright, is*

seated between the two policemen. The car is moving slowly, Benz driving.

FOGARTY: Yeah, he's coming out of it. Good idea to drive around the block while we talk to him; I think it helps some. You say your name is Joe Bailey, kid?

Joe nods.

FOGARTY: But you don't know the number of your house, the house you ran out from?

Joe shakes his head, and a touch of fear returns to his eyes. Obviously the idea of returning to be alone in the flat again terrifies him. He isn't telling.

FOGARTY (*to Benz*): He couldn'ta come more than a couple blocks that way, and it'd been somewhere on Dearborn. He was running too fast to make any corners.

BENZ: Two blocks is a lot of territory. Where are your parents, Joe? Where's your mother?

JOE: W-working. She's a w-waitress.

BENZ: What restaurant?

Joe shakes his head again.

FOGARTY: Where's your old man? Your father?

JOE: A m-m-movie.

FOGARTY: Well, guess we'll just have to take him in to the station. Hell, all the Goddam red tape and everything. (*He is obviously reluctant to do so, and so is Benz. He tries again.*) Joe, if we drive up and down Dearborn Street a few blocks, don't you even know the outside of your house when you see it? Can't you point it out to us?

Joe's lips clamp tightly. He shakes his head violently.

FOGARTY: Hell, the kid's afraid to go back, Charlie. He knows where he lives all right; he had a nightmare and he's afraid to be alone again. He's— How old are you, Joe?

JOE: S-Six.

FOGARTY: Any kid six knows his own house when he

sees it, and his address, too. He won't tell us because he's afraid to go back. I'd like to tell off his old man, leaving him alone like that, his age. (*Sighs*) Well, we'll just have to take him in.

A new kind of fear shows in Joe's face. These policemen have been friendly; he is not afraid of them. But being taken in — he thinks to jail — is something else again. But to go back to the house and be there alone is unthinkable. Neither of the policemen happens to be watching his face or the sudden terrific struggle that is going on there. He opens his mouth as though he is going to speak, clamps it shut again, and then

JOE: Pop went to the Walton Theater on Walton Street with two men one of them was named Montoya.

He has blurted this out so rapidly that the words almost run together and it is said in a flat monotone. For the first time in this sequence he has spoken without stuttering. Both policemen turn to look at him curiously because of the sudden change in his manner, and because of the odd flat way in which the sentence was spoken. For a second there is silence.

FOGARTY: That's only a few blocks, Charlie. Let's go there and find his old man. I'd like to tell him off.

BENZ: How'd you find him? We can't carry the kid all through the audience or anything.

FOGARTY: If it's the same Montoya—Say, kid, is this Montoya's first name Tony? Does your old man call him Tony?

Joe nods.

FOGARTY: I know him, then. He's been in lineup. He's a bad boy. Drive around there, Charlie. You keep the kid in the car and I'll go in and spot Montoya and find the kid's father that way.

BENZ: Okay.

FADE OUT

FADE IN

17. *Front of Walton Theater. Camera in middle of street takes in a lobby, ticket booth (closed) and sidewalk and curb in front. Montoya, Anders and Alvin Bailey push their way through the double exit door that leads from the foyer into the lobby. Each of the three has his right hand in his suit coat pocket. Montoya carries a briefcase in his left hand. All three are trying to walk casually but are, despite the effort, both furtive and quite tense. When they are about halfway through the theater lobby, walking toward the camera, the squad car containing Benz, Joe Bailey and Fogarty pulls into the curb and stops; car cuts off view of ticket booth and one side of lobby, but not the side along which the three men are walking.*

Squad car door on curbside opens and Fogarty gets out. He has taken only a step and is still beside the car as the three men come into sight around the ticket booth — into sight of Fogarty, Benz and Joe, that is; they have been in sight of the camera since they came through the door from the foyer.

The three men stop. Fogarty stops. The two groups (Benz and Joe still in the car) are face to face about ten feet apart.

Fogarty isn't stupid. At least he isn't stupid enough not to notice those three right hands in coat pockets, the briefcase, the fact that there is a tension you could cut with a knife. Fogarty goes for his gun.

JOE: Pop! *Alvin Bailey starts and looks at the squad car. There are so many emotions on his face that they add up to blankness. The dome light in the car went on automatically when Fogarty opened the door and, as the door is not yet closed, it is still on. We can see Joe clearly, kneeling on the seat, his face close against the windshield.*

MONTOYA (*rapidly, under his breath*): Shoot it out! *His gun is coming out of his pocket as he speaks. Dutch Anders is drawing his, too. Fogarty is a fraction of a second ahead of either of them in getting his gun clear.*

ALVIN: No! Don't! The kid!

He is turning as he speaks—frantically. His hand is out of his pocket too, but without a gun in it. He throws himself in front of Montoya and makes a grab for Montoya's automatic just as guns start to go off—Fogarty's, Anders' and Benz's. Benz is trying to reach across with his left hand and push Joe down out of danger while he fires through the windshield. Montoya's gun goes off, too, but Alvin Bailey is in the way of the shot he's trying to get off.

Before Montoya can get off another shot, he goes down. A shot of Benz's fired through the windshield has caught him in the right shoulder. On the sidewalk, he is trying to shift his gun to his left hand when another bullet hits him—in the head.

Meanwhile Anders and Fogarty have been shooting it out. Fogarty's draw is a fraction of a second sooner and faster and he gets off the first shot; it hits Anders somewhere for it knocks him a little back and off balance. His one shot goes wild and Fogarty's second shot kills him instantly; he falls.

Fogarty, who has been too engrossed with Anders to take in the fact that Alvin Bailey's hand has come out of his pocket without a gun or that Bailey has tried to stop Montoya from shooting, swings around and fires at the only figure left standing—Alvin Bailey. He is lining up the sights for a second shot when he sees that Bailey hasn't a gun in his hand. Fogarty lowers his own gun slightly but keeps it ready. Bailey is turning around slowly. His face, as it faces the camera, is utterly blank and we see blood on the front of his shirt (his coat is slightly open). He continues to turn until he is facing the squad car, his knees starting to buckle. Then he falls forward. This scene has taken a long time to describe but actually, from the time the two groups caught sight of each other, takes only a very few seconds.

CUT TO

18. *View through squad car windshield from front, camera close, lens slightly above radiator cap. Dome light is still on inside (as the door is still open). Through the windshield we see Joe Bailey's face, frozen with horror. He is still kneeling on the seat. We do not see Benz's face as clearly because of the two holes in the windshield in front of him and the cracks in the glass radiating from them, so Joe's face stands out clearly in comparison and is the center of interest.*

MUSIC: *Rachmaninoff's* Isle of the Dead. *There is no action or motion (except of the camera) in this scene. As far as the actors are concerned, it is a still. But the camera begins to move backward away from its position just above the radiator cap. No character— among the three living or the three dead— moves a muscle as the camera recedes. By the time it is back twenty feet from its starting point we can see all six of them, equally motionless. It continues to recede at constant pace until the squad car and the figures around it become tiny, puppet-like.*

Motionless, they recede and vanish into distance and into the past. The music swells in volume and then, with the picture

DISSOLVES.

The Story

10

He hadn't wanted Dixie to see his room after he'd seen the nice one Dixie had at the Wyandotte. He'd planned to be downstairs waiting at the curb or in the doorway when Dixie came. But Dixie got there ten minutes early and spoiled that idea. Not that it really mattered.

Dixie rapped on the door at ten of six, just as Joe was buttoning his shirt, and Joe let him in. "Hi, Dixie," Joe said. "Hell of a time to be getting up. Middle of the night. Haven't had breakfast yet, have you?"

Dixie shook his head. "We'll get something. It'll be eight by the time we're actually shooting." He wandered over to the dresser where the gun lay and picked up the sheath knife that lay beside it. Joe had forgotten to put it away.

"Nice shiv, kid," Dixie said. "Know anything about using one?"

"Not outside of sharpening pencils," Joe said. "I won it on a punchboard once."

Dixie slipped the blade back in the sheath and put it down. Joe had his shirt buttoned by now and was reaching for his coat. He asked, "How about the gun? Shall I wear it on the way out?"

"Sure. Get used to it."

Dixie's car, at the curb, turned out to be a black Ford sedan, a '47. Dixie started to get under the wheel and then asked, "Want to drive, Joe?"

"Sure," Joe said. "I like to drive but don't get much chance to. Haven't got a car of my own right now."

Dixie went around and got in on the other side. "That's what Mitch told me; that's why I suggested it. You ought to pick up some kind of a jalopy for yourself."

"Like to," Joe said. "But they tell me it's against the law unless you pay for it."

"Maybe you'll have one pretty soon. You got to know how to drive, Joe, and I mean drive good. Yeah, you're doing all right. But don't break any speed limits or get in an accident when we got guns in the car."

"You didn't bring them all, did you?"

"No, just the twenty-two thirty-two you're going to shoot to start with. And Maggie. But you're not going to shoot Maggie. She's a lot of gun, kid. Bucks like a bronc unless you know how to handle her. First time I ever shot a Magnum I wasn't expecting anything and it jerked so I missed the whole damn target by a couple of yards. Yeah, you drive okay for a guy who hasn't a car of his own."

"Anywhere special you want to eat breakfast?"

"Head out through Shorewood; that's the way we're going. We'll eat somewhere out of town."

They had ham and eggs at a roadside restaurant that was just opening for the day. Dixie told Joe where to turn off the highway about twelve miles farther north. They kept going along worse and worse roads until finally one petered out entirely after they hadn't passed a house for at least two miles.

Joe had pictured himself shooting at tin cans or bottles, but Dixie had, it turned out, brought regular pistol targets, a whole stack of them.

He said, "What the hell good does it do to pop at something and only know that you miss it, when you do miss it? You got to know if you're shooting high to the right or low to the left or what."

They found a good tree to mount targets on and Joe did a lot of shooting for about an hour and a half, some of it snap shooting at close range, some of it target shooting—with the gun cocked and carefully sighted—from farther back. He used up several boxes of cartridges for the twenty-two and fired a dozen rounds from the thirty-eight Terrier. He found he did better at snap shooting with the Terrier, despite its shorter barrel. It was lighter and felt better in his hand.

Dixie was satisfied. He said that Joe was doing damned well for a first try. He agreed that the Terrier was a good gun for Joe and promised to get him one the next time he went to Chicago, which would be within a week or two. Mitch, he said, would either pay for the gun or advance the money for it.

They went out again the next day, Thursday, but not quite so early. After that Dixie told him he wouldn't have a chance to go again until Monday of the following week, but he loaned Joe the Terrier and the holster and told him to practice wearing it at least part of the time and to practice fast drawing and dry shooting in his room.

Joe wore the gun until he got dressed for his date with Ellie Thursday evening, but he left it home then. Guns and women, he'd already learned, didn't mix. Not women like Ellie, anyway.

Maybe, he thought, he'd better quit seeing Ellie. But he liked her; he didn't want to quit seeing her.

"Well, Ellie, what'll we do? Movie again, or would you rather dance for a change? Or what?"

"What would you like to do, Joe?"

"Well—anything you want. But I was thinking maybe we could call up and see if a friend of mine and his wife are going to be home. Like you to meet them sometime—but it doesn't have to be tonight, if you'd rather do something else."

"Sure, Joe. Call them."

Joe called; the Lorgans were home, wanted him to come. That was good because, if for no other reason, it would save money and Joe was getting a bit low. Today was a week from the time Mitch had last given him money, so more was due. But Mitch hadn't come into the tavern, so he was down to about seven bucks. If the date cost him much it would leave him strapped.

Ellie said she liked beer a little better than wine so on the way to the Lorgans' he picked up some cans of Blatz. Jeannie was putting the baby to bed and, after introductions, Ellie joined her in the bedroom.

Ray frowned at the beer. He said, "What's the idea, Joe? Think I can't afford to be a host, so you always bring something? I was going to go down and get something as soon as you got here; didn't do it sooner because I forgot to ask over the phone what your gal liked to drink. Who is she, by the way, besides being Ellie Dravich?"

While Ray opened beer cans, Joe told him how he'd met Ellie and something about her.

"Seems like a nice kid," Ray said. "Anything serious?"

"No," Joe told him.

Ray handed him a glass and lifted one himself. He said, "Then here's to nonmaintenance of the status quo. You ought to get married, Joe."

"Why?" Joe asked. "To make myself what you call a slave to Capitalism?"

"There's that, yes. But here's a thought for today, Joe. I mean it as seriously as hell. It's better to be a slave to Capitalism than to be a capitalist. The really horrible thing about any system of slavery—literal or figurative slavery—is that, in the long run, it's more degrading to the master than to the slave. The worst thing that can happen to a man is for him to have power over a fellow human being."

"You mean that Uncle Tom had a better time than Simon Legree?"

"I think that, basically, he was happier. Not that I don't think the Simon Legrees shouldn't be eliminated. Or at any rate the power of the Simon Legrees. They themselves if they won't give up that power. And the sad part is, Joe, there are enough of us Uncle Toms to take it away from them, if we all got together on it. Do you know, Joe, how few families control ninety percent of the means of production in this country?"

"Not exactly, no. But more than there are men who control the means of production in Russia."

"Who's talking about Russia? Damn it, Joe, I've explained over and over again that I'm a communist, lower case, not a Stalinite. I believe that communism—Marxian communism—is the right system, the only system under which a worker will get a fair share of what he produces. The Russians pay lip service to that ideal, but Russia is an oligarchy and, yes, the people there are worse off than they would be under Capitalism. But the fact that there can be something worse than Capitalism doesn't mean that Capitalism is good; it just means Russia took the wrong turn at a crucial point."

"Which means I should marry Ellie?"

Ray Lorgan sighed with exasperation, partly feigned and partly serious. "I don't give a damn if you marry Eleanor Roosevelt. My point is that our argument about not wanting to be a slave isn't valid if your alternative to being one is to become something worse."

Joe said, "All right, I'll be serious. What do you think is better?"

"To be a slave who *thinks*. One who tries to see a way out—not for himself as an individual, but a way for society as a whole to end a system whereby the few exploit the many. When enough slaves figure that way, they'll take over the means of production and end slavery. But until that time comes, Joe, the only course an honorable and self-respecting man has—"

Jeannie, coming out of the bedroom with Ellie, interrupted him. "Where's our beer? You could have brought it to us, couldn't you?"

Ray grinned at her. "Then you'd have stayed in there twice as long. Karl asleep?"

"No, but I think he will be pretty soon. He's quieted down. Glad you brought Ellie, Joe. Your taste is improving."

Joe grinned at that, but was a bit embarrassed because he knew Jeannie was needling him about the last time he'd brought a girl around, a few months before. Not that the girl had got drunk or had broken dishes or anything like that, but she'd been so obviously out of place and so obviously bored that even Joe had been embarrassed.

Ray opened more cans of beer and the four of them sat around the table and talked and talked, about everything and nothing. Joe was glad to notice that Ellie could carry her end of the conversation. Maybe she wasn't as intellectual as Ray and Jeannie but she had at least moderately intelligent opinions on most things that were discussed.

A mention of the use of atomic energy in the world of the future reminded Joe of Krasno. He said, "I was talking to a really cheerful bird the other day. He doesn't think there's going to *be* any world of the future. Says another war is inevitable—that it may come next week but *will* come in a few years—and that it'll be fought with A-bombs and we'll all starve to death or shoot each other with bows and arrows fighting over crusts of bread. Think we will, Ray?"

Ray said, "I don't know. Ready for some more beer, Ellie?"

He got up to open another can and Jeannie went into the bedroom to see if the baby was asleep. A few seconds later, she opened the door a crack and said, "Joe, he isn't asleep yet and I want you to see him. You haven't seen him for a while."

Joe went into the bedroom. Jeannie was standing by the crib and she put her finger to her lips and then motioned him over. The only light in the room was from a dim bulb in a lamp on the dresser, but it looked to Joe as though Karl's eyes were closed. He tiptoed over.

Jeannie said, "He *is* asleep; I just said he wasn't so I could call you in here. We won't wake him if we talk quietly and I want to tell you something."

"What, Jeannie?"

"Don't talk anymore about—what you were talking about. Will you, Joe?"

"You mean—about the next war? Of course not, if you don't want me to."

"Not for my sake, Joe. For Ray's. By the way, Joe, you've got an awful nice girl there in Ellie. Better latch onto her."

"Sure. But what's this about Ray's sake?"

"I don't want him to think about it, Joe. He thinks it's coming, and he thinks it's a death sentence for—for all three of us. He feels about it so strongly that he's sorry we—" She made a little gesture toward the sleeping baby.

"Good grief, Jeannie. I'm sorry I mentioned it. Look, *you* don't think—?"

"I don't know, Joe." She looked down at the baby and then up at him, her face a little pale, suddenly. "Why should I lie about it, Joe? Of course it's going to happen. The war, at least. But the—the result, the aftermath—maybe it won't be—well—" She looked down at the crib again. "Better go, Joe. I don't want Ray to guess what I was talking about."

Joe went. From the door he looked back and saw that Jeannie was still looking down at the baby and that she was crying.

He managed to grin at Ray as he came through the door. He said, "Some kid you got, Ray. Almost as ugly as you are, but on him it looks good."

Ray nodded. He said, "That was the second last can I just opened, Joe. And the evening's a pup. I'm going down for some more. Want to come along?"

"Sure," Joe said. "Didn't realize what lushes we all were or I'd have brought more."

They waited half a minute until Jeannie came out of the bedroom, so they wouldn't be leaving Ellie alone. Joe was relieved to see that you couldn't tell that Jeannie had been crying.

He and Ray walked up to Wells Street for the beer. It was a place that sold both package goods and drinks across a bar and Ray said, "How about a shot, Joe, while we're away from the females?" after he'd bought the beer.

"Sure," Joe said.

He could tell Ray wanted to talk, but Ray waited until they had their drinks before he opened up.

"Joe, about this coming cataclysm you mentioned. Don't talk about it in front of Jeannie, will you? She—Oh, hell, it's my fault. I got a few too many drinks a few times recently—not drunk, but enough to loosen my tongue—and did too damn much talking and I know it worried her." He moved the bottom of his glass in wet circles on the bar. "It *is* coming, Joe, but it's one of those things it doesn't do any good to talk about—especially to someone you love. It's like—well, if somebody's got cancer, for instance, they know they're going to die, but just the same it's not a nice thing to talk about to them."

Joe said, "Good God, Ray, you're exaggerating. A war may happen, sure, but it isn't *that* inevitable. And if it does happen, hell, we lived through the last one."

"The last one was a lead pipe cinch, Joe, compared to what the next one would—will be. Oh, I know I'm being selfish about it—at least being selfish on Karl's behalf if not my own."

"I don't get it," Joe said. "What's selfish about wanting to go on living?"

"Just this: it *may* lead to a better world, and I'd like to see a better world—even if I'm not here to see it, if you know what I mean. The two big systems, both of them rotten to the core, Joe, may destroy one another and whatever comes out may be better than either. In fact, it's got to be, or it too will destroy itself. The only thing is that I wouldn't take even odds on the chance of any one individual—you or Karl or me—surviving to see it. Let's have one more drink."

"If it's on me," Joe said. He managed to get the bartender to take his money instead of taking from Ray's change.

Ray lifted his glass. "To you and Ellie, Joe. May you

have a couple of happy years together before a wheel comes off."

Joe drank and then laughed. "I told you it wasn't serious, damn it," he said. "Not that I don't like Ellie, but I don't want to get married."

"Why not?"

"I've—got other plans."

"What? To be a two-bit gangster? I'm sorry, Joe. Forget I said that."

It had hurt, somehow, because Ray had said that. Even though he had taken it back in the same breath. But there wasn't any anger at Ray Lorgan. Just hurt. He said, "I didn't even hear it," and said it as lightly as he could.

"One on me," Ray said, "and we'd better get back and join the ladies."

Joe glanced at Ray and saw that his face was just a trifle flushed, and he'd already noticed that Ray's tongue had thickened just a faint bit. So he said, "I don't want another one, Ray. Let's get back."

Ray nodded and they went out. It had started to drizzle, very slightly, but they had only a block and a half to go so it didn't matter.

They were halfway there before either spoke and then Joe remembered something that had puzzled him at the time.

He said, "Ray, you said that what you think's going to happen—and I still think you're wrong about it—worried you because of Karl more than yourself. Not that it's any of my damn business, but how come you didn't rate Jeannie in there? I mean—hell, you and Jeannie aren't splitting up or anything, are you? Don't answer that if you don't want to."

He thought Ray wasn't going to. Ray didn't say anything until they were almost at the door. And then Ray stopped walking. Joe was a step past before he realized; then he stopped and turned to look at Ray.

Ray said, "I think I'll answer that. Do you remember what I said—metaphorically—a few minutes ago about cancer not being a good subject of conversation if you're talking to someone who has it? Well, don't bring that subject up in conversation tonight, Joe."

Joe just stared at him.

Ray said, "Yes, I mean Jeannie. We learned six weeks ago. She's probably got less than a year. But for another month or two she can stay up, live a normal life, not let anybody know. We decided not to let anybody know for that long. She said she wants—for a little while—to pretend that she's still—all right."

Joe said, "Oh, Christ, Ray."

"I—couldn't help telling you. Maybe because you asked a question—why I didn't rate Jeannie in there—that I couldn't answer without telling you. For God's sake don't let Jeannie know I told you." His lips twisted a little. "I told you I talk too much when I've had a couple of drinks. Can't keep my God damn mouth shut. I had to pop off about the end of the world and get Jeannie worried about Karl living through—Let's go up."

He stepped forward again and took Joe's arm, but Joe hung back. He said, "Christ, Ray, I can't go up this minute. I—I couldn't act normal. I couldn't look at Jeannie without giving away that I knew. You go up; I'm going to walk around the block once first. Tell them—tell them anything."

"I'll go around the block with you."

They walked once around the block in the thin cool rain. They didn't talk much. When they got back to the door Joe still didn't want to go up but he realized they had to sooner or later so he said it was okay.

Jeannie looked up as they came in and said, "Did you boys fall down a manhole?"

Joe made himself grin at her. "Well, it was this way, Jeannie; we met these two broads on Wells Street and—"

An hour or so later he took Ellie home in a cab; it was raining fairly hard by then. He put his arm around her in the taxi and felt very tender toward her. In the downstairs hallway of her rooming house he kissed her good night very gently and didn't even suggest that he drop into her room for a minute. A possibility he'd had in mind earlier in the evening didn't seem—well, *right*. Not tonight anyway.

Ellie said, "I like your friends a lot, Joe."

"Yeah. They're swell people. Well, 'night Ellie."

"Joe—"

He turned back. "Yeah?"

"I—don't like to tell you this, Joe, but it would be better if you didn't see me at the restaurant."

"Huh?" Then he got it. "Oh. Your Uncle Mike, you mean? He doesn't like your going with me?"

"Yes, Joe. I'm sorry, but he doesn't like it. Not that he can forbid me to go with you or anything. I'm of age and he's not my guardian. But—it's just unpleasant, that's all."

"Yeah, I can see how you'd feel about it, if he feels that way. What does he say about me? What does he think I am?"

"Nothing really bad, Joe. But he knows you used to sell policy tickets and—"

"He ought to," Joe said. "He used to buy 'em from me. Is it any worse to sell them than to buy them?"

"And he keeps asking me how you're making a living now, Joe, and—well, it's embarrassing that I can't tell him. You can understand that, can't you?"

"Sure," he said unhappily. He thought, I'll either have to quit seeing her or tell her—well, tell her about Mitch's plans and what I'm waiting for. Then if she objects to that and doesn't want to go with me when she knows I'm going to work in a gambling house, that's that.

"I hated to spoil our good night, Joe, by mentioning it, but—well, I thought it would be better if you didn't drop in tomorrow or the next day. If you think we should talk about it any, we can talk Sunday evening. You're coming here for dinner, don't forget."

"Okay, Ellie. I guess we'd better do a little talking, but it can wait till then."

"What time do you want to eat?"

"Anytime you say, but how's about my picking you up around two o'clock, like last Sunday, and we can go to the beach or somewhere in the afternoon before we eat."

"I don't think we'd better, Joe. I want to make some Italian spaghetti for us, and it takes a long time; you've got to simmer the sauce for hours, so I'll have to be here. Tell you what, though; don't eat a big lunch and we'll plan to eat about five. Then there'll be plenty of time afterwards. We'll have time to talk a while, and still time to go somewhere in the evening, if you want to."

"Fine," Joe said. "Okay, Ellie. I'll see you at five Sunday."

He kissed her good night again, and left.

State Street is a good street for catching cabs inbound, but he didn't wait or even watch for one, in spite of the rain. His suit needed pressing anyway, he told himself.

Death walked with him, Jeannie's death. It didn't seem possible to believe that Jeannie Lorgan had less than a year to live, less than a few months before she'd be in a hospital waiting to die. That was the horrible part—knowing, waiting.

Horrible for Ray, too. He tried to think how it would be to be married to—well, to Ellie and to know that she was under sentence of death. To sleep beside her, knowing that inside her body was a monstrous thing, incurable, eating

142

away at her life—

But he wasn't going to marry Ellie. Damn it, he wasn't going to marry anyone. Tie himself down like that? Never.

Sunday evening would probably end it, anyway. And that would be to the good. She was messing up his life—making him want two different things that were incompatible. Or were they, really? Well, he'd find out soon enough.

But for tonight he knew he'd have to get his mind off things before he could go to sleep. Luckily there was a drugstore still open on Wells Street and he found a science fiction magazine that he hadn't read yet, so he took it home with him.

In his room, he remembered that he hadn't been practicing the draw with the thirty-eight as Dixie had told him to do. He took off his wet suit but left his shirt on and strapped on the shoulder holster. He practiced a few minutes, but it felt silly—and looked even sillier in the mirror—to be wearing a shoulder-holstered gun with his pants off. He took off the gun, finished undressing, and lay down on the bed to read.

The lead story was an atomic blowup story and he skipped it without consciously figuring out why. He read all of the rest of the magazine and by that time it was two o'clock and he was sleepy enough to go right to sleep after he turned out the light.

If he dreamed, he didn't remember his dreams.

12

He went into the tavern earlier than usual, not much after noon, because he didn't want to take any chance on missing Mitch, if Mitch came in. He had a little less than three dollars left, which would see him through till tomorrow if it had to, but he always felt uncomfortable when cash on hand was low. That was a hangover from the days when he and his mother had had to live on her slender earnings as a waitress. Her small salary usually went for rent or other major items and, from day to day, they lived on the tips she got, which weren't many in most of the restaurants she'd worked in. He didn't like, now, to think back about those times. Of course they hadn't been so bad after he was in high school; he'd been able to earn money after school most of the time, at least enough so that he had a little spending money. But there's nothing like a dose of poverty to make one appreciate how wonderful money—big money, like Mitch had—would be.

He sat in one of the booths by himself, because he didn't want Krasno to start talking to him as he had a few days ago. There were a few customers at the bar, but they might happen to leave all at once and then he'd be stuck there, alone, and Krasno might start talking to him.

Joe sat facing the window. Just before two he saw the blue convertible pull into the curb. Mitch got out; Joe was glad to see that he was alone. If he'd come in with somebody, Joe couldn't very well have reminded him about the money, and Mitch might not have remembered.

Mitch came in and saw Joe sitting there right away. He said, "Hi, kid. How're things?"

"Fine," Joe said.

Mitch came to the booth as though he was going to sit down across from Joe and then changed his mind and said, "Let's go in the back room to talk, Joe."

It sounded serious, the way Mitch said it. Joe hoped it didn't have anything to do, negatively, with the forty dollars he had coming.

He got up from the booth. Mitch had turned around and

caught Krasno's eye; he was holding up two fingers for Krasno to make two drinks. He jerked his head toward the back to show Krasno where to bring them.

Joe followed him into the card room at the back. Mitch sat down as he had the last time, with his feet up on the table. He said, "This is kind of private, Joe. Let's wait till Krazzy has come and gone. You know I'm getting fed up with that old bastard. He talks too much. You don't talk, Joe. That's something I like about you. I can say something to you and I know it won't go any farther."

"Sure," Joe said.

"By the way, you lined up for the party tomorrow night? Got yourself a dame, I mean?"

Joe nodded. His best out on that party would be to call at the last minute and say his date had fallen through. Then he wouldn't have to come. Mitch would understand that he wouldn't want to come alone.

"Good," Mitch said.

Then there were Krasno's footsteps shuffling toward the door and they both waited until he'd come in and put the drinks down on the table between them. Mitch had to put his feet down to reach his drink; then he put them up again as he sat back, but a little to one side so he could watch Joe's face.

When the door had closed and Krasno had walked away from it, Mitch said, "Joe, how'd you like to be a partner in The Gold Mine?"

"The what?"

"The Gold Mine — that's what I'm calling the place I'm going to open in Waukesha County. Good name, huh? Makes the marks think they can come in and mine gold. Well, a few of them will. Most of them will leave some of their own instead."

"It's a swell name," Joe said. "But you're kidding me

about being a partner. What'd I buy in with? Two dollars and seventy-five cents?"

Mitch chuckled. "Take a little more than that, but we can get it." He stared at Joe speculatively and then said, "Dixie tells me you're getting good, Joe. Or rather, that you're a natural with guns. If you weren't, it'd take you plenty long. And what's a hell of a lot more important, he thinks—like I thought already—that you've got guts and that you're shooting for the big time. Are we right, Joe?"

Joe nodded slowly. His throat felt a little tight.

"I knew it," Mitch said. "Okay, Joe, here's the deal. There are four of us going to raise the dough we'll need. Me and Dixie and you and a guy you don't know yet, in Chicago. He knows the game, even better than Dixie does."

"Which game?" Joe asked. "Running the gambling joint or raising the money to get it?"

"You're a smart kid, Joe. The way to raise the dough, sure. I'm going to be the big wheel in running the joint, once it's going. And listen, Joe, I want you to understand one thing—I don't mean you're in for a full fourth or anything like that. An eighth, maybe. It's the others of us that have the experience and know what we're doing."

Mitch put his feet down and leaned forward, elbows on the table. "Here's the way it stands, Joe. You don't need to worry about what fractions the others of us are getting, only your own. Right? Well, there's a slight difference of opinion. Chicago thinks you ought to settle for a tenth interest and a tenth of the take. I said an eighth. It's one or the other and it depends on how you do. By the time the moolah is raised, we know. But it'll be anyway a tenth and—well, I can't name a figure exactly but it'll be from three hundred a week up, depending. A joint that doesn't net three grand a week isn't in business. If you get an eighth, it should run you about four hundred."

Joe's lips were dry and he licked them. Three or four hundred dollars a week. That was *money*. That was blue convertibles and good apartments and girls like Francine. That was everything you could want.

Mitch said, "You're interested, Joe?"

Joe nodded.

"Then I'll tell you how you happen to be in on this. I liked you ever since you started working for me — and I figured you were a guy I could count on in a pinch, that you had guts and you weren't going to be a punk all your life. That's why I kept you going — the few bucks a week I fed you weren't going to break me, and I wouldn't lose you. Right away, when the heat went on over that policy business in the Sixth Ward, I figured it wouldn't last long. And I'd been doing all right, Joe. Don't tell the income tax department, but I made myself somewhere around forty grand last year, and more than half that much up to the time the heat went on in July this year.

"And I was figuring on getting you ready to handle things for me, Joe, whenever I wanted to go out of town a while. To spend a month in Florida, maybe, or follow the tracks a little. So while I thought the heat wouldn't last long, I kept you going. Worth it to me to keep you. But I finally figured that the heat's going to stay on a long time. That God damn John Doe investigation's just getting started and it may run a year. And meanwhile the cops are afraid to shake hands with their best friends for fear someone will see it and think money's passing."

Joe nodded again. "I figured it'd be on a long time, too. That's why I was going to tell you last week maybe I'd better take a job or something."

"So I got in with Dixie and this other guy and figured this deal. I thought you'd want in on it — I figured you had nerve and ambition enough, kid. But Dixie and the other guy said nix, not unless they had a say in it. That's one reason Dixie's been taking you out, see? The other guy said he'd take Dixie's word. And Dix says you're okay, kid, so you're in. Right?"

"Right," Joe said.

"But not too sudden, Joe. I know this is new to you and I don't want a snap decision. You think it over and give me an answer tomorrow night at the party and that answer goes. I don't want you in, Joe, unless you're sure."

Joe thought about three hundred dollars a week. He said, "I'm sure now, Mitch."

"Won't take a yes now. Because when you say it, kid, you're *in*. You're not going to back out on us, understand? Tomorrow night, if you still think so, I'll give you some of the details — at least the first job we plan." His face changed. "It'll be too late then, Joe."

"I'm sure," Joe said. "I'm sure now."

"Need money?"

"Well, I'm a little low."

Mitch took out his wallet and put a ten dollar bill on the table. "That be enough to tide you over till tomorrow night?"

"Sure, Mitch."

"Okay, I'll give you some more tomorrow night — if you still feel the same about it. If you don't, if you want to chicken out, that's your chance. And I'm going to tempt you to do it, even, this far: If you do, we're even. I've given you — let's see — counting that, somewhere around two and a quarter —"

"Two hundred and thirty," Joe said.

"All right, two thirty. But if you don't want to go in with

148

us, that's washed off anyway. I gambled that much on you and lost; that's all. I don't want you to come in, if you're chicken, just because you figure you owe me money. Fair enough?" He waited for Joe's nod. "And if you come in, you don't pull out. Fair enough on that?"

"Sure," Joe said.

"We'll have another drink on it. You want to get 'em for us, Joe?"

Joe took their glasses into the bar. His was empty, too, although he didn't remember drinking it. Krasno grinned at him. "He giving you the works, kid?"

Joe didn't answer him. He thought, Mitch is right about his talking too much. He knew Mitch would fire Krasno in a minute if he told Mitch everything Krasno had said about him last Monday.

But, come to think of it, Krazzy had been pretty right in what he'd said. Mitch probably was down to his last ten thousand bucks. Mitch had just said he'd been clearing forty thousand a year. And from the way he spent money he must have spent most of it. Maybe he didn't have even ten thousand in actual liquid cash left out of it. Certainly not enough to finance a swanky gambling house. And old Krazzy must have guessed some of the rest of it, too; he'd asked Joe if Joe was getting dragged into anything.

Well, he was. Only he was getting dragged into the big money.

He took the drinks back and Mitch said, "Here's luck, Joe!" as he lifted his glass.

Mitch took half of his at a swallow and then sipped the rest. He said, "Joe, we're going to make a good thing of it. There isn't a decent mob operating in Milwaukee. It's all amateur stuff, except sometimes someone comes up from Chi. Know what the trouble with most mobs is, Joe?"

"What?"

"They operate till they get caught. We're not. We're going to set ourselves a quota and make it, and then parlay that quota by buying The Gold Mine and going legit. That's the McCoy, Joe; we're really going to do it. You good at poker, Joe?"

"Fair. But I've never played for high stakes."

"Then that's something else we'll have to teach you. It's different when you're playing for money instead of marbles. And you'll have to sit in on games once in a while. And—you fast at figures? How'd you be on a roulette wheel?"

"I'm pretty good at figures, Mitch. Dunno how I'd be on a wheel." Joe grinned. "Have to get myself a new suit, though. Croupiers are supposed to work without pockets, aren't they?"

Mitch laughed. "Joe, I'd trust you even *with* pockets. You wouldn't cross me, would you, Joe?"

"Hell, no, Mitch."

It was after three when Joe left. He'd had three drinks and he felt them plenty. Not that he couldn't handle three drinks, except that these were on an empty stomach; he'd eaten a very light breakfast a long time ago. He knew he'd better eat something and he'd started for the Dinner Gong before he remembered that he wasn't supposed to go there. He thought, damn Mike Dravich.

And then he remembered that this really changed things. He'd better stop seeing Ellie. Completely. It wouldn't be fair to her not to, and Ellie was a good kid. He wouldn't cross her any more than he'd cross Mitch. Oh, sure, he'd keep the date for Sunday night, but he'd tell her—well, the simplest thing would be to tell her enough of the truth that she'd do the breaking off and not want to see him any more.

150

Only damn it, he wanted to keep on seeing her.
He wanted that and the big money, too. You can't have
everything, he told himself.

13

It was a minor bad break that Mitch had put so much empha-
sis on the party – wanting his definite decision then, and
holding back all but ten bucks of whatever Mitch was going
to give him. But he still didn't want to go if he could get out
of it. He could still phone Mitch at the last minute, and at
least try to get out of going. He could give Mitch his decision over the phone. It meant he probably wouldn't see
Mitch again till Monday to get more money and he'd have
to stretch the ten to last that long, but he could do that all
right.

He waited till nine o'clock to phone. Mitch answered
and when Joe had made his stall, Mitch said, "The hell with
a dame, kid; come on out. Look, it ain't a big party and it
ain't all couples. I just invited a few people, that's all. We'll
probably have a poker game and if you're a stag, that's swell.
You can help entertain some of the women."

So that didn't leave Joe any out at all, especially as he'd
said he was all ready to come until his date fell through. He
said, "Okay, Mitch. Be seeing you then." He even made it
sound cheerful, because he didn't want Mitch to guess that
he hadn't wanted to come.

He deliberately took his time getting there and arrived
at half past ten.

It wasn't a wild party, after all. There were six men there
when he arrived, counting Mitch. There was Dixie, and
a tall thin man with a horse face who was introduced to

him as Gus Bernstein—of Chicago. There was Jay Wendt, whom Joe had already met once, who was a lawyer, Mitch's lawyer. And there were two friends of Mitch's, one of whom he'd already met and one he hadn't; they were Bill Murdock, who'd been an alderman once, and a man named Wayne Corey.

Besides Francine, there were three women. One, a faded blonde who looked as though she'd once been a chorine, was Wayne Corey's wife. The other two were prettier, but not as pretty as Francine; they were introduced as Jane and Gert, last names weren't mentioned. Apparently Murdock had brought Jane and Dixie had brought Gert. Gus Bernstein and the lawyer had come without women.

There wasn't any shortage of liquor. The kitchen table was piled with it. Mitch waved a hand at it through the doorway. "Go make yourself a drink, kid. We're on our own. I had a jig lined up to make drinks for us, but he didn't show up. And damn if *I'm* going to be bartender."

Bernstein and Francine were by the table making drinks. Mitch followed Joe out into the kitchen and said, quietly, "Beat it a minute, huh, Francy? Business."

She closed the kitchen door after her as she went out. Mitch said, "Well, kid?" to Joe and Joe nodded.

"Attaboy. Gus, Joe's a good kid. We can count on him."

Bernstein nodded. "If you and Dixie both say so."

"You said you wanted to talk to him, Gus. Better get it over with. I'm going to get a little poker started. Going to play, Joe?"

"Can't afford it, Mitch."

"We're going to play low stakes. I want to drink, and I don't play high when I drink. We'll make it a twenty dollar buy-in; I'll stake you to twenty, Joe."

He peeled out three twenties from his wallet and handed them to Joe. "One of 'em's a buy-in on the game for you. Be seeing you."

He went back into the living room; Jane and Murdock came in for drinks, passing him in the doorway. Gus Bernstein said, "Let's get some fresh air, Joe. Stuffy in here." He picked up a drink and went out the back door; Joe, his own drink in his hand, followed. They sat on a bench a dozen yards from the house. There was enough moonlight so they could see one another.

Gus said, "Well, kid, you're in, if both Mitch and Dixie say so. Here's the setup. I'm running things in the field, when we're actually on a job. Mitch is picking 'em. This is his territory and he knows it better than me or Dixie. All you got to do is what we tell you—and don't get trigger-happy. Ever killed anybody?"

"Once," Joe said.

14

You're a little drunk, not with booze because you're on your first drink. With excitement and the fact that this is it, the big time, the real thing. You're in. The guy talking to you is an honest-to-God holdup man, in the chips. And you're going to be in the chips, too. Blue convertibles and women like Francy and everything you've ever wanted. All of it can be bought and this is the way you get money, big money.

And he asks you if you've ever killed anybody.

"Once," you say. You mean your father; you got him killed, didn't you? You called copper on him. And the cops killed him and since then you've hated cops—and hated yourself. You're a patricide and you're a killer just as much as if you'd pointed

a gun at your father and pulled the trigger. You're no damned good anyway and you might as well cash in on it.

"Once," you say, and from the way you say it, calmly, you know he believes you, because, damn you, it's true. And he does believe you and it was the right answer.

Because he says, "That's good, kid, both ways. Once doesn't mean you're trigger-happy. And it means you've got the guts to do it if you've got to. Was it on a job?"

"Let's skip the details," you say. "I answered your question."

That was the right answer, too. You can tell by the way he says, "Sure, Joe." He was feeling you out to see how well you could keep your mouth buttoned. You won on that point.

He says, "Mitch is lining us up something for week after next. That'll be our first job, and Mitch says it's a pushover. Well, let's get back to the party."

Yeah, you can tell by his voice that you went over, that he respects you now and talks to you as an equal. You're in. You're all right with Gus.

You follow him back and you're walking on air. You're a big shot now, or on the way to being one. You're not a punk anymore. This is what you meant to be. You feel different, you walk different.

Sure, maybe you're going to get killed. But you can get killed walking across the street. You can get killed if they drop an atom bomb on you. You can do worse than get killed—cleanly, suddenly, with a bullet or a lot of bullets, like your father got killed. Sure, you can do worse. Jeannie Lorgan. How'd you like that? Christ.

Maybe you even want to get killed that way. Remember reading about a Freudian death wish when you were reading up on psychology? But that's a lot of crap. You don't want to die. You just want money and power badly enough to take a reasonable chance to get it. And not too much of a chance. Thanks to Mitch you're starting in the big time, with boys who know their business.

But just the same, if you do get killed, what better way than by a cop's bullet— to make up to your father for getting him killed that way?

And not that he's watching you— from Heaven or Hell or anywhere else— but if he did know about what you're doing now, or planning to do, wouldn't he understand that you were trying to make up for what you did to him? And wouldn't he understand that you had to, that you had to show him you don't condemn him for having had the guts to take a gun and go out after what he needed? That you don't think you're any better than he was?

Won't that maybe wash it out? Or, no matter what you do, can you ever wash out the fact that you murdered your father?

You realize that Mitch, sitting at the table in the living room, is talking to you. "Sit in a while, Joe?"

"Sure," you say.

15

Four of them started the game. Mitch, Murdock, Dixie Ehlers, and Joe Bailey. Wendt, the lawyer, didn't play poker. Bernstein and Corey said maybe they'd sit in later. Mitch didn't try to argue anybody into playing, although a four-handed game wasn't too good. He probably realized that if more than four played at once, the women would object. Not that it would have done them any good.

Joe turned back one of the twenties and got twenty whites at a quarter each and fifteen reds at a buck. He lost only a two-bit ante on each of the first two hands and then dropped four dollars on a back-to-back pair of treys, drawing two more cards to them and then dropping when they didn't improve and two other pairs showed up on the board.

The next hand broke him. He had tens backed and caught another one on the fifth card. He had five bucks in the pot by that time and when Murdock, who'd paired a jack on the last card, bet twenty dollars, Joe saw he was the only one left to call and shoved in his last ten dollars to call as much as he could of the bet. Murdock might possibly have a third jack but two pairs was more likely, especially as he needed the case jack; Mitch had turned down one of them.

Murdock turned another jack, though. Joe said, "You win," and started to throw in his cards. Mitch put out a hand; he said, "Do you mind, Joe?" When Joe nodded he looked at the hole card Joe had had, the third ten, without showing it to the others. He nodded. "Good boy. You had to call all right. Just wondered. Want another twenty?"

Joe said, "Yeah, but on me." He gave Mitch another twenty. That would cut him pretty low for the next week, but he'd get by somehow.

He got down to ten dollars before he won his first pot, but that brought him up to thirty-five; it would have been considerably more if he could have called the full amount of the final bet. He played cautiously and didn't drop much more than the ante in the next half dozen hands. Then he started with a jack and queen of diamonds and got an almost unbelievable hand for stud—a king-high straight flush. Even better, there was competition against him and he was looking down its throat. Dixie had three fours showing and Murdock had a possible ace-high flush in clubs but with the cards too assorted to make it even possibly another straight flush.

He went all in on that one and got called both ways. He

had ninety-five dollars in front of him when he'd raked in the pot. Mitch grinned at him and told him he'd better quit while he was ahead, but Joe grinned back and asked why he should quit while he was getting rich. He played along another half hour without any particular luck, either good or bad. Once he won a small pot that covered his antes and minor investments—for one or two cards—on the others. Once he sensibly turned down four hearts on the fourth card when Mitch, with a pair of aces showing, bet fifty dollars into him. Considering the cards out, he had about one chance in seven to draw a fifth heart and the percentage wasn't there; there was less than a hundred in the pot, counting Mitch's fifty dollar bet. It would give him two to one on his investment on a one in seven chance, so he folded and got an approving nod from Mitch that showed Mitch had figured those odds too.

A few minutes later Bernstein and Corey came over and wanted in and Joe said he'd sit out for a while. So did Dixie, who was just about even.

Joe cashed in ninety and gave Mitch back the twenty Mitch had staked him with. Counting out his own twenty, he was fifty bucks ahead and felt swell about it. Particularly about the fact that he'd had sense enough to quit while he was ahead, but without doing so right after he'd won the big pot that had put him there.

Dixie said, "Come on, Joe. Let's get ourselves some drinks."

Joe mixed himself a strong one. He didn't care, now, if he got a little tight. In fact, he wanted to.

He did.

16

It's late, but you don't know whether it's one o'clock or three and you don't care. The phonograph is playing Stardust *and you're dancing with Francy, her body — that beautiful body you saw naked on the beach — is pressed against the rhythm of the music. You want Francy so bad that you can taste it. But it's a pleasant kind of torture because you're drunk enough to think that nothing's hopeless, even getting Francy. Not tonight, and not just once, but to keep and to live with. And you're on the way to having enough money to do that little thing. There's Mitch, but Mitch changes girls. And you're not in the money yet, anyway. You've got ninety-five bucks, but that's peanuts.*

Maybe you should sit in the game again and run it up. No, you're too near drunk now. Your judgment's impaired. You'd get reckless and lose it the first big hand that came up. Hang onto it. It's peanuts in the long run, but it isn't peanuts to you right now. A new suit. But more would be a down payment on a car. A jalopy, but the first step toward a convertible. The hell with it; you're dancing with Francy. To Stardust. *And in the stardust of a —*

She whispers, "I'm glad you came, Joe." She laughs a little. "You didn't want to, did you? Did you really have a date that fell through, or wasn't that a stall to keep from coming?"

You say, "You're too smart for me, Francy."

"Afraid of me, aren't you?"

"Yes," you say.

The records ends, and Francy goes to change it. You're a little dizzy. You sit down — on the arm of a chair, for fear if you sit down in it, Francy will sit in your lap. That would be wonderful, but Mitch is right over there in the poker game. Dixie is back in the game again, now, and he's got a lot of chips in front of him. Looks like he's the big winner. They're using the blues now, five buck chips. Mitch must be losing, from all the chips out; of course you don't know how many were bought. Anyway it's a steeper game now, too steep for you. You showed them you could play; now be smart and stay clear.

Francy's back; she sits in the chair on whose arm you're sitting. If you could only drop your arm around her. Those breasts. Her dress cut low. You can almost see the aureoles around the nipples. To kiss them. To put your face between. Quit looking. Her hair brushing your hand on the back of the chair.

The faded blonde that's Corey's wife passed out on the sofa, sitting up, her mouth open. Two gold teeth. Gert dancing with Bernstein. Thought he was in the game. No, Murdock and Corey. Wendt and Jane gone. Bedroom? Maybe; door's closed. Or maybe outside. Nice outside. Fresh air. Go? No, Francy. And if you go out with Francy—

Mitch. He'd know. But—

A million dollars.

You could, unless Francy has been kidding you ever since. No, not that way. Not outside. A bed, all night. Everything or nothing. For now, nothing. Don't look down.

Except for Mitch. God damn Mitch.

You're crazy, Joe. You haven't got that kind of money. Yet.

"Let's go get a drink, Joe."

"Sure, Francy. Want me to get you one?"

She goes along, but she lets you make the drinks. "Let's have Toms, Joe. Remember how I showed you how to make 'em?"

"Sure." *Sugar in lemon juice. Gin, soda, stir. You'll never forget anything that day. Francy lying there, first you think white bathing suit, fraction of second. Golden triangle. Nippled breasts. Francy, not suit. White. Light golden tan legs, shoulders. Golden hair, loose.*

"Easy on the gin, Joe. Not that I don't like 'em strong, but."

"Sorry, Francy. Thinking about something else." Wish you could tell her.

She laughs. "Bet I could guess."

Damn her, she could, she has. You laugh it off. "What else could I be thinking about?" Keep it kidding.

You got to keep it kidding. You go back with drinks. Francy sits on sofa, next to passed out faded blonde. Contrast. You sit next, look like you were afraid of her if you didn't. Only you are afraid.

Jane back, and Wendt. Bedroom? Must have been; didn't pass through kitchen. And bedroom door now ajar. Was closed. Wendt wandering over to watch poker game. Jane looking through phonograph albums.

You stare at Jane over the top of your glass, sipping. You wonder, why not? She'll pick a record, you ask her to dance. Then. She came with Murdock, but he pays no attention. Facing bedroom door at poker table, but Wendt took her in there, and out. Just a pickup, then, to Murdock. Wouldn't matter.

Francy would know. So what? Francy and Mitch.

Francy touches your arm. "I wouldn't like you if you did, Joe."

You don't stop to wonder how she knew. You ask, "You would care, Francy?"

"I think you know that, Joe."

And you do know. You knew that Thursday afternoon. Francy wants you, too. God knows why. Ninety-five dollars. Chemistry.

You're scared now. She puts a hand on the back of your hand and it's like a burn. A little hard to breathe.

"Joe, I feel the drinks a little. Let's take a walk outside."

You're in the kitchen, opening the door for Francy. The night air, dim moonlight. You're walking down toward the water, Francy holding your arm.

You walk down the little slope to the cove; you're out of sight of *the house. Francy stops and turns toward you. You're supposed to put your arms around her. And.*

You're almost sober. The night air.

"Francy," you say.

"Yes, Joe?"

"Francy, I want you so bad I can't see straight. But not like this." You are sober. A little while ago your tongue was getting thick. It isn't now. Your mind is clear as glass. "Maybe I'm a God damn fool, Francy, but I want more or nothing."

"You're a funny boy, Joe. Maybe that's why I like you. I—I see what you mean."

"And I'm right, Francy."

"I think you are. I never thought of it that way, exactly, but I think you are. All right, Joe, shoot for more."

You ask, "Mitch?" You don't have to use any more words than that.

"I—I don't like him much, Joe. Listen, I'm going to start breaking with him gradually. Or making him break with me—that's better. He'll think he's getting tired of me; he'll never even guess I'm doing it."

"I'm going to make money, Francy. Big money, soon."

"Do that, Joe. And when you do—"

She turns away, looking out over the water. Shimmer of moonlight over the water. Over Francy's golden hair.

"Joe, I'm going to take a dip. I love cold water. Do you?"

She is pulling down her shoulder straps, kicking off her slippers.

You know what that would mean. There's a limit. You make yourself laugh. You say, "Francy, I couldn't take it. I'm running."

And you don't run, but you walk. Back toward the house. Her soft laugh and "'Bye, Joe," follow you.

You won't let yourself run but you walk almost blindly, think-

ing what a God damn fool you are for being such a God damn fool. You walk almost blindly, that is until you're near the kitchen door and then you see the door is open and someone is standing in it, silhouetted against the light.

Mitch. You can't see his face, but it's Mitch. No one else would fill that much of the doorway.

He says, "Hi, Joe. Where's Francy?" He comes down the steps.

Don't get scared.

Keep your voice calm.

"She wanted to take a swim. I thought I'd better come back."

Your face is in the light. Mitch is looking at your face. You can't see his. You want to brace yourself but that would give you away.

Mitch laughs. It's all right. An amused laugh. He says, "You're all right, Joe. Don't think I don't know how long you were out there, and it wasn't long enough. And you wouldn't have come back alone."

He shook his head. "But how you didn't, I don't know. That little bitch has been needling you all evening. I'm not blind even when I'm facing the other way."

He claps you on the shoulder. "Let's have a drink, Joe."

You say, "Sure, Mitch." You hate him. You hate him for knowing. Does he think you're loyal, though, or yellow?

The two of you go back into the kitchen and have drinks together. Mitch says, "Gus likes you, Joe."

You don't give a damn about that. The kitchen feels hot and close. You lean against the wall because you're not sober now, you're drunker than you were before. You say, "That's good, Mitch," because you've got to say something, and your tongue is thick again.

Mitch claps you on the shoulder again and you find you don't like it. He says, "Joe, if that little bitch of mine got your pants

162

hot for you, give Jane a jump. She's a party girl. Should've told you; I forgot."

You realize Mitch isn't sober, either. He sways a little as he goes back toward the other room and the poker table.

There's a glass in your hand and you drink what's in it and make another one, strong. You might as well get drunk.

You get into the other room without spilling it and no one's sitting in the comfortable overstuffed chair so you take it and sip your drink and you're drunk. You know you're drunk because your eyes are heavy and the room sways.

But you aren't paying attention to the room anyway; you're looking through the wall and the kitchen wall and the night and the bank and seeing Francy swimming there in the cold lake. Her naked warm body in the dark cold water.

You'd go back out there again now if you dared. But you realize that the reason you hadn't the first time was not the fancy stuff you said. You were afraid of Mitch. That's all. You were afraid of Mitch. And with him waiting there in the back door, probably going to walk down there to see, it was a damn good thing.

You're drunk. Things are blurred. Vague. Francy's back. She says, "Hi, Joe," and laughs when you don't answer because this isn't Francy. Francy is in the water, swimming, naked. This isn't Francy. You close your eyes.

17

Sunlight was slanting through the windows when Joe woke up. He was lying stretched out on the sofa in Mitch's living room and someone had taken off his shoes and loosened his tie and collar. His mouth tasted horrible. He swung his feet off the edge of the sofa and sat up. For a few seconds he felt dizzy and then he was all right except that he wanted a drink of water worse than anything in the world.

He looked around as he stood up. At first glance the place looked like a shambles; then he saw that it was the ordinary debris of a party. There were glasses all over, two or three broken ones. Bottles standing around, too, brought in from the kitchen after people had tired of walking that far for refills. The card table was still up and the cards were scattered across it, a few of them on the floor. But the game had met an orderly end, obviously, for the chips were neatly racked at the side of the table at which Mitch had sat. Ashtrays were overflowing and abandoned cigarettes had burned themselves out on the arms of chairs and elsewhere. It looked as though the party had gone on quite a while after he had passed out.

The bedroom door was closed. Maybe Mitch and Francy were asleep in there, or maybe the whole party had moved elsewhere and he had the house to himself. He didn't care which, just then.

Without putting on his shoes he went out into the kitchen. It was in worse shape than the living room. Someone had been sick on the kitchen floor; Joe hoped it hadn't been he.

He let water run, splashing some into his face while it got cold, and then drinking two glasses of it. He went back into the living room to look for his shoes and found them under the phonograph. The phonograph, he noticed, was still running, although there wasn't a record on it; he turned it off. He turned out a couple of lamps that were still burning, too, and then still carrying his shoes he got his hat out of the clothes closet and let himself out of the front door as quietly as he could. He put his shoes on sitting on the steps outside and then started walking toward the bus.

The first cheerful thought came to him while he was walking; he remembered the money he'd won. He looked into his wallet to be sure it was still there and it was. Ninety-five dollars exactly; forty that Mitch had given him, fifty he'd won, and five he'd had left out of the ten Mitch had given him Friday.

He caught a bus after a short wait and by the time it got him downtown he realized he was hungry enough to eat a big breakfast. Apparently, from the state of the kitchen at Mitch's, there'd been some eating done at the party, but it had been after he'd passed out.

While eating he remembered his five o'clock date for spaghetti at Ellie's and wondered, for the first time, what time it was. His wristwatch had run down, but the restaurant clock told him it was eight o'clock, and he set his watch by it. He must have slept a good four hours at Mitch's, then, maybe longer. It had probably been at least two o'clock, maybe three, when he'd gone under. And if it was eight now, he must have wakened about seven. Well, if he stowed away a good breakfast now, as he was doing, he'd have to remember to eat a light lunch, if any, so he'd be ready for the meal at Ellie's.

He got home by nine and set his alarm for two o'clock, but he woke at noon and couldn't go back to sleep. He bathed, dressed, and went downstairs for a light lunch. He had plenty of money to do anything he wanted for the afternoon but he still felt logy and didn't want to do anything. He bought a magazine and went back to his room to read.

At three o'clock he was called downstairs to the phone; he almost hoped the call was from Ellie, calling off the date.

Somehow he didn't feel in the mood to see Ellie – or anyone else. The call was from Mitch.

"Hi, kid," he said. "Just wondered if you got home okay and everything."

"Sure, Mitch. Had a swell time. Sorry I made a goof of myself passing out."

"You weren't the only one, Joe. But you missed the best part of the party, after the game. We really had the joint jumping. We'd have took you home but you were out so cold we'd have had to carry you up the stairs, and I figured you'd be as well off on the sofa."

"Sure, Mitch. You – uh – home?"

"No, at the flat downtown. We ended up there. All but you and the Coreys. His frau went out early; we took them home on the way downtown. You had the place to yourself after about four in the morning. I just phoned there and there wasn't any answer so I thought I'd see if you got home okay."

"Sure, Mitch. I got out about eight o'clock."

"You play pretty good poker, Joe. And you had sense enough to get out in time, too, before the drinks hit you. Glad you came out ahead. Look, it was fifty bucks. Dixie said to tell you he knows how to invest it for you in – what you need. He says that'll buy you one."

"That'll be swell, Mitch. When'll I see you? Or Dixie?"

"I'll be in at the tavern tomorrow afternoon. Dixie's going down to Chi; he'll do your shopping for you. And he says he'll pick you up Tuesday morning to go out and – uh – practice. Okay?"

"Fine. I'm sorry I made an ass of myself passing out, Mitch."

"That's okay, Joe. You didn't do anything worse than going to sleep. Frankly, I wanted to see whether you'd get talkative, or fighting drunk or anything. And you didn't. You were under control, and that's what's important. You don't get in trouble going to sleep when you drink."

Joe went back upstairs feeling better after learning he hadn't made a fool of himself—worse than he knew already, at any rate—at the party.

He felt pretty good by the time he got to Ellie's room at five. The spaghetti sauce, simmering on the little gas stove in the kitchenette, smelled wonderful. And Ellie, in a gingham apron, looked pretty. She put up her lips to be kissed, and he kissed them lightly, putting his hands on her shoulders but not drawing her to him.

"Ready in about fifteen minutes, Joe," she said, going over to stir the spaghetti. "Hungry?"

He sniffed appreciatively. "Ravenous."

The only two chairs in the room were straight chairs and both were pulled up ready at the table. Joe sat on the bed; it was a daybed, not a regular one, so that was all right.

He watched Ellie working and thought how pleasantly domestic she looked, how nice—in some ways—it would be to have someone comfortable like Ellie instead of someone who could drive you nuts, like Francy could.

Why didn't women come both ways? Or did they? Maybe a girl like Ellie, if she really loved you—

But Ellie was out. It wouldn't be fair to her to keep on seeing her, under the circumstances. She might fall for him and he might fall for her, and Ellie—well, Ellie just didn't fit in with his plans.

He couldn't picture Ellie as—he grinned at the thought—a gun moll.

She happened to glance at him and catch the grin. "Am I that funny, Mister Bailey?" she wanted to know. "In this apron, I mean?"

167

"You look wonderful in an apron," he told her. And he was surprised to find he wasn't kidding her or flattering her. Ellie seemed prettier everytime he'd seen her. "If you want, you can wear it when we go out this evening."

"Are we going out? I thought we were going to talk, Joe."

He felt uncomfortable; suddenly he didn't want to talk—he didn't want to have to tell her maybe this was the last time they should see one another.

He said, "Oh, sure. But that doesn't mean we can't go somewhere too. I'm rich tonight."

From her face, he knew he'd said the wrong thing. That was the whole trouble; Ellie couldn't understand where his money came from, since he'd told her he wasn't working and hadn't been working for quite a few weeks. That was what was between them and he'd mentioned it at the wrong time.

She turned back to the stove and said, "It's ready, Joe, soon as I put it on. Might as well come to the table."

It was good spaghetti, cooked just right, and the sauce was excellent. He ate so much of it that he groaned aloud when she brought out apple pie. "You've got to eat it, Joe. I baked it myself."

It was wonderful pie and he didn't burst, after all. But he felt too comfortable and happy to move and they sat a long time over coffee and cigarettes.

They talked a lot, but about nothing.

Joe ground out the butt of his second cigarette. "Let's break the dishes instead of washing them; I'll buy you some new ones. And let's go somewhere."

"All right, Joe." She said it so quietly and so seriously that for a moment he didn't realize what she'd said. Then it penetrated.

He said, not brilliantly, "Huh?"

She smiled. "I don't mean it literally about breaking the dishes. I just mean I'll stack them; I can do them some other time. But we can go out. We don't have to talk."

"It's early, Ellie. Only half past six. We can do the dishes; I'll wipe them for you." He wanted to ask exactly what she meant about their not having to talk, but decided he'd better not. "Where'd you like to go?"

"Oh, anywhere."

"Say, it's a nice evening, or going to be. Let's take a drive, huh? Up along the lake or somewhere. I can rent a car at the drive-yourself place; I've done it a few times before. And we don't have to go far or put many miles on it; it won't cost any more than if we went to a show or something."

"All right, Joe. If that's what you want to do." She glanced at the window. "I don't suppose there's any hurry; it's getting dark already. I might as well do the dishes, if you don't mind."

He helped her clear off the table and then she chased him away, telling him the kitchenette was too small for two of them and she could do them faster by herself.

He lounged on the daybed, picking up a magazine and then putting it down again. He wondered what she meant by saying they didn't have to talk. He'd come here wanting to talk, but knowing that what he intended to tell her – without any details, of course – would probably mean the end of their seeing one another.

But it was so comfortable, so nice being with Ellie that he found himself hoping already that they *wouldn't* have to break things off. Did Ellie feel the same way about it? Was that why she'd said what she'd said about their not talking?

They got the car and he drove east and then north along the lake, just driving leisurely, enjoying the evening. He stopped in Doctors Park, just north of Fox Point, and parked so they were facing the lake and could look out over the moonlit expanse of it, framed in the black-green of the trees under which they parked.

His arm, across the back of the seat, dropped across Ellie's shoulders and pulled her closer to him. She put her head on his shoulder and he turned and kissed her. Her hand rumpled his hair.

They looked out at the moonlit water. "It's beautiful out there," Joe said.

"Yes."

"But it's more beautiful in here."

"Yes, Joe."

He thought, I mustn't say things like that; I mustn't kiss her again.

He kissed her again, and it was very wonderful.

A little too wonderful, he decided. He started the car's engine and began to back out to the main road again. Ellie pulled away to her side of the seat and he could feel her looking at him, wondering at him. But she said nothing, nor did he, until they were on Fox Lane again and heading north.

Then she asked, quietly, "Are you afraid of me, Joe? Afraid I'm going to seduce you?"

"You know better than that, Ellie. Don't talk like that."

"What *are* you afraid of, Joe?"

What *was* he afraid of? Candles and axes. Mitch. Tying himself down to domesticity and a time clock. Not *getting* anywhere. Atom bombs and needing a gun to get a crust of bread. Yes, there were plenty of things he was afraid of, but they didn't have anything to do—not directly, anyway—with why he'd pulled the car out of the park. He knew why that was; he was afraid of hurting Ellie.

He wanted to say, "Damn it, Ellie, don't fall in love with me. I'm not worth it, from your point of view. I'm not the kind of man you want." But you couldn't say that, not just that.

He said, "I'm afraid of a lot of things, Ellie."

"What, Joe?"

"Well, candles and axes—"

"Joe, when I said I didn't want to talk—that I'd decided not to—I didn't—Joe, we've got to talk, now."

"All right, Ellie. Go ahead."

"Not while you're costing yourself a fortune driving a rented car miles and miles and miles. Turn around and start back the other way. Or stop somewhere. Stop under a light if you're afraid of me."

He laughed at that, and made the laugh almost ring true. And then he thought of Francine and last night—and how this was so like and so different from what had happened with Francine—that the end of the laugh *did* ring true.

Ellie laughed with him. She said, "Oh, Joe, why can't we keep it funny? Why can't we just have fun?"

"Sure, Ellie."

He turned at a side road and headed back. He said, "We just passed a juke joint. Shall we go in and have a beer or something? I'll feel safe there."

"If you want, Joe."

Why can't we just have fun? Ellie had said. Joe tried to think back when he'd had fun. It jarred him. He couldn't quite remember when, unless it had been these dates with Ellie. And always, on them, this worry, this thought, this fear—And they'd been fun anyway, until tonight, and tonight was different. Why? It took him half a minute to place what was different. *Now it was too late for him to back out of the deal with Mitch.*

Or could he? It would be damned unpleasant to do, now, and now he'd definitely owe Mitch back the money Mitch had given him.

But damn it, he didn't *want* to back out.

Why had the big chance he'd waited for, and Ellie – and Francy – all come along at the same time to mix him up on what he really did want?

He pulled in at the roadside tavern and parked the car. He took Ellie inside and they found a booth; there were others there but the place wasn't crowded. Ellie said she wanted beer, so he ordered a bottle for himself, too. The juke box was playing *To Each His Own,* and Ellie's eyes met his across the table.

She said, "Joe, if we're going to sit somewhere, we might as well do it in town. You're paying on that car by the hour as well as by the mile, aren't you?"

He was so relieved that he laughed again. "Ellie," he said, "quit worrying, will you, about how much things cost."

"I suppose I should, Joe. Especially tonight."

Why did she say *especially tonight?* Because, to her also, this had been important because it was going to be the *last* night? But hardly that; she'd said she'd decided that they shouldn't talk. Had she intended breaking things off between them tonight without even talking it over?

He asked, "Why especially tonight, Ellie?"

"Because – I don't know. I'm all mixed up. There were things I wanted to ask you, things I thought I wanted to know about you before we kept on seeing one another – especially after what Uncle Mike said. And then tonight, at supper, when you said that about breaking the dishes, I suddenly thought – I thought, I don't *want* to talk. I thought, let's just go out and have fun."

He was looking at her very seriously. "You were afraid

that if we did talk you'd learn something you didn't want to know. Something that would spoil everything?"

"Yes, Joe. That's close enough, anyway."

"You poor kid," he said. "Did you expect me to tell you I was a — a monster or something?"

"I — I know you're not, Joe. If you were *bad*, I couldn't like you as much as I do. But, well, I did worry where you got money when you're not working, not even looking for a job, and then tonight — just suddenly — I decided, *what business is it of mine?* It isn't dishonest; you couldn't be. It's probably nothing worse than selling numbers tickets, and if you don't want to talk about it, that's your business.

"And it isn't like — well, if we ever got serious and were going to get married or anything, then it would be different. But we're just having dates, having fun. So I decided I was being silly."

"What if I told you I was a bank robber, Ellie?"

"Then *you'd* be being silly, expecting me to believe anything like that. Joe, let's skip the whole thing. I mean it. I meant it, only when you acted like that when we were out in the park — I mean, when you kissed me and then — well, practically *ran away*, I — *Are* you afraid of me, Joe?"

"I guess I am."

"Why?"

"I guess because I like you too much, Ellie. That's the only answer to that. Or maybe I mean I was afraid of myself because I like you too much."

Ellie laughed. "I guess that's what I've been afraid of, too. I mean, of my getting to like you too much."

"But now you aren't afraid anymore, huh?"

"I guess not. Why can't we just have fun without worrying whether it might get serious or not? But Joe, whether we worry about money or not, it's silly to pay rent on that car and not use it. Let's take it back; we can sit and drink beer downtown as well as way out here."

"All right, Ellie, if it really worries you. Like to go back to the Violina Room?"

"I'd love it."

They took the car back and had a drink and listened to music—real, not juke box music—at the Violina Room. At eleven Ellie said she was tired and he took her home. In the hallway downstairs, he kissed her good night, and the kiss skyrocketed. They clung together and he whispered, "Ellie—may I come up?"

"Please, Joe—no," she whispered back.

He could have, if he'd persuaded. The "please" told him that she wanted him as badly as he wanted her. And yet it stopped him more effectively than anything else she could have said. He kissed her again, marveling how wonderful her lips felt against his, how soft her body was against him.

He walked home wondering if he was in love. Damn it, he'd *have* to stop seeing Ellie now, even if she didn't want to ask questions about where his money came from. Whether he was in love with her or not, she was falling in love with him. And that wasn't fair to her. Ellie wasn't the kind of girl you could have an affair with unless she loved you. And he'd end up hog-tied, married. Only he *couldn't* marry her, not with his other plans what they were—and it was too late to back out of the deal with Mitch now.

For the first time he almost wished he *could* back out.

Hog-tied or not, it would be wonderful being married to Ellie.

He called himself all kinds of a damned fool for even thinking about it.

174

The Sportcast

SERIES THEME (*Rachmaninoff's* Isle of the Dead, *in waltz time*) *for five seconds.*

CLEM ABEL: This is your favorite sports announcer, folks, Clem Abel, going to bring you today another in our famous series of sportcasts. And we've got something unusual lined up for you today, folks. Not baseball, not football, not even chess. That's one broadcast, folks, that chess broadcast last week, that I've really got to apologize for. The only thing I can say is that it hurt me worse than it did you. Imagine me having to think of things to keep talking about between moves! You were only bored stiff, but I was scared stiff. I dreamed about knights for days and I was in a daze for nights. Honest. But today — hang onto your seats — we're not broadcasting a game of chess. We're broadcasting a game that's *always* exciting, even when you played it when you were kids and it wasn't for keeps. The good old game of *Cops and Robbers!* Now I'll have to qualify that a bit; there *may* not be any cops — or then again there may; you can't ever tell until the game is under way. But there are going to be robbers. We have inside information — never mind from where — that a crime is going to be committed within the next half hour. Now it may not be a very important crime, unless something backfires, but there's always the possibility of that happening and we want to be there if it does. Now let me remind you of one thing, folks: *This is a confidential matter.* Our Sponsor agreed to it

175

only under those circumstances. You are *not* to report to the police anything—anything whatever—that you hear on this broadcast. It wouldn't be fair if you did. No matter what happens, you're going to keep your mouths buttoned tight. Understand? All right, now I'll tell you what the setup is. I'm sitting in the backseat of a car and I've got my walkie-talkie set right here in my lap. Following us, but keeping a fair distance behind so it won't interfere with us or attract attention is the station's pickup truck. It picks up what I'm saying into this mike and rebroadcasts it via shortwave to our main station—that's WTMJ, *The Milwaukee Journal* station—and it's broadcast from there at six hundred and twenty kilocycles and that's what your set is tuned in on. Which reminds me to check up right now before we go any farther. Am I coming in all right, Hank?

VOICE: Pickup truck speaking. Reception excellent.

CLEM: You don't have to be so formal about it. Now how about a check with the studio.

ANOTHER VOICE: Studio. Reception good. Broadcast going out as scheduled.

CLEM: Technicians always talk that way. Dunno why; sometimes I think they aren't really people. Anyway, I guess you're all hearing me okay. I'm in the backseat of a car about forty miles from Milwaukee and heading toward our fair city at a moderate speed. We're not on a main highway. I don't know why we aren't; I'll see if I can find out for you in a minute, but first I want to introduce the men I'm riding with—the ones in the front seat, I mean; I'm here all alone in the back seat, except for Mike. That's just a pun, folks; I meant I'm here alone with my microphone. Don't want to confuse the picture by having somebody miss the pun and think there's really someone named Mike back here with me. The two men in the front seat are named Joe Bailey and Dixie Ehlers. Joe's driving. I'll hold the mike forward over the seat and see if he'll say a word to us. Joe.

JOE: Yeah? What do you want?

CLEM: You don't know you're about to commit a crime, do you, Joe? Anyway, that's what they told me. Is it right?

JOE: That's right.

CLEM: Is this your car, Joe?

JOE: No, it's Dixie's. I wish I had one. He's letting me drive it a while.

CLEM: What are your plans, Joe?

JOE: You mean for right now? I'm just driving back to Milwaukee, that's all. We were out practicing, just a few miles back.

CLEM: How does it happen you're not on a main highway?

JOE: just getting to know the country around here. Dixie says we should go different places and by different routes, so we get to know all the roads, the unimportant ones as well as the main ones. It might come in handy once in a while, sometime.

CLEM: How old are you, Joe?

JOE: How old would you guess?

CLEM: Oh, twenty-two maybe.

JOE: That's close enough.

CLEM: All right, folks, now you've met Joe Bailey. Now we'll introduce you to Dixie Ehlers. That's him up front, the one not driving. Will you say something to the folks, Dixie?

(*Pause.*)

CLEM: Guess he isn't in a mood for talking. He won't even look around, let alone answer my question. But I'll tell you what little about him I can see from here. He's smaller than Joe, an inch or so, but he's older; I'd say about ten years older. And he doesn't talk much. Not to me, anyway. But I think he's about to say something to Joe Bailey. I'll shut up—hard as it is for me to do that little thing—and let you listen.

DIXIE: Joe, slow down a minute.

JOE: Sure.

DIXIE: That place just ahead. Turn her around there and head back the way we came.

JOE: Sure, Dixie. We forget something, or what?

DIXIE: Kid, I'm going to blood you a little.

JOE: Huh?

DIXIE: See how you act when the heat's on. We just passed a little filling station. Let's go back and fill up. And I don't mean our gas tank. It'll be peanuts—probably twenty or thirty bucks apiece, if that much—but it's a sitting duck, and I just want to see how you take it. Now take it slow past here. Not slow enough to attract attention; I mean, go by about twenty-five, so I can take a good look. It's right ahead there. You can see the sign but you can't see the station on account of the trees. But you just watch the road; I'll do the looking.

CLEM: Yes, folks, I can see the sign Dixie is pointing to and we're almost there. I'll watch out of the window and—yes, I can see the station now. It's back only the width of a driveway from the road, but because there are trees all around it, you can't see it until you're quite close. You can, of course, see the sign; that's how you know to slow down if you want gas. It's a nice-looking little station; there's only one man there, and he's sitting in a chair tilted back against the wall, out front. He's reading a newspaper and doesn't look up as we go by. It looks

178

like a lead-pipe cinch, even to me. But I wonder just how Dixie's going to handle it. We're past now.

DIXIE: Slow down, Joe. Park right here, only pull off the road a little. That's it. Anybody goes by and sees the car here they'll just think we stopped here and walked back in the woods to take a piss.

CLEM: Sorry, folks. If I'd guessed what he was going to say, I'd have turned the mike off for a second. But those things happen when you're giving a live, unrehearsed broadcast and the people you're following are people like Dixie. All we can do is apolo—

DIXIE: Yeah, this is good. Now here's the setup, kid. Wait, your gun ready?

JOE: Sure.

DIXIE: Not that you'll need it on a pushover like this, unless something unexpected happens. But that's what you've always got to be ready for. Now the guy hasn't seen us, hasn't even seen our car. He didn't look up either time we passed. It'll be a cleaner job if he never gets a look at our pusses at all. So we're going to walk around through the trees and come up on the station from the back, see? We'll be sure there are no cars pulled in or going by and then I'll step around put a gun on him and take him inside.

JOE: Won't he see your face when you do that?

DIXIE: Nah. I'll pull down my hat brim and turn up my coat collar. All he'll see is Maggie. And that much only for a second; I tell him to turn around and I follow him in. I'll take care of getting the dough, and of him. Your job is to step around to the front from the other side, and stand there in case any car pulls in. You send 'em away. Tell 'em the station's closed and you're waiting for the guy who runs it to come back but he isn't coming soon, or

179

something. Anything to get them to drive off. Hell, I'll be inside only a few minutes anyway; probably no car'll pull up.

JOE: What do I do if somebody pulls up that knows the guy and says, "Where's Elmer?" or something?

DIXIE: Then, kid, you use your noodle. But don't get scared; I'll be back of you.

CLEM: They're starting to get out of the car now. Dixie Ehlers has opened the glove compartment while they were talking and has taken out a sap—a blackjack, if you don't know what a sap is, folks. I was wondering whether he was going to take time inside the filling station to tie up his victim. I guess the sap answers that. Well, they're out of the car now, walking back into the woods. I'm getting out, too. It might be interesting to go along with them, to see what other things Dixie is telling Joe. I can see that they're talking, or Dixie is, anyway. But I think we'll take a shortcut and go right along the road instead of through the trees. That way we'll get there sooner and be set up to watch whatever happens. So I'm walking along the road now, out of the car. It's only about a hundred yards. No car has come along yet. Wish I didn't have to carry this gosh darn walkie-talkie set with me. A car's coming now, from in front of me, but it doesn't seem to be— No, it didn't even slow down. It's past me already and keeping on going. That's *one* car they won't worry about. I kind of hope a car does stop while they're transacting their business, just so I can see how Joe Bailey acts. He looks a little scared, to me. I mean, he did look scared back there when he was getting out of the car. I can't see him now, of course. Now I'm almost in front of the filling station and I can see it. The proprietor—somehow he looks like a proprietor and not just somebody working there—is still leaning back in his chair reading. Now I'm standing right in front of him, but he doesn't see me. He won't, of course, unless I speak to him; that's the rules of the game. I'm here, you see, but I'm not really here either. But you know that, by this time. I think I'll really be here, though, long enough to put him on the air for you. We've got at least a minute or two yet; Joe and Dixie will take a good look around before they show up. *Hello, there.* Yes, he's looking up from his paper.

PROPRIETOR: Hello. Anything I can do for you?

CLEM: No, not a thing. Just want to introduce you to the audience that's listening, before the holdup happens.

PROPRIETOR: Holdup?

CLEM: That's right, you don't know about it yet. Well, just forget I told you and let it be a surprise. For that matter, it's *supposed* to be a surprise. What's your name?

PROPRIETOR: Frayter. Harvey L. Frayter. And I was born in Green Bay, Wisconsin, in nineteen hundred.

CLEM: Well, that makes you just forty-eight, doesn't it? I mean, since it's nineteen forty-eight now.

PROPRIETOR: That's right; I'll be forty-eight next month, October.

CLEM: You own this station?

PROPRIETOR: Yes.

CLEM: Got much money in the register? Or on you?

PROPRIETOR: Only about thirty bucks in the register. But I got about ninety bucks in my wallet. Hundred and twenty, altogether.

CLEM: Do you always carry that much?

PROPRIETOR: No, I don't. But I own a house in Beaver Dam and rent it. My tenant paid me two months rent this morning, sixty dollars. He was a month behind. He paid it in cash, and I had thirty before that, so I got ninety now. Why?

CLEM: I'm afraid you won't have it long, Mr Frayter. Here comes Dixie Ehlers around the corner of the station right now. Don't look; you're not supposed to know he's there yet. He's got his hat pulled down low over his eyes and his coat collar turned up and his chin buried in it. You won't be able to see much of his face, and I wouldn't advise you to look very long after he tells you to turn around and face the other way. He's got his hand under his coat, resting on Maggie's butt. That sounds a little obscene, but it isn't; Maggie is what he calls his Magnum revolver. Know anything about Magnums, Mr Frayter?

PROPRIETOR: I've heard of 'em. They're the guns that'll shoot right through bulletproof glass.

CLEM: And bulletproof vests, too. You're not wearing one, are you, Mr Frayter?

PROPRIETOR: Me? Don't be silly.

CLEM: And you aren't going to be silly and resist, are you?

PROPRIETOR: For a hundred and twenty bucks? My life's worth more than a hundred and twenty bucks to me.

CLEM: That's good, Mr Frayter. I'm glad you feel that way about it. For your own sake, I mean. This would make a better broadcast for our audience if you resisted, but I hate to see a man killed just to amuse people. Well, we'd better stop talking now; Dixie is coming toward you. He's been looking and listening to be sure no car is in sight or in hearing along the road. Now look down at your paper again and just forget everything I've told you so you'll be surprised.

DIXIE: Put 'em upl

182

CLEM: (*laughing*) You should have seen that man jump when Dixie stuck the gun in his ribs. Dixie walked up so quietly that Frayter didn't hear him at all. He jumped right up out of the chair and nearly knocked the chair over doing it. He's staring at Dixie with his eyes wide.

DIXIE: Turn around the other way. Walk inside.

CLEM: He's doing it like a lamb. It's only two steps to the door of the station. He walks in and Dixie follows him. Dixie's pulling the door shut and that's the signal for Joe Bailey to come around the other side of the station. He stands there and looks around; there's nothing in sight, no car coming from either direction. Joe goes over and sits down on the chair Frayter was sitting in. He looks pretty tense. Inside the station I can hear the cash register opening. Joe jumps up out of the chair. I wonder—Oh, I hear it now, too. A car coming. Guess Joe's ears are better than mine because he heard it first. Yes, there's not only a car coming, but it's slowing down as though it's getting ready to turn in here. Must have seen the sign. Can't see the car yet, but—Yes, here it comes pulling into the station. It's a dark green Buick, about a forty-six model. It's got an Ohio license; that's good, because it's probably a tourist rather than someone who might know Harvey Frayter and get suspicious at whatever song and dance Joe's going to hand him. There's only one man in the car. He's big, but he doesn't look like a cop. He's pulling into a stop in front of the pump. Joe is walking over to him, managing to walk and act pretty casual, under the circumstances. Let's beat Joe there, though, and find out who the man is. Pardon me, sir.

DRIVER: Yes?

CLEM: Hope you won't mind me asking you a few questions. This is a special broadcast of a crime. But you aren't supposed to know that a crime is going on unless you get suspicious from something Joe does or says. That's the fellow behind me, waiting to talk to you. May I ask your name?

DRIVER: Harvey Oglethorpe.

CLEM: Harvey, huh? That's a coincidence, Mr Oglethorpe, I mean that your first name should be Harvey. That's the first name of the owner of the station here, only his last name is Frayter and yours is Oglethorpe. Not much similarity in last names, anyway. But you don't need to worry about Mr Frayter, Mr Oglethorpe; he's being taken care of. Inside the station. You're from Ohio, Mr Oglethorpe?

DRIVER: Yes. From Columbus.

CLEM: Well, well, the state capital. I was there once, some years ago. I remember the squirrels on the grounds around the capitol building. Tame. Used to come right up and take peanuts out of your hand. Are you on vacation here in Wisconsin or are you here on business?

DRIVER: A little of both. I had some business in Green Bay, but I thought I'd combine a vacation with it. I've got my business over with now, and today I'm just driving around sightseeing. Beautiful country.

CLEM: Isn't it? Most beautiful state in the United States.

DRIVER: It's nice, but I wouldn't go that far. I like California better. I want to go there to live someday.

CLEM: Well, we don't think California can hold a candle to Wisconsin, but we won't argue about that. You pulled in here for some gas, Mr Oglethorpe?

DRIVER: Sure. This is a gas station, isn't it?

CLEM: Well, just at the moment the circumstances are peculiar. But I'll step out of the way and let you talk to

Joe Bailey about that. All right, Joe, take it away. Joe's stepping up to the car now, folks.

DRIVER: Ten gallons, please. The ethyl.

JOE: Sorry, mister, the station isn't open. And I don't work here; I'm just waiting for someone.

DRIVER: Oh. hell. How far is it to the next station?

JOE: Less than half a mile. Can you make it okay?

DRIVER: Guess so. Got about a gallon left, if the gauge is right.

JOE: Sorry.

DRIVER: That's all right.

CLEM: It's all okay, folks. The car with the Ohio license is pulling out again and Joe is walking back to the chair. Guess everything's okay and nothing's going to happen. Joe starts to sit down and then doesn't as he sees the door of the station opening a little. Guess Dixie's going to check that everything's all right.

DIXIE: Coast clear?

JOE: Sure.

CLEM: Dixie is stepping out, folks. Guess he's all through inside and it's all over but the getaway. He pulls the door shut.

DIXIE: Come on, kid. Back the way we came, so nobody will notice us walking from the station to the car.

CLEM: They're walking around behind the station again. I don't think we need to follow them; I think they'll walk fast and not do any talking. We don't have to worry about being seen so I'm walking along the road to the car. It's a beautiful day, folks, and Wisconsin is certainly the most beautiful state in the union, despite what that man from Ohio thought. And especially at this time of the year. I think September is the most beautiful month in

185

Wisconsin. Well, there's the car, just as they left it. I'll get in the backseat again, just as I was before. And—yes, here come Joe and Dixie. They're getting in the front. Joe's walking around the car to get in the driver's seat again. His face looks blank, but as though he's holding it carefully blank. He's a criminal now, folks; he's committed his first crime—unless you count swiping things from dime store counters, things that all kids or anyway most kids, if they're brought up like Joe, do. And if you don't count selling pool tickets and things like that as crimes. Wonder what he's thinking about. He's starting the car now. I'll ask him for you. Joe, what are you thinking about?

JOE: So many things at once that I'm all mixed up. I guess I'm thinking about Ellie mostly.

CLEM: Not about Francy?

JOE: Ellie, mostly. But I guess I can't keep on stringing Ellie along, now. And that leaves Francy.

CLEM: Except for Mitch. Don't forget Mitch.

JOE: I wish I could. My God, I wish I could.

CLEM: On account of Francy, you mean?

JOE: I didn't mean that. I mean, my God, I wish I'd quit Mitch while there was time. I wish I was out of it.

CLEM: Maybe you'll get out of it like your father got out of it.

JOE: There's that. I guess—well, I guess I got it coming, on account of that.

CLEM: You still blame yourself for your father's death?

JOE: (*dully*) I got him killed, didn't I? If it wasn't for that—

CLEM: You'd wish you were out of it even more than you do? Is that it? But how about the big money and being a big shot? Don't you still want all that, Joe?

JOE: Sure, but—

186

CLEM: But you want Ellie too. To marry, I mean, not just to sleep with. You know she's in love with you, don't you, Joe?

JOE: I don't know. I don't want to get married. Tied down. I don't know *what* I want. Lay off of me, will you?

CLEM: Okay, Joe. I'll lay off of you. I guess you're pretty mixed up. And you're just a kid. You aren't really twenty-two, are you? You're about twenty, aren't you?

JOE: (*sullenly*) Nineteen.

CLEM: And a holdup man with a gun in a shoulder holster.

JOE: Lay off of me.

CLEM: Sure, Joe. Go ahead and talk to Dixie. I'll shut up.

JOE: How much did we get, Dixie?

DIXIE: A hundred, kid. Almost on the head. Thirty in the register and seventy in the mooch's pocket. Fifty bucks apiece. I'll split it with you when we get home.

JOE: Did you sap him?

DIXIE: Yeah, lightly. Didn't hurt him. He may not be out over a few minutes, but so what? There wasn't any phone in the joint, and we're practically back to the main highway now. Not a thing to worry about, kid, even if he's talking to cops already. He couldn't describe either of us, don't know what kind of a car we got, anything. Yeah, here's the highway. We're completely clear now. Like taking candy away from a baby.

JOE: Yeah. Except that the guy who stopped for gas got a plenty good look at me. He could identify me, all right.

DIXIE: Didn't get him suspicious, did you?

JOE: No.

DIXIE: Then what you worried about?

JOE: Nothing, I guess. Where we going?

DIXIE: Drive yourself home, kid. I'll slip you your fifty

when we get there. And then I'll take the car. I'm going to start casing a job for the four of us this afternoon, something Mitch picked. But I can do it better alone.

CLEM: Well, guess that's all that's going to happen, folks. Sorry—for your sakes—that there wasn't any more excitement than that. But that's the way it goes, sometimes. Some days you just can't lay away a corpse. And now my time is up, so this is Clem Abel saying good-bye to you until next week—and reminding you once more, before I fold up my walkie-talkie like the Arabs and silently steal away, that this broadcast was by special permission of our Sponsor and with the strict understanding with Him that it is to be held completely confidential, especially from the police. That's all, folks, and good-bye till next week.

MUSIC: *Up and under, into Station Break.*

The Story

18

By Thursday he *had* to see Ellie. Tuesday, after the holdup of the filling station, he hadn't wanted to. Wednesday he'd tried to see her. He'd gone to her room at eight-thirty in the evening, time for her to have been home from work. But she wasn't there.

He tried again half an hour later and decided she must have gone somewhere, probably to a movie.

Thursday noon he was in his room. He'd just got back from another trip with Dixie—nothing exciting had happened on that one—or he could have gone to Ellie's place before she went to work at eleven. Now he'd missed that chance for today but he *had* to see her when she got off at eight this evening.

That meant he had to get in touch with her before she got off duty; otherwise she might have other arrangements by then.

He felt miserable because it was going to be the last time, probably, that he *would* see her. He told himself that he had to talk to her, to make a clean break, whatever he told her. It wasn't fair to let things taper off like this and besides it made him feel lousy. The only thing to do was to tell her enough that he *couldn't* see her again, ever. Then he could go about the process of getting her off his mind, forgetting her. And she could forget him. This way, everything was up in the air. Things couldn't stay like that; it made everything too complicated. He felt awfully glad that Ellie had moved away from Mrs Gettleman's; it would have been bad to keep running into her in the hallway or going in or out, after they'd broken things off.

He wondered if her uncle was at the restaurant. If not, he could phone her there. For that matter, if Mike wasn't there, he could even drop in and have a sandwich and coffee and fix things to see Ellie when she got off.

He went downstairs and walked over Wells Street toward the restaurant, taking the opposite side of the street so he could see in better. He didn't have to go all the way; from diagonally across the street he could see Mike at the cigar counter.

He swore to himself, turned around and walked back. He couldn't phone, either. The phone was on the wall near the cigar counter and Mike would answer it and recognize his voice.

By the time he got back home, though, he had the answer. He knocked lightly on Mrs Gettleman's door. She opened it and said, "Yes, Joe?"

He smiled at her. "Mrs Gettleman, I wonder if you'd do me a big favor. You remember Ellie Dravich, the girl who lived here for about a week? I've got to get in touch with her about something important. And I've got her phone number at work but they've got a rule against girls who work there getting calls from men during working hours. But it *is* important that I talk to her. Would it be too much to ask for you to phone there and get her on the line and then let me talk to her?"

She frowned and, for a moment, looked uncertain; then she said, "All right, Joe. But then after you're through talking, you come back here. There's something I want to talk to you about."

"Sure. And thanks a lot, Mrs Gettleman."

The phone was in the hall just outside Mrs Gettleman's door, so she could hear it ring and answer incoming calls. Joe gave her the number and nickel and stood close while she dialed the number. He heard her ask for Ellie Dravich and then, a few seconds later, say, "Oh. All right, thanks."

She put the receiver back and turned to Joe. "Not there yet," she told him. "Working a little different shift today; she doesn't start till one o'clock."

Joe looked at his watch; it was a quarter after twelve. He said, "Gosh, I can catch her in her room then, before she starts for work. Thanks an awful lot, Mrs—"

"Joe, I want to talk to you. Come on in my place a minute."

"But I'm in a hurry now. Can't I see you later?"

"All right, I'll tell you here, in that case. Joe, I want that room. I'm sorry, but you'll have to move when your week's up."

He was startled out of being in a hurry. "Huh? Why, Mrs Gettleman? Have I done something, or what?"

"Well—I'm not going to stand here in the hallway and talk. If you want to come in—"

"Will you be here in an hour? Will an hour from now be all right? Gosh, I want to talk to you about it. I don't understand. But I might miss Ellie if I don't go right away—and that's important, too."

"All right, Joe."

He didn't want to get to Ellie's room out of breath or he

might have run. He walked rapidly. He tried to think out what he was going to say to Ellie but the moderately startling ultimatum Mrs Gettleman had just handed him kept getting in the way. Why, all of a sudden, had she given him notice on his room? He and she had always got along fine, and he was one of her most quiet tenants. He didn't even have a radio. True, he got in late lots of times, and slept late mornings, but that didn't inconvenience anyone. He was quiet about it. And sleeping late couldn't matter; she never made her rounds of straightening up rooms on the third floor until afternoon anyway.

He couldn't even guess what she'd decided was wrong, and he was impatient to get back and find out. He hoped—and thought—that he could talk her out of whatever it was. His room wasn't much and he could probably find another one without too much trouble, but he'd got used to it now and liked it. And it was handy to Mitch's, to town, to Ellie's—although he suddenly realized that didn't matter because he wouldn't be seeing Ellie anymore anyway.

He reached Ellie's without having decided what to say at all except that it might take longer than a few minutes and he'd better settle, now, for arranging to see her after work tonight. Somehow he felt relieved that it could be accomplished and still postponed.

She came to the door when he knocked. She said, "Why, Joe, how'd you know I'd still be here? I don't start till one today, but how did you find that out?"

"My secret spy system, Ellie. May I come in a minute?"

She stepped back and held the door open. "Not *much* longer than that, Joe. I have to leave pretty soon. But I'm all ready to go, so we can talk a few minutes."

He pushed the door shut behind him and looked at her. "Ellie—" He got lost there.

"Joe, you sound as though something's the matter. Is it?"

"Well—"

"Are you in trouble, Joe? Is there anything I can do?"

"No it isn't that, Ellie. Listen, I've got to tell you something, but not in a few minutes. If you're starting at one today, what time do you get off? Ten?"

She nodded.

"Can I see you then? It's important, Ellie."

"All right, Joe. Only don't pick me up at the restaurant. I'll come back here; I'll be here by a quarter after."

"That's fine, Ellie."

"Joe, how *did* you know I start late today? You didn't go to the restaurant, did you, or phone there?"

He told her about his landlady having made the call.

"I'm glad you told me so I won't be surprised when I learn there *was* a call. I'll just say I left the number with two or three people while I was looking for a housekeeping room and that probably it was one of them."

"Sure. Listen, Ellie, I—"

"Don't tell me now, Joe."

She knows already, more or less, what I'm going to tell her, he thought. And she doesn't want to hear it, any more than I want to say it, either now or at ten-fifteen this evening.

He stood looking at her and suddenly he didn't want to tell her, now or ever, anything that would end things between them.

Damn it, he loved Ellie.

And yet that very fact—something he'd realized just now for the first time—made it more important than ever that he didn't hurt her. And he couldn't go on seeing her without hurting her, not possibly. If she wasn't already in love with him, she would be if they kept on seeing one another. And what business did a girl like Ellie have falling

193

in love with a holdup man, a man who'd participated in a holdup only day before yesterday and who couldn't back out now because it was too late? Hell, he'd better not even see her tonight. That would just make it worse for both of them. He'd not even break the date; he just wouldn't come. She'd sit and wait for him and get mad and that would be the best thing. Better than any final scene between them, for her. For him, too, maybe.

She said, "I'd better go, Joe. It's ten minutes of. And—whatever it is—we'll talk it out tonight."

"Sure, Ellie."

But he had to kiss her good-bye. It would be all right now, because she wouldn't know that's what it was.

He went forward the one step that separated them and put his arms around her. His lips found hers and for a moment her arms went up around him, her hands behind his head pulling it down against hers. Nothing exploded; there were no pyrotechnics in that kiss, only tenderness. Tenderness and peace.

Then Ellie was pushing him away. "I've got to go; I'll be late."

She almost ran down the two flights of stairs, her heels clicking on every step. Joe followed her, dazed and unhappy, not quite believing that this was really the end. It had seemed, that kiss, so like a beginning, something completely new to him.

She was out the door ahead of him; she was waving an empty taxi to a stop. It swung into the curb and she turned quickly, talking fast. "Got to take it, Joe, or I'll be late. 'Bye." She turned back and started to run toward the cab.

For a second, just long enough for it to be too late for him to run after her, Joe stood rooted. There had been tears in

Ellie's eyes when she had turned back toward him before running.

He called after her, "'Bye, Ellie. Ten-fifteen."

He knew he was going to keep that date in spite of everything.

He walked home slowly, trying to think it out. He thought: *I'll tell her the truth— well, most of the truth, not the details. Then it's up to her. Maybe she loves me enough that she won't care. And after a few months it'll be all right; we're going to raise some money the hard way, but after that the risk will be over. She shouldn't object just to me working in a gambling place; that may be illegal, but it's not dishonest and not dangerous. And then— then it'll be all right. Maybe we'll even get married. If she loves me enough to marry me without tying me down to a job that won't pay anything, that'll be all right.*

Being married to Ellie, he knew now, would be very wonderful. At least it would be if he had the several hundred dollars a week he'd be making after they opened the place. Ellie in expensive clothes, furs, in a fine apartment, with a maid so she wouldn't have to do all the work. What a jump that would be from being a waitress. Yes, he'd put it to her that way. He'd be sure she understood that he was heading for big money, and soon. And he'd make sure, too, that she understood it was too late now for him to back out even if he wanted to.

Give her all the factors, if not all the facts, and tell her that he loved her. Then it would be up to her. If she didn't love him enough—

It never occurred to him that she might love him too much.

He was back in front of the rooming house before he remembered that Mrs Gettleman had wanted to talk to him.

195

He hadn't had time to wonder why. And there wasn't any use wondering now; he could find out in a minute.

Mrs Gettleman said, "Come in, Joe," when she opened her door. He followed her into the living room of her three-room apartment. "Sit down."

Joe leaned against the edge of the door instead, holding his hat in his hand and wondering what on earth she was leading up to. Whatever it was he wanted to get it over with. He said, "I can't stay long, Mrs Gettleman. I—I've got an appointment."

"About getting a job, Joe?"

He thought, *My God, that's what's worrying her. She knows I'm not working and I guess she's afraid I'll run out of money and not be able to pay my room rent. But it's none of her business, as long as I do pay it.*

He almost decided to tell her that it was none of her business. But he didn't want to move if he didn't have to. He'd be moving soon anyway, because soon he'd be able to afford a nice swanky room, maybe even a small suite, at some nice residential hotel, but it would be annoying to have to take another cheap room now and get settled down in it.

So he said, "I'm working now, Mrs Gettleman. Just started. A selling job on commission. Don't know how much I'll be making but you don't need to worry about the rent. It'll be that much anyway."

"That's good Joe. I'm glad to hear it. But that *isn't* what I'm worrying about."

Then what is? he wondered. No use asking; she'd tell him. So he just looked at her questioningly.

"Joe, yesterday morning you opened a package of laundry while you were getting dressed and you left it lying on your bed. I had to move it to make up the bed. So I thought I might as well put the laundry in the bureau drawers for you. And when I opened the top one, I saw that gun. And I don't know much about guns, Joe, but I know a little. Enough that I don't want you to try to tell me that's a target gun, not with that short a barrel and in a shoulder holster. And, Joe, I'm sorry but I don't want any trouble and that's why you've got to move. By Monday, when your rent is up."

He was glad she'd gone on; it had given him time to think after her first use of the word *gun* had told him what was wrong. He was ready with a story by the time she paused; it might sound thin, but it was better than nothing.

"Mrs Gettleman, I've never used that gun and don't expect to. I got it almost by accident. A guy owed me some money—twenty-five bucks—and couldn't pay it and offered me the gun for it. The gun's worth more than that, so I took it. I'm going down to Chicago soon and I'm going to sell it while I'm down there; I'll probably get thirty or thirty-five for it and be ahead on the deal."

She was studying his face; Joe could see she was trying to tell whether he'd told the truth or not. She was wavering. A little more—

He said, "If it worries you to have it in the house here, I'll take it away till I get rid of it. Mitch won't mind my leaving it at the tavern. He knows about it; I thought maybe he'd want to buy it to have a gun to keep back of the bar so I told him about it and how I got it. But he already had one."

She was almost convinced. Not quite. "But it's loaded, Joe. I looked. Why would you keep it loaded if that's true?"

He laughed. "I cut my teeth on that idea, Mrs Gettleman. My father used to be a good pistol shot and had several guns—" (He thought fast: Have I ever told her anything at all about my father? No, never mentioned him.) "—and one of his favorite ideas was that nothing is quite as dangerous as an unloaded gun. He said if you have a gun around, keep it loaded and *know* it's loaded and then you won't fool around with it and have an accident. I had that drilled into me, as a kid—partly, I guess, so I wouldn't ever handle his guns. And when Pete gave me the gun there was a box of bullets with it, so I keep it loaded."

"You aren't going to carry it to Chicago to sell without unloading it, are you?"

Good, she believed him.

"Oh no, not for that. I'd probably scare the dealer I offered it to. But I'll give him the box of bullets along with the gun."

"I'm glad, Joe," Mrs Gettleman said. "What's your new job, Joe?"

Ordinarily he could have stalled her on that, told her anything or nothing. But not right now; he'd have to tell her something that would check. If he mentioned the name of a company, she might phone them to be sure, if her suspicions came back about the gun. Hell, Mitch would front for him.

He said easily, "Not a new job, Mrs Gettleman. Back to the old one. The heat's off enough that we're selling pool tickets again." He grinned at her. "And that's illegal, but you can't squawk about that because you used to get one from me yourself once in a while, if not oftener."

He saw the catch in that, too late. Mrs Gettleman was a baseball fan, and she'd been one of his most regular customers, although always for small stakes, generally two-bit tickets.

"That's good, Joe," she said. "And I don't even have to look at the paper to pick tomorrow's winners. I'll take fifty cents' worth."

"I'm sorry," he said. "Mitch thought it was too late in

the season to start baseball. We're just working stock exchange figures."

"How does that work, Joe?"

He couldn't tell whether she was suspicious or not. He said, "The advances, declines and unchangeds — last figure on each. You take a three-figure number, say six-nine-two, and if that corresponds with the last digit of the number of stocks that advanced and the last digit of the number of stocks that declined and — "

"Oh, sure, I know how that works, Joe. I used to take a ticket on that once in a while, but I wish you were selling baseball tickets."

"So do I," Joe said. He found he could breathe easily again; it was going to be all right. "That way you can back your judgment. On the stock market figures, it's pure luck and the odds against you two to one. You get five hundred to one, if you win. But actually the odds are a thousand to one against you."

"By the time the series start, you'll be handling baseball again?"

"I hope so," Joe said. "Well, I got to be getting — "

"Wait a minute, Joe. I *will* take a numbers ticket but just for a quarter. I'll take — umm — six-six-six; that's the number of the Beast in the Apocalypse, isn't it? And if you haven't got a slip with you for today, bring me one for tomorrow."

Joe was caught and there wasn't any out. He looked down miserably. He said, "I'm afraid I wasn't telling you the truth about that, Mrs Gettleman. I mean, we're not selling tickets yet. But we will be soon and I just said that because I wasn't wanting you to worry about me not having a job. I've still got money saved, Mrs Gettleman, and I was just waiting until the pools *do* start operating again."

He looked up at her then, but it wasn't good. She was shaking her head slowly. "I'm sorry, Joe. If I can't believe you about that, I can't take your word for the rest of it. I'll want your room by Monday; that's the day you're paid up to."

"But Mrs Gettleman, that's pretty short notice. Aren't you supposed to give me a week?"

"Joe, if you're still here after Monday, I'll tell the police about that gun. If what you're telling me about it is true, you won't mind telling them."

He said, "All right then; I'll be gone by Monday." Miserably he had to tell one more lie to save the remnants. "Not that it would worry me, but the cops would check with the guy who gave it to me and I don't want to get him in trouble. So okay, if that's the way you feel about it."

He started for the door on a note of injured dignity.

"Joe," Mrs Gettleman said. He turned. Maybe it had worked.

It hadn't.

"Joe—you're a good boy. Be careful. Don't get yourself in trouble."

The worst of it was that he couldn't hate her, because she was in the right. All he could do was keep up the lie, pretend to be angry when he wasn't. "I'll find another room, Mrs Gettleman."

Upstairs in his room he wondered why he'd come up. There wasn't anything there.

Except the room itself. He looked around it and tried to tell himself, *It's a lousy room anyway. What the hell does it matter that I got to get another one?*

He tried to get mad at Mrs Gettleman and couldn't.

He lay down on the bed and stared angrily at the two pictures on the wall—the photograph of the store with

LEIBER AND HENNIG lettered on the windows and the ugly chromolithograph of the shepherd with the flock of sheep.

Why the hell should it annoy him to have to move out of a dump like this?

Things came in focus, finally. What a soft sap he had been making of himself!

19

The reasoning part of your brain keeps telling you it's a lot of crap and finally the reasoning part of your brain wins out and you see things straight. You've been a sap in a lot of ways, but now you know it.

Of all the God damned things to do—letting yourself think you're in love—love, for God's sake—with a waitress who isn't even outstandingly pretty or smart or anything else. And because she's soft for you and you know you can have her, you think so anyway, you get so soft yourself that you don't even lay a hand on her. You even get fuzzy-brained enough to think about marrying her.

You're on the verge of the big time, the big money, getting what you want, and you go soft like that. You've got to be tough.

Can you imagine Mitch being soft like you've been acting? Can you imagine Mitch thinking about marrying a waitress and going straight and living on a few dollars a week he'd have to work like a dog to get? How can you ever be a big shot if you let yourself even think like that?

So you want Ellie. All right, what are you waiting for? Go ahead and sleep with her. Tonight. It's not going to hurt her, damn it. You won't knock her up if you use precautions. Isn't she the one who changed her mind about wanting to talk seriously, about wanting to know how you lived without having a job? Doesn't that mean she doesn't want *to know?*

Then what are you being a sap about? Either go ahead and sleep with her or else don't keep the date at all and never see her again. No explanations. Just drop it. One way or the other.

Tonight at a quarter after ten. You told her you had to talk to her about something important. All right, what's more important than that? You want her.

Why shouldn't the two of you enjoy yourselves and one another for a while? Tell her nothing. Even if she asks, tell her nothing. She'll worry about it and after a while she'll break things off and that will be that, but look what you'll have had meanwhile. And why not?

But that isn't all you want from Ellie. You want the peace and contentment and happiness that she could—

Cut it out. You can't have everything. You aren't going to live forever; you might as well have what you can while you can.

Suppose you get killed, like your father did.

All right then, it's settled. Tonight you quit being foolish. Tonight you sleep with Ellie. If she's willing. She will be. If you do it right. Don't talk. Just make love to her. Kiss her. Your hand on her breast, as you wanted to do when you parked the car that night. You could have then. You ran, instead. What were you afraid of?

She probably wants it as bad as you do. Why does she think you haven't? Maybe she thinks you're queer or something. No, she can't think that. Probably thinks you're afraid to.

Well, weren't you? But not for the reason she thought.

All right, it's settled. If she won't, then it's settled, too. If she won't, that'll end things and it might be even better that way. For her sake.

For Christ's sake, quit thinking about her sake. It isn't going to hurt her.

It's settled; forget it. One way or the other it's settled, as of tonight. Only you wish it was tonight right now, now that you've decided.

Ten minutes after two. Eight hours and five minutes. Maybe you should start looking for another room. No, you've got till Monday, plenty of time. Ads in the Sunday paper. Find one better than this crummy place. Pay more if you have to; you're ahead of the game with the fifty from the holdup. Be way ahead if the fifty you won in the poker game hadn't gone to buy the gun.

Oh well, lots more coming. First big job next week. Maybe hundreds your cut. Maybe take room where Dixie stays. Wyandotte. No hurry; you've got enough to move in a hotel Monday if you don't find a good bet Sunday. Nothing to worry about.

Except have to be more careful with the gun. Locked suitcase, like Dixie. So hotel maid won't find. Silly, leaving it in sight if drawer pulled open. Lucky Mrs G. didn't call police. What could you have told police? Nothing, without involving Mitch and Dixie. Have to keep mouth shut and take the rap. Couldn't be much just for having unregistered gun. But you'd have a record then. So you'd have a record. Your father had a record, didn't he?

Are you any better than he was? You should have a record for murder right now. You got him killed.

While you're moving anyway, why not double apartment with Ellie? If things go well tonight. No, you'd end up marrying her probably. You'd go soft. You can't *go soft. Besides, Mike. Mike Dravich would find out sooner or later. Probably kill you or try to. You're not afraid of him but it would make row. Police.*

Too dangerous. But get room, while you're at it, where you can have company. Francy? If Ellie says no tonight. Francy in your room. Mitch walks in. Mitch more dangerous than Mike.

After tonight you'll know. Think about tonight. How wonderful—

Somebody calling you?

203

He opened the door as Mrs Gettleman called his name a second time. She heard it open. "Telephone, Joe."

He went downstairs to the phone.

"Joe?" It was Ray Lorgan's voice. "You doing anything tonight?"

"Sorry, Ray, I am. Why? What'd you have in mind?"

"Nothing startling. Thought you might drop in a while and keep me company. I'm taking Jeannie to the hospital early this evening; she's going to stay there overnight, just for a checkup. I'm taking her after dinner and I'll be home by nine o'clock. If you could drop around then or later, we could talk a while. And I thought maybe you might even stick around overnight. With Jeannie gone you might as well, if we talk late."

"Wish I could, Ray. But—well, I have other plans."

"Okay, Joe. But look, I'm going to be there anyway; have to on account of the kid. And I probably won't want to turn in until after twelve. So if whatever you're doing gets itself over with by—oh, eleven or even half past, come on around."

"Sure, Ray. But don't look for me. I'll probably be busy pretty late."

"All right. If you're not here by half past eleven I'll not look for you. And if you do come, don't bring a bottle. There's stuff on hand. Come if you can, Joe."

"Don't look for me, Ray. I won't be able to make it unless a wheel comes off. 'Bye."

"So long."

A wheel came off. There was an envelope pinned on Ellie's door with his name on the front. The note inside it said:

Joe: I'm leaving town; I've quit my job with Uncle Mike. Please don't try to find me. I've written you a letter explaining why and put it in the mail so you'll know tomorrow. But I guess maybe you know now. I guess we both know what would happen if I stayed in Milwaukee. If you don't understand, the letter will explain. And tell you how sorry I am. Goodbye, Joe.

Ellie.

It made him feel hollow inside to know how right Ellie had been. She'd not only been smart enough to know what was going to happen but *good* enough to take what she must have known was the only safe and sensible way to avoid it.

Well, that was that.

It made him feel like a louse, but then why shouldn't it? He'd *been* a louse. He'd had no business to keep on seeing Ellie, after the first date or two with her. After he'd seen that she was falling for him. After he'd learned what kind of a girl she was. Instead, he'd strung her along while he tried to make up his mind whether to drop her or have an affair with her. He had it coming all right.

He went to Ray Lorgan's, after all.

He wished that he hadn't when he found Ray slightly drunk already and bent on getting drunker. But Ray was almost pathetically glad that he had come and Joe figured he'd been lousy enough for one evening without walking out on Ray when Ray needed company. He stayed and tried to get a little tight himself, but the liquor didn't seem to have any effect on him.

And he didn't feel like talking, but that didn't matter because Ray did enough talking for both of them. His tongue got thicker and his thoughts less coherent, but he talked until one o'clock—about every subject on earth and some quite a bit farther than that, every subject except one. Jeannie wasn't mentioned once, by either of them.

But finally Ray's voice ran down. He sat staring blankly, saying nothing.

Joe asked, "Hadn't you better turn in, Ray?"

"Sure, guess so. Stay?"

"I don't think I'd better. I—" He couldn't think of any reason why he shouldn't except that he didn't want to; he didn't want to sleep where Jeannie usually lay. But he couldn't say that; of all things, he couldn't say that.

"Wish you would, Joe. I—I drank pretty much. Might sleep too sound to hear Karl if he wakes up and cries. You'd hear him. You wouldn't have to know what to do. Just shake me or slap me awake."

"Well—"

"If you don't, I won't dare go to sleep. For fear I won't wake up if Karl does. I'll make coffee and try to sit up all night."

Joe sighed. "Okay, Ray, you win."

In the bedroom, by the light of the shaded lamp, Joe stalled, pretending one of his shoestrings was in a hard knot that he couldn't open. If Ray went to sleep, as he looked as though he might do, the moment his head touched the pillow, then he wasn't going to get in bed at all. He was tired enough himself that he could do all right in the overstuffed chair in the far corner. He managed to be only partly undressed by the time Ray got into bed. And he could tell by Ray's breathing that Ray went to sleep instantly.

Joe tried to make himself comfortable in the chair. In the morning, if Ray woke first, he'd say that Ray had tossed around so much in his sleep that he'd decided to try the chair instead of the bed. Ray wouldn't know whether he'd tossed or not.

Joe couldn't get to sleep. He thought about Ellie and that hollow feeling came back. As though part of him was missing.

He tried to quit thinking. What was the use of thinking, now? It was all over, wasn't it? She was gone and he didn't even know where she'd gone. Back to Chicago, probably.

And a good thing. It had been Ellie, thinking about Ellie, that had messed him up. Here he was on the edge of the big money and he'd thought, almost seriously, about chucking it for a dame. Only he couldn't have chucked it even if he'd wanted to. It had been too late to do that. And now it was too late to decide he wanted Ellie instead, and there wasn't any choice anymore. It was all simple now; all he had to do was go ahead with his plans, Mitch's plans.

That's what he wanted to do, wasn't it?

It was all simple now. All he had to do was to quit thinking about Ellie. He'd never have Ellie now. He'd forget her in a day or two. When the letter from her came tomorrow he wouldn't even read it. He knew what would be in it already. The note in the envelope pinned on her door had told him. He'd tear up the letter when it came.

He tried to forget Ellie by thinking about Francy. Someday he'd have Francy. Not right away, but someday. He tried to think about that, but Ellie kept getting in the way.

And the hollow feeling came back, worse than before.

The Video

1. *Panel reading "Sydney Science Series, No. 8."*
MUSIC: A few bars of "Liebestraum," full orchestra, from recording.
Fade to:
2. *Closeup of program announcer, seen against background of complicated electrical panel containing many dials, switches and other apparatus.*
ANNOUNCER: For number eight in our science series, we bring you something truly unusual. Something that has never been attempted before on a television program. Ladies and gentlemen we are going *to telecast a dream.* Our guest expert in charge of this program is Dr Albert Orr, late of London and Cambridge, currently a practicing— (*Glances left.*) I'm afraid I can't pronounce that word, Doctor. What are you?
VOICE FROM OFF SCREEN: I am an electroencephalographist.
ANNOUNCER: Ah, yes. Currently a practicing electroencephalographist of Adelaide, South Australia. We have brought him here to Sydney especially to arrange this history-making electroencephalographistic

broadcast. I shall let Dr Orr explain to you how it works. Ladies and gentlemen, Dr Orr.

Waves hand left and camera pans left to a closeup of Dr Albert Orr, seen against background of another section of same complicated electrical panel. He bows slightly.

DR ORR: Thank you. I will be as brief as possible so we can get to the demonstration itself. First, as you all know, the electroencephalograph in its original crude form, as first described by Berger in 1929, was merely a machine designed to picture in graphic form the tracings called electroencephalograms, popularly known as "brain waves." Originally it was necessary for the sleeping subject to wear a helmet. A more recent development has been radioelectroencephalography, which eliminates the need for the helmet; the machine can pick up and amplify the thought waves of any brain to which it is attuned, even at a moderate distance, tuning out conflicting impulses from other brains in the same manner as a selective radio tunes out interference from unwanted stations. But radioelectroencephalography was merely an intermediate stage of the science. The next step, a great step forward, was—(*Smiles deprecatingly*)—photoradioelectroencephalography, which enables us to see—or to project upon a screen, as a television screen—the actual *pictures* in the mind of the subject to which the machine is attuned. Recently we have taken what I believe is the final step. Through a method which I myself developed, we are able to share the actual feelings and sensations of a sleeping subject, actually *to participate in his dream.* This is called psychophotoradioelectroencephalography, and, properly, I am called a psychophotoradioelectroencephalographist. But since that is a difficult word for the average layman readily to remember, I still call myself simply an electroencephalographist. I regret one thing; on this particular program we are unable to let our audience share in the feelings and sensations of our dreamer, except through my description of them. A special headband is required and, to date, only one of them exists. (*Raises hand to show band.*) I have it here; I shall wear it during this telecast and shall give you a running commentary of the feelings that accompany the pictures of the dream. And now while I make final adjustments and tunings, I shall turn you back to Mr Worcester, your program manager, who will tell you the circumstances under which this dream is picked up and telecast. Thank you.

Cut to: 3.

Medium shot of program announcer, seated at desk.

ANNOUNCER: This dream will come to you from a city in the Midwest of the United States of America, a city which shall be nameless on this program. Here in Sydney, New South Wales, Australia, it is six p.m. It is, therefore, four o'clock in the morning in the American city, an excellent time to set our trap for shadows. We have chosen a point of origin almost halfway around the earth for two reasons. First, the time differential; second, to minimize to the vanishing point the possibility that any one of our audience might chance to know the dreamer and guess, from portions of the dream or characters in it, who the dreamer is. Thus we assure him the privacy that dreams deserve. The setup is simply this: The representative whom we sent to Mil—to the American city chosen at random has erected in some part of that city the very special aerial which picks up the brain waves, as Dr Orr has called them. They are relayed here by special arrangement; the visual parts of whatever dream our representative tunes in on will appear before you on the screens of your television sets; Dr Orr will wear the apparatus, the headband, which will enable him to share the feelings and sensations that accompany the dream, and will give you a running commentary. Are you ready, Dr Orr?

Cut to:

4. *Long shot that takes in announcer seated at desk and Dr Orr standing before microphone in front of panel of complicated dials and instruments. He wears the headband, from which a wire is plugged into panel.*

DR ORR: Yes, we are ready. I can see the screen from here; a camera is being adjusted in front of it and at the right moment I shall give the signal for the telecast to switch to that camera so you can see the dream; you will still hear my voice as you see it. We have been fortunate, for my colleague in America seems to be tuning in on what is indubitably the start of a dream. There are vague images roaming through the mind of the dreamer — and therefore roaming across the screen. They are becoming sharper, more focused. When they are sharp enough for identification, we shall switch to the other camera. The only sensation I share thus far is one of vague uneasiness. The dreamer is not happy; he is worried about something …Getting sharper, but still not identifiable as pictures. Incidentally, Mr Worcester a moment ago referred to our arrangement as a trap for shadows; I hope we shall not trap any truly unpleasant ones…Ah, I think we're ready now. (*Turns to Announcer.*) Will you please tell them to cut in the other camera? Thank you.

Announcer nods. Cut to:

5. *Vague, poorly defined scene, not immediately identifiable, but*

clarifying slowly into the windshield of a car, seen from inside car. Car is moving along dark streets.

DR ORR: The sensation of uneasiness, even fear, is increasing. I'm inside a moving car. I'm not driving. Someone else is. I seem small. Crowded in between two big men. Going somewhere to do something horrible. I don't like this at all. Wish we'd tuned in to some other brain wavelength...

Car stopping in front of a theater. Three men coming out. One is clearly seen. Others shadowy.

I'm a child. And I feel I'm going to do something horrible. I've got a gun in my hand; it seems to be named Maggie. I don't get that, why a gun should be named Maggie. I'm pulling the trigger, shooting through the windshield.

Red flashes; windshield shattering. The three men are falling like tenpins.

Now things are blurring; I feel horror-stricken at what I've done. God, I've killed my own father!

Blood is running in the gutter, gallons of it.

Because—it's got something to do with an object—no, two objects—which are so horrible that I can't think of them; there's a psychic block and I can't remember right now what they are or why I'm afraid of them, but I'm worse afraid of them than I am of death. In fact, I'm not afraid of death at all...

Screen blurs momentarily, then one of the three men gets up and walks toward the car; he holds something in his hand, something that is invisible but gives off light.

What you see now is strange; the man—he's my father—is holding something in his hand—*to light you to bed*—

He holds it up and is peering through the shattered windshield. His face is the face of a corpse.

I get that phrase, but I can't see or recognize the object. It gives light, though. He's dead, but he's looking at me. I'm horribly ashamed of what I've done, shooting him. I love him. But he's got something in his other hand, too, that I'm horribly afraid of also. It's something *to chop off*—Thought blurring.

The windshield becomes a closed door.

Ah, this is better. I thought we were heading for a nightmare. But I have a feeling of happiness now. I'm going to open that door to something I—

Door opens showing a pretty girl in a cotton dress standing inside waiting; there is love in her eyes and her arms open wide for an embrace.

Yes, her name is Ellie, and she's my wife; I'm coming to her. She's waiting for me to kiss her, but I can't. There's something...

Two men appear standing behind the girl. Each has a gun in his hand.

That's it; that's why I can't put my arms around her. I daren't, no matter how much I want to...Those men—Mitch, Dixie.

Policemen appear, two at each of two windows, with tommy-guns. They start firing into room. Neither of the men even notices them although bullets thud into their bodies.

I'm shooting at the policemen. I'm horribly afraid Ellie will be killed. I've got to get them before they can get her...

The girl screams and suddenly changes to a different girl, a very voluptuous blonde, naked; the area of her body covered by a bathing suit, were she wearing one, is creamy white; the rest of her lightly golden tanned.

Francy; this is Francy. Oh, God, she'll get hurt, too. And I want her. I start toward her, but now Mitch is starting to shoot at me, too. I can't live long with five of them shooting at me, but none of the bullets seem to be hitting. God, how beautiful Francy is. Francy...

Sudden switch to inside car again, through windshield.

Ah, this is better; this is something I want; something I'm going to have. And Francy is beside me. This is a different car, and this time I'm driving.

Superimposed over the view through the windshield is a view of the exterior of the car; it is a brand new convertible, robin's-egg blue in color, very long, low, shiny. Superimposed view fades.

It's *my* car. I think the girl beside me is Francy, but it could be some other girl equally beautiful. And she's mine, too.

Smooth lighted road unwinding into windshield.

We're driving out into the country to a gambling house, one that I own. I'm rich, and I'm still young. But something is wrong; something is going to happen. I'm getting afraid again...

Girl standing in road, same girl as seen before in cotton dress, staring toward car, crying.

Ellie! We'll run her down. I'm swinging the wheel trying to avoid hitting her! Can I –

Car swerves; big tree coming toward car; car crashes into tree. Blackness with red flashes. Suddenly white, resolving into white walls and ceiling, as of hospital room.

I'm in a bed; I can't move a muscle; it's as though I'm encased in a solid cast from head to foot. Or maybe paralyzed.

White door of room opening. Door closes.

Who's coming?... No one.

We see window and through window scene of a city; hospital is on a high hill, as entire city can be seen.

I'm staring out the window now. Did I turn the car in time?

Suddenly the gigantic mushroom of an atomic explosion lifts itself. There it goes; that's the end of everything. We'll all be killed now, or fight for bones with dogs. *Smoke fades. City is gone.* I feel a wave of utter despair that everything is gone now. And I lie here helpless; can't move a muscle. Ellie killed. What was it all for?

Room is changing, becoming a bedroom, same bedroom we heard described in radio sequence and saw in movie sequence; the bedroom in which Joe slept as a child in Chicago. I'm becoming smaller; I feel that I'm becoming a child again, but I'm still lying in a bed and I still can't move. I've a feeling that something horrible is coming, the *ultimate* horror. Oh, if I could only move, only *run.* I'm helpless, waiting for it. Oh, Christ, *here it comes!*

Room grows dimmer, almost completely dark. Then what little light there is seems to be running toward one side of the room and coalescing there in a tiny flame, a candle flame, and a dim white candle shape takes form under the flame. It begins to move slowly closer, gaining in size as it comes. Oh Good God, *now I know what they are!* The two things too terrible to think of. I'm thinking of the rhyme; it's running through my head, louder, louder. *Here comes a candle to light you to bed, and here comes a chopper to chop off your head. Here comes a candle to light you to bed, and here comes a chopper to chop off your head. Here comes* A CANDLE TO LIGHT YOU TO BED, AND HERE COMES A CHOPPER TO CHOP OFF YOUR HEAD.

In a far corner of the room the shadows gather; they too are coalescing. The light has become the candle; the darkness is becoming an inhuman figure, holding in its hand the horror to end all horrors—the ax.

215

*HERE COMES A CANDLE TO LIGHT YOU TO
BED, AND HERE COMES A CHOPPER TO CHOP
OFF YOUR HEAD. HERE COMES A CANDLE
TO LIGHT YOU TO BED, AND HERE COMES A
CHOPPER TO CHOP OFF—*
Picture wavers and begins to break up.
Screen goes blank.
VOICE OF ANNOUNCER: Dr Orr! Are you all right?
VOICE OF DR ORR: Oh God, I guess so. I'm awake. Some-
one just shook me and said, "Joe, wake up. Wake up,
Joe!" And I woke—I mean that whoever was having that
horrible nightmare woke up. Are we still on the air?
VOICE OF ANNOUNCER: Yes. Hey, cut camera one back
in. The screen is blank.
6. *Same as scene 4, showing announcer at desk, but now
standing; Dr Orr still at microphone in front of panel; he has
taken off headband and is wiping forehead with handkerchief;
he is trembling and quite shaken.*
DR ORR: A truly terrible experience. God help the young
man who was having that nightmare.
ANNOUNCER: Have you any comments, Doctor? Could
you analyze the dream?
DR ORR: Not without knowing the subject's past. Obviously, however, he has a guilt complex concerning his
father's death, though his dreaming of shooting his father
was probably symbolic. And he has a terrible phobia
concerning a nursery rhyme; he must have had some
horrible childhood experience. That is all I care to say.
ANNOUNCER: Thank you, Dr Orr. (*Turns to camera.*) As we
still have five minutes before the next scheduled program,
we shall fill in with a brief cartoon comedy—an importa-
tion, as was the nightmare you have just seen, from the
States. Ladies and gentlemen—Mickey Mouse!
Cut to film.

The Story

21

Beginning of the last day.

He was fully awake now, sitting in the kitchen, listening to the irregular throbbing of the percolator on the gas stove. It had been fifteen minutes since Ray had shaken him out of the nightmare. The kitchen clock said twenty minutes of five; the panes of the windows were still black with night.

He shivered a little.

Ray said, "It's cool in here, Joe. Wait, I got an extra bathrobe; I'll get it for you."

Joe stood up and shook his head. "Don't bother. I'll get the rest of the way dressed. I'm not going to be able to go back to sleep."

"Hell it's only half past four or a little after. *I'm* going back to sleep as soon as you've had a cup of coffee to shake off that dream."

"I can't," Joe said. "I'll scram in a few minutes."

He went back into the bedroom as quietly as he could

and gathered up the clothes he had taken off, taking them out into the kitchen to put them on.

"You'll have to wait an hour for a streetcar," Ray said.

"I'll catch a cab. Don't worry about me, Ray. I'm okay. Just that some fresh air and traveling will do me good before I even try to go back to sleep."

"Well, there's one point I'll give you," Ray said. "If you do go to your own place to go back to sleep you can sleep till noon if you want to. If you stay here, I'll have to roust you at eight. That's when I'm leaving for the hospital to pick up Jeannie. Good thing, in one way, this happened. I went to bed too tight to set the alarm. Might have overslept if you hadn't waked me."

"How did I wake you, Ray? What was I doing?"

"Whimpering in your sleep. It wasn't loud; probably wouldn't have waked me except that I automatically have an ear tuned for the kid waking up. I thought it was him at first."

"I didn't scream?"

"No." Ray put coffee cups on the table and got the percolator from the stove. "Why? Do you?"

"Not since I was a kid. Not for several years, anyway. Used to have pretty bad nightmares when I was a kid."

"How do you know you don't now? I mean, Joe, you weren't making enough noise to wake anybody up in another room, and you don't room with anybody, so how can you be sure you don't make noises like that lots of nights?"

"Well—I think I'd have waked up and known about it if you hadn't waked me. And, by the way, thanks. I'm glad I just woke you and not Karl."

"How come you were sleeping in the chair?"

"Guess I was a little tight, Ray. I got a little dizzy bending

218

down to take my shoes off and I leaned back in the chair to rest a minute and the next thing I knew you were shaking me."

Ray grunted. "And I thought *I* was drunk. What were you dreaming about?"

"I don't remember. I never remember dreams. And I don't think I have nightmares like that. Not often, anyway. It was probably because I was sleeping sitting up, or something."

"Joe, have you got anything particular on your mind? Or are you in any kind of a jam?"

Joe sighed. "No. I'm all right. Anybody can have a nightmare once in a while, can't he?"

"Depends on why, and what it's about. Still seeing Ellie, Joe?"

"No. She left town. Went back to Chicago, I guess."

"Too bad; she was a swell girl. You ought to have latched onto her and married her."

Joe sighed and stood up. "Maybe I should have, but I didn't. Well, thanks for everything, Ray. The liquor and the coffee and waking me up. I'll push on so you can get back to sleep. Unless you want me to stay here—and awake—so I'll hear Karl if he cries."

"That was just a gag to get you to stay. Drunk or sober, I'd hear him. I heard you, didn't I?"

Outside, the sky was beginning to lighten with the dawn. Joe took a few steps toward Wisconsin Avenue, the best place to catch a cab, and then decided to walk home. It was almost twenty blocks, but the walk would do him good and might tire him physically so he could go back to sleep after he got there.

But the cool air of early dawn got him wider awake instead.

He felt ashamed of himself for having pulled so childish a stunt as to have whimpered in his sleep and to have waked Ray. And he realized, it must have been pretty loud and pretty bad whimpering to have made Ray shake him out of it.

And the dream, the nightmare, *had* been bad. He couldn't remember anything about it except that it had concerned the —

You damned fool, he told himself, *still afraid of the very words. Think them: the candle and the ax.*

He thought them, and they brought back vaguely the feeling of terror that had been in the dream. Yes, he'd dreamed about the candle and the ax. And before that, hadn't there been something about Francy and about Ellie? And before that — but he couldn't remember anything back before that.

He had to quit thinking about Ellie, he thought. She was gone now. Lost. And a damn good thing for both of them.

He didn't have any problems now, once he had Ellie off his mind.

Francy? Why should Francy be a problem? All he had to do was wait for her. Or why even that? There were plenty of women — well, some, anyway — who were as beautiful as Francy. And within a few months, even a few weeks maybe, he could have his pick of them.

Of course if Francy and Mitch *did* break up meanwhile —

Oh God, it would be wonderful to have Francy. Even *once.*

What if he got killed *before* —

He wished a tavern was open somewhere along the way home. But they'd all closed at two o'clock, of course, and none of them would be open this early. For the first time in his life he wanted a drink in the morning. Or was this really the morning rather than just the end of the evening?

You could still see a star or two, although the streetlights had just gone off.

He stopped and looked up at one and wondered if the science fiction stories he liked to read above all else were really right. *Were* there planets circling around other stars besides the sun and *were* there living beings, intelligent beings, on them? Why hadn't he been born a few centuries later so that if mankind was going to develop interstellar travel, he could get in on the adventure of it? That is, if mankind didn't blow himself up sooner in an atomic war and set himself back at the start of civilization again. Funny that so many science fiction stories dealt with that very possibility, and that people as diverse as old Krazzy and Ray Lorgan should agree with the stories.

I wish I was on Mars right now, he thought.

Maybe, probably, there wouldn't be any air there, or not enough air to breathe, anyway, and he'd die in a few minutes of cold or of suffocation—or maybe some bug-eyed monster would get him before he could die otherwise. But wouldn't it be worth almost anything that happened just to have stood on Mars?

Or would he have the guts to take the chance if he were really offered it?

Hadn't Francy offered him a chance at Mitch's party that he'd been afraid to take? Was he more afraid of Mitch than of the things that could happen to him on another planet?

Why had he thought *that?* What's Francy got to do with Mars?

And then he thought—why not? Francy is like Mars; Ellie is like Earth.

Mars and Francy are far above me and very beautiful and deadly dangerous.

Ellie—yes, Ellie is like Earth. And he could have had Earth if he hadn't flubbed his chance wanting more.

Wanting—the similes were getting better—the world with a little red fence around it. The little red fence was money. Well, he'd get the little red fence now, but he'd lost the—

Cut it out, he told himself, *you're going to forget Ellie. You've got to forget her, whether you want to or not. You've lost her. She had the right answer; she solved things for you and herself.*

You're going to tear up her letter when it comes without reading it. You know what it's going to say and that everything in it is right and it's going to hurt.

Ellie had your number.

So has your landlady, Mrs Gettleman. She knows you're a criminal. And she and Ellie are right. Isn't there money in your pocket right now from the robbery of a filling station?

Well, isn't that what you want?— money. And how else can a punk like you get big money?

Are you yellow? You don't know. It's mixed up because you're not afraid of cops or of getting shot. But you're afraid of Mitch all right.

It was almost six and fairly light by the time he got back to his room. He undressed and went to bed but he wasn't either tired or sleepy. He rolled and tossed for almost two hours before he decided it was useless to try to sleep.

It was eight o'clock then and he began to wonder what time the mailman came around for the morning delivery. Once or twice, going out or coming in, he'd seen the mailman putting letters on the table in the hallway downstairs, but he couldn't remember now what time it was. It might have been as early at eight-thirty or nine o'clock. It probably was; if it was later than that he'd probably have seen the mailman oftener.

Anyway, he couldn't go to sleep. He got up and took a shower. For some reason he dressed more carefully and meticulously than usual. Maybe just to kill time. He put a high polish on his shoes and tied his necktie three times before he got the ends to come out to the exact length he wanted them. He managed to make it nine o'clock by the time he was ready to go out. Surely the mail would be there by now.

It wasn't. Or, at any rate, there wasn't any letter from Ellie. There were two or three letters on the table, but they might have been ones from the day before. There were eighteen rooms in the building, some of them double, so a lot of people got mail there and usually there were several letters on the table left over from previous deliveries. He wished now that he'd looked on his way in at six o'clock to see which letters were there; then he'd know for sure whether the mailman had really been there yet this morning.

He waited around a little while, maybe ten minutes, thinking the mailman would come any minute, but he didn't. He went out to the sidewalk to see whether he could see him coming, but he couldn't.

It was still cool; about sixty degrees, he decided (it was sixty-two, to be exact). He almost decided to go back and put on a heavier suit. But it would probably warm up during the day.

He looked again, both directions—although he was fairly sure the mailman came from the west—to be sure he wasn't in sight either way. Of course he might be inside a building that had a lot of mailboxes, putting letters into them. He waited long enough, looking first one way and then the other, to be sure that wasn't the case; surely he couldn't stay inside one building longer than five minutes or so.

He decided he might as well have some breakfast and surely by that time the mail would be there. He started walking west, the direction from which the mailman would come; maybe he'd run into him.

It wasn't until he was almost to the Dinner Gong that he thought of the place and—why shouldn't he have breakfast there?

Mike Dravich might or might not be there—he came and went at irregular hours, sometimes spending the whole day and evening at his restaurant, sometimes only a few hours—but why should he worry about Mike now?

But Mike wasn't there. Joe sat down at the counter and ordered breakfast. He recognized the waitress by sight although he didn't know her name. Her shift overlapped with Ellie's and she just might know where Ellie had gone. Not that he really wanted to know.

But when she brought his breakfast he asked casually, "Where's Ellie Dravich?"

"She left town."

"Go back to Chicago?"

"I don't know. I don't think so; she'd said she didn't like Chicago, so I don't think she'd go back there."

"Left kind of suddenly, didn't she?"

"Suddenly is right. I don't know what got into her. Must have got a telegram or something."

Good, Joe thought; at least nobody here, except maybe Mike, knew why Ellie had left. She must have told Mike the truth, or at least part of it, to explain her walking out on him so suddenly.

"What happened?" he asked the waitress. "She just walk out?"

"Didn't even start, yesterday. She was supposed to start at one. She came in then, but she talked to Mike and then

224

went out again. Mike told me later that she'd quit and was leaving town, but he didn't say where. Funny, I asked him that and he wouldn't tell me where."

Mike had been smart, Joe thought; he realized that the other waitresses might be pumped. And that meant Ellie had told Mike the truth.

He kept an eye to the front while he ate, thinking he might see the mailman go past. He didn't, but while he was drinking his coffee Mike Dravich came in. Joe met Mike's eyes squarely, almost hoping there was going to be trouble.

There wasn't. Mike paid no attention to him; he walked on past as though Joe wasn't there and went into the kitchen. A minute later he came out without his coat and hat and went behind the cigar counter at the front of the store.

Joe deliberately took his time finishing the coffee.

His check was for fifty cents. He went to the cigar counter and put it and a dollar bill on the rubber mat beside the register. He hoped Mike would say something, anything.

Mike didn't. He rang up the amount of the check, put Joe's change on the pad and turned to stare out of the window, as though Joe wasn't there at all.

There wasn't anything to say, anything to do. Joe picked up his change and went on out.

He walked back to the rooming house and the mailman still hadn't been there. He began to worry whether the mailman was coming at all. Was this a holiday maybe, that he'd forgotten about? No it was Friday, September 10th. Last Monday had been Labor Day; there wasn't any holiday this soon after Labor Day.

But it was almost ten o'clock. *Why* wasn't the mailman here yet? Or had he been past and left no mail for anyone in the building? Or had Ellie changed her mind about sending the letter?

He took out of his pocket the note he'd found on her door and read it again. "I've written you a letter explaining why and put it in the mail so you'll know tomorrow."

Yes, she'd already mailed the letter and even if it had been late in the day when she'd mailed it, it would certainly have been picked up in time for the first delivery today.

He walked once around the block and as he turned the final corner he saw the mailman coming out of the rooming house. He hurried his steps.

The letter was there, on the table. There wasn't any return address, of course, but he recognized Ellie's small, precise handwriting from having read so often the note she'd left on her door for him. It was postmarked 3:00 p.m. She must have returned to her room right after one o'clock and written that letter first, before she even started to pack. If it was postmarked at three o'clock, she must have dropped it in a box well before then.

He didn't want to open it there in the hallway beside the table. He went up to his room holding it in his hand. He closed the door behind him and walked over to the window where the light was best. He started to tear an end off the envelope and then realized he might tear part of the letter that way. He picked up the hunting knife from the dresser and slit the top of the envelope carefully. He put the knife back in its sheath and then sat down on the edge of the bed and took the letter out of the envelope. It wasn't a long letter, not much longer than the note on the door had been.

Dear Joe:

I guess you know, I guess I've showed, that I love you. Too much, Joe, for me to keep on seeing you. You know and I know what would happen. What would have happened tonight—last night, when you read this—if I had stayed.

Either that or you would have told me something I found out I didn't want to hear—and I guess you know what I mean by that, too. Either way, Joe, there would be only unhappiness for both of us, or for me anyway. For you, too, I guess, whatever happened. And I haven't been in Milwaukee long enough to make it matter otherwise whether I stay or not, so the only sensible thing is for me to go away before either of us is hurt. Don't try to find me, Joe. I'm not going back to Chicago and I'm not going to tell anybody where I am going. Please understand and don't hate me for running away.

Yours,
Ellie.

He didn't know how many times he read it through, sitting there, on the edge of the bed, still with his hat on.

"Yours, Ellie." She could have been, if he hadn't wanted other things worse—or thought that he wanted them worse.

For the first time in hours he remembered that he had decided to destroy this letter without opening it.

Might as well, now. There was only one thing to do—to forget Ellie. He couldn't find her if he wanted to. Well, now he could burn the letter and the note that had been on the door and that would be that. He walked over to the dresser and tore both the letter and the note into little pieces into the ashtray and touched a match to them. It made a bigger fire than he had anticipated but only for a moment and then there were only black ashes and gray ashes and that was that. Except that he could have repeated both the note and the letter almost word for word even now that they were burned.

It was half past ten. Maybe he could sleep for an hour or

so; he didn't feel either sleepy or tired now, just dull and miserable. But he took off most of his clothes and lay down on the bed to see if he could at least doze. He couldn't. At eleven he gave up. He got dressed again. When he tied his tie he found himself looking at himself in the mirror as though he expected his own face to look different, somehow. But it didn't. Even his eyes looked clear and straight out of the mirror back into his eyes. They shouldn't have. He remembered the phrase Ray had used to him once a week or two ago and tried it on himself softly. "Two-bit gangster." Ray had apologized in the same breath he'd said it in. Joe Bailey didn't. But the Joe Bailey in the mirror didn't bat an eye; he didn't even look ashamed of himself.

He went downstairs and outside.

It was still cool but getting a little warmer and beginning to cloud up a trifle. He wondered if it was going to rain. It wasn't. (Increasing cloudiness and slightly warmer Friday night; Saturday partly cloudy and—but Saturday doesn't matter. This is the last day, remember?)

22

He had himself fairly well straightened out mentally by half-past two when he dropped in the tavern on Clybourn.

At the moment, there weren't any paying customers in the place. The beat cop was there, talking to Krasno, and a glass of whiskey stood between them on the bar. Joe knew the cop wouldn't drink the whiskey while he was being watched, so he went on through to the can and stayed there a minute; when he came out the whiskey was gone and so was the cop. All cops are crooks, he thought, only they haven't got the nerve to do anything crookeder than being cops.

He sat down on a stool at the bar.

Krasno asked, "A beer, kid?" and Joe nodded.

Krasno drew one and put it on the bar. "Mitch was in earlier. He's coming back, though. Going to meet someone here. A dame."

"Francy?"

"I guess that was the the name. How you doing, Joe?"

"Fine," Joe said.

"Look to me like you're worrying about something. Kid, is Mitch getting you in over your head?"

"I'm all right. Don't worry about me."

Krasno leaned on the bar. "Kid, you're making a mistake. You aren't cut out for what you're going in for. Know why?"

Joe looked down into his beer and didn't answer.

Krasno said, "You got too much conscience, Joe. You're too good a kid. Everything you do wrong is going to worry you. Look, you don't want me to talk like this to you; you wish I'd shut up and mind my own business. But you got too much consideration to tell me to go to hell, haven't you? You feel sorry for me because I'm just an old geezer that hasn't sense enough to mind my own business and you think I don't know what I'm talking about, but you're too nice a guy to tell me to go to hell. I don't know what Mitch and this Dixie are getting you into, Joe—but you're too nice a guy for it. You're not tough like they are. You think you are, but you aren't. You want to be but you never will be. I can prove it to you."

"How?"

"Let's hear you tell me to shut up. I don't mean just 'Lay off of me, Krazzy.' I mean let's hear you say 'Shut up, you old son of a bitch.' And mean it."

"All right, so I don't like to hurt people's feelings. So what?"

"Think I could talk to Mitch like this? Or Dixie? Not and keep either my teeth or my job. Not that I care a hell of a lot about the job. Trouble is with you, Joe, you're fundamentally a decent guy. Not that that's a trouble unless you try to force yourself to be something you aren't."

Joe moved his glass in slow circles on the bar. He said, "What about this atomic blowup you always talk about? If that's going to happen, what does anything I do matter?"

"Hell kid, are you happy *now?* Sure, I think war's coming and that—well, to put it mildly, it's going to change our way of living plenty. But I *could* be wrong. I have been, once or twice in my life. And even if I'm right, it might be years off. And how about those years? You'll never be happy as a criminal, kid; you're not the type. You're too decent. You'll hate yourself all the time."

Joe thought of looking at himself in a mirror and saying "Two-bit gangster" that very morning.

He wished Krazzy would shut up. He said, "Lay off of me, will you? I know what I'm doing. I'm all right."

"Okay, Joe. I'll lay off of you in a minute. But you'll never lay off of yourself. You'll never have a minute's peace as long as you let Mitch lead you around by the nose. If you haven't got guts enough to break with him otherwise, get the hell out of Milwaukee. Go somewhere and get yourself an honest job—or if you're too damn lazy to work, go somewhere the heat's not on and go back to selling numbers tickets. That's just as hard work as anything else you're likely to do, but you probably don't think so. And get yourself a decent girl—not one of these bitches like Mitch runs around with—and get yourself straightened out."

Joe said, "Krazzy, you're a good guy, but I don't want—"

He happened to look up then and stopped. Krasno was

looking at the backdoor, the one that led back to the toilets and the private room. Krasno's face was suddenly pale, almost sick with fear.

Joe turned and saw that Mitch was standing there. He'd come in the back way and they hadn't heard him. Joe wondered how long he'd been standing there listening. Long enough, from his face.

He said, "*Get out!*" to Krasno.

Krasno took the bar apron off and Joe saw his hands were shaking a little. He had to pass within a yard of Mitch to get his coat and get out from behind the bar.

Joe thought, *God, I hope he has sense enough to keep his mouth shut and not say a word; maybe then Mitch won't touch him. If Mitch does—*

But he didn't dare carry out that thought. Mitch was big, twice his size. Mitch could twist him into a pretzel.

He almost held his breath as Krasno passed Mitch. He could feel Krasno's fear. He didn't turn his head as Krasno walked behind him toward the door. He was afraid if he turned to watch or if he said a word, Krasno might say something to him. And he knew that if Krasno said another word, even "So long, Joe," it might be too much. Mitch would come after Krasno, even though he was now safely past the biggest point of danger and throw him out bodily. Krasno must have known that, too. He went out without saying a word. He even closed the door very quietly behind him.

Mitch said, "The God damn punk." Not to Joe, just to himself. He didn't say a word to Joe. He walked to the phone and dialed a number.

"Harry?" he said. "Mitch talking. Can you come in early today, right away, and work through?...Yeah, I just fired Krasno...Huh? None of your God damn business. Do you want the extra hours at double time, or not?...Sure, I'll pay double between now and seven if you come down right away. And I'll have another day man by tomorrow. Okay, Harry."

He put down the receiver and said quietly, "Go latch the front door, Joe. I don't want any customers in here till Harry gets down. He says he can make it in fifteen minutes."

While Joe was throwing the latch, Mitch went back of the bar and made two stiff drinks. He came around the end of the bar carrying them and headed for one of the booths.

He said, "Come on, Joe. We got some talking to do." His voice was quiet, but Joe didn't like the tone of it. But the drinks were a good sign.

He sat down in the booth across from Mitch and for seconds Mitch just looked at him. Joe realized that he himself hadn't said a word since Mitch had come in. Unless Mitch had—But no, he hadn't said anything to Krasno that Mitch could be angry about; he'd told Krasno to lay off; that was all. He hadn't agreed—out loud—with a single thing Krasno had said.

Mitch said, "Joe."

"Yeah?" He had to clear his throat to get it out.

"What was the idea of sitting there letting Krasno fill you with stuff like that? Why didn't you tell him to shut his God damn yap?"

Because Krasno was right, he wanted to say. He said, "I wasn't agreeing with him. What'd it matter what he said?"

"I'm wondering something, Joe. Maybe you're too damn soft. If you haven't even got the guts to tell off a mug like *him,* how can you—Listen, Joe." His hand came across the table suddenly and clamped on Joe's shoulder; his fingers dug in. They hurt.

232

"Listen, Joe. You're in too deep now to rat on us. You aren't thinking of taking Krasno's advice, are you?"

Joe took a deep breath. He said, "No. But take your hand off of me, Mitch."

Mitch laughed and pulled back his hand. He said, "Attaboy, Joe. I just wanted to be sure you had the moxie to say that or do something. You'll be all right, kid. Just don't get softhearted about punks like Krasno. Say—" His eyes narrowed. "How'd he know as much as he did? You haven't told him anything, have you?"

"Hell, no. He was just guessing. He knows the numbers game is off, and what with Dixie and me still hanging around, he'd have had to be pretty dumb not to guess *something*, Mitch."

Mitch nodded slowly. "Guess I was dumb to keep the old bastard around. Should've fired him long time ago. Well, he'll never show his face around here again. He better not."

Mitch leaned back and picked up his glass. "To crime, Joe."

"To crime," Joe said.

The drink was too strong; Joe didn't like it at all, but then he never cared much for whiskey and water. Mitch had downed half of his at a gulp, but Joe took only a sip.

Mitch said, "Gus is coming up from Chi today. He's going to stay up here this time. We're getting into action next week, Joe."

Joe nodded.

Mitch said, "Want to play a little poker late this evening, Joe? Gus and Dixie are coming over this evening—to the flat on Prospect; I've closed the Fox Point place for the year. We got some talking to do—and you're not in on this first conference, Joe, but if you do all right next week you'll be in on the other ones. But later, around eleven, I've asked some other guys around to make up a game. If you're not doing anything, drop around and take a hand."

Joe said, "I'd better wait till I'm a little more in the chips, Mitch. Your poker's kind of steep for me until then—even if I was lucky last time."

"Suit yourself, kid. If you change your mind, drop in. It's stag this time. Even Francy won't be there. She's going out of town overnight." He looked at his watch. "Francy ought to be along pretty soon. She's going to pick up the car from me here. Which reminds me; you haven't got any plans for the next half hour or so, have you?"

"No, Mitch."

"I think before Francy gets the car, I'm going to take a run downtown and see if I can pick up a day man for the bar. You wait here, Joe, and let Harry in when he comes. And when Francy comes, tell her I'll be back in half an hour or so. Give her a drink."

"Sure, Mitch."

Mitch walked to the door and opened it. He said, "Latch it behind me, Joe, and don't open up till Harry gets here—unless Francy gets here first and you let her in. Better tell Harry to check the register before he starts."

"Sure, Mitch."

Joe latched the door and, through the glass, watched Mitch get into the convertible and drive off.

He went back to the booth and sat down again, but this time on the side Mitch had been sitting so he could face the door. His shoulder hurt and he rubbed it with his hand. He put his hand out in front of him, a few inches above the top of the table. It was shaking a little.

It had been a close thing with Mitch.

He wondered what he'd have done if Mitch had hurt Krasno. Oh, Mitch wouldn't *really* have hurt him; he was

234

too smart to get in trouble doing something like that. But he might have slapped him around a little, using the flat of his hand so he wouldn't mark him. As mad as Mitch had been, it was a wonder that he hadn't touched Krasno.

And if he had—? Well, he hadn't, so why worry about that?

What *could* he have done? Mitch was built like an ox. And Krasno *had* stepped out of line. You couldn't blame Mitch for firing him, under the circumstances, if you saw it from Mitch's point of view.

Only, damn it, so much of what Krasno had told him was right. He, Joe, wasn't tough like Mitch. Whether you called it *decent* or *soft* it was the same thing. Was he really cut out for—

A taxi was stopping in front and Francy was getting out of it.

Joe had the door unlatched and open by the time she got there. She said, "Hi, Joe. You look better than the last time I saw you."

Joe flushed a little; the last time Francy had seen him he'd been passed out cold, and he wasn't proud of that. He said lightly, "For that crack, I'm going to lock you in."

Francy watched him throw the latch. She said, "Oh, goody. You're going to *rape* me."

"Not here and now. Mitch will be back any minute. But I'll make you a drink instead. Whiskey sour or Tom Collins? Those are the only two I can make."

He walked around behind the bar and Francy perched on a stool in front of it. He looked at her for an answer as to what drink she wanted and she was frowning at him with mock seriousness. "Joe, all I taught you to make was a Tom. Who taught you to make a whiskey sour? Have you been cheating on me?"

235

He grinned. "Why, Francy, I'm surprised you'd think that. My *mother* taught me how to make a whiskey sour." The funny thing was that that was strictly true. A whiskey sour had been Flo Bailey's favorite drink; she *had* taught him how to make it.

"I'll forgive you, then. All right, make it a sour, Joe. It's getting a little cool for Toms."

When he was almost finished with the drinks, she walked across to a booth and sat there. He brought the drinks over and sat down on the opposite side of the booth.

She sipped hers. "Nice sour. You do know how to make them. How have you been, Joe?"

"Fine, Francy." He grinned. "At least better than I was the last time you saw me, out cold."

"Joe, why did you do that? Afraid of *me?*"

"Not exactly."

"Partly, then." That was flippant, but her voice suddenly was serious. "Joe—"

"Yes, Francy?"

He looked at her and it was back again, his wanting her. Back as strongly as ever.

And why not? Wasn't *this* the way to get over thinking about Ellie? Francy he might have someday; Ellie never. Why not let himself think about Francy and want her? Why not concentrate on wanting her until it drove all the conflicting things out of his mind? Francy was the goal at the end of the path he had chosen—and chosen irrevocably. By thinking about Francy—

She still hadn't answered his "Yes Francy?" He said it again.

She put her hand on his. "Joe—I don't like Mitch anymore. I never did, really. I'm going to break with him pretty soon."

"That's—I'm glad, Francy."

"Joe, are you afraid of Mitch?"

He couldn't lie outright; he hedged. "Well—he's bigger than I am, Francy. He could knock my ears off, whether I'm afraid of him or not. I'd be dumb not to recognize that, wouldn't I?"

She sounded disappointed. "I suppose you would."

He glanced toward the door; their hands were not in line of vision from it. He put his hand on top of hers. He said, "But Francy, listen, you want me to have money, don't you?"

"That's a silly question. Of course."

"Then I can't break with Mitch. Not for a while, whether I'm afraid of him or not. And listen, I don't like Mitch either. I thought I did, once, but I've found out I don't. But if I'm going to get into the money, and soon, I've got to stick with him for a while. You understand that, don't you?"

"Yes, Joe. But—you do like me, don't you?"

"I'm crazy about you, Francy. I want you so bad I can't see straight. But what good's that going to do me if I'm broke?"

She started to pull her hand back but he held it between his. She said, "Do you think you've got to buy me, Joe Bailey?"

"I don't mean that. But damn it, Francy, I want you all the way. I want to be able to give you everything you want."

Her hand didn't try to pull loose anymore. "I see what you mean, Joe. Yes, I want you to have money. We—we could go places, Joe."

"We're going to. Francy, you can break with Mitch—when you're ready—so everything will be okay, can't you? I mean, so he won't care what we do after that—if he doesn't guess that we'd planned before to do it."

She laughed a little. "Any woman could do that. Don't worry; he'll think the decision is his."

"That's wonderful, Francy. It's terrible waiting, but—"

"Is it, Joe?"

She leaned forward; her knees were pressing against his under the table. Her lips were slightly parted; her eyes invited him. "*Is* it terrible waiting? I'm glad. I want you too, Joe."

"My God, Francy. But—"

"Mitch gave me walking papers for tonight. He's having a conference and then a poker game. Told me to take the convertible and go amuse myself so I'd be out of the way. I'm going to drive down to Lake Geneva for overnight. Does that give you any idea, Joe?"

He took a deep breath. How would Mitch ever find out? And wouldn't it be almost worth it if he did? God, to sleep with Francy *tonight!*

She smiled. "I guess the way you're looking at me is enough of an answer, Joe. How about a kiss to seal the bargain?"

He took only the quickest glance toward the door before he leaned across the table and kissed her. It was just like the first kiss between them, the time in the car when she'd driven him to the bus line, except that this time the table was between them. Table or no, he felt it down to his very toenails.

He sat back, still breathing a little hard.

Someone was rattling the door. Joe got up quickly. It was all right; it was Harry, the night bartender, and he couldn't have seen them. Joe let him in.

He said, "Hi, Harry. Shall I leave the door unlatched for business or do you want time to get ready?"

"Leave it open. All I got to do to get ready for business is take my coat off and put an apron on." Harry saw Francy as he walked past the booth. "Hi, Francine."

Joe said, "Mitch will be back in a few minutes. He wants you to check the register before you start."

Harry nodded. Joe went back to the booth across from Francine. He said, "Maybe we better sit at the bar; it'll look better when Mitch comes back. But first, when and where?"

"I'd better pick you up, Joe, because I haven't much idea when. I'll be leaving sometime between six and seven, I think, but it might be a little later. If you tell me where you live and stay in your room from six o'clock till I get there—"

"Sure. Swell." He told her where and then stood up and spoke loudly enough for Harry to hear. "Shall I bring you another drink here, or shall we sit over at the bar and keep Harry from being lonesome?"

They were sitting at the bar, on adjacent stools but not too close together, when Mitch came back a few minutes later. He was cheerful. "Got a good man lined up for tomorrow," he said. "Francy, the gondola's yours, but how about dropping me off at the Schroeder? When you finish your drink."

When Mitch and Francy had left, Harry asked, "What'd old Krazzy get bounced for?"

Joe said, "For doing what I'd be doing if I told you."

"Huh? Oh, talking too much. Well, Krazzy always did have too big a mouth. Another drink, Joe?"

Joe had two more. He didn't know whether it was for Dutch courage because he was scared or to celebrate because something so wonderful was going to happen. *Tonight!*

The Stage

SCENE: *Joe Bailey's room. The room, however, is expanded, enlarged, to the full size of an average stage. The few pieces of furniture—a bed, a dresser, a wardrobe cabinet, a magazine rack, a small table, two straight chairs—stand in their proper relative positions, but seem lost in the comparative vastness of the stage. In the wall opposite footlights is one window. The shade is up and we see it is early evening. The door to the hallway (the only door) is at left and is closed. Unless we count the window, it is the only actual entrance to the room, but the wings at both sides of the stage are open, enabling the actors to enter and leave as though walking through the end walls of the room.*

It is a few minutes after 6:00 p.m., September 10, 1948. At the rise of the curtain we see Joe sitting on the edge of the bed waiting for Francy's knock on the door. He is fully — and nattily — dressed, except for his panama, which lies on the bed ready to hand. He is fidgeting, playing nervously with the hunting knife and its sheath. He starts, standing suddenly at the sound of a voice from the wings.

VOICE OF ELLIE: (*From offstage, right*) Joe! Joe!

JOE: Ellie! What are you doing here? (*Ellie enters from right wing, walks toward him hesitantly.*)

ELLIE: Don't do it, Joe. Don't go with that woman. Please.

JOE: (*Frowning*) What business is it of yours, Ellie? Things are through between us, remember? And for the best; I agree with you on that. What you said in your letter was true. I'm trying to forget you because it *was* true. And you left town, didn't you? So what business you got being jealous?

ELLIE: (*Pleadingly*) It's not jealousy, Joe. Oh, sure, I hate the thought of your sleeping with that—with Francy, yes. But it's because of what she'll do to you. She'll drag you down, dear.

JOE: Down from where? She can't drag me down till I get *up*. What am I? Nothing, yet.

ELLIE: You're a nice guy, Joe. You're *good*. You don't like to hurt people. You're decent. She can drag you down from that. And she will.

JOE: It's none of your business, Ellie. We're through. I'm trying to forget you. All right, if it makes you any happier to know it, I'm in love with you, whatever that means. But that's *why* I'm going with Francy tonight, to make me forget about you. Since I can't have you anyway—

ELLIE: Why can't you, Joe?

JOE: You know why. I'm a criminal. Could you be a—a gun moll? A criminal's wife, even? You aren't the type, Ellie. That's what's wrong between us; that's why I can't have you. It wouldn't be fair to you!

ELLIE: (*She laughs softly.*) Are you so blind, Joe Bailey, that you can't see you're contradicting yourself? If you were a *criminal*, deep down inside, you wouldn't care whether it was fair to me or not.

JOE: (*Desperately*) I *am* a criminal, Ellie. If I wasn't before, I am one now. I've robbed a filling station.

ELLIE: And that's the only thing thus far and your share was—how much?—only fifty dollars. You can send it back anonymously and the slate will be clean.

241

JOE: Send it back out of what? That's about every cent I have in the world just at this moment. And how about all the money I owe Mitch? Look, Ellie, don't get me wrong; I'm not even *thinking* about backing out of my deal with Mitch. But if I did, wouldn't I owe him back all the money he's been advancing me? It's—well, right up to now it's two hundred and seventy dollars? Where'd I get that kind of money? Even if he'd let me back out if I wanted to, how could I pay him back?

ELLIE: With fifty from the station, Joe, that's three hundred and thirty dollars you owe. That wouldn't be much with both of us working for a while. With tips, I make about forty dollars a week. You could easily make that much honestly, once you got started. And, Joe, we could live on not much more than half of that for a little while, and live well and happily, Joe. You could pay back twenty or thirty dollars a week and get it all paid off in a few months. And I've got money saved up, Joe; I'd gladly give it to you out of that except I know you wouldn't want it that way.

JOE: Ellie, please. Please go away and let me alone. I never meant to fall in love. God knows life's complicated enough without that. And besides, I don't know where you are. I couldn't find you if I wanted to.

ELLIE: You could if you wanted to badly enough. Somehow.

JOE: All right, maybe I could. But I'm not going to, Ellie. You were right the first time when you ran away from me. I'm no good and I'm going to keep on being that way. I'm going to have money, big money, and everything I've always wanted. I've been poor and broke all my life and I'm sick of it. (*Francy enters through the wings at the left—not the real Francy, of course; for she would have come in through the door and not through the wall. Neither Joe nor Ellie notices her; Joe keeps on talking and Ellie's eyes—now beginning to fill with tears—are on Joe's face. Francy saunters toward them and stops behind Joe.*) Damn it all, Ellie, you understood that once. That's why you left, isn't it?

ELLIE: I left because I was afraid of myself, Joe. I loved you too much; I knew what would have happened last night, if I'd stayed. I'm weak, too, Joe. You can't expect me to have all the strength between us.

JOE: That's not what I'm talking about, Ellie. Listen, when I was a kid after my father died—even before, because he was out of work—we always had to live in lousy dumps and never had enough money, never had a car, or anything. I was ashamed of the clothes I had to wear to high school, I hated them. I hated not having enough money to go places. Part of the time, when Mom was out of work, we were on relief. And when I got on my own—even *before* then—I decided that I wasn't going to be broke all my life. I was—I *am*—going to have money no matter what I have to do to get it. You can't change that in me, Ellie. So go away, please go away, and let me alone.

FRANCY: Attaboy, Joe. (*Both Joe and Ellie turn to face her. Francy looks only at Joe.*) I'm really surprised at you, Joe, even thinking you could fall for a—a dumb little waitress like that! But if you want her, go ahead. Get married and make a sap of yourself, keep your nose to a grindstone all your life.

ELLIE: (*Fiercely*) You keep out of this! Isn't it better to work at an honest job than to get himself killed as a—a gangster? *You* don't care about him or you wouldn't want him to do that. You don't love him. Why—why, you're sleeping with another man right now!

FRANCY: (*Looks at Ellie with amusement.*) Not just at this moment. Right now I'm getting into my car—all right, it's

Mitch's car—to come here and pick up this wonderful boy-friend of yours. And do you know what we're going to do?

ELLIE: Sure I know. That's what I'm trying to stop him from doing. For his own sake. Because I love him and you don't. You—you just have hot pants for him. (*Francy laughs.*) You know Mitch would find out sooner or later and—Oh, Francy, *please*. If you must have Joe, wait—and make him wait—until you've broken with Mitch! I don't want him killed! He's going to be in enough danger without that!

MITCH: (*His voice comes from offstage, left.*) Joe! Hey, Joe, you home?

JOE: (*Frantically*) Hide! Both of you, quick! (*They run. Ellie runs around the bed and lies down behind it. Francy gets into the corner between one side of the wardrobe and the wall—right under the chromolithograph of the shepherd leading his sheep.*)

MITCH: (*Still from offstage*) Hey, Joe, are you there?

JOE: Sure, Mitch. Come on in. (*Mitch enters from the left wing — as it were through the wall of the room.*)

MITCH: Hi, Joe. Coming over to the poker game tonight?

JOE: No, Mitch. I can't make it. Got a date.

MITCH: With Francy? (*Laughs.*) Don't get scared, Joe. I don't guess I'd mind too much, if I found out. Francy's getting a little too bitchy for me recently. I'm going to toss her out on her beautiful little fanny any day now. Too many women in the world to have trouble with any one of them.

JOE: Gee, I'm glad you feel that way, Mitch. I was worried. You don't mind if I go to Lake Geneva with Francy tonight?

MITCH: Not unless I find out, kid. But you damn well better not let me find out. I—I don't know what I'd do, Joe,

244

if I happened to get mad about it. I'd be sorry afterwards, but I might kill you. I got a hell of a temper. I almost slugged Krazzy this afternoon—and I'd have probably killed the old bastard if I had, so I'm glad now that I didn't. But I had a hell of a fight with myself keeping my hands off him. You ever feel that way, kid?

JOE: No. But back to Francy. You don't care, if you don't find out? I mean, you feel it wouldn't be disloyal to you?

MITCH: Kid, I was young myself once. I wouldn't expect you to think about me, if you had a chance at as pretty a little piece as Francy. That is, I wouldn't if I had time to think it over. If I found out sometime when you were handy I might pull your arms off and make you eat them, but not if I had time to think it over.

JOE: Okay, Mitch. If you find out, I'll try not to be around when it happens. But listen, Mitch, there's something more important.

MITCH: What, kid?

JOE: Mitch, I'm just asking this to find out. Don't get excited. How would you take it if I—changed my mind about going in with you and Dixie and Gus Bernstein?

MITCH: You're kidding me, Joe. You can't really mean that.

JOE: I—I don't think I do, really. But I want to know. Just in case.

MITCH: (*His face darkens; he takes a step toward Joe.*) Why, you—you Goddamn punk, I think you mean it. And if you do—

JOE: (*Stands his ground.*) If I do, what? Providing I pay you back the dough you've advanced me? (*At the start of this speech the figure of the ghost of Alvin Bailey, Joe's father, has entered from the right; a green spotlight follows, bathing it in ghostly radiance.*)

245

MITCH: (*His face is black with anger; he takes another step toward Joe.*) Kid, you try to pull something like that on me now and here's what I'll do to—

ALVIN BAILEY: Joe! (*Mitch turns and sees the ghost behind him.*)

JOE: Dad! What are you doing here? (*Mitch starts to back away from the frightening figure, his face pale. He breaks suddenly and runs past Joe, heading for the wardrobe alongside which Francy is hiding; he jerks the door open and jumps inside, pulling the door closed again from inside the cabinet.*)

ALVIN BAILEY: (*Sepulchrally*) Murderer. You killed me, Joe.

JOE: I know, I know. But what can I do about it now? I was just a kid; I was only six, and—I don't remember for sure, but I must have hated you ever since that Christmas Eve when I saw you with—(*He cringes.*) with the—you know what I mean. Can you blame for that?

ALVIN BAILEY: Do you still hate me, Joe?

JOE: No, no! I'm trying to make up for what I did. Can't you see that that's at least part of the reason why I—(*Suddenly and with enough noise to make Joe stop talking and look, the picture on the wall over Francy's hiding place flies back to reveal a trap door in the wall. Out of the hole in the wall projects the head of Dr Janes, the psychologist whom Joe once visited.*)

DR JANES: Joe, you know better than that. (*Points at ghost.*) That is not your father!

JOE: You mean—?

DR JANES: I mean this. Watch. (*He extends both hands toward the ghost and addresses him very solemnly.*) I conjure thee in the name of Adler, Freud and Holy Ghost. Be thyself! (*The green light that has bathed the figure of Alvin Bailey fades. Bailey puts a hand to his head and stares at Joe in confusion.*)

ALVIN BAILEY: Joey, Joey, what am I doing here? (*The head and shoulders of Dr Janes pull back into the wall; the trap door snaps shut; again it is the picture of the shepherd leading his sheep.*)

JOE: You were telling me I killed you, calling me a murderer.

ALVIN BAILEY: (*Horrified*) Joey! My son! Are you crazy, or am I? You killed me? No! You didn't, Joey, you didn't!

JOE: I got you killed. I led the coppers to you.

ALVIN BAILEY: But not on purpose, Joey! You were a little boy. You were only six. You didn't know what I was doing that night, you weren't old enough to know. You were just a scared little boy that wanted his father.

JOE: Oh, Pop, I wish I could be sure of that. (*He sits down on the bed again and drops his head into his hands.*) I've tried to remember just what I thought that night—and I can't! I can't remember for sure whether I knew or not; I can't remember what I was thinking.

ALVIN BAILEY: You weren't thinking anything, Joey. You were a little six-year-old boy scared out of his wits by a nightmare. Oh, Joey, have you been blaming yourself all these years?

JOE: (*Miserably*) Yes. And because I blamed myself for getting the coppers to kill you, I got this— (*He gets up and goes to the bureau; from the second drawer he takes the revolver and holster.*) That's why I've got this, Pop. Since I got you killed, I thought I'd have to—

ALVIN BAILEY: But you didn't, Joey.

JOE: I—I don't know, now. I thought I was sure. But, anyway, the cops killed you and I've hated cops ever since.

ALVIN BAILEY: Joe, the cops didn't kill me! It was Montoya; he shot me when I tried to stop him from shooting at the cops.

JOE: But a policeman's bullet hit you and then you fell.
ALVIN BAILEY: I was dead already, Joey. Montoya's bullet killed me. But I was still on my feet a fraction of a second later when the policeman's bullet hit. It hit a dead man, Joey. Montoya killed me. And, Joey—I can see into your mind a little bit now and I see you've got something else wrong.
JOE: What, Pop?
ALVIN BAILEY: You think I was a criminal, Joey. And I wasn't. I mean, down deep I wasn't, any more than you are. Oh, sure, I was bartender in a speakeasy and that was illegal, just like your selling pool tickets was illegal. But the only reason I went with Dutch and Montoya that night was that I was desperate for money. That wasn't like now, Joey. That was in the bottom of the Depression and I'd tried *so* long to get a job and I couldn't get a job. If I could have got a job, Joey, I'd never have gone that night. And you can get a job, Joey; they're easy to get in nineteen forty-eight, especially for a young man like you without a record.
JOE: You mean that was the only crime you ever committed?
ALVIN BAILEY: The only real one, yes. Just like you've committed one real one, Joey. I helped hold up a theater and you helped hold up a filling station. We're even, Joey, on that. Except that you were lucky and I was unlucky. (*The window has been opening since Alvin Bailey started to speak. Mrs Gettleman looks in the window.*)
MRS GETTLEMAN: Joe Bailey! What are you doing with a *ghost* in your room! (*She sees the holstered gun still in Joe's hand.*) And a gun! (*She looks down behind the bed where Ellie is hiding.*) And a woman! Joe Bailey, you'll have to move out as soon as your week's up. I'm giving notice to you right now. And get that ghost out of there *at once!*

ALVIN BAILEY: (*Grinning*) Joey, I guess I'd better go. Good-bye, son. (*Exit, right.*)

JOE: (*Facing window*) But Mrs Gettleman, you don't understand. That was my father, and you've driven him—(*The window slams shut and Mrs Gettleman vanishes. Joe faces right and calls.*) Pop! Pop! Come on back. It's all right now. (*He stands a moment but when there is no answer and Alvin Bailey does not return, he walks to the wardrobe in which Mitch has been hiding and jerks open the door. Mitch steps out; he still looks pale and frightened.*)

MITCH: Is that ghost gone, kid?

JOE: Yes. And you've got to go too. I've got something to think out and I don't want you around while I do it. (*He puts gun back in drawer as he talks and then picks up the hunting knife—which still lies beside the bed where he had dropped it when he rose to speak to Ellie—and puts it on top of the dresser.*)

MITCH: You can't get rid of me that easy, kid. I might want to help you decide whatever you're trying to think out.

JOE: No, Mitch. Beat it.

MITCH: (*Glaring at Joe but walking to side of stage*) Okay, kid, if you feel that way about it after all I've done for you. You Goddamn-well better decide the way I want you to decide, though. (*He laughs, an ugly laugh.*) Think I'll toss you in something to remember me by. (*He walks off, right, and a second later, while Joe still faces that way, Krasno is thrown bodily onto the stage from the right wing. He lands hard and lies there prone, panting. His face is covered with blood and he has obviously taken a terrible beating.*)

JOE: Krazzy! What happened? Did Mitch—(*He runs to Krazzy and helps him to his feet; Krazzy sways a bit but can stand.*)

KRASNO: Who do you think did it, Santa Claus? Sure it was Mitch. It's all right, kid; I'm not really hurt. He'll do worse to you, if he can, but he won't kill you. With him planning everything he's planning, he isn't going to lay himself open to a murder rap unless he has to. And unless he thinks you're going to call copper on him, why would he have to?

(*At the start of Krasno's speech Francy peers out from behind the wardrobe. She smiles and starts to disrobe. She steps out of her shoes, peels off her stockings and starts to pull her dress off over her head. Neither Joe nor Krasno notice her.*)

JOE: Gosh, Krazzy I'm sorry. Is—is there anything I can do for you?

KRASNO: Not for me, Joe, but for yourself. You can get out of this mess.

(*Francy throws her dress and stockings across the top of the wardrobe; she takes off her brassiere.*)

JOE: It sounds easy, Krazzy. But—there are so many angles. I'm in so deep already, in so many ways. Ellie's lost already for one thing.

KRASNO: You can find her. If you try hard enough, you can find her.

(*Francy takes off her panties and adds them and the brassiere to the dress and stockings on the wardrobe.*)

JOE: And I haven't got a job—oh, I suppose I can get one. And all that money I owe Mitch and what I'd have to send back to the filling station—and the question what Mitch would do to me—and Francy—

KRASNO: Do you love Francy?

JOE: Well, no, not the way I love Ellie. But look—Francy's coming here, any minute now. I'll have Francy *tonight* and—

(*Francy, still standing with the wardrobe between her and the two men, smiles.*)

KRASNO: But, Joe, if you go with Francy, you'll be tied to Mitch and to crime because you'll need money—or think you will. You can't have Francy without having money.

JOE: *Tonight* I can. And oh God, she's so beautiful, Krazzy. You should have seen her as I first saw her, lying there on the beach at Mitch's, sunbathing, naked. I thought at first she had on a white bathing suit—just for a second—because her legs and arms were light golden tan and her body as white as milk and her breasts so round and beautiful and—I can almost see her like that now.

FRANCY: (*Stepping into sight from behind wardrobe, stark naked*) Almost, Joe? Why make it almost? Look at me, Joe. Think of tonight. What else matters, past tonight?

JOE: Francy!

(*Ellie stands up behind the bed, first staring, then glaring, at Francy. She starts around the end of the bed.*)

ELLIE: Joe! No! You love *me*, Joe. Remember, you love *me*.

(*Joe doesn't hear her. He takes a step toward Francy. Krasno takes Joe's arm and tries to hold him back.*)

FRANCY: (*Smiling sensuously, beckoning*) Kiss me, Joe.

(*Ellie runs between them. She is tearing at her own clothes, trying to take them off, rip them off. Her dress rips down the front, is thrown aside.*)

ELLIE: Joe, look at me. I've got a body, too. You'll find as much pleasure in it as in Francy's—more, because *I love you.* And I want you, Joe; I wanted you so bad I had to run away from you because—Am I not a woman, too, Joe? Am I not beautiful, too?

(*Francy, trying to pull Ellie out of the way, grabs the back of Ellie's bra; it pulls away in Francy's hand. Ellie tears off her step-ins and she, too, stands naked before Joe. She seems even more naked than Francy because she still wears her shoes and stockings.*)

FRANCY: (*Laughs scornfully.*) Joe Bailey, if you'd rather have a dumb little dame like that—go ahead. But don't forget what kind of a life she'll tie you down to. And don't forget I'm on my way here right now; I'll be knocking on your door in a few minutes—and that you don't even know where *she* is!

ELLIE: (*Desperately, crying now*) You can *find* me, Joe.

KRASNO: Don't be a goddam fool, Joe. Sure you can find her. And are your pants so hot you can't wait a little while for something worth waiting for? You fool, Joe, Ellie *loves you.*

(*Joe backs away from both of them, sitting down on the bed as he sat at the opening of the scene. He drops his head into his hands.*)

JOE: Lay off of me, Krazzy. Lay off of me!

(*Two figures reenter simultaneously, Alvin Bailey from the left and Mitch from the right. The five of them crowd around Joe—Ellie and Francy, both naked; Krasno, Mitch, Alvin Bailey. None of them pays any attention to any other, all are looking at and talking to Joe Bailey who, with his hands over his face, now sees none of them but still hears what they say.*)

KRASNO: Lay off of yourself, kid. Give yourself a break.

MITCH: (*Blackly*) Kid, you saw what happened to Krasno, didn't you? Well, you rat on me now and God help you. I'll put you in the hospital so long that you'll be an old man when you get out.

ALVIN BAILEY: Joey, Joey! You aren't a criminal, you can't be one! Joey!

FRANCY: Tonight, Joey. And I'm coming up the stairs now. I'll be here in a minute, less than a minute. Really here, Joey. In the flesh. Think of kissing these breasts, Joe, of —

ELLIE: (*Sobbing*) But you love me, Joe. And I love you. Oh, Joe, *don't* —

FRANCY: Not even hours, Joe! Here and now, in half a minute, I'll knock on your door. I'll come in if you ask me. If you kiss me — as you did that time in the car, why — Joe, you can have me here and now, besides tonight at Lake Geneva! Within minutes, Joe!

ELLIE: No, Joe, no! It's not that I'm jealous — although there's that, too. But if you answer when Francy knocks, you're — you *are* in too deep, Joe. You'll never get out. You'll go ahead and be a criminal. You won't be able to change your mind after that. Francy won't let you.

JOE: (*Speaking without looking up*) Let me alone, Ellie. We had our chance. We didn't take it.

MITCH: Kid, God help you if you try to back out on me now!

JOE: (*Still without looking up, wearily*) Shut up, Mitch. You're not in on my deciding this.

ALVIN BAILEY: Joey!

(*Ellie drops to her knees in front of Joe. He looks up, for the first time since he has sat down on the bed and his eyes, on a level with hers, stare at her as though he never saw her before. He is looking at her face, into her eyes, not at her body.*)

ELLIE: (*Softly*) I love you, Joe.

JOE: Can I find you, Ellie? Is it too late? I love you, Ellie.

ELLIE: I love you, Joe. What more can I say than —

(*There is a knock at the door. As at as signal the other five besides Joe suddenly run to the wings — Mitch and Francy left; Alvin Bailey, Krasno and Ellie right. By the second knock, a second or less after the first, Joe Bailey is alone on the stage. He*)

253

stands up and looks at the door uncertainly. A third knock. Very quietly, he sits back down on the bed. A pause of several seconds and then a fourth knock, louder, and with a final sound to it.)
FRANCY'S VOICE: (*From beyond door*) Joe!
(*Joe sits very quietly and does not answer. After a few seconds more, we hear the click of high heels moving away from the door and then starting down a flight of stairs. For seconds after the footsteps have died away to silence, nothing happens. Joe sits still. Slowly from the right wing floats a lighted candle; it comes about ten feet onto the stage and stops, poised about four feet above the floor. It burns steadily and does not flicker. Lights on that side of the stage dim and a vague shadowy figure follows the candle out on stage; it is a shadow, but it holds something in its hand that gleams brightly in the flickering light of the candle, something that might be a hatchet or an ax. The shadow figure stops halfway between the right wing and the floating candle. The bright blade moves back and forth slowly in a small arc, a menacing arc.*

Joe Bailey sits facing forward, an exalted look on his face; he does not turn and see the candle and the chopper. Instead, as the curtain falls slowly, he rises and walks toward the bureau. Neither the candle nor the chopper moves and, unless the curtain rustles, there is no sound whatsoever as it falls.)

The Story

23

The last evening. The first hurdle was past; Francy was gone. And by now she'd be driving away and it would be too late to get her back even if he weakened. Now or any other time. He knew that Francy wasn't the kind of girl you'd have a second chance to get after standing her up once.

Joe Bailey opened the second drawer of the dresser. He took out the gun and the holster and stood looking at them for a second. He took the gun out of the holster and unloaded it. He put the bullets back into a box of them that had been in the drawer beside the gun. He got newspaper out of another drawer and made a package of gun, holster and box of bullets.

Paper and a pen. He sat down at the table with them. He poised the pen over the paper and hesitated.

What? — "To the Police: If I am killed, Stanislaus Mitchell is the man who — "

The hell with it. If Mitch killed him, what would be to gain? What satisfaction that Mitch might — or might not—spend most of the rest of his life in jail? No worse than that, for there is no capital punishment in Wisconsin. And Mitch would live longer in jail than out of it, probably. And what would it matter to Joe, either way? Nothing.

He stared at the still blank paper. Write to Ellie, telling her what he was going to do? Send it care of Mike, hoping Mike would forward it? No, nothing to be gained there either. If he survived the encounter with Mitch, he'd find her. If he didn't, getting any letter he might write would only make her feel worse.

Write to Ray? Why? Ray had enough trouble of his own; Ray's tragedy—Jeannie with less than a year to live—dwarfed his own problem to insignificance. Why bother Ray?

There was only one thing to write that was worth writing. He wrote it:

I.O.U. $270. Joe Bailey

He folded the paper and put it into his coat pocket.

He thought: *Obit for Joe Bailey— I. O. U. $270.*

He walked back to the dresser and looked at himself in the mirror. He looked calm, he thought. Almost too calm.

Anything else before he left? His eyes, looking about the room, fell finally on the hunting knife in its sheath lying on top of the dresser. Yes, that. Then Mitch wouldn't beat him up. He might kill him, but he wouldn't beat him up.

He picked up the hunting knife and held it a moment. Then, quickly, he unfastened his belt and ran it through the loop of the sheath. He buttoned his coat over it and stepped back from the mirror to see if the knife showed. It didn't. He unbuttoned the top button of his coat to see if that would enable him to draw the knife quickly, and it did. He looked at the reflection in the mirror of himself holding the knife and thought: *Hell, I probably wouldn't use it, no matter what Mitch does. But my having it just might stop him from doing anything short of shooting me.*

He put the knife back into the sheath. Another look about the room. The chromolithograph of the shepherd leading his flock. The enlarged photograph of the dry goods store with *Leiber and Hennig* lettered on the windows. For the hundreth, and last, time he wondered vaguely who Leiber and Hennig were or had been.

He went down the stairs. As he passed the phone he thought momentarily of phoning old Krasno at the Antlers to tell him what he'd decided. No, he'd wait and tell Krasno afterwards, if it all came out all right.

It was still not quite seven o'clock when he left the building. He crossed to the south side of the street to have a better chance of catching an inbound empty cab. One came along almost right away, and he hailed it.

Getting rid of the gun was the next thing; he wanted it irrevocably gone by the time he saw Mitch. He took the cab only to Plankinton and Wells; from there he walked across the Wells Street bridge. Halfway across he leaned over the railing and, at a moment when no other pedestrian was near, dropped the package containing the gun and bullets into the dark waters of the Milwaukee River. Across the bridge, he was able to catch another cab within a block.

He gave the address of Mitch's apartment on Prospect and then sat back in the cab and tried not to think. No use thinking now, no use planning, until he found out whether he was going to get out of Mitch's apartment alive.

The cab swung into the curb.

"Will you wait?" he asked the driver.

"Have to charge you waiting time if I do. How long?"

257

"I don't know," Joe said. He took out his wallet and found two singles and handed them to the driver. "If I'm not down by the time that much waiting time is used up, don't wait any longer."

The dome light of the cab showed Joe's face to the driver. The driver said, "Sure. That'll cover quite a while; the fare was only — say, are you all right? Your face looks — uh — pretty pale."

"I'm all right," Joe said.

He got out of the cab and went into the apartment building. There was an elevator, but it wasn't at the first floor level. Mitch's apartment was on the third and Joe walked. Rapidly up the first flight of stairs and slowly up the second. For the first time he remembered that Dixie Ehlers and Gus Bernstein, the man from Chicago, were to be at Mitch's this evening. But maybe it was too early for them to be there; it was only seven-twenty. He hoped they wouldn't be. Then he hoped they would.

He rang the bell of Mitch's apartment and waited.

The door opened and Mitch stood there. "Joe," he said, a bit surprised. "Look, kid, the poker game isn't till ten or eleven o'clock. Glad you decided to come, but — well, we're still talking. Can you kill some time and come back in a couple of hours? We'll be through talking by then, even if the poker game isn't — Say, Joe, is something wrong with you? What's the matter?"

"Nothing's the matter, Mitch," Joe said. "I'm all right. From your point of view that's all wrong, but I'm all right. Listen, Mitch, I'm quitting."

Mitch's face darkened. His hand shot out and caught Joe's shoulder, pulling him inside the apartment. His other hand slammed the door behind them. He said, "Listen, Joe, I told you —" His fingers tightened, dug into Joe's shoulder, much harder than they'd dug in across the booth at the tavern. They hurt like hell.

Joe said, "Cut it, Mitch. Look down."

Mitch looked down and saw the bright blade of the knife, its point lightly touching his shirt just above the belt buckle. He let go of Joe's shoulder and jumped back.

He said, "What the hell, Joe?"

Joe said, "Keep your hands off me; that's all. Shoot me if you want to, but keep your hands off me."

"*Shoot* you? Listen, Joe, what the hell's wrong with you?"

"Dixie and Bernstein both in there?"

"Sure. In the next room. What—?" Mitch watched the knife blade warily. His face looked just a little greenish.

"Let's go," Joe said. "Let's get it over with."

Mitch backed away as though he didn't dare turn his back to the knife. Joe followed, keeping the distance between them. Mitch backed through the doorway. Past him, Joe could see Dixie and Gus Bernstein in the living room beyond the foyer. Dixie was on the sofa, Bernstein leaning forward in an overstuffed chair.

Suddenly there was a gun in Dixie's hand. It wasn't Maggie; Dixie had been traveling light tonight. It was a thirty eight like the one Joe had just dropped into the Milwaukee River.

Joe grinned at him. He said, "Hi, Dixie." His eyes flicked quickly back to Mitch, who was closest. But Mitch was still backing away from the knife.

Bernstein's hand was in his coat pocket, but whether it was on a gun or not Joe didn't know. It didn't matter, and if Bernstein had one he didn't bother to draw it after a quick cross glance at Dixie and the sight of Dixie's revolver leveled at Joe's chest.

259

Bernstein said disgustedly. "Jesus Christ, a psycho. Mitch, you saddle us with a psycho. That's all we need, a psycho."

Joe said, "Hi, Gus. Tell 'em, Mitch."

Mitch had kept backing until he was between Bernstein and Dixie. Then, seeing Dixie's gun, he stopped. He said, "Joe says he wants to quit, that's all. Why the frog-sticker, I don't know."

Joe realized that he was still holding the knife slightly out in front of him; he dropped his hand to his side. He said, "Just that I'm not going to let you beat me up, Mitch. Tell Dixie to shoot if you want to. But keep your Goddamn hands off me otherwise. If anyone touches me without shooting me first, somebody's going to be cut up."

Mitch shook his head slowly. "I don't get it, Joe. After all I did for you—"

"All you did for me was advance me money, and I'm going to pay it back. Here's an I.O.U. for the exact amount, Mitch. It boils down to the fact that I've changed my mind. And there's only one question: What are you going to do about it?"

"Goddamn it, Joe," Mitch said. "I don't get it."

Bernstein laughed. "You don't get it," he said viciously to Mitch. "*I* get it all right. I took your word for letting the kid in on things and you turn out to be crazier than he is. Look at his face. He's a psycho."

Joe said, "There's only one point to be settled. Shoot me, or don't. This knife isn't going to stand up against Dixie's gun. There's only one thing you're not going to do to me, and that's anything less than killing me. That's all this knife's good for."

Dixie said, "Mitch?"

Mitch's face had calmed down now. The anger was out

260

of it and it was calculating. He said, "We'll talk it over. Keep the gun on him, Dix. Shoot him if he moves – forward or backward, either one. What do you think?"

Dixie said, "I'm thinking."

"That job you did with the kid. Can he pin it on you?"

Dixie shook his head slowly. "My word against his. The mooch couldn't identify either of us. Not that I'd want to be picked up for it." He looked questioningly at Joe.

Joe said, "Don't worry, Dixie. I'm not going to talk. Laugh if you want to, but I'm going to send back my share of it. But anonymously, and you can worry about your share."

Bernstein looked at Mitch and laughed shortly. He didn't have to repeat "A psycho." His laugh did it for him. He asked, "Does he know any of our plans? *Anything?*"

Mitch said, "No. What do you think, Bernie?"

"By me it's off, either way. Deal me out. If he calls copper, they'll be on us like a ton of bricks; we'll need alibis any time an ice cream cone is swiped from a kid during recess at school, and we can't be sure he won't if we let him out of here. And if you shoot him – or tell Dixie to – I'm still out. He's your boy, Mitch; they'll trace him to you and ask too many questions if he turns up with a hole in his head. Besides, don't you see he's practically asking for it?"

"So what?"

"So he probably left a note or told seven people he was coming here and who to talk to if something happened. The hell with it. I'm going back to Chi."

"Now, Bernie – "

"I tell you, Mitch, I'm *out* of it. Has he got anything on you?"

Mitch said, "Dixie?"

"I'm with Gus. Mitch, whether we shoot him or not, Milwaukee's going to be too hot for a while."

Joe felt a little dizzy, but he was leaning back against the jamb of the door, so it didn't show. Something white was lying on the rug in front of him; it was the I.O.U. he had written for Mitch. He didn't remember dropping it, but there it lay, so he must have. But the knife was still in his right hand, his fingers gripping the hilt of it so hard that they hurt. Things were blurring a little. Mitch and Bernstein were out of focus slightly and so was Dixie's face. Only Dixie's revolver was clear and sharp. He almost wished Dixie would shoot and get it over with. But they were still talking.

Then Mitch was saying, "Get the hell out of here, Bailey." It was the first time Mitch had ever called him Bailey instead of Joe or kid. He was thinking about that and didn't even move until Mitch said, "Get the hell out of here, I said."

He heard Bernstein laughing as he backed out, backed all the way to the outer door with the knife ready so Mitch wouldn't come after him.

Then he was in the cab, without any clear memory of having walked down two flights of stairs. And the cab was moving so he must have given directions to the driver although he didn't have any memory of that at all. He remembered suddenly about the knife and quickly glanced down to see if it was still in his hand, but it wasn't. A quick gesture assured him that it was back in the sheath on his belt and that his coat was buttoned over it. Everything was under control and he must even have told the cab driver where to go. He held out his hands and looked at them; they were shaking a bit but that was understandable after the risk he'd taken in Mitch's apartment. But that had been worth it; this way there was a clean break and he didn't worry now about Mitch coming after him or anything. If Mitch had wanted him shot, it could have been done there and then with less risk than at any later time and place. No more worry even about being beaten up. Undoubtedly that had been Mitch's first thought, but the knife had saved him. And once his first blind temper had abated, Mitch would see he had nothing to gain by coming after him.

Yes he was through with Mitch, completely, except for sending him the money to cover that I.O.U., and he wouldn't have to see him personally to do that.

The cab was pulling up to the curb in front of the Dinner Gong restaurant. Joe could see through the window even before the cab stopped that Mike Dravich wasn't behind the cash register. But Mike just might be still at the back so he told the driver to wait. He ran into the restaurant.

"Where's Mike?" he asked the first waitress he saw.

She glanced back at the clock. "Ought to be here in about twenty minutes," she said. "Said he'd be back at eight."

"Where is he now? Home, at the Tower Hotel?"

"I don't know. Maybe."

He realized he hadn't asked this waitress about Ellie. "Do you know where Ellie Dravich went?"

"Who? Mister, I just started work here today."

Then Mike had hired her to replace Ellie. He thanked her and ran back to the cab. "Tower Hotel," he said. It was only a few blocks, but as long as he'd told the taxi to wait, he might as well use it.

He knew the number of Mike's three-room apartment at the hotel. Back while the numbers game had been going hot, he'd taken tickets up to Mike several times on days Mike hadn't gone to the restaurant. So he took the elevator up without having to announce himself at the desk and risking Mike's refusal, via telephone, to see him.

He rang Mike's bell. Mike opened the door and Joe walked in and closed it behind him. Mike's surprise, his involuntary step backward, enabled him to do it. Joe said, "Listen, Mike. I want—"

"Get the hell out of here!"

"Mike, listen! I've *got* to have Ellie's address. It's all right now; everything has changed. But I've got to know—"

Surprisingly Mike had taken another step backwards. He said, "All right, Joe." His voice was strange.

Joe didn't get it. Alongside where Mike stood now was Mike's desk. There was a letter rack on the desk, with a number of letters—they looked like personal rather than business letters—neatly arranged in it. If Ellie had written him, the letter would be in that rack, surely.

But Mike wasn't turning toward the desk; he was backing toward the door of the other room. He said, "Listen, Joe, I can get you Ellie's address, but I'll have to phone the restaurant for it. I had a letter from her, but it came to me there and—will you wait just a minute?"

Joe said, "Sure."

It was easy, too easy. Something was wrong with the way Mike was acting. Mike had kept facing him until he was nearly to the door of the other room, then he went through quickly and closed the door behind him. Quietly, his footsteps making no sound on the rug, Joe started toward the door after him.

He didn't get all the way there, the first try. The mirror in the wall beside the door stopped him. He caught sight of himself in it. His suit coat wasn't buttoned any more and the sheathed knife in his belt showed plainly. And his tie was twisted way around to one side; that must have happened when Mitch had grabbed his shoulder. Good God! No wonder Mike –

He buttoned his coat and straightened his tie as he went closer to the door and put his ear near it. Mike's voice was soft, but he could hear it. "Police? This is Mike Dravich, Tower Hotel, Apartment number –"

Joe backed away. He tiptoed to the letter rack and took the envelopes out of it. Yes, second from the top. Ellie's handwriting. He'd seen it only twice – once on the note she'd left pinned to her door, once on and in the letter she'd sent to him the afternoon she'd left town – Lord, *yesterday* afternoon; it seemed like weeks – but he knew it as well as he knew his own handwriting. Postmarked Racine, Wisconsin, 8:00 P M, September 9. And there was a return address in the upper corner, but he didn't take time to read it; Mike might be back any second. He stuffed the letter into his inside coat pocket and put the other letters back in the rack, trying to make them look just as they had before.

He was back standing where he'd been standing, just inside the closed outer door, when Mike came back.

Mike still looked nervous. He said, "They can't find the letter right away, Joe. They're looking for it and they'll call back in a few minutes. Sit down for a minute."

Joe didn't want Mike to suspect that he knew what the call had really been so he pretended to hesitate before he shook his head. He said, "Thanks a lot, Mike, but I've got to be somewhere right away. I'll drop in the restaurant later for it; if you're not there they can give it to me."

"Wait, Joe; they'll call back in just a minute."

In just a minute the cops would be here and he'd have a sweet time explaining that knife. Joe shook his head and backed out. He said, "I *can't* wait, Mike. I'll drop in the restaurant later."

He was outside and going down the stairs before Mike could say anything more. He rounded the corner to Wisconsin Avenue quickly, almost running.

It was still seven minutes of eight, and he knew that the North Shore Line trains for Racine left every hour on the hour. And he was at Eleventh and Wisconsin, five blocks from the station. He wouldn't be able to make it on foot. He ran diagonally across Wisconsin Avenue so he could hail an inbound cab on the south side of the street. He got one within two minutes; it made the lights and got him there on the dot of eight.

The fare was thirty-five cents but he didn't wait for change out of a dollar; he sprinted into and through the station. The train was half a minute late in pulling out and he made it.

He found a seat next to a window and sat down, breathing hard, but very happy, happier than he could remember ever having been before. He was on his way now to Ellie; he'd be in Racine in about forty minutes. He'd be seeing Ellie within an hour if his luck held out.

He remembered the letter and took it out of his pocket. The return address was the Cleveland Hotel, 610 Winetka Street. The letter was already slit across the top; he hesitated only a moment about opening it. There might be something in it he should know before he saw Ellie and she hadn't been close enough to her uncle for the letter to be extremely personal. As long as he'd stolen it, he might as well read it.

It was just a brief note. It read: *Dear Uncle Mike: Just to let you know where I'm staying, the Cleveland Hotel. Just for a few days. I'll start looking for a job tomorrow. If I find one and like it, I'll look for a regular room somewhere and let you know as soon as I have a permanent address or if I decide not to stay in Racine. I hope you found another girl to take my place. I'm awfully sorry I had to leave you without notice. And thanks again. Ellie.*

Good, he thought. She'd still be at the hotel, then. She wasn't going to look for another room right away.

He put the letter back into his pocket and relaxed in the seat. He thought that if Ellie would marry him, maybe it would be a good idea if they both stayed in Racine. It would be a clean break from Milwaukee and he could find a job there as easily as anywhere else, probably. He started to wonder what kind of job he'd look for, and then shoved that to the back of his mind. It didn't matter; anything would do to start. He'd live anywhere, do anything, to have Ellie.

At the Racine station he hurried to a phone booth and called the Cleveland Hotel. Yes, Ellie Dravich was registered there, but her room didn't answer.

He went outside and caught a cab for the hotel. Surely, she wouldn't be out late. Possibly, on her first—no her second—night in a strange town she'd gone to a movie. Or, just possibly, she'd found a job on her first day of looking for one and was working an evening shift. He groaned, thinking that she might be away until midnight or even one or two o'clock if that was the case.

The Cleveland was as he'd expected, a small inexpensive hotel, a walk-up. There wasn't any lobby where he could wait. Well, there was an easy answer to that; a room couldn't cost much. It had been only minutes since he'd phoned for Ellie so he didn't ask for her again. He asked for a room instead.

"Dollar and a half, sir. In advance, if you don't have baggage."

He paid it and signed the register, noticing Ellie's signature half a dozen names up the page. Her room number was 302. Good, he could rap on her door once in a while without having to make the desk clerk curious with room-to-room phone calls. He felt even more cheerful when the clerk turned the register around and wrote *305* after his own signature. He'd be almost across the hall from Ellie; if he left his own door ajar he could probably hear when she came in.

There wasn't any bellboy to escort him; the clerk merely gave him the key and directions to his room. Joe walked up. He found 302 first and tapped lightly on the door but Ellie was still out. That didn't disappoint him; he hadn't really expected her to have come home in the few minutes that had elapsed before his phone call and his arrival.

He went to his own room and looked at it. It was a cheap hotel room like any cheap hotel room. He left the door a few inches ajar and sat down on the bed to wait. Someone in the room next to his started to draw a tub of water. The sound was so loud that he couldn't hear footsteps outside if there were any to hear. He went to the door of his room and looked both ways along the hall but no one was in sight. Down the hall just past his room there was a glass case mounted on the wall. He shuddered a little, knowing what those glass cases in hotels like this one always contained – a hose and a fire axe. Fire axes were horrible-looking things; he'd always averted his eyes whenever he walked past a glass case like that, knowing what would be in it.

It had been only a few minutes, but Ellie *could* have come in without his hearing it, with that water running. He went to her door and rapped on it again. There wasn't any answer.

He went back to his own room and stood leaning against the jamb of the door until the water stopped running next door and he could hear. Then he sat on the bed again. He

268

wondered why he was so nervous and jittery. He held out his hand and found that it was still shaking a little. Not much, but it wasn't steady.

Hell, it was probably still reaction after the scene with Mitch and Bernstein and Dixie. That was still only a couple of hours ago. And no use denying, even to himself, that he'd been scared stiff. But it had been damn lucky, he felt now, that all three of them had been there. If he'd faced it out against Mitch alone, he'd still be worried what the reaction of the others would be when Mitch told them. This way, he'd got it over with all at once. He didn't have a thing to worry about now.

Except what Ellie was going to say. And why was he worried about that? He wasn't. She'd said in her letter to him that she loved him. And now that he wanted to get a job, to marry her, to do things her way because it was the right way, why should that worry him? Yesterday she'd loved him; surely she couldn't have changed her mind in a single day. And she'd run away from him, but not in anger—he needn't doubt that she'd give him a hearing. And believe what he told her. Especially as he'd almost leaned backwards to be honest with her all along.

After ten minutes he went to her door again, knowing that he was being ridiculous, knowing that a door couldn't have opened and closed that near his own door without his having heard it.

He went back to his room and sat down again, feeling hollow inside. And suddenly he realized why: he *was* hollow inside! He hadn't eaten a bite in over twelve hours! He'd had breakfast around nine and hadn't eaten since. He'd been getting hungry by the time he left Mitch's tavern but Francy had been picking him up sometime between six and seven so he'd deliberately refrained from eating so

269

he could eat with Francy somewhere on the way to Lake Geneva. No wonder he felt a little funny by now.

He left his room and walked downstairs to find a restaurant. Funny, he thought, if he happened to walk into one Ellie was working in, while she was on duty. Not that that was likely to happen, but it could.

24

He was only a dozen steps from the door of the hotel, walking toward the main street, when he saw her coming. She had just turned the corner, a quarter of a block away. She hadn't seen him yet.

He hurried his steps; she still hadn't noticed him by the time they were only a few yards apart.

"Ellie!" he said.

She saw him then all right. "Joe!" Surprise and happiness were about equally blended in her voice. And then they'd both stopped, and Joe's hands were on her shoulders. He talked fast, to ward off any rebuke for his having followed and found her.

"Ellie darling, it's all right; everything has changed. I found out how much I love you and I've broken with Mitch and I'm going to take a job so we can get married if you'll marry me."

"Oh, Joe! Do you really —? Where can we talk, Joe? We can't stand here."

"Your room?"

"We couldn't. They wouldn't let you come up with me. Unless — no, I couldn't suddenly change the registration; I registered as Miss."

"We can change that at Waukegan. We can get there in an

hour or two and get married right away. Or if you want to talk first—and I want you to be sure, Ellie—we can go into the hotel separately and I can come to your room. I took a room there too—just across the hall from yours."

"Oh. Where were you going just now?"

Joe grinned. "A very unromantic errand, Ellie. I had a busy day, getting straightened out, and haven't eaten anything since breakfast."

"Then you're going to eat right now, Joe Bailey. I won't even *talk* about getting married to a man who's starving. Come on." She took his arm and started back the way she had come.

"Anywhere you say, Ellie," he told her. "But the nearest place would be the best."

"Can you walk two blocks?"

"If I have to."

"You have to, then. On my way home from the movie just now, I passed such an interesting little place that I almost decided to stop in by myself, but I wasn't really hungry, so I didn't."

"And a good thing. Look what you'd have missed."

"Uh-huh. Such a romantic-looking dimly lighted little restaurant, nothing but candlelight—" She was looking up at his face. "Why, Joe, what's the matter?"

"Nothing," Joe said. "Or—well, I'll tell you later. It's all right now. Are you working, Ellie?"

"I found a job, but I don't start till Monday. I've two full days free before then. But, Joe, your face changed—kind of tightened up—just a minute ago when I was talking about that restaurant. What was it I said?"

"It's nothing, Ellie. Well—I suppose I might as well tell you now. It was when you said 'candlelight'; I've had a—you know what a phobia is?"

271

"Like acrophobia, when you're afraid of high places? I have that, a little. I guess most people have. And some people are afraid of closed places; I forget what that's called."

"Claustrophobia. I'm afraid of — of candles and axes. That sounds silly, doesn't it? But I know how the phobia started, and I'm getting over it. I used to have nightmares about them, but I don't anymore. It's something I'm growing out of."

"Joe, then we'll go to another restaurant."

"No, I *want* to go there. Look, Ellie, this is something childish that I've got to get over, and there's no time like now for starting. And besides, I'm almost completely over it."

"But maybe you shouldn't — "

"I should. And I'm going to tell you all about it tonight. It'll do me good to talk about it. I guess one reason I didn't get over it sooner and more completely is that I've never talked about it. Not even to Ray. Except once to a psychologist that my mother took me to see, and he explained it all to me. Is this the place?"

"Yes. Are you sure — "

"Sure, Ellie. Come on."

He was ready for the candles and the candlelight and it didn't bother him, much. He led Ellie to a booth and kept his eyes on Ellie and then, after the waitress came to them, on the menu, not looking directly at the candle until after they'd ordered. He turned and deliberately looked at it, then, and it was all right. He didn't feel anything at all.

He grinned at Ellie. "See; it's all right now. Cured."

"That's wonderful, Joe. Do you want to tell me — "

"Sure." He told her. The nursery rhyme. His waking up out of deep sleep to see the candle and the figure with the chopper.

"How horrible, Joe." She put her hand on his.

He told her about the nightmares he'd had as a child. "But it's all over now. I can even say that nursery rhyme now without worrying about it. Listen: Here comes a candle to light you to bed, And here comes a chopper to chop off your head. But that's one rhyme we're not going to teach our children if we have any. *Are* we going to have any, Ellie? I mean, do you want children?"

"I think one or two maybe. But not right away. We're young, Joe, even to get married, let alone have children right away."

"But you *will* marry me?" He was looking at her anxiously, but hurried on before she could answer. "Wait, Ellie. Don't answer yet. There's something I've got to tell you first."

He told her, briefly, everything that mattered about the entanglement with Mitch and the one crime he'd participated in.

"It puts us off to a bad start, Ellie. Over three hundred dollars in the hole. I'm going to pay back that two-seventy to Mitch and I'm going to send back, anonymously, the fifty that was my share of the holdup. If you'd rather wait to marry me until I'm in the clear—"

"Don't be silly, Joe. Think how much faster we could pay it back if we're *both* working, and married."

He sighed with relief. "I hoped you'd say that, Ellie. It's true—and besides it would have been awful to have to wait. And—about waiting; shall we go on to Waukegan tonight and get married?"

She hesitated. "Let's go tomorrow, Joe."

"But, Ellie—"

She put her hand on his again and smiled. "Haven't I told you I love you, Joe? We—we won't need separate rooms tonight even if we wait till tomorrow to—make it official."

"You're wonderful, Ellie. And I was *such* a damn fool. My God, let's get out of here. I haven't even kissed you yet."

"Can't you lean across the table Joe?"

"No, I want the first one to be a real one, without a table between us. And anyway here comes the waitress with our check. And that gives me an idea." He leaned toward the candle and blew it out.

"Joe, what?"

"Shhh. You'll find out."

The check was two dollars and ten cents. Joe put three dollars in the waitress' change tray and smiled up at her. He said, "That's even, if you don't notice a minor theft that's going to happen." He took the six inches of unburned candle out of the wall bracket and wrapped it in a paper napkin, then put it in his pocket.

The waitress obviously didn't notice. She said, "Thank *you*, sir," and left them.

Ellie frowned at him. "Joe, you're silly. Tipping ninety cents to get a nickel's worth of candle."

"A honeymoon by candlelight. What's ninety cents, Ellie?" He reached across the table and smoothed out her frown with a gentle finger. "After tomorrow we'll start worrying about saving money."

"All right Joe. Are you ready?"

Joe was ready. They walked arm in arm back to the hotel. Joe waited outside, out of sight of the desk clerk, a few niinutes after Ellie had gone in, so they wouldn't be seen going up together. Five minutes by his watch, but it seemed like five hours.

25

It was a wonderful kiss, worth waiting for; he was glad now that he hadn't kissed her across the table at the restaurant. But it ended in minor anticlimax; Ellie moved back from him and said, "Joe, what on earth—?" And looked down at his coat front at the level of his belt.

Joe laughed. "Good Lord, I'm still wearing the knife I bluffed Mitch down with." He took it out of the sheath and showed it to her. "Won it on a punchboard once. But now we ought to have it framed; it probably saved me a hell of a beating tonight."

He put it down on the nightstand and put out his arms again, and Ellie came into them.

"Oh, Ellie, I was such a damn fool."

"I was, too, Joe, to run away."

"No, Ellie. If you hadn't, maybe I wouldn't have seen things straight—in time. Ellie, shall we—?"

"Yes, Joe. Yes."

He took the candle from his pocket and unwrapped the paper napkin from around it. He looked at Ellie. "Do you mind, Ellie? I'd—I'd like to light it and leave it lit. I think it would be wonderful to go to bed by candlelight. And—Lord, if there's even a trace of my phobia left, there wouldn't be after that."

Ellie lighted it, putting it upright in the middle of an ashtray so it could burn itself out without setting fire to anything, and Joe turned out the electric light.

"It's beautiful," he said. "Dim and—just right. Put it on the dresser?" He laughed. "*Here comes a candle to light me to bed.* Oh, Ellie, that's beautiful now. Everything's beautiful."

Everything was very beautiful.

It was a little after midnight when he woke, or almost woke; not that he knew or cared what time it was. He was warm, tired, happy, snuggled up against Ellie's body. He moved enough to put his arm back around her and cup her breast in his hand. Still half asleep, he snuggled more closely against her, knowing only that he was more happy, more contented, than he had ever been before in his life.

There was dim light against his closed eyelids, but he didn't remember or care what it was.

Drifting. Nine-tenths asleep now. The light. Oh, yes; *here comes a candle to light you to bed.* Beautiful, but— He stirred restlessly. There was something that came after that. Something horrible, but he couldn't remember what it was. The candle was beautiful, he knew now; he'd been afraid of it, too, but it was the other thing, not the candle, the—forget it. Go back to sleep.

Don't remember, try not to remember, But you're going to remember; you're dreaming—no, you're awake. All right, get it off your mind. The rest of it. You know. *Here comes a chopper to chop off your head.* Only that's silly; there isn't any chopper. Why not? There'd been a candle to light him to bed. Was it still there, still burning? The dim light against his closed eyelids. Too near asleep to open them. Forget. Closer to Ellie. There isn't any—

The loud sudden knock at the door.

He sat up, and Ellie was sitting up, too, and he clamped his hand quickly over her mouth so she wouldn't scream or wouldn't say anything that—whoever or whatever was outside the door would hear.

The knock again, louder. Ellie as scared as he; she was rigid, not struggling to get loose from his tight hold. Be very quiet. Someone outside saying something. Footsteps.

Going away? A crash of glass. Footsteps coming back. The knock again.

He glanced in sudden stark terror at the candle and then back at the door just as the crashing sound came and the bright blade of the ax bit clear through the thin wood on the first stroke and caught the gleam of candlelight.

The candle that lighted him to bed.

And here comes.

He let go of Ellie but only to save her first. He grabbed for the knife lying on the nightstand beside the bed —

The blade of the chopper came through the door again.

Psychopathic Killer Slays Girl, Self

RACINE, WIS., Sept. 11 (AP) — Shortly after midnight last night police broke their way into the hotel room of Ellen Dravich, 19, Milwaukee, seconds too late to prevent a murder and a suicide. Joseph Bailey, 19, also of Milwaukee, fatally stabbed Miss Dravich and then himself while police, after their knocking had not been answered, were chopping through the door with a fire axe from a case in the hotel corridor.

The police were acting on information from Mike Dravich, Milwaukee, an uncle of the murdered girl. Early in the evening, according to Dravich, Bailey had called on him and demanded the address of his niece, who had left Milwaukee the day before in order to avoid the unwelcome attentions of Bailey.

Appeared Demented

Dravich said Bailey appeared to be demented and had had a knife in his possession. He had refused to give Bailey the address and had called police, but had been unable to detain Bailey until the police arrived.

Dravich had gone to his restaurant on Wells St. after that and had worked until almost midnight. On his return to his room at the Tower Hotel he recalled that a letter from Miss Dravich had been on a desk in the room in which Bailey had been alone for a few minutes. He looked for the letter and found Bailey had stolen it.

Squad Car Sent

He immediately called the police to tell them Bailey had obtained the address and he feared for the girl's safety. Milwaukee police phoned Racine police and a squad car was dispatched to the hotel, arriving just too late to prevent the crime.

Both Miss Dravich and Bailey died immediately.

Bailey was not known to Milwaukee police and does not appear on their records but, according to Dravich, he was a small-time criminal and a hanger-on of the numbers racket.

The Joke

The big man in the flashy green suit stuck his big hand across the cigar counter. "Jim Greeley," he said. "Ace Novelty Company." The cigar dealer took the offered hand and then jerked convulsively as something inside it buzzed painfully against his own palm.

The big man's cheerful laughter boomed. "Our Joy Buzzer," he said, turning over his hand to expose the little metal contraption in his palm. "Changes a shake to a shock; one of the best numbers we got. A dilly, ain't it? Gimme four of those perfectos, the two-for-a-quarters. Thanks."

He put a half-dollar on the counter and then, concealing a grin, lighted one of the cigars while the dealer tried vainly to pick up the coin. Then, laughing, the big man put another coin—an ungimmicked one—on the counter and pried up the first one with a tricky little knife on one end of his watch chain. He put it back in a special little box that went into his vest pocket. He said, "A new number—but a pretty good one. It's a good laugh, and—well, 'Anything for a Gag' is Ace's motto and me, I'm Ace's salesman."

The cigar dealer said, "I couldn't handle—"

"Not trying to sell you anything," the big man said. "I just sell wholesale. But I get a kick out of showing off our merchandise. You ought to see some of it."

He blew a ring of cigar smoke and strolled on past the cigar counter to the hotel desk. "Double with bath," he told the clerk. "Got a reservation—Jim Greeley. Stuff's being sent over from the station, and my wife'll be here later."

He took a fountain pen from his pocket, ignoring the one the clerk offered him, and signed the card. The ink was bright blue, but it was going to be a good joke on the clerk when, a little later, he tried to file that card and found it completely blank. And when he explained and wrote a new card it would be both a good laugh and good advertising for Ace Novelty.

"Leave the key in the box," he said. "I won't go up now. Where are the phones?"

He strolled to the row of phone booths to which the desk clerk directed him and dialed a number. A feminine voice answered.

"This is the police," he said gruffly. "We've had reports that you've been renting rooms to crooked boarders. Or were those only false roomers?"

"Jim! Oh, I'm so glad you're in town!"

"So'm I, sweetie. Is the coast clear, your husband away? Wait, don't tell me; you wouldn't have said what you just said if he'd been there, would you? What time does he get home?"

"Nine o'clock, Jim. You'll pick me up before then? I'll

282

leave him a note I'm staying with my sister because she's sick."

"Swell, honey. What I hoped you'd say. Let's see; it's half-past five. I'll be right around."

"Not that soon, Jim. I've got things to do, and I'm not dressed. Make it—not before eight o'clock. Between then and half-past eight."

"Okay, honey. Eight it is. That'll give us time for a big evening, and I've already registered double."

"How'd you know I'd be able to get away?"

The big man laughed. "Then I'd have called one of the others in my little black book. Now don't get mad; I was only kidding. I'm calling from the hotel, but I haven't actually registered yet; I was only kidding. One thing I like about you, Marie, you got a sense of humor; you can take it. Anybody I like's got to have a sense of humor like I have."

"Anybody you *like?*"

"And anybody I love. To pieces. What's your husband like, Marie? Has *he* got a sense of humor?"

"A little. A crazy kind of one; not like yours. Got any new numbers in your line?"

"Some dillies. I'll show you. One of 'em's a trick camera that — well, I'll show you. And don't worry, honey. I remember you told me you got a tricky ticker and I won't pull any scary tricks on you. Won't scare you, honey; just the opposite."

"You big goof! Okay, Jim, not before eight o'clock now. But plenty before nine."

"With bells on, honey. Be seeing you."

He went out of the telephone booth singing "Tonight's My Night with Baby," and straightened his snazzy necktie at a mirror in front of a pillar in the lobby. He ran an exploring palm across his face. Yes, needed a shave; it felt rough even if it didn't show. Well, plenty of time for that in two and a half hours.

He strolled over to where a bellboy sat. "How late you on duty, son?" he asked.

"Till two-thirty, nine hours. I just came on."

"Good. How are rules here on likker? Get it any time?"

"Can't get bottle goods after nine o'clock. That is, well, sometimes you can, but it's taking a chance. Can't I get it for you sooner if you're going to want it?"

"Might as well." The big man took some bills out of his wallet. "Room 603. Put in a fifth of rye and two bottles of soda sometime before nine. I'll phone down for ice cubes when we want 'em. And listen, I want you to help me with a gag. Got any bedbugs or cockroaches?"

"Huh?"

The big man grinned. "Maybe you have and maybe you haven't, but look at these artificial ones. Ain't they beauties?" He took a pillbox from his pocket and opened it.

"Want to play a joke on my wife," he said. "And I won't be up in the room till she gets here. You take these and put 'em where they'll do the most good, see? I mean, peel back the covers and fill the bed with these little beauties. Don't they look like real ones? She'll really squeal when she sees 'em. Do you like gags, son?"

"Sure."

"I'll show you some good ones when you bring up the ice cubes later. I got a sample case full. Well, do a good job with those bedbugs."

He winked solemnly at the bellboy and sauntered across the lobby and out to the sidewalk.

He strolled into a tavern and ordered rye with a chaser. While the bartender was getting it he went over to the jukebox and put a dime in, pushing two buttons. He came back grinning, and whistling "Got a Date with an Angel." The jukebox joined in – in the wrong key – with his whistling.

"You look happy," said the bartender. "Most guys come in here to tell their troubles."

"Haven't got any troubles," said the big man. "Happier because I found an oldie on your jukebox and it fits. Only the angel I got a date with's got a little devil in her too, thank God. Real she-devil, too."

He put his hand across the bar. "Shake the hand of a happy man," he said.

The buzzer in his palm buzzed and the bartender jumped.

The big man laughed. "Have a drink with me, pal," he said, "and don't get mad. I like practical jokes. I sell 'em."

The bartender grinned, but not too enthusiastically. He said, "You got the build for it all right. Okay, I'll have a drink with you. Only just a second; there's a hair in that chaser I gave you." He emptied the glass and put it among the dirties, coming back with another one, this one of cut glass of intricate design.

"Nice try," said the big man, "but I told you I *sell* the stuff; I know a dribble glass when I see one. Besides, that's an old model. Just one hole on a side and if you get your finger over it, it don't dribble. See, like this. Happy days."

The dribble glass didn't dribble. The big man said, "I'll buy us both another; I like a guy who can dish a job out as well as take one." He chuckled. "*Try* to dish one out, anyway. Pour us another and lemme tell you about some of the new stuff we're gonna put out. New plastic called Skintex that – hey, I got a sample with me. Lookit."

He took from his pocket a rolled-up object that unrolled itself, as he put it on the bar, into a startlingly lifelike false face. The big man said, "Got it all over every kind of mask or false face on the market, even the expensive rubber ones. Fits so close it stays on practically of its own accord. But what's really different about it is by gosh it looks so real you have to look twice and look close to see it ain't the real McCoy. Gonna be an all-year-round seller for costume balls and stuff, and make a fortune every Halloween."

"Sure looks real," said the bartender.

"Bet your boots it does. Comes in all kinds, it will. Got only a few actually in production now, though. This one's the Fancy Dan model, good looking. Pour us two more, huh?"

He rolled up the mask and put it back into his pocket. The jukebox had just ended the second number and he fed a quarter into it, again punching "Got a Date with an Angel," but this time waiting to whistle until the record had started, so he'd be in tune with it.

He changed it to patter when he got back to the bar. He said, "Got a date with an angel, all right. Little blonde, Marie Rhymer. A beauty. Purtiest gal in town. Here's to 'er."

This time he forgot to put his finger over the hole in the dribble glass and got spots of water on his snazzy necktie. He looked down at them and roared with laughter. He ordered drinks for the house—not too expensive a procedure, as there was only one other customer and the bartender.

The other customer bought back and the big man bought another round. He showed them two new coin tricks—in one of which he balanced a quarter on the edge of a shot glass after he'd let them examine both the glass and the coin, and he wouldn't tell the bartender how that one was done until the bartender stood a round.

It was after seven when he left the tavern. He wasn't drunk, but he was feeling the drinks. He was really happy now. Ought to grab a bite to eat, he thought.

He looked around for a restaurant, a good one, and then decided no, maybe Marie would be expecting him to take her to dinner; he'd wait to eat until he was with her.

And so what if he got there early? He could wait, he could talk to her while she got ready.

He looked around for a taxi and saw none; he started walking briskly, again whistling "Tonight's My Night with Baby," which hadn't, unfortunately, been on the jukebox.

He walked briskly, whistling happily, into the gathering dusk. He was going to be early, but he didn't want to stop for another drink; there'd be plenty of drinking later, and right now he felt just right.

It wasn't until he was a block away that he remembered the shave he'd meant to get. He stopped and felt his face, and yes, he really needed one. Luck was with him, too, because only a few doors back he'd passed a little hole-in-the-wall barber shop. He retraced his steps and found it open. There was one barber and no customers.

He started in, then changed his mind and, grinning happily, went on to the areaway between that building and the next. He took the Skintex mask from his pocket and slipped it over his face; be a good gag to see what the barber would do if he sat down in the chair for a shave with that mask on. He was grinning so broadly he had trouble getting the mask on smoothly, until he straightened out his face.

He walked into the barbershop, hung his hat on the rack and sat down in the chair. His voice only a bit muffled by the flexible mask, he said, "Shave, please."

As the barber, who had taken his stand by the side of the chair, bent closer in incredulous amazement, the big man in the green suit couldn't hold in his laughter any longer. The mask slipped as his laughter boomed out. He took it off and held it out for examination. "Purty lifelike, ain't it?" he asked when he could quit laughing.

"Sure is," said the little barber admiringly. "Say, who makes those?"

"My company. Ace Novelty."

"I'm with a group that puts on amateur theatricals," the barber said. "Say, we could use some of those—for comic roles mainly, if they come in comic faces. Do they?"

"They do. We're manufacturers and wholesalers, of course. But you'll be able to get them at Brachman & Minton's, here in town. I call on 'em tomorrow, and I'll load them up. How's about that shave, meanwhile. Got a date with an angel."

"Sure," said the little man. "Brachman & Minton. We buy most of our makeup and costumes there already. That's fine." He rinsed a towel under the hot-water faucet, wrung it out. He put it over the big man's face and made lather in his shaving cup.

Under the hot towel the man in the green suit was humming "Got a Date with an Angel." The barber took off the towel and applied the lather with deft strokes.

"Yep," said the big man, "got a date with an angel and I'm too damn' early. Gimme the works—massage, anything you got. Wish I could look as handsome with my real face as with that there mask—that's our Fancy Dan model, by the way. Y'oughta see some of the others. Well, you will if you go to Brachman & Minton's about a week from now. Take about that long before they get the merchandise after I take their order tomorrow."

"Yes, sir," said the barber. "You said the works? Massage *and* facial?" He stropped the razor, started its neat, clean strokes.

"Why not? Got time. And tonight's my night with baby. *Some* number, pal. Pageboy blonde, built like you-know-what. Runs a rooming house not far from—Say, I got an idea. Good gag."

"What?"

"I'll fool 'er. I'll wear that Fancy Dan mask when I knock on the door and I'll make her think somebody *really* good-looking is calling on her. Maybe it'll be a letdown when she sees my homely mug when I take it off, but the gag'll be good. And I'll bet she won't be *too* disappointed when she sees it's good old Jim. Yep. I'll do that."

The big man chuckled in anticipation. "What time's it?" he asked. He was getting a little sleepy. The shave was over, and the kneading motion of the massage was soporific.

"Ten of eight."

"Good. Lots of time. Just so I get there well before nine. That's when—Say, did that mask really fool you when I walked in with it?"

"Sure did," the barber told him. "Until I bent over you after you sat down."

"Good. Then it'll fool Marie Rhymer when I go up to the door. Say, what's the name of your amatcher theatrical outfit? I'll tell Brachman you'll want some of the Skintex numbers."

"Just the Grove Avenue Social Center group. My name's Dane. Brachman knows me. Sure, tell him we'll take some."

Hot towels, cool creams, kneading fingers. The man in green dozed.

"Okay, mister," the barber said. "You're all set. Be a dollar sixty-five." He chuckled. "I even put your mask on so you're all set. Good luck."

The big man sat up and glanced in the mirror. "Swell," he said. He stood up and took two singles out of his wallet. "That's even now. G'night."

He put on his hat and went out. It was getting dark now and a glance at his wristwatch showed him it was almost eight-thirty, perfect timing.

He started humming again, back this time to "Tonight's My Night with Baby."

He wanted to whistle, but he couldn't do that with the false face on. He stopped in front of the house and looked around before he went up the steps to the door. He chuckled a little as he took the VACANCY sign off the nail beside the door and held it as he pressed the button and heard the bell sound.

Only seconds passed before he heard her footsteps clicking to the door. It opened, and he bowed slightly. His voice muffled by the mask so she wouldn't recognize it, he said, "You haff—a rrrooom, blease?"

She was beautiful, all right, as beautiful as he remembered her from the last time he'd been in town a month before. She said hesitantly, "Why, yes, but I'm afraid I can't show it to you tonight. I'm expecting a friend and I'm late getting ready."

He made a jerky little bow. He said, "Vee, moddomm, I vill rrreturrrn."

And then, jerking his chin forward to loosen the mask and pinching it loose at the forehead so it would come loose with his hat, he lifted hat and mask.

He grinned and started to say — well, it didn't matter what he'd started to say, because Marie Rhymer screamed and then dropped into a crumpled heap of purple silk and cream-colored flesh and blonde hair just inside the door. Stunned, the big man dropped the sign he'd been holding and bent over her. He said, "Marie, honey, what—" and quickly stepped inside and closed the door. He bent down and—remembering her "tricky ticker"—put his hand over where her heart should be beating. *Should* be, but wasn't.

He got out of there quickly. With a wife and kid of his own back in Minneapolis, he couldn't be—Well, he got out.

Still stunned, he walked quickly out.

He came to the barbershop, and it was dark. He stopped in front of the door. The dark glass of the door, with a street light shining against it from across the way, was both transparent and a mirror. In it, he saw three things.

He saw, in the mirror part of the door, the face of horror that was his own face. Bright green, with careful expert shadowing that made it the face of a walking corpse, a ghoul with sunken eyes and cheeks and blue lips. The bright-green face mirrored above the green suit and the snazzy red tie—the face that the makeup expert barber must have put on him while he'd dozed—

And the note, stuck against the inside of the glass of the barbershop door, written on white paper in green pencil:

CLOSED
DANE RHYMER

Marie Rhymer, Dane Rhymer, he thought dully. While *through* the glass, inside the dark barbershop, he could see it dimly—the white-clad figure of the little barber as it dangled from the chandelier and turned slowly, left to right, right to left, left to right...

It's Only Everything

This morning a quite handsome and very young man came to our door. He was, it turned out, a Jehovah's Witness and had come to bring me salvation. Probably to sell me something too, but the conversation never quite got around to that.

I told him that I was an ardent atheist, but this did not discourage him in the slightest. He kept on talking and I, hung over and in pajamas, kept on listening—because in seeing him I saw myself, in a way in which I *could* have gone, *if* there were a God and *if* upon a certain occasion he had deigned to alter a miniscule part of the cosmos and perform a miracle for me. *I* was the persuasive young man, sans miracle.

This is a bitch piece, and what I am bitching about is the apathy of Christians—of members of most religions, but since I am writing of this country, mostly of Christians, so-called.

I can best lead up to telling what I'm bitching about by telling of my own experience as a Christian, back when. Perhaps I should say as an almost-Christian; I saw a truth that very few Christians see, but still I never quite made the grade. The turning point came with my mother's death, when I was fourteen years old.

My parents were not religious people; my father was an admitted atheist, my mother a mild agnostic. Nevertheless, they came to the conclusion, when I was eight or nine years old, that I, their only child, should for my own sake be exposed to religion, should be given a choice. For my sake they joined a church —Presbyterian as it happened, probably because it was the nearest one—and enrolled me in its Sunday school. A few years later (they grabbed 'em young in those days) I was "confirmed" and became an actual member of the church.

The years of my life between nine and fourteen were, thanks to this exposure to Christianity, the most mixed-up period of my life. I thank the God in whom I do not believe that they are long over.

You see, I was cursed with logic. Even so young, I realized that the lukewarm, passive Christian against whom I am bitching, and who made up—then and now—the vast majority of my contemporaries, could not see or did not choose to see, what to me was immediately obvious: the simple fact that in the acceptance of a *revealed* religion, and particularly Christianity in any of its forms, there are no shades of gray. Either there is personal immortality or there isn't. Either the son of God—and the son of God in a very special sense, not in the sense in which we might

294

all be sons of God—was crucified to save us, or he wasn't. (Proofreader, please don't make that he into a He.) If he was, and arose from the dead, then that fact transcends in importance *all else.* In that case our brief stay here on Earth is only preparation for Eternity, and belief in Christ and salvation through him is the only thing in life even worth considering. *Nothing* else should matter.

I was torn, unable to understand (as I am still unable to understand) people, my contemporaries and predecessors, who give or gave lip service to the special divinity of Christ and the worship of God and who do or did spend less than their full time and effort and thought in carrying his gospel to the ends of the Earth—and to the rest of the universe, whenever we get there.

It seemed to me, and still seems to me, simple common sense. I think Christianity is superstition, but if it *isn't* there is no Mister In-between; it's the *only* thing that matters a good God damn. Either God, through his son, has revealed himself to us, or he hasn't.

Yes, I remember my mother's death. But more vividly I remember the occasion, a few weeks before it, when I learned—and it came to me suddenly—that her death was inevitable and imminent. I'd known she was ill. I'd even known it was cancer. But doctors had given a note of hope, and I'd never *let* myself believe the truth, or I'd shoved it into the back of my mind and refused even to consider it. My mother just *couldn't die.* Then I learned that she *would.*

I ran out of the house crying. The pathetic fallacy was its usual pathetic self: there should have been thunder, lightning, high wind and a driving rain. But there was none of these things, nor even darkness, except inside my soul. It was a balmy spring evening and the streets of Cincinnati were brightly lighted. As I ran until I was breathless and then walked, for many miles, I prayed—God, how I prayed. And went beyond prayer to promise God that if he would cure my mother, would pass the miracle of making her well again, I would devote the rest of my life to him, would become a missionary to Darkest Africa or wherever he might send me.

I remember the night of my mother's death. I had been sent away from home and was staying the night with our Presbyterian minister. (He loved to have boys sleep with him; he made no passes but found every excuse for physical contact and chaste caresses—what a poor, tortured guy *he* must have been. And what a good man.)

I heard the phone ring in the middle of the night and heard him answer it, knew from his end of the conversation that my mother had just died.

I played possum when he came back to bed, but I was very wide awake. I felt grief, of course, but my passion had already been spent and my grief was calm. Mostly my feeling was one of relief; I was saved from a fate worse than my mother's death.

I knew that I had *not* believed, that Christianity except for a part of its code of ethics and by no means all of that, was a mess of crap. Or superstition, for those who find that last word offensive. It was *such* a relief to be able to become, or to admit that I was and really had been all along, an atheist. To know that henceforth I could be governed by mind unwarped.

All this went through my mind this morning, forty years later, while I stood, half awake, listening to that very pleasant and very sincere young man who was a Jehovah's Witness. I was honest with him, but gentle.

Because I saw in him again, all over and clearly as I saw at the age of fourteen, that either he was right or I was right, and that there is and can be nothing in between.

And, listening to him I thought the obvious: that there, but for the grace of God in not existing, or at best or worst for his grace in not concerning himself with the affairs of mice and men and not giving a damn about a sparrow's fall or mine, went I. The I that might have been had he fooled me and passed a miracle.

I dug that young man. He was wrong and silly, but I dug him. I dig St Francis of Assisi and Jesus of Nazareth, and whirling dervishes and anybody else who goeth whole hog with the courage of his convictions. I may not like him, but I understand him. I cannot and never will understand, and hereby spit in the eye of, any passive believer in a revealed religion who gives less than his whole life and thought to what, if it be true, is a matter of such personal and cosmic import that nothing else is worth a thinker's damn.

green press INITIATIVE

Millipede Press is committed to preserving ancient forests and natural resources. We elected to print *Here Comes a Candle* on 50% post consumer recycled paper, processed chlorine free. As a result, for this printing, we have saved:

24 Trees (40' tall and 6-8" wide)
10,066 Gallons of Waste Water
13.9 Million BTU's (Total Energy)
1,110 Pounds of Solid Waste
2,191 Pounds of Greenhouse Gases

Millipede Press made this paper choice because our printer, Friesens Corporation, is a member of Green Press Initiative, a nonprofit program dedicated to supporting authors, publishers, and suppliers in their efforts to reduce their use of fiber obtained from endangered forests.

For more information, visit www.greenpressinitiative.org

CW01022271

A KILLING near WATERLOO STATION

Book 5 in the Mayfair 100 series

Lynn Brittney

IRIS BOOKS

IRIS BOOKS

First published by Iris Books, London in 2023

Iris Books is an imprint of Write Publications Ltd

© Lynn Brittney

The rights of Lynn Brittney to be identified as the author of this book
have been asserted, in accordance with the Copyright, Designs and Patents Act
1988. This publication is protected under the Copyright laws currently existing
in every country throughout the world.

ISBN 978-1-907147-87-6

All rights reserved. No part of this publication may be reproduced,
stored in a retrieval system, or transmitted, in any form or by any means
without the prior written permission of the publisher. Any person who does
any unauthorised act in relation to this publication may be liable to
criminal prosecution and civil claims for damages.
This book is sold subject to the condition that it shall not, by way of trade
or otherwise, be lent, resold, hired out or otherwise circulated without the
publisher's prior consent, in any form of binding or cover other than that in
which it is published and without a similar condition including this condition
being imposed on the subsequent purchaser.

Design by Kate Lowe

Printed in the United Kingdom

This book is dedicated to the heroic,
but largely unknown, government departments,
The Pigeon Carrier Service and
The Train Watcher's Units, who provided
invaluable service to the Allied war effort.

Cover photograph courtesy of The National Railway Museum.

The author would like to acknowledge the valuable and detailed research done by:

Panayi, Panikos, *Prisoners of Britain, German civilian and combatant internees during the First World War,* published by Manchester 1824 (Manchester University Press).

Foley, Michael, *Prisoners of the British, Internees and Prisoners of War during the First World War,* published by Fonthill Media.

Lt. Col. A.H Osman, *Pigeons in the Great War, A complete history of the Carrier Pigeon Service during the Great War 1914-1918,* facsimile edition published by The Naval and Military Press Ltd.

Bird, J.C, *Control of Enemy Aliens in Great Britain, 1914-1918,* published by Routledge Revivals, part of the Routledge, Taylor & Francis Group.

Landau, Henry, *The Spy Net, The Greatest Intelligence Operations of the First World War,* published by Biteback Publishing.

Greenwood, John Ormerod, *Quaker Encounters, Volume 1, Friends and Relief,* published by William Sessions Ltd.

Fry, A.Ruth, *A Quaker Adventure, The story of Nine Years' Relief and Reconstruction in Europe,* published by Friends Service Council.

Also, special thanks to the following organisations:

The Society of Friends

The Port of London Authority

The Western Front Association

The Imperial War Museum

Network Rail

CONTENTS

CHAPTER 1:   The Brutality of a Modern War   1

CHAPTER 2:   Innocent Alien Enemies   17

CHAPTER 3:   Trouble from the Sky Again   34

CHAPTER 4:   An Abduction in the Night   47

CHAPTER 5:   Fumes and Feathers   59

CHAPTER 6:   Are the Pigeons Important?   71

CHAPTER 7:   "Where are the Women?"   88

CHAPTER 8:   The Search Along the River   101

CHAPTER 9:   The Mystery Corpse   114

CHAPTER 10:   The Secrets in the Clothes   130

CHAPTER 11:   Who is WL?   149

CHAPTER 12:   Diplomatic Intrigues   161

CHAPTER 13:   Thelma's Secrets   178

CHAPTER 14:   Missing in Action   195

CHAPTER 15:   Too Many Fingers in this Pie!   211

CHAPTER 16:   New Friends   224

CHAPTER 17:   Mattie gets her Wish   237

CHAPTER 18:   The Watchers are Watched   252

CHAPTER 19:   A Two-Pronged Attack   267

CHAPTER 20:   A Government Crisis   281

EPILOGUE: 296

A Reminder...

During World War One, there was a mass exodus from London of tens of thousands of young men, who volunteered for the armed services to fight the Germans and Austrians. These men left behind jobs, which were quickly filled by women.

But there were two London workforces they were not allowed to join – the Metropolitan Police and the City of London Police. Some determined women's organisations set up 'volunteer' women's police bodies. They had no legal powers and Scotland Yard grudgingly used them as factory supervisors, for crowd control and for air raid management.

Chief Inspector Peter Beech, in May 1915, was called to a case where a young aristocratic woman, Lady Murcheson, was implicated in her husband's murder but she refused to speak to a man. This situation led him to ask the fairly progressive Commissioner of the Metropolitan Police, Sir Edward Henry, if he could set up a secret team of, mostly, amateur female detectives, who would be assisted by hand-picked regular policemen, to deal with certain crimes. The Commissioner agreed and the team was set up in Mayfair – telephone number Mayfair 100.

The team consists of Chief Inspector Beech (invalided out of the army with a damaged leg), Detective Sergeant Arthur Tollman (a retired detective of great experience, who had come back into the force at the outbreak of war) and young Constable Billy Rigsby (former professional soldier and boxer, invalided out of the war with a scarred face and damaged hand).

The female members of the team are Doctor Caroline Allardyce (works at the Women's Hospital in Euston), Miss Mabel Summersby (pharmacist at the Women's Hospital and lover of forensic science and cameras), Mrs Victoria Ellingham (received legal training but women were not allowed to practice as lawyers), Lady Maud Winterborne (mother of Victoria Ellingham), and Constable Rigsby's mother, Elsie, and aunt, Sissy. From time to time the team call upon the expertise or assistance of others, who may have special talents or knowledge.

The Mayfair 100 series © Lynn Brittney

CHAPTER ONE

LONDON, OCTOBER 1915

THE BRUTALITY OF A MODERN WAR

Edith Cavell, a 49 year-old, genteel, middle class English nurse had been shot as a spy by the Germans. Britain was outraged.

Breakfast in Lady Maud's house in Mayfair was a sombre affair as Maud, Caroline, Victoria, Billy and Tollman surveyed the many newspapers scattered across the table. The Times had produced the first shock of the day as it fell through the letterbox, its lurid headlines proclaiming the barbaric execution, by the Germans, of a woman. Lady Maud had immediately dispatched Billy to buy as many different newspapers as possible, "even the tabloids – I shall make an exception just this once," she said dramatically, as though she was confessing to imbibing an illicit glass of cheap sherry.

By the time Peter Beech arrived, with his own copy of the Daily Telegraph, Lady Maud was reading out loud an account in the Guardian of Nurse Cavell's heroic death, pausing now and then to wipe away a tear.

"The heroism shown by Miss Cavell and some weeks ago by Mme. Louise Frenay, who was executed at Liege, influenced, says the correspondent, even the German firing squads, of whom the majority did not aim at the victims. The result in the case of Mme Frenay was that she was wounded in the leg, while Miss Cavell was hit by only one of the twelve bullets, the commanding officer in each case being obliged to give a *coup de grace* by shooting the wounded woman with a revolver placed at the ear." Maud's voice trembled as she fought back against her distress. Tollman tutted and shook his head. Billy's face became quite red with rage, whilst everyone else's faces were just a picture of sorrow.

"It says here," said Caroline quietly, indicating another newspaper, "that the German military chaplain was with her to the end and afterwards gave her a Christian burial. So, I suppose that's important."

"It comes to something when they are now executing women," murmured Tollman.

Victoria, ever logical, replied "Yes, but if she really was a spy, I suppose that under German military law, they feel that they were entitled to execute her."

"Victoria!" Maud rebuked her daughter sharply, "The Germans have shown over and over again that there is no depth of barbarity to which they will not sink! First, they decide to bomb women and children in Britain with their dreadful Zeppelins, then they decide to use poison gas on our troops…"

"Apparently, we have now used poison gas *against* the Germans in Loos," Beech pointed out.

"Two wrongs don't make a right!" snapped Caroline and Beech rolled his eyes at Tollman.

"All I am saying, Caroline, is that this war – this type of war in which we are now engaged – seems to have unleashed levels of barbarity on both sides, that we have never known before." Beech was trying to be reasonable.

"But our side has never shot any women as spies. Have we, sir?" asked Billy, flushed and in a righteous mood.

"Not yet," countered Beech, "but our allies have shot them."

There was a murmur of protestation around the table but Beech persisted. "Since this war began, the French and the Belgians have executed several women accused of being German spies. It just hasn't been reported in the press but I have seen the official statements."

There was a stunned silence and everyone looked at Beech with a mixture of horror and embarrassment. He rashly decided to continue. "We have several German spies being detained in prison, in Britain, at the moment and two of them are women. They have yet to be sentenced. I have no idea whether the women, if found guilty, will be shot but the men certainly will. You have to realise…" he looked around at everyone, "…that this is *war*. If women are doing the jobs of men, then they put themselves in harm's way, like men. The women who work in munitions run the risk of being a target for sabotage or bombing, just like the men who worked there before them. If they are working as spies, they run the risk of the ultimate penalty, just like the men."

Tollman nodded, understanding Beech's explanation, and the women around Maud's breakfast table were forced to swallow the bitter pill of equality in wartime. Billy Rigsby, however, found it difficult to accept that chivalry was completely dead.

"Well, I wouldn't shoot a woman – spy or no spy," he said firmly and was rewarded by a smile from Caroline and a pat on the hand from Lady Maud.

Tollman decided to change the subject and tapped his finger on an article in The Times that had been pushed off the front page by Nurse Cavell. "Has anyone registered that Bulgaria has entered the war now, on the German side?"

Lady Maud snorted derisively, "Well, Bulgaria's such a small country, Mr Tollman, I doubt whether it will make much difference in numbers to the enemy."

Tollman nodded, "That is true, Lady Maud, but unfortunately, it will make a difference to police work in Britain."

Caroline looked quizzical. "How so, Mr Tollman?"

"Because, Doctor, we shall now have to round up all Bulgarian men and put them in internment camps with the Germans, Austrians and Hungarians. I hazard a guess that, at any one time, there are probably at least a thousand Bulgarians in London. That's a lot of manpower and time required from the Metropolitan and City police forces." Tollman looked disgruntled at the thought.

Beech suddenly remembered the real reason he had come round so Mayfair so early this morning. "Good Lord! I quite forgot! The Commissioner called me in at an ungodly hour this morning to tell me that all able-bodied policemen will be on protection duty in London today. Because of the Edith Cavell story in all the newspapers, he is expecting a rash of retribution. We are to offer our assistance in protecting any women of foreign extraction whose businesses or homes might be attacked or looted by a vengeful British public. Sir Edward feels that it will be worse than the aftermath of the sinking of the Lusitania."

Caroline hurriedly gulped down the last of her lukewarm tea. "In which case," she said, making for the hallway, "I had better get over to the hospital as soon as possible. After the Lusitania revenge attacks, our wards were flooded with women who had been beaten, or whose faces were cut by breaking glass in shop windows. It wasn't pretty at all."

"I shall never forgive the Germans for dragging everyone down to the level of beasts," Lady Maud said with feeling, "but no matter how much I despise them, I could not bring myself to take vengeance on innocent people who just happen to have Germanic names. What has this war done to everybody?"

"What indeed, Lady Maud," said Tollman, wearily getting up from his chair to face the task of policing the streets. "I, for one, am getting too old to take on ignorant thugs who decide to amuse themselves with a bit of foreigner-bashing. Billy," he tapped Rigsby on the shoulder, "You and I had best get back to headquarters and get allocated a district to patrol. I'll insist that we stick together. I need your brawn and you need my brains."

Billy laughed and went to collect his greatcoat. The weather was definitely autumnal now and if he was going to pace the streets, he wanted to be warm.

Beech suggested that he accompany them but first he counselled Maud and Victoria to stay indoors today. "I doubt that any troublemakers will come Mayfair way. They'll probably be heading for the east and north of London, where they know there are a lot of German-owned bakeries, cafes and other businesses – but you never know. No sense in going out if you don't have to." Lady Maud agreed and said she would also keep the staff indoors as well.

"Come back for supper tonight," she said to the men as they left. "We want to hear about your experiences today."

"Do we really, Mother?" Victoria asked, after the policemen had gone. "I for one have read about enough brutality in Belgium and France today, without hearing about Londoners letting everyone down by brutalizing women and children in their homes."

Mother and daughter sat in silence, contemplating the horror of what the day might bring, out on the streets.

"You're right, my dear," said Maud, after a while. "Let's clear away these newspapers and offer a silent prayer for everyone in London today who bears a foreign name."

* * *

Tollman and Billy Rigsby were strolling purposefully along the Commercial Road in Whitechapel, keeping alert for any signs of trouble. Policemen usually based at Scotland Yard had been dispersed to help out in, as Chief Inspector Beech had stated, the east and the north of London, where the second-generation European immigrants lived and ran their businesses. Even though it was not yet past ten in the morning, distant sounds of shouting, breaking glass, police whistles and the clanging bells of police wagons could be heard. The Commercial Road, usually a busy throughfare, bustling with horse-driven carts, motor vehicles and people, was as quiet as the grave.

"It's unnerving," observed Billy, "not a soul around anywhere."

"Not surprising though," replied Tollman. "The minute

those newspapers hit the streets this morning, everyone knew there would be trouble, and sensible people are staying indoors or staying away from the places where rioting is likely to occur."

Suddenly, a group of men, carrying wooden sticks and faces set with grim determination, came running out of a side street. At the sight of Constable Rigsby, with his intimidating height and bulk, they slowed down and attempted to conceal their makeshift weapons.

"Oy!" shouted Tollman, pointing at the men, "Put those sticks down!"

"Do as you're told!" shouted Billy, picking up speed, "Or we'll nick the lot of you!"

The men reluctantly handed over the implements, some of which were very nasty indeed, being improvised clubs with nails protruding from them.

"Names and addresses," said Tollman curtly, taking out his notebook and pencil. "And don't think about giving us the runaround with false details because we will find you anyway. I've got a particular memory for faces. You, for example..." and he pointed at a young man with ginger hair and a beard, whose face instantly flushed. "By the look of you, I'm willing to bet that you are related to that charming Scots family of villains – the Drummonds." The man's face flushed a deeper red and Tollman knew he had hit his mark.

"What do you need our names and addresses for? We ain't done nothing," complained another of the group.

"Well, that's the point, isn't it?" said Tollman sarcastically. "If you do foolishly decide to commit a crime, we know what you look like, what your names are and where to find you? See? It's what we policemen call 'a deterrent'."

"A what?"

Tollman sighed. "Look, son, as it stands, me and my colleague here could nick the lot of you for carrying weapons with the intent to use them. Got it?" The group of young men nodded. Tollman continued. "But we are not going to nick you, we are going to let you off with a caution...thank you very much, sir...don't mention it..." Billy grinned as Tollman carried on a conversation with himself and then continued, "But I want your names and addresses because it is obvious that you lot are so thick that you think you can just carry on as if nothing had happened. And I'm telling you that if I find that so much as a window has been broken or an old lady upset in the next half a mile, I'm sending a whole posse of policemen round to your homes and I'm pinning whatever happens on YOU. Got it now?"

The men all looked uncomfortable and the one who had questioned Tollman was the first to mumble his name and address to be scribbled in the book. Meanwhile, Billy went to find the nearest row of dustbins, outside a pub, and put all the homemade wooden clubs inside, then emptied the slimy contents of another dustbin on top of them.

"Just in case you thought that once we were round the corner, you could help yourself to your nasty weapons, I thought you might like to know that they are all covered in pig swill now and you might think better of it." He winked at Tollman, who nodded with satisfaction.

Details taken, the group of disgruntled men moved off,

back the way they had come, muttering amongst themselves, whilst Billy and Tollman continued their promenade down the Commercial Road.

"Today," Tollman pontificated to Billy as they took their measured steps along the pavement, "is an example of what I call 'distasteful policing' – truly distasteful." Billy said nothing and waited for Tollman to expand on his thought. "You see, it doesn't upset me to deal with a violent crime, when it's one villain against another. If members of the criminal fraternity want to beat each other to a pulp over some imagined grievance or botched crime, I'm all for it. I'll happily sit and watch, and pick up the pieces when it's over. But, today, these mindless people who go out to deliberately damage property and maybe even hurt defenceless women and children, just to satisfy some mob anger against people with foreign surnames…well, it's distasteful, to say the least. But you can't get through to them, see? They are just a mob, with no independent thought or conscience. Makes me sick."

Before Billy could answer, they both heard screaming and shouting and they looked around to try and gauge from which direction the sound came.

"Down there!" said Billy urgently, "Sydney Street!" and he began to run. Tollman did his best to keep up but he found himself lagging behind Rigsby and was forced to pace himself.

As Billy rounded the corner, he saw a young woman screaming as a group of men and women were smashing shop windows behind her, whilst one youth was daubing the words **"GERMAN PIGS"** in black paint across the brickwork beneath the windows. The young woman was not screaming in fear, but in rage, as she tried to stop some of the women taking goods from the shop.

Billy blew his whistle and shouted "Stop or I will arrest you!", which caused the mob to scatter and drop their looted goods. One youth, out of sheer nastiness, turned and threw the black paint tin at the young woman before he scarpered. It hit her shoulder and splashed all down the front of her dress, at which point she gave up and sank to the pavement in a spasm of sobbing.

Billy momentarily toyed with the idea of running after some of the mob but then decided that the girl needed help more than he needed to make an arrest. Her sobbing had subsided and she was now shivering with delayed shock. Her dress was not only covered in paint, but one sleeve was practically hanging off and she had a bruise on her cheekbone. Billy quickly took off his greatcoat, helped her up, and wrapped her in the heavy coat, as she clung to him in a daze. Just then Tollman arrived, out of breath and dismayed at the scene of devastation before him.

"What's your name, Miss?" asked Billy quietly, as he continued to support her.

"Mattie," she said shakily and she hesitantly pointed at the damaged sign above the shop doorway which said "Grunwald's Haberdashers."

"Mattie Grunwald? Is that your full name?" Billy asked, just to confirm and she nodded.

"Do you live above the shop, Miss Grunwald?" asked Tollman, and when she nodded, he added "Then let's get you inside and make you a cup of tea, before we take you to see a doctor and have you thoroughly checked over for any injuries."

Mattie allowed herself to be led inside and she opened a back door which led to a hallway and some stairs. She stood and surveyed her shop, part of which was still intact, and began to cry again, with bitter frustration.

"Don't worry, Miss," Billy said comfortingly. "We'll help you sort this out. But let's get you upstairs and change your clothes first, eh?"

Mattie nodded and led the way up to a little sitting room. As Billy changed direction on the landing, he could see that Tollman was picking up all the looted goods from the pavement and bringing them into the shop.

"Sit down and I'll make us a brew," Billy said to the girl and when she protested about needing to get out of her paint-soaked dress, he told her that it could wait. "Keep warm under my coat and drink some hot tea first." He bustled about in the little kitchen area and began to boil a kettle on the stove. As he waited for it to boil, he glanced out of the window and smiled to see that Tollman had now found a broom somewhere and was sweeping up broken glass on to a sheet of cardboard and emptying it into a dustbin.

Pretty soon, all three of them were quietly sipping tea in the little sitting room and trying to coax Mattie out of her state of shock and fear. Bit by bit, some gentle questioning from Tollman gleaned the information that, before the war, she had lived here with her father, who had come over to Britain in 1880, as a young man. He had met and married Mattie's mother and they had set up the haberdashery shop. Mattie had been born in 1895 in the little flat where they were drinking tea. Her mother had died in 1905. Then, not long after the outbreak of war, her father had been taken away by the authorities and interned as an enemy alien. But Mattie was lucky because he had been interned in Alexandra Palace, in north London, and she was able to visit him every Sunday. Many of the men were interned in places that were nowhere near London and their women and children had no prospect of visiting them at all. Tollman shook his head sorrowfully and Billy looked at the pretty girl in front of him, with her pale face, dark eyes and black hair and his always generous heart just broke for her. *A poor slip of a girl, being left all alone to run a shop, with no father or husband to protect her,* he thought, and he was filled with rage.

Mattie excused herself to go into the bedroom and get changed and when she came out, in a pale pink dress with her long hair brushed and swept back off her face, Billy realized how thin and fragile she looked. She held out his greatcoat and thanked him, then apologized. "I'm sorry but it has got paint on the lining now." Billy assured her that it didn't matter and the police would clean it or give him another one.

"Now, we should see about getting you somewhere to stay, Miss Grunwald," said Tollman briskly. "You can't stay here. The lock on the front door of the shop has been smashed and, in any event, it's not safe here for a young woman on her own."

Mattie looked alarmed. "But I can't leave the stock in the shop. It will all get stolen! Besides, this is my home! What am I to do?" Tears began to fill her eyes. Soft-hearted Billy sprang to put his arm around her and Tollman patted her hand.

"Look," Tollman began, with a practical note in his voice, "Do you have a relative that can come and stay with you?" Mattie shook her head, so Tollman continued, "Do you have any trusted friends that can come and stay and help you run the shop?" Mattie thought for a moment, and Tollman was hopeful, but then she shook her head again. "Right," Tollman sounded a little defeated and he took another swallow of his tea, while he mulled over the problem. "Have you got a telephone here?" he finally asked.

Mattie nodded and said, "Yes, it's in the back of the shop. Behind the dressmaker's dummy."

Tollman grunted acknowledgement and searched his pockets for his "Useful Information" notebook before he exited to make some telephone calls. Mattie looked at Billy for an explanation but he just smiled and shrugged.

"Mr Tollman will sort everything out, don't worry. Now how about another cup of tea before we take you to a doctor? Mattie nodded and moved over to an armchair, where she could sink back into it and close her eyes. Billy could see that the bruise on her cheekbone seemed to have got larger and her eye was beginning to close. *I can't imagine why anyone would want to hit a defenceless young girl like that*, he thought to himself, *whether she's German or not. None of this is her fault.* He was beginning to get quite worked up about it when, fortunately, Tollman came back into the room with a look of satisfaction on his face.

"I'll have another cuppa, since you're making it," he said cheerfully to Billy, which cause Mattie to open her eyes. Billy dispensed more mugs of tea and waited for Tollman to explain his solution to Mattie Grunwald's present predicament.

"I've just got off the telephone to Eustace King," Tollman said, looking at Billy with a smile.

"What, Eustace, the retired copper, now a private detective?" Billy asked.

Tollman nodded. "The very same," he said, with a note of satisfaction in his voice. "I remembered that his wife, Lily, is very fond of sewing. She makes all sorts of things for neighbours – christening robes, children's clothes and the like. So, I asked Eustace if he and his wife, as a favour to me, could come over for a week and look after this shop."

Mattie gasped with pleasure at this solution.

Tollman held up a warning finger, however, and said, "I am, though, going to ask that you agree, Miss Grunwald, to something that I consider important to your future safety."
Mattie asked what that might be and Tollman continued. "We don't know how many of these riots might happen in the future, if the Germans take it into their heads to commit another act that outrages the British public, so I am going to suggest that the name of your shop is changed and Eustace puts a notice up in the window saying 'Under New Management'. It will be a ruse, if you like, to stop ignorant folk round here from getting it into their heads to smash the shop up again. We'll find you somewhere to stay for the week and then you can quietly come back to your flat here and no-one will be any the wiser. But, I think you should consider, in future, employing a strong young lad to help you out – do deliveries and such like."

Mattie thought for a moment and then said suddenly, "I can go to the Quakers for a week. I help out there sometimes as a translator and they would find me somewhere to stay."

Tollman looked interested. "What's this Quakers' place then?"

"St Stephen's House, in Westminster, next to Scotland Yard. I'm surprised you don't know it. They run an emergency service there for Germans, Austrians and Hungarians in distress." Mattie explained.

Tollman looked surprised. "I know the building very well," he said, "but I thought it was just government offices."

"The Quaker's Emergency Relief Committee rents rooms from the National Peace Council," she elaborated. "I can probably stay in one of the hostels they rent for families that have lost their homes. I started helping them out when my Pa was taken into custody. The Quakers do a lot of things for men interned in the camps as well. That's how I found out about them."

Tollman was impressed. "Sounds like an ideal solution and Billy can take you there by way of Charing Cross Hospital. He can get you looked over." He nodded at Billy, who returned the nod. "Meanwhile," Tollman continued, "I shall wait here for Eustace and Lily. Any instructions you want me to give them?"

Mattie thought for a minute and said, "I'll write down the number of the wholesaler in case they run out of anything. They won't have to pay for supplies because I get it on thirty-day credit. I've just paid the rent and gas bills, so that's taken care of. I'll write down the telephone number of St. Stephen's House in case they need to get hold of me. I'm terribly grateful for you organizing this, Mr Tollman. I should have been afraid to sleep here tonight." She was on the verge of tears again.

"That's quite alright, Miss. Now you go and write down your instructions, get some clothes together and Billy will take you to Westminster. Meanwhile, I'm going to telephone one of the police- trusted glaziers and a locksmith to sort out the shop front."

Mattie smiled and winced – the bruised cheekbone was swollen and throbbing now. She would be glad to be out of Whitechapel for a while.

CHAPTER TWO

INNOCENT ALIEN ENEMIES

"Doctor Allardyce!"

Caroline straightened her aching back at the sound of her name. She had spent the best part of the morning bent over an operating table trying to do her best possible stitchwork on the faces, necks and arms of countless women patients, who were covered in lacerations from being attacked by a baying London mob.

"Yes?" she turned round to face the orderly who had spoken her name. The woman handed her several white folded paper packets of powder. "Miss Summersby has sent these up for you from the pharmacy, Doctor, and she said to tell you that she is running low on powdered aspirin at the moment but she has some more on order."

"Thank you," Caroline took the packets and put them in her pocket and then turned back to her laborious stitching. "Nearly finished Mrs Goschen," she smiled wearily at the white-faced Austrian woman, with very poor English, who was bravely enduring the stitching of multiple lacerations on her arms. Caroline had understood from the woman's mime that she had held her arms up to protect her face when an angry group of men had thrown stones at her and her fellow workers in the Austrian bakery where she worked. The two other women with her had a better command of English and they had been able to explain that they all worked in Brandt's Patisserie shop in the King's Cross Road. Caroline knew the shop and had often bought some apple cake – Apfelkuchen - from their shop on her way to the omnibus shop. She realised, with regret, that it would probably close down now.

Since Caroline had arrived at 9.30 that morning, there had been a tide of hysterical women and children arriving at the hospital. Many were battered and bruised, some were just frightened and because their children had vomited with terror, had brought them into hospital to be checked. Matron and her nurses had mostly rushed around dealing with grazed knees, dispensing cups of tea and trying their best to calm everyone. The thing that was causing these women the most distress, and they spoke of it with the hospital staff, was that all their menfolk were in internment camps and they were frightened of what harm might befall those men if the whole of civilian Britain was up in arms against "The Enemy".

Everyone in the hospital had been grateful for Mabel Summersby's command of German. Caroline, faced with a tide of hysterical patients in the hospital foyer when she arrived, had sent an orderly to fetch Miss Summersby at once. Mabel had appeared and was able to instantly dispel the shrieks and wails of the women and the crying babies and children by standing on a chair and shouting firmly,

"Seien Sie ruhig, meine Damen! Hier seid ihr alle in Sicherheit! Die Ärzte werden sich gut um Sie kümmern!" (Be quiet ladies! You are all safe in here! The doctors will take good care of you!)

A wave of relief had spread over the crowd and the noise reduced to a level of quiet snuffling and murmuring. Then the medical staff had been able to move through all the women and children, assess their needs and start medical treatment accordingly. Mabel had bustled back to her pharmacy in the basement of the hospital, as she had assessed that salves, antiseptics and pain relief would be required.

By lunchtime, there was a lull in the numbers of injured and frightened women coming through the doors. Mabel, during that morning, had found a blackboard and easel, in one of the rooms used for training, and she brought it down to stand in the inner entrance of the hospital. On it, she had chalked, in German, as she had announced earlier, BE CALM. YOU ARE SAFE HERE. THE DOCTORS WILL TAKE GOOD CARE OF YOU. Matron had pronounced Mabel 'A Saint' because that one blackboard notice had the effect of instantly reassuring everyone who came through the door. So, there were no more hysterics and everyone was able to get the help they needed.

Caroline went down to the pharmacy to spend her lunch break with Mabel. Lady Maud's cook, Mrs Beddowes, had pressed a package of chicken sandwiches into her hand before she left the house and she knew that they would be too much for her to eat by herself. She also knew that Mabel had a habit of rushing out of her flat in the morning without bringing any lunch.

As they sat together munching the sandwiches in companionable silence, Mabel suddenly said, "It makes you ashamed to be British, doesn't it?"

Caroline nodded, "I know what you mean. I never thought I would spend a morning patching up women and children who have been attacked by London men. I mean I've always had to deal with the odd marital dispute, where the husband has knocked the wife about, but not a great crowd of women who are the victims of vicious and illogical violence."

Mabel nodded. "War makes beasts of everyone." Then she turned to Caroline and asked, "I suppose you read about Edith Cavell this morning?"

Caroline sighed. "Yes. Maud had every single newspaper – even the tabloids. She sent Billy out to get them. Quite shocking and sobering. We had a big heated discussion about it over breakfast. Peter surprised me though..."

Mabel raised an eyebrow, "In what way?"

"Well, he more or less said that if women wanted to do the job of men, as in being a spy, then they should expect to be punished when they are caught. You know...shot...like Miss Cavell."

Mabel finished eating her sandwich and looked at the clock on the wall.

"I have to be honest, Caroline, and say that I think Peter Beech is right."

"I do too," Caroline replied, "but I wasn't going to give him the satisfaction of telling him so."

Lunch over, Caroline went back upstairs to the main treatment area and Mabel bustled about, preparing to receive more supplies. Caroline was perturbed to see that the crowd of women and children had not diminished. If anything, it was even larger and she recognised many patients that had already been treated. Matron approached her with a look of concern.

"Doctor, we can't get rid of those who have been here since this morning. They say they are too frightened to go back to their homes." She looked at Caroline with desperation. "We can't just make them leave and, frankly, I don't know what to do."

Caroline understood the predicament. "Matron, I think this is a public order matter and I'm going to telephone the police. They have to find a solution to this."

※ ※ ※

Tollman was supervising the locksmith and the glazier, when Ernest and his wife, Lily, arrived from Clapham.

Lily was beaming and seemed thrilled at the thought of running a haberdashery for a week. She gave a brief greeting to Tollman and rushed into the shop, admiring and fondling all the lace, ribbons and sewing threads like a woman possessed.

Ernest gave Tollman a rueful smile. "Perked her up no end, this assignment," he said, nodding in Lily's direction. "She's been a bit down since the youngest son left home to get married and the daughter has moved to Grimsby." Tollman felt a pang of envy at the thought of Ernest's home being devoid of offspring. *What I wouldn't give for my lot to tie the knot and leave me to a bit of peace and quiet,* he thought ungraciously and immediately regretted his momentary lapse of fatherly affection for his three quarrelsome daughters.

"It's only for about a week," Tollman said, by way of apology. "The poor girl, who lives here, needs to get herself sorted out before she can come back. There's a nice flat upstairs," he added. "You should be quite comfortable."

Just then, the glazier, who had been measuring up the smashed front window, interrupted Tollman to tell him that he was going back to his workshop to cut the glass and would return late this afternoon to finish the repair. Tollman nodded and said "You'll have to report to this gentleman here, when you return," he indicated Ernest, "and give him your bill. I'll make sure it's paid as quickly as possible." The man shook Tollman's hand first and then Ernest's hand, giving him his business card before he departed.

Ernest looked up at sign above the shop which read 'Grunwald Haberdashers.' "That's going to need changing – and that," he said firmly, pointing at the wall where the thugs had daubed GERMAN PIGS. "I think I'll get a tin of paint and sort it out myself, Arthur. Do you know where the nearest ironmongers is?"

"On the Commercial Road, Ernest. Just round the bottom of Sydney Street."

Ernest nodded. "Can you stay here for a bit, while I go and get some paint and a brush? Just in case any nasty people come back?"

Tollman nodded. "Of course. I hope you can cope if there is any trouble, Ernest?"

Ernest smiled grimly, withdrawing a black hornbeam cosh from his inside jacket pocket. "Not only have I got my little helper here, but I've also got my old warrant card to flash, in case anyone tries it on. The missus knows what's what, anyway...look..." and he pointed to the unbroken part of the front window, where Lily was taping up a notice which read

**PREMISES ARE NOW UNDER
ENGLISH MANAGEMENT**

"Good," Tollman knew that Ernest was the right man for the job. "Well I'll stay here and make your missus a cup of tea, whilst you go and get your paint." Ernest left on his mission.

Lily was bustling about in the shop, making approving noises as she patted every shelf of fabric and sorted every box of pins.

"I'll show you upstairs, Mrs King," offered Tollman affably.

She beamed and said "Do call me Lily, please. After all we've known each other for years, Arthur!" Tollman smiled and inclined his head in agreement, stretching out a hand to show the way up to the flat. Lily gathered up her skirts and climbed the stairs ahead of him.

"I'll put the kettle on, shall I?" he asked and she nodded, all the while taking in the neatness of the flat and nodding quietly in approval at the cleanliness and charm of the surroundings. She picked up a framed photograph of Mattie and her father and smiled. "Is this the girl you rescued this morning, Arthur?"

Tollman put his spectacles on and looked at the photograph. "That's her. Just a slip of a thing she is. There were about eight or nine people trying to hurt her and smash up the shop."

"Poor thing." Lily put the photograph down and accepted a cup of tea, then she sat in the armchair and looked pleased with herself. "I'm sorry for the girl but I have to confess to being excited at this opportunity to run a haberdasher's shop. I just wish it wasn't under such circumstances, Arthur."

"You were the first I thought of this morning," Tollman said. "I knew you loved sewing and I thought, Ernest and Lily

– the perfect combination of brains and brawn..." He laughed.

Lily chuckled. "I hope I'm the brains, Arthur! Although Ernest says I've got a mean right hook when I'm riled!"

"Well, that may come in handy. Be very careful, Lily. Don't open the shop without Ernest by your side. People are in a nasty mood at the moment and they are unpredictable – especially around this area."

Lily grimaced. "Yes, I wouldn't like to run a shop in the East End of London, myself. Too rough. Now, between you and I..." her voice sunk to a conspiratorial level, "there's a little shop in Clapham I've been watching. It's a tobacconist' shop at the moment, run by an elderly lady, and it doesn't get much business. It's on the corner of Queenstown Road but, and here's the advantage of it, it's right opposite a school and two factories full of women, who would, I'm sure, love to be able to buy their sewing bits and bobs when they come out of work. But don't tell Ernest!" she said hastily, "I'm hoping he can be persuaded over the course of this week. It's got a nice flat over the top of it, not much of a stroll to Clapham Common for a bit of greenery. Nice pub for Ernest in the other direction, going towards Queenstown station..."

"I know it!" interrupted Arthur, "Queen's Arms, isn't it?"

"That's the one! Got a nice pub garden and does good food. Anyway, Mum's the word, Arthur. Let's see how this week pans out, first."

There was a knock at the flat door and it was the locksmith, saying his job was finished and asking where he should send his bill. Tollman gave him the department in Scotland Yard and he took his leave, passing a returning Ernest, paint and brushes in hand, purposefully coming up the stairs.

"Just made some tea, Ernest," offered Tollman and he was rewarded by a smile of acceptance.

"Well, this is nice," said Ernest, looking around the flat. "You alright there, Lil?" he asked his wife, who had taken her shoes off and was resting her feet on a pouffe.

"Happy as a pig in clover, Ernest. I really am. Any more tea in that pot, Arthur?"

Ernest winked at Tollman, who grinned. *Little does he know what his missus has planned for him,* he thought and he chuckled.

※ ※ ※

Billy decided that he was rather taken with Mattie Grunwald. She had lovely eyes and quite a sparky personality. She was intelligent and self-sufficient – he marvelled at her efforts to keep her father's business going while he was interned. During their bus ride from Whitechapel to Charing Cross, Mattie seemed to recover from the morning's ordeal of being attacked and some of her resilience began to show through. Billy even managed to make her laugh a few times by recounting some of his escapades in the army and the police. She asked him to take off his gloves so she could see his scarred and rigid hand and, in a moment of tenderness that took Billy by surprise, she stroked his hand and then kissed his cheek. By the time they reached the hospital, Mattie was holding Billy's good hand, as though they had been friends for a long time, and Billy was beginning to feel the warm glow of a burgeoning relationship with a member of the opposite sex. Life was looking up!

The hospital at Charing Cross was like a madhouse. There were women and children everywhere, in distress. Mattie looked dismayed.

"Every hospital is going to be like this," she said, looking at Billy with the light of anger in her eyes. "I must help. A lot of these women won't speak good English."

Billy nodded. The noise was deafening and he was unsure what to do. Mattie strode up to the nearest harassed doctor, who was stitching up a woman's jaw, which had been split open by a blow of some kind.

"Excuse me…" she began and the doctor looked up, saw her bruised cheek and assumed she was another patient.

"You'll have to wait," he said tersely, "There are others with more serious injuries."

Mattie gritted her teeth and replied forcefully, "No, you don't understand. I can help. I speak German."

The doctor looked at her again, and then at the uniformed Billy who had appeared behind her, and his face softened. "I beg your pardon, Miss," he said, in an apologetic tone, "I didn't realise that you were offering to help. There are several nurses over there, cleaning wounds and dealing with those who don't need surgical intervention. Perhaps you could go over there and translate for them?" he pointed at the far side of the room.

Mattie nodded and turned to Billy. "Can you do something for me?" Billy waited for instruction and Mattie continued. "Can you go to the Emergency Committee Headquarters in the National Peace Council Building? You know where it is, don't you? Right next to Scotland Yard!"

Billy said "Of course I do. What do you want me to say?"

"Explain to them that you have come from this hospital and how bad the situation is and probably how bad the other hospitals will be, and ask them to send someone to all of them to sort out temporary accommodation for the women and children. They'll take notice of you, 'cos you're a bobby."

Billy agreed and said he would come back to the hospital afterwards to help her but she shook her head.

"No, Billy, I'm fine, honestly. After you've been to St Stephen's, go into Scotland Yard and tell your bosses what is going on. I don't think they realise how bad it's going to get." Billy hesitated and Mattie took his hand. "*Then* you can come back and find me. I won't leave the hospital until you come back, honest." She gave him a reassuring smile and Billy, satisfied that he was doing the right thing, gave her a bold peck on the cheek and set off on his mission, but he noted that Mattie had blushed and was smiling.

Westminster was bustling with army uniforms, coming and going from the War Office, as usual, and Billy decided to leap on to the platform of a passing omnibus and hitch a lift down past the Parliament Building and Big Ben to St Stephen's House and Scotland Yard.

With a grateful wave to the omnibus conductor as he jumped off the platform to the street, Billy then ran into St Stephen's House. The building was not only a huge rabbit warren, but the corridors were jammed with Germans, Austrians and Hungarians, some with suitcases, all patiently waiting patiently in line for assistance from the Committee.

"Anyone here speak English?" shouted Billy, but everyone looked at him fearfully – policemen not being regarded by them as necessarily friendly. However, one elderly man, sitting on a small trunk, said quietly, "I do, constable, what do you want to know?"

Billy looked relieved and said, "I'm looking for the offices of the Emergency Committee."

The man, and anyone within earshot, smiled. "Just follow this line of people, son," said the elderly man. "It goes up the stairs and along a corridor on the first floor. You'll see it."

Billy thanked him and began to edge his way along the corridor, made narrow by the press of people. He was forced to continually say, "Excuse me please," as he struggled to pass them on the stairway, and then he managed to traverse the first-floor corridor until he came to the office, staffed by three women, who were dealing with the supplicants.

As he entered the room, taking his helmet off to be able to duck under the door frame, the women administrators looked up at him with concern.

"Is there a problem, Constable?" asked a woman, busy rifling through a filing cabinet.

"Yes, madam. I have been sent here by Mattie Grunwald…" he was relieved to see the woman break into a smile of acknowledgement at Mattie's name, "She is assisting at Charing Cross Hospital, which is packed with aliens who have been attacked or driven out of their homes. She suspects that all the hospitals will be the same and she asked if you could send someone to each of them to help them with accommodation? Most of the people don't want to go back to their homes." He looked at her hopefully.

The woman sighed. "Of course they don't," she said sadly. "No one thought it would be as bad as this…" she trailed off, trying to marshal her thoughts. "Right," she said briskly, galvanised into action, "Annie!" she called to one of the women, "Telephone all the vicars and caretakers on our lists and ask them to make their church halls and meeting rooms available. Mary! Telephone the headquarters of the Boy Scouts and the Territorial Army HQ in Sloane Square and tell them we need all the camp beds they can lay their hands on…and blankets…and pillows, if possible. Constable!" she turned back to Billy. "Would you be so kind as to tell the people lined up in this building that we are about to sort out overnight accommodation? And could you escort our Mr Fotheringhill back to Charing Cross Hospital? We'll contact Scotland Yard to tell them we need some help at the other hospitals."

"I'm just going next door to Scotland Yard, Miss," Billy said helpfully, "I can get something organised."

"Oh, would you, please? That would be wonderful." She was grateful and held out a hand to shake his. "My name Ethel Brown. Here's our leaflet," she handed Billy a small publication, "it's got our telephone number on it. If you could get your colleagues to telephone us and we can sort something out. I'll just go and get Mr Fotheringhill." She bustled out of the room.

Billy went out into the corridor and shouted "Listen up!" in his loudest voice. Everyone stopped talking and looked at him expectantly. "The ladies in the office are now trying to sort out overnight accommodation and I'm going next door to get the police involved in helping. So just be patient and you people at the top of the stairs pass the information on to the people down the stairs."

The hubbub started up again and he could hear people shouting the information in German or Hungarian to the people beyond them. A tall, thin, bespectacled man appeared and tapped Billy on the shoulder. "I'm Herbert Fotheringhill," he said breezily, "I understand we're going to Charing Cross Hospital?" He seemed businesslike and was clutching a briefcase.

Billy shook his hand and said, "I have to go and see my boss first, so if you wouldn't mind waiting in Scotland Yard while I sort things out?" Mr Fotheringhill was amenable, so they began the lengthy process of wending their way through the crowds lining the corridors and stairs.

Chief Inspector Beech was on the telephone to Caroline, when Billy knocked and entered.

"Ah…just a moment, Caro," he said as he put his hand over the mouthpiece. "I've got Doctor Allardyce on the phone, asking me for help as her hospital is overwhelmed with foreign aliens who have been attacked…" he explained to Billy.

Billy held up his hand to stop the conversation and replied, simply, "I've sorted it, sir. Tell Dr Allardyce that someone from the Emergency Committee for the Assistance of Germans, Austrians and Hungarians in Distress will be attending her hospital very shortly, that is if we can find a constable to accompany each of them."

Beech looked impressed at Billy's news and relayed the

information to Caroline, then put the receiver down. "Doctor Allardyce was greatly relieved," he announced with a smile. "Now, Rigsby, tell me what I need to do to facilitate this assistance you have organised."

Billy explained what had happened up until now and that he was to accompany Mr Fotheringhill, who was sitting outside Beech's office, to Charing Cross Hospital.

"The Committee, which is just next door here, has asked if we can provide a constable to accompany their people to each of the major London hospitals."

Beech reached for the internal telephone. "I should think that ten men would do, wouldn't you?" he asked Billy, who agreed. He dialled the number of the front desk. "Sergeant Stenton? Chief Inspector Beech here. Could I ask you to come to my office, please? Matter of some urgency."

"May I go now, sir?" Billy asked. He was anxious to get back to Mattie at the hospital. Beech nodded and Billy left, passing Stenton on his way out. Confident that everything would now be set in motion, he apologised for the delay to the patiently-waiting Mr Fotheringhill and they set off in the direction of Charing Cross.

The scene that greeted them was just as chaotic as when Billy had left and he anxiously scanned the room for Mattie, fearing, for a moment, that she had left without him. But then he saw her, bending over an elderly lady, bandaging her ankle. Billy pushed his way through the crowd, Mr Fotheringhill dutifully following, and tapped Mattie on the soldier.

"So, they've got you nursing now, have they?" he asked with a grin and she smiled back at him, relieved he had returned.

"You can see how shorthanded they are, Billy! I'm only helping out with the easy stuff, like bandages and slings. The nurses are doing the antiseptics and medicines."

"This gentleman is from the Quaker's Committee," he indicated Fotheringhill, who shook Mattie's hand warmly and thanked her for getting the police alerted to the scale of the problem.

"We are in the process of arranging temporary accommodation for all these people, but I need to make a list of those in need," Fotheringhill said and he opened his briefcase to take out a clipboard with paper attached and a pen. "Is it possible, Constable Rigsby, that you could blow that splendid whistle of yours and get everyone's attention?"

Billy took out his police whistle and gave a long and shrill blast. Everyone was silenced and even the medics were looking on with shock.

"MEINE DAMEN UND HERREN…" Fotheringhill shouted, in a surprisingly booming voice for such a reed-thin individual. He then carried on in German to explain that those who wished accommodation for the night, and possibly beyond, to line up in an orderly fashion on the left-hand side of the room, and he would take their details. Everyone was further impressed when Fotheringhill repeated his announcement in Hungarian, and people began to quietly shuffle towards the left of the room.

Mattie was about to follow them when Billy caught her arm and held her back. "Oh no you don't! he said, "I'm not having you dossing down in a church hall with all these people."

"Then where am I supposed to go?" she asked in irritation.

"I'm taking you to my mother and auntie's house. They'll look after you properly. You'll have a room to yourself and all the food you can eat."

Her eyes widened in amazement. "Won't they mind a complete stranger staying with them for a week?"

Billy smiled. "Not the women in my family. They love looking after people. Right pair of mother hens, they are. So, grab your little suitcase and let's be off. I'll take you to Belgravia…"

"Belgravia!" Mattie exclaimed, "Are you some sort of toff, then?!"

Billy laughed. "Do I sound like a toff?"

Mattie shrugged. "I don't know, I've never met one. But you must be rich if you live in Belgravia!"

"I'll tell you all about it on the way," he said, taking her hand and leading her through the crowd. "Let me just tell Mr Fotheringhill that I'm taking you away but I will be back to help him with the evacuation."

Chapter Three

TROUBLE FROM THE SKY AGAIN

It was almost 11 p.m. when Billy finally got back to Lady Maud's house in Mayfair. He expected everyone to be in bed and was surprised when he opened the front door to hear voices coming from the parlour. He gingerly peered in to see Beech, Caroline, Victoria and Maud, all drinking tea and having a lively discussion.

"Constable Rigsby!" Maud said in a concerned voice, "Peter has been telling us about your resourcefulness today. Have you had anything to eat?"

Billy shook his head and confessed to be rather hungry and rather tired.

"Victoria, go and get Billy some soup and sandwiches, dear. Mrs Beddowes will be asleep by now." Maud asked.

Billy protested but Victoria said, "No, no. It will be no trouble, Billy. After the day you've had, and mother and I have done nothing more than read the newspapers all day!" and she made a quick exit through the door.

Billy sat down gratefully. He desperately wanted to take his heavy police boots off but decided against it in present company.

"So how did it all go, Rigsby?" asked Beech.

Billy explained, in great detail, from the point of Mr Fotheringhill making the announcement in the hospital. "He made detailed lists of everyone that needed a bed for the night, by which time, a boy came with a message from the Quaker's Committee to say that forty of the people on Mr Fotheringhill's list were to go to the Friend's Meeting House in St Martin's Lane and the rest were to go to the underground cellars in the Banqueting House in Whitehall."

Both places were within walking distance but the people needed the reassurance of a police escort, so Billy had found himself walking a crocodile of assorted families up St. Martin's Lane and then going back to Charing Cross Hospital to walk the rest down Whitehall. Mr Fotheringhill had accompanied him down to the Whitehall location and then they had both carried on to St Stephen's House and Scotland Yard. After checking in with the exhausted ladies of the Emergency Committee, who had performed a monumental organisational task for hours during the course of the day – all parties closed up the office and made their weary ways home. And not before time. As Billy had stepped off the night omnibus from Whitehall to Mayfair, he saw the familiar searchlights on the river, moving across the sky, and he heard the whistles and rattles in the streets of the Marshals who were heralding the arrival of a Zeppelin raid.

Victoria appeared with a mug of steaming vegetable soup and a plate of bread and cheese and Billy's eyes lit up. Just as he gratefully took his first mouthful of soup, there was a sound of an explosion – a little too close for comfort – which caused everyone to react.

"My goodness!" exclaimed Maud, "I thought the Germans were under orders not to bomb near the Palace?"

"Mm." Beech furrowed his brow in concern. "So did I, Maud. But I dare say there might be the odd renegade Zeppelin captain who may feel that those instructions don't apply to his airship." Beech got up and looked out of the window.

"Peter, you must stay here tonight. I insist."

Beech nodded and said it was probably wise. "What about you ladies?" he enquired. "Perhaps you should go down into the kitchen?"

There was a resounding "No!" from all three ladies.

"I've had a hell of a day," Caroline decided to abandon being ladylike in her language, "And I want the comfort of my bed, thank you."

Beech could see that the women were obdurate and he gave up trying to persuade them. Billy, who had drunk his soup and eaten his bread and cheese in record time, was now trying to fight against his eyes closing.

"Well, I think we should all go to bed now, don't you?" and Victoria nudged Billy from the edge of oblivion and said, "Bedtime Billy."

Billy Rigsby needed no persuading and he stumbled gratefully out to the study where his king-sized camp bed awaited.

"I shall put two of these very comfortable armchairs together", announced Beech.

"And I shall fetch you a couple of blankets, Peter" said Victoria and she disappeared.

Maud and Caroline, one by one, gave Beech a fond kiss on the forehead, bade him good night and left him to shuffle armchairs around.

Victoria came back with the blankets and a pillow and stood there awkwardly, whilst Peter Beech draped blankets in place on the chairs, added cushions, and made his makeshift bed.

"Well, good night, Peter." Victoria's tone of voice was brisk.

Beech felt a momentary stab of irritation and he asked curtly, "How's it going with that solicitor chap that you are stepping out with?"

Victoria flushed and said frostily, "David. His name is David."

"Yes." Beech avoided looking at her. "Things progressing well, are they?"

"Yes. Thank you. Good night." Victoria left hurriedly and Beech felt at once, shame that he had been so ungentlemanly, and pleasure at her discomfort. He settled down in the armchairs and felt irritable that he had been so petulant and wondered when he was ever going to get over the fact that Victoria appeared to have rejected him twice now.

* * *

Elsie Rigsby stood at the window of the basement kitchen of their house in Belgravia and watched the searchlights piercing the sky in the distance. She could hear the thump, thump of the guns along the river, trying to hit an invisible airship that was quietly cruising above the clouds. Then there came a loud explosion, which made her jump and her sister, Sissy, rush over to be at her side.

"That was a loud one, Else," she said, anxiously scanning the blackness to see if there was any evidence of fire, caused by a bomb hitting its target.

"Nowhere near here, though," Elsie answered. "I reckon it's just that the wind is blowing in this direction and it made it sound nearer. Look!" She pointed over to the left of the window where they could just make out a faint glow. "East End copping it again," she said sadly. "As if those people haven't suffered enough."

The two women fell silent, both reflecting on their luck to be living in a grand house in Belgravia, acting as caretakers, after being bombed out of their previous house in North London.

Just then, obviously woken by the explosion, Mattie appeared from the bedroom, followed by the trembling dog, Timmy, who had been fulfilling his usual function of sleeping on a visitor's bed just to 'guard' them.

"Is it bad?" she asked, rubbing her eyes. She had been deeply asleep and had been roused with a jolt.

"Not for us, lovey," said Elsie, moving to the sink to fill the kettle. "But you should be glad you're not in the East End tonight. It looks like they're getting a pasting again. Let's all have some cocoa, shall we? Help us get back to sleep again."

"You warm enough, Mattie?" Sissy took a shawl from the back of the armchair and draped it round the girl's shoulders then she picked Timmy up and cuddled him until his little warm body stopped trembling.

Mattie smiled. "Billy was right," she said, "You two are like a pair of mother hens."

Sissy laughed. "Billy would know! He's had the pair of us fussing around him ever since he was born!" Then she said thoughtfully, "Mind you…for all that…Billy has not grown up to be spoilt and selfish, has he Elsie?"

"No," Elsie agreed. "He's a rare one, alright. For a man. He's soft-hearted, and would give you the shirt off his back, if need be, and yet he's tough enough when the occasion demands."

"Yes," agreed Mattie quietly, "Billy's special."

Elsie and Sissy looked at each other. Sissy winked and Elsie smiled. Ever since Billy brought Mattie to their house, earlier that evening, they had sensed that the two youngsters liked each other. Billy had been more than anxious to make sure the girl was well looked after and Mattie had kissed his cheek with unusual tenderness when he left to go back to Charing Cross Hospital.

So, Sissy had bathed Mattie's cheek and put some antiseptic ointment on it, whilst Elsie had made her some dinner. Then they had watched her eat, whilst gently probing the girl to find out about what had happened that day, and about her work and life in general. By the time Mattie had finished her meal she didn't realise that the two women had thoroughly vetted and silently approved of her.

Then they had displayed their confidence in the girl by telling her about their lives and about Billy and the special team in Mayfair. Mattie had been entranced.

"So, you get to work for the police, on special jobs, in secret?" She had been astonished and delighted to hear that women were working undercover for Scotland Yard. "Fancy that! A titled lady, a doctor, a lawyer and a pharmacist and you two!"

Sissy had chuckled. "Yes…us! We're the unqualified members but sometimes we can go where posh ladies can't," and she had explained about the past work they had done – Elsie pretending to be a ladies' maid, Sissy assisting at an autopsy, both of them working in a canteen, and so on. Mattie had said she was both full of admiration and a little envious.

"I always wanted to do something useful," she had said wistfully. "I didn't want to be running a shop all my life."

Elsie had admonished her. "Mattie! You have been running a business, all on your own, without any protection, in a rough part of London. You've done more than most women could possibly do!" Sissy had agreed and they had all fallen into reflective silence.

Then the Marshal had passed by with his rattle, announcing the approaching Zeppelin raid and it was decided that Mattie should sleep down in the basement with them, rather than up in one of the guest bedrooms. Sissy would share a bed with Elsie.

Now, they were all drinking cocoa and listening to the distant thump of the guns, the shrill clamour of bells, heralding the movement of fire engines around the London streets, and wincing whenever there was the sound of an explosion when a bomb found its mark.

"How many is that, now?" asked Sissy.

"Well, I've counted four, so far," said Elsie.

"I hope Billy's safe!" said a distressed Mattie.

"He will be, love," Sissy reassured her. "If he's around Charing Cross, he's much too close to Buckingham Palace to get bombed. The Kaiser has forbidden the Zeppelins to bomb his own family."

Mattie seemed reassured and said she might try and go back to sleep. Sissy and Elsie agreed that they would also try and get some rest.

As the two sisters were laying side by side in bed, Sissy

whispered to Elsie, "I think she's a very nice girl, don't you?"

Elsie agreed. "It doesn't matter to me that her father is German. I think it's a disgrace that people are attacking women with German names."

"It's just ignorance and blind hatred," murmured Sissy. "Though I don't know that you can entirely blame them when the Germans are bombing them out of their homes like this." Elsie grunted and Sissy continued. "'Course, if she married Billy, she wouldn't have a German name anymore."

Elsie chuckled. "Trust you to put the cart before the horse, Sis! The two of them have only just met! Don't go picking out wedding hats just yet!"

But Sissy was already gently snoring, so Elsie smiled and turned on her side to surrender to sleep herself.

* * *

Ernest and Lily King were unable to sleep, of course, because they were right in the middle of the bomb trail being created by the Zeppelin. They were somewhat used to the raids because where they normally lived, in Clapham, they were also a target area, being along the favoured bomb route which began with the giant munitions complex at Woolwich; progressing towards various docks on the south bank of the River Thames; the major railway termini at London Bridge and Waterloo; then culminating in the giant power station at Battersea. However, having read in the papers how much the East End of London was favoured as a bombing route, they were apprehensive.

"Maybe we should go round to the Whitechapel tube

station," suggested Ernest, looking out of the window at yet another fire engine driving past.

"Too late for that now, love," said Lily, covering herself with a blanket as she sat in the armchair. "Besides, we need to be here to deal with any fire, if it breaks out. We promised Arthur Tollman we would look after this place for that poor girl and we can't back out now."

"I should have thought about it, before I said yes," Ernest grumbled. "I knew that it would be a moonless night, because of the weather forecast, and the Krauts always choose a moonless night to send the Zeppelins over."

"Stop fussing, love and put the kettle on. We'll have a cup of tea and some biscuits. We're in no more danger here than we were in Clapham."

"Yes, but in Clapham we have a cellar, Lily" Ernest said pointedly.

"To be honest," Lily retorted sharply, "I'd rather be hit directly by a bomb than be buried alive in a cellar. Now shut up and make the tea, Ernest. We must make the best of it. It will all be over soon. The Zeppelin will have to return home because it will run out of bombs and fuel. It's already passed over us. You can tell that all the fire engines are heading north – up past Whitechapel towards Bethnal Green."

Ernest knew that his wife was right and he took comfort from that. "Right!" he said, with a bit more cheerfulness in his voice, "Where are these biscuits, then?"

* * *

Billy woke up with a start, in the middle of the night. He had been having a nightmare again, about being in the trenches and the German guns were pounding his position before the battalion were about to go over the top. He was trying to run away, because he knew what was coming and he was shouting at his mates to do the same, but they weren't taking any notice of him.

He sat up, feeling groggy, and realised that he could hear the noise of the big guns on the river, firing into the sky, in the vain hope of hitting an airship. Then, in the darkness, he could see a shape in the doorway and Billy squinted to try and make out who it was.

It was Beech. He had heard Billy cry out and had come to help.

"Bad dream, Billy?" he asked, softly. He rarely called Billy by his first name, so he was obviously very concerned.

"Yes, Mr Beech," replied Billy, turning on the standard lamp by his bed, feeling foolish and drained from the sweat that had drenched his underwear.

"Here," Beech strode into the room and gave Billy a glass of brandy. "Drink it up. It will make you feel better." Then he sat down in a nearby chair and sighed. "Bloody air raids. They cause me to have nightmares too. The sound of those guns just takes me right back to that hellhole of Mons. Sometimes I wake up feeling sick."

Billy nodded in sympathy and took a large swig of the brandy. "Do you think we will ever get over it, Mr Beech?"

Beech shook his head. "Not while these heavy guns keep firing in London. Maybe…once the war is over…and we can go back to a peaceful existence, with no disturbing sounds other than the occasional automobile backfiring, we can begin to put it all behind us."

"We were only in one battle, Mr Beech," Billy reflected, "Imagine the state of those men who have survived several battles and are still in the trenches."

There was a moment's silence while the two men contemplated the awful reality of the mental condition of the men who had been fighting on the front for over fourteen months.

"Want another brandy?" asked Beech, after a while. Billy nodded and Beech left the room to replenish Billy's glass and pour himself one. When he returned, Billy was peering through a crack in the curtains.

"East End again," he said, accepting the drink from Beech and sitting down again. "Poor buggers."

"It's because they live near the docks and all the factories..." Beech said, stating the obvious.

"Which they have to, because that's where they all earn a living. It isn't fair to kill civilians – children as well - is it Mr Beech!?" Billy spoke bitterly and forcefully.

"No." answered Beech, "It isn't fair. Whatever lunatic in Germany thought up poison gas, and airships, and bombing civilians in their homes, will answer for it to God, I hope. But, sadly, the machinery of war is so powerful that now, we are aping most of the German's tactics – well, not the airships, of course, because we haven't got any – but you can be sure that our lunatics are trying their hardest to create some, so that we can do the same. Reason and fairness fly out of the window when it comes to all-out war, I'm afraid. It's all about power."

Billy gave a mirthless chuckle, as he finished his brandy. "We're beginning to sound like pacifists, Mr Beech, and, as a once-professional soldier, I never thought I would say that." Beech grunted in sympathy and Billy continued, "Those Quakers today, sorry yesterday, I 've lost track of time…they are the sort of people that once I would have despised. You know – refusing to fight when the likes of me have to do it for them. But, when I was involved in the business of protecting the foreign civilians, I found myself really admiring them – the Quakers – the organisation and support that they have created. Finding safe places and beds for all those people. The government hasn't done that. All those johnnies in uniform in Whitehall…not one of them would have lifted a finger to make citizens – even though they were foreigners – safe. No, it falls to the Quakers and their like, to organise, raise money and such. Mattie was telling me that they even pay for enemy aliens to go back to their original country, if that's what they want…"

"Mattie?" asked Beech.

"This girl that Mr. Tollman and I rescued from a gang trying to beat her up and smash her shop."

"Ah," Beech nodded. "Made an impression, this Mattie, did she?"

Billy grinned. "I suppose she did, sir."

"And where is Mattie now? In one of these Quaker places?"

"No, I took her to my mother and aunt in Belgravia."

"Oh? You must have thought her special then." Beech chuckled quietly. "I envy you, Rigsby. You can form relationships with a certain amount of ease. I find it very difficult indeed."

"My mother would say that I form attachments to ladies much too easily," Billy grinned and dropped his head in embarrassment.

"Well, good luck to you, Rigsby." Beech stood up and collected Billy's empty glass. "Now that brandy should help you sleep and I suggest you try and dream of this young lady you've met and wipe all memory of the trenches from your mind."

CHAPTER FOUR

AN ABDUCTION IN THE NIGHT

It was a subdued team that gathered for breakfast in the morning. Lady Maud tried to make some conversation but she failed, as everyone seemed to have had such a restless night and they were not in the mood for lively chatter. Billy appeared to have a headache and Caroline gave him a packet of powdered aspirin she found in her pocket. Victoria was quite moody. Beech was a little terse and to make matters worse, Mrs Beddowes sent the maid, Mary, up to the breakfast room with a tureen of porridge and an apology that eggs and bacon were in short supply at the moment. Everyone looked glumly at their porridge and only Billy decided to eat it but he sprinkled his powdered aspirin on it first, followed by liberal spoonfuls of honey. This made Caroline laugh and she commented that she would remember that as a means of getting small children to take their medicine.

The telephone rang and Mary answered, then popped her head around the door to announce that Sir Edward Henry would like to speak to Chief Inspector Beech. Everyone looked interested as Beech stepped out into the hallway to take the call. At that moment Tollman arrived and he loitered by the door, eavesdropping on Beech's conversation, then entered the breakfast room with a smile on his face. Everyone took that to mean that they were being given an assignment and the mood at the table lightened.

"Porridge?" offered Lady Maud, lifting the lid on the tureen in front of her, surveying its contents with mild distaste.

"Don't mind if I do, Lady Maud." Tollman was feeling a bit peckish as he had been unable to have a bacon sandwich this morning, due to his daughter Daphne informing him that no bacon was to be found anywhere in Clapham. He was on his third spoonful when Beech returned to the room.

"We have a job and it's a curious one," he announced and everyone looked interested. "It appears that last night, just after the Zeppelin raid started, two women were abducted from a train just outside Charing Cross station…"

"What? And nobody saw anything?" Tollman was astonished. "How can you abduct two women from a train full of passengers?"

"Well quite!" added Lady Maud.

"Ah, well that's just it, Tollman," Beech answered. "Apparently, it is required, in the event of a Zeppelin raid, that all trains must stop wherever they are on the tracks and put out all their lights. The two women, for reasons we do not yet know, were travelling in the guard's compartment, and the only other person in that compartment was the guard, who was coshed over the head and is now in hospital. The railway company, with great foresight, have sealed off two carriages and have placed it in a siding for us to examine. I wonder, Caroline, if you could ring Miss Summersby and see if she is available this morning to do a forensic examination?"

"Fortuitously, Mabel and I both have a day off today, so I will telephone her and then pick her up in a taxi cab. Where do you want us to meet you?"

"Sir Edward says that we are to meet up at London Bridge Station." Beech replied, then he turned to Tollman. "I suggest that you and Billy go to Guys Hospital at London Bridge and try to interview the hospitalised guard."

"Anything I can do?" asked Victoria, hopefully.

Beech looked regretful. "I'm sorry, Victoria. Nothing at the moment. When we get some more information about the case, I'm sure there will be some tasks for you."

Victoria looked irritated, and briefly harboured the feeling that Beech was deliberately excluding her, but then her usual commonsense prevailed and she accepted that, as he had said, there was nothing for her to do, at the moment.

Caroline decided to eat a slice of toast before she left. Meanwhile, Billy was on his second bowl of porridge, donated by Victoria, who had no appetite. Everyone, however, seemed to have perked up a little. Tollman finished his cup of tea and porridge and motioned to Billy that they should be off to the hospital.

Maud said, looking up from her newspaper, "Do be careful, everyone. The newspapers appear to be still full of sensational stories about Edith Cavell. I shouldn't be surprised if people carry on with their vengeful campaign against German immigrants."

"The trouble with this war," said Tollman with feeling, and everyone looked up at him with interest, sensing that he was about to say something very important, "The trouble with this war," he repeated, "is that the flames have been fanned, even before the war, by irritating propaganda."

Maud sensed a lively argument brewing and she was tempted to delay Tollman leaving but, wisely, she said, "Mr Tollman, that is the opening for a very interesting discussion and you don't have time to develop it now, more's the pity. So, I insist that you stay to dinner tonight, so that we may discuss this further!"

Tollman grinned. He always relished a debate with Lady Maud. She had a quick mind and an appreciation of politics that few men, let alone women, possessed.

"It would be an honour, Lady Maud." Then he briskly said, "Billy! Hurry up with that porridge – we have work to do!" Billy swallowed the last spoonful and sprang to his feet. His headache had gone and his stomach was full, so now he could face the world.

Beech was already out on the pavement, hailing a taxicab, when Tollman and Billy came through the front door.

"We might as well share this ride," said Beech, "as we are all going to the same place," and he issued instructions to the cab driver to make for London Bridge station.

* * *

Mabel's flat is so cluttered! Caroline thought to herself as she sat on the sofa waiting for Mabel to gather together all the paraphernalia she would need for the examination of the railway wagon.

When Mabel had opened the door this morning, flustered, with her hair still in rags, her first comment to Caroline was a disappointed, "So there's no actual body to examine?"

"Not yet," Caroline had replied. "But if these poor abducted women suffer a terrible fate, there surely will be."

Mabel had murmured something about 'not wishing for the worst but…' and then bustled off to dress and gather her forensic implements together.

Caroline had moved several scientific papers off the sofa, because there was nowhere else to sit. Then she sat there patiently waiting for Mabel, who kept talking to herself as she bustled from one room to another trying to remember where she had left certain items on her list.

Caroline had cast her eye around the living room and that was when she came to the appreciation of how cluttered everything was. Mabel's pharmacy at the hospital was meticulous – bottles ranged in height on shelves, colour coded, neatly written labels everywhere – yet, at home, she appeared to live in a state of utter chaos. On the dining table, which, Caroline reasoned, should be empty apart from, possibly, a vase of flowers, there were at least three experiments in various stages of completion. Interconnecting tubes, vials and flasks, containing strange substances jostled for space with a Bunsen Burner and a fat file of notes. Every item of furniture that could seat a human being, instead played host to piles of papers, newspaper clippings and photographs. In foreign languages, no less! Caroline glanced at the papers that she had moved. At least one appeared to be written in German, another in French and a third looked like it was Russian or Greek.

"Nearly ready," puffed Mabel, as she limped through the living room with two baskets of implements and deposited them by the front door.

"Mabel, you're limping!" said Caroline in alarm.

Mabel looked confused and then looked at her feet. "Ah,

yes, I've only got one shoe on, that's why. I'd better go and find the other one."

"And take the rags out of your hair!" Caroline called after the retreating Mabel. Privately, Caroline doubted that Mabel ever looked in a mirror. Sometimes her attire was utterly shambolic.

Finally, they were ready to go. "Mabel, do you have your keys, your handbag and something to write with?" Caroline asked, prompting Mabel to turn around and disappear into the bedroom and return with her handbag.

"Finally ready!" said Mabel with a smile.

* * *

Tollman and Rigsby were navigating the magisterial colonnade of Guy's Hospital after being told by the front desk that the train guard who had been brought in last night was in the Accident Ward. When they got there, the Nursing Sister told them that he had been moved to Cornelius Ward as he was recovering from his head wound. So, they went out to the quadrangle, back into the colonnade and then into another quadrangle, to find the correct ward.

"Like a bleedin' cathedral in here, isn't it, Mr Tollman?" said Billy, very aware that his studded boots were making a terrible noise on the marble floor.

"It is a cathedral, of sorts," replied Tollman. "A cathedral built for the worship of medicine. I once came here to the main operating theatre to watch an autopsy. Ranged seats like in the music hall, so all the students can see every gory detail.

Everywhere has got these high vaulted ceilings, like in a cathedral, and there's stained glass windows and a couple of chapels I believe. It is a veritable house of worship for the medical profession."

"Mm," Billy wasn't impressed. "I bet all this grandeur doesn't prepare these doctors for life on the front line, operating in a tent with little or no pain relief on the poor buggers who copped it at the last advance."

Tollman laughed mirthlessly. "You're right there, son. This place just trains them for a life of dealing with privileged patients in Harley Street. It must be a hell of a shock for them in the Royal Army Medical Corps."

They arrived at Cornelius Ward and Tollman went up to the Nurses' Station to flash his warrant card and enquire about "Mr Willam Durden, the train guard who was brought in last night with a head wound."

One of the nurses duly took them the full length of the ward and then round the corner to William Durden's bed, where the man was being propped up on his pillows by another nurse. Tollman and Billy approached and sat either side of the bed. Tollman introduced himself and Rigsby. Billy took his helmet off, and Durden looked resigned to answering questions.

"How are you, Mr Durden?" enquired Tollman solicitously.

"How do you think?" was the testy reply, "I've got a whacking great lump on my head, a thumping headache and I feel sick."

Tollman commiserated. "Yes, of course. I'm sorry about this but you do understand that we have to ask you some detailed questions about the unfortunate incident last night?"

Durden nodded and winced. Nodding was not a sensible thing for him to have done in his present condition.

Tollman continued. "What can you remember about yesterday evening, in the lead up to you being attacked."

Durden thought for a moment and looked at Billy, who was poised to take notes. "Now, I'll do my best to recall everything," he said as a warning, "but, at the moment, it's a bit fuzzy, so don't take it as gospel."

"We understand," Tollman assured him.

Durden then recounted what he could remember of the evening. He said that he had been reading in the guard's wagon. He had hoped to have a conversation with the two women who were travelling in the wagon but they seemed disinclined to chat.

"Describe these women, if you can," asked Tollman.

"Both young. One was foreign, from her accent, I would have said French or Belgian. The other one sounded like she came from London. She wasn't common but she wasn't upper crust either. They both had fairly plain clothes on and hats. Nothing fancy. I asked them why they wanted to sit in the guard's wagon and the London one said something about they 'wanted to sit together and have a bit of privacy' and the passenger carriages were too full. They both had War Office travel warrants."

"Did they?" Tollman was interested in this little fact. "Do you know where they got on the train?"

"Undoubtedly Southampton – that's what the travel warrants said. Southampton to Waterloo. Same for the pigeons."

"Eh?" Tollman was momentarily confused, "Did you

say, pigeons? As in the grubby things that fly around London?"

Durden nodded – and winced again – he kept forgetting that movements of his head were not a good idea.

"The foreign woman seemed to be in charge of two baskets of pigeons. In fact, she got quite hoity-toity with me when I moved one of the baskets to check the label. She said 'Please don't disturb the pigeons, they don't like it.' She was sharp, like, when she said it."

"What did the label on the pigeon baskets say?" Tollman asked and Billy could tell that he was intrigued.

Durden thought for a moment. "It wasn't the standard label…the one that says 'Pigeons for Liberation by Station Masters'…but it *was* a government label. I think it said something like 'Pigeons to be Collected by Authorised Person' and then it had some department's name underneath but I can't remember that."

"So, what would normally happen to those baskets of pigeons?" Tollman asked and Billy wondered why he was so bothered about the birds, but he knew better than to interrupt.

"Well, when we arrive at Waterloo, I would have taken them to the Station Master, and, presumably, he would contact the person supposed to pick the pigeons up."

"I see." Tollman thought for a moment and then said, "Carry on."

"I'm a bit parched, Sergeant," insisted Durden. "Can you organise a cup of tea?" Tollman nodded at Billy, who went off to find a nurse. "He's a big lad," Durden commented, watching Billy as he strode up the ward. "I bet he's useful in a fight."

Tollman gave a wry smile. "More than you know, Mr

Durden. Constable Rigsby used to be a heavyweight boxing champion in the army."

"Did he now?" Durden was impressed. Billy came back and reported that tea was on its way and was slightly unnerved by Durden giving him a very warm smile and a wink.

"While we are waiting for the tea, Mr Durden," Tollman persisted and Billy took up his notepad again. "Perhaps you could tell us if, during the long journey from Southampton, you overheard any of the conversation between the ladies?"

"Ah, now, I should have mentioned that I only took over the guard's position at Basingstoke – that's where I live, you see. I do the Basingstoke to Waterloo section. Another guard does the Southampton to Basingstoke bit."

"Do you have a name for the guard you took over from?"

"Of course, we regularly work the same shifts. It was Charlie Preston. Big ginger-headed bloke. Lives in Southampton, unfortunately, so you'll have to go and see him there, or catch him while he waits at Basingstoke for the down-line train."

"Right." Tollman paused whilst a cheerful nurse, who had obviously taken a shine to Billy, arrived with three cups of tea. She smiled at Billy, who smiled back, then, as she left, Durden winked at Billy.

"She ain't bothered by that scar on your face, son," he said, nodding in the direction of the retreating nurse and winced again, cursing under his breath that he kept forgetting his head and neck were injured. Billy laughed.

"Now," Tollman doggedly persisted. "You were reading, you say, and you didn't hear any of the two women's conversation at all, is that right? Or did you hear snippets?"

Durden screwed his face up and thought. "I heard one or two things. After the Frenchie told me off about the pigeons, as I turned away, I heard her say, 'I won't be happy until they get to Doughty Street,' then just before we got to the old Blackfriars Road Station, the London woman said, 'No, I can't, I have to take an urgent message to my father.' Those were the only two things I heard them say before we got the word that an air raid was starting and we had to pull in to the old Blackfriars Road Station and put all lights out."

Billy was writing furiously and Tollman was digesting Durden's statement carefully.

"So, what happened when the lights were out?" Tollman finally asked.

Durden finished his tea, "I stood up and said, 'Stay where you are ladies, until the lights go back on,' then I heard a noise behind me but before I could turn round and put my torch on, my cap got knocked off and I got hit hard on the back of my head. I remember the pain and falling down – that was when I hit the front of my head as well – and I think I heard a little yelp from one of the women and that was it. Nothing, until I woke up a bit in the ambulance. Apparently, the train slowly carried on to Waterloo and then the porters opened the guards wagon door and saw me laying on the floor, so they commandeered one of the troop ambulances lined up outside the station. That's it. I was in and out of it all, until I got here and they patched me up."

Tollman sighed, as if he wasn't really satisfied but then he said to Durden, "Thank you Mr Durden. We may have to come back and ask some more questions. Meanwhile," he scribbled down a telephone number on a piece of paper from his notebook and handed it to Durden, "that's my phone number, Mayfair 100, do you think you can remember that?"

Durden was about to nod, but thought better of it and simply said, "Yes."

Tollman and Billy rose to leave. "If you think of anything else, no matter how trivial, give me a ring."

"Mayfair 100," said Durden, glancing at the paper. "Gotcha."

CHAPTER FIVE

FUMES AND FEATHERS

Beech was waiting patiently for everyone - anyone really. He had said goodbye to Tollman and Rigsby, as they peeled off to go to Guy's Hospital, and had placed himself directly outside the ticket office, at the appointed time, as requested by the Station Master, Mr Grimble. He had been waiting for almost twenty minutes when he spied Caroline and Mabel bustling on to the station concourse from the taxicab rank and two bowler-hatted gentlemen advancing towards him, with purpose, from the other direction. The men reached him first and one doffed his hat, extended his hand and said "Chief Inspector Beech?" After shaking hands with Beech, he introduced his companion, "This is Mr Arnold, our Munitions Officer, and the reason I am late for this appointment."

Mr Arnold shook Beech's hand and smiled. "I do apologise Chief Inspector but I was on the telephone with the Ministry of Munitions. They were complaining, as usual, and I had the devil of a job to get rid of them."

Caroline and Mabel arrived and set down all their baskets. "So sorry we are late, gentlemen," said Caroline. "But it takes us some time to get together all our equipment to undertake a thorough and detailed examination of a crime scene." She extended her hand and both Grimble and Arnold looked surprised.

Beech introduced everyone, "This is Dr Allardyce, a medical doctor and Miss Summersby, a pharmacist with a particular talent for crime analysis. Caroline and Mabel, this is

Mr Grimble, the Station Manager and Mr Arnold, the Munitions Manager." Everyone shook hands and Caroline was gratified that neither of the two men made any comment about women doing scientific police work.

Introductions completed, Mr Grimble explained that they had uncoupled the two wagons at Waterloo and removed them to the siding at London Bridge. Apart from the porters and ambulance crew removing the injured guard, the two wagons had been sealed and locked and no one had touched anything inside.

"Why two wagons?" asked Mabel.

Mr Grimble looked at Mr Arnold and nodded for the Munitions Manager to take up the story. "The second wagon was carrying material vital to the munitions industry…" he began.

"Gracious! Nothing explosive, I hope!" exclaimed Caroline.

"No, doctor," Arnold smiled, "It is bags of fruit stones and nut shells to be made into charcoal for the filters on gas masks. They are experimenting with them. Apparently, it makes much better charcoal than wood."

Mabel's eyes lit up, "How fascinating," she said with enthusiasm, "I had no idea we were so resourceful with material that would normally just be thrown away!"

Mr Arnold nodded. "The reason we have left the two wagons together is because the villains must have come through the cargo wagon to enter the standard guard's wagon, as the door that leads to the forward passenger carriages, is usually kept locked. Also, the fruit stones and nut shell sacks were loaded at an unscheduled stop at Farnborough. We picked up the consignment left from a local jam factory and the nut shells came from a local toffee factory. It's possible that the villains got on at Farnborough too."

"You say 'villains'? More than one?" asked Caroline.

Mr Grimble pointed out that two women had been abducted and one man alone could not accomplish that. "It could very well have been more than two," he added, upon reflection. "One to knock out the guard and another two to capture the women."

Beech suggested that they get on with the business of examination of the wagons and Mr Grimble led the way through the labyrinth of the station, that ordinary passengers never see, and out on to the sidings, where an assortment of trains, carriages, engines, wagons and open wagons were sitting, under a roof of corrugated iron. The carriages that were obviously for passengers were being cleaned by an army of women, wearing long aprons and trousers, and wielding mops, buckets, cloths, hoses and scrubbing brushes. Down the end of one track were the two wagons, with a set of portable steps leading up to a cargo-loading double door. Mr. Grimble nipped up the steps and produced keys to unlock the padlock keeping the doors closed. He then pushed the doors apart and came back down the steps.

"Ladies, if you would like to go up into the wagon, we will hand your equipment up to you."

Mabel and Caroline ascended the steps, but Mabel insisted that they stop at the top step whilst she examined the floor of the wagon. First, she retrieved a battery-operated storm lamp from one of the baskets and held it up over the floor space, which was scarcely wider than one and a half feet in depth – the rest of the wagon being taken up by a padlocked cage stuffed full of bulging sacks.

"There are a lot of footprints here, in the dust, but only three sets that actually go to the right, to the next wagon. The rest of the footprints go backwards and forwards in and out of the cage area." She then retrieved a tape measure from her baskets and asked Caroline to write down the measurements. "I'm measuring right boot marks going towards the guard's wagon. I have one that is thirteen inches long – very big man, must be over six foot with feet that large – another one at ten inches long and another at nine and a half inches long with what looks like a jagged hole in the sole in the front right-hand side." Mabel straightened up and put the tape measure away. "So, possibly three men." She swept the storm lamp from side to side to see if there were any more distinguishing marks. "There is nothing else on the floor but I would suggest, as the floor space is quite narrow, that there may be finger or hand marks on the walls and the back of these doors, Mr Beech."

Beech realised that he was being asked to organise a fingerprint squad and he would need to find a telephone for that. "Can we lock up this wagon then, please, until I can arrange for a fingerprint specialist to come here?" Beech asked Grimble. "And transfer these steps to the other wagon, so that the ladies can examine that in detail?"

Mr Grimble nodded but Mr Arnold looked very disappointed. "Do you know how long this might take?" he asked in a concerned voice, "Because I've already had an earful from the Ministry of Munitions this morning about this consignment being held up and the wagon itself being out of use. There's a shortage of wagons at the moment, mainly because they're not unloading and returning them fast enough at the various munitions factories," he added, by way of an apology.

"Well," Beech replied, "If one of you could take me to the nearest telephone, I'm sure I can get a fingerprint man here within the hour. Once we are done with that, then I'm sure the wagon can be removed." Mr Arnold seemed satisfied.

"I'll take you to my office," he said, "and Mr Grimble can assist the two ladies." Grimble was happy with the suggestion. Caroline and Mabel came down the steps and the two railwaymen moved them in front of the doors of the other wagon. Grimble then unlocked the padlock on the second set of doors and stepped down. Caroline and Mabel ascended the stairs one more and again Mabel held her storm lamp aloft.

"Oh, I won't be able to get much from here!" she exclaimed in annoyance. "It looks like there has been a dreadful scuffle of some sort, judging by the disturbance of dust and the fact that there are several footmarks, big and small around the edge of this central area, leading to the door. But the central area itself appears to have been swept away by something."

Mr Grimble looked a little uncomfortable and said apologetically, "I'm afraid that is caused, probably, by the porters retrieving the unconscious guard. They did it in rather a hurry because they said there was a funny smell in the wagon that made them feel light-headed."

Mabel and Caroline stuck their heads further into the wagon, looked at each other and both said "Chloroform". The sweet sickly odour was unmistakeable. Mabel held her storm lamp up high in order to fully illuminate the interior of the wagon. "There," she said, pointing at a sponge lying on the floor over by some wooden seating. "I'm going to cover my face and retrieve that," she announced to Caroline, "Could you take the lid off a large glass jar so that I can immediately put it in there and seal it?" Caroline nodded.

Mabel fished some clean gauze out of one of the baskets and held it over her nose and mouth whilst she stepped into the wagon and deftly picked up the sponge with her gloved hand and Caroline held the open jar at arm's length whilst Mabel pushed the sponge in. Then Caroline swiftly screwed the lid on and allowed herself to breathe again.

"It's definitely chloroform." said Mabel, coming down the steps and taking a few deep breaths of fresh air. "Apart from the telltale smell, chloroform is a pretty good solvent, as I know to my cost when I have spilt a little. Underneath the sponge, the varnish on the wooden floor of the wagon had bubbled up. That sponge has been laying there all night."

"Would the men have used that sponge on the face of one of the women and accidentally dropped it?" Caroline asked.

Mabel shook her head. "In my capacity as anaesthetist in the hospital, I know that chloroform takes at least five minutes to work if you apply it on a Schimmelbusch mask. I think the kidnappers threw that sponge into the wagon during the confusion of the air raid, when the lights were out. The fumes would have had plenty of time to work before they grabbed the women, who would have been very confused and almost unconscious before they were dragged out. Chloroform vapours can linger in the air for months, it can be very dangerous."

"The kidnappers must have worn masks then." Caroline pointed out.

Mabel pointed at Mr Grimble, who was wearing a cumbersome canvas satchel on his hip, attached to a canvas strap slung from his right shoulder. "Yes, like that. That is a gas mask, isn't it, Mr Grimble?"

"Why yes!" Grimble replied, "But this type is very new. The railway personnel are trying them out for the Ministry of War. It's a restricted issue, mind. Not even the troops on the front line have got these yet. Invented by some Russian, I'm told."

"Yes, Zelinsky and Kumant, I've read the paper," Mabel said.

"Of course you have, Mabel," observed Caroline dryly.

"So could I borrow your gas mask so that I can do a better investigation of this wagon, Mr Grimble?" Mabel asked hopefully.

"Delighted, dear lady!" Mr Grimble took his bowler hat off and lifted the gas mask strap off his shoulder and over his head. He then asked Mabel to take off her hat and he put the strap around her neck. "You see the mask goes over the face." he said, taking the mask portion out of the satchel and holding it in front of her face, "whilst the charcoal filter portion" – he tapped a metal container attached to the bottom of the tube running from the mask – "is kept in the satchel." Mabel gingerly put the gas mask over her face and the elastic straps around her head. She turned her head from side to side.

"That has to be the most frightening thing I have ever

seen," observed Caroline, finding the sight of Mabel quite amusing.

"It's a bit claustrophobic," admitted Mabel in a very muffled voice from inside the mask. "But I shan't be wearing it for long." Then she grabbed one of the baskets and stepped into the wagon and began meticulously scouring the floor for any clues. Caroline, watching from outside the wagon, saw her pick up various things and deposit them in glass jars. Labelling them as she went along.

Now she's fastidious and organised! Thought Caroline as, she watched Mabel at work. *If only she was the same in her home!*

Beech returned at that point, announcing that he had telephoned the Yard and organised a fingerprint man and two constables to guard the wagons. He had left poor Mr Arnold on the telephone to the Ministry of Munitions. It seemed, from Arnold's raised voice that the Ministry was none too pleased at having a wagon out of action. He peered into the wagon and saw Mabel wearing the gas mask. "Good Lord! Is that Mabel Summersby in that contraption?" He was about to go up the steps and into the wagon when Caroline pulled him back.

"Mabel is wearing a prototype gas mask because the air in that wagon is dangerous, Peter!" Beech stepped back immediately and apologised. Caroline continued "There was a sponge soaked in chloroform on the floor, which has tainted the air, but Mabel is determined to get as many pieces of evidence as she can."

"I suppose the wagon that's connected will be affected as well?" Beech asked, pointing at the adjoining goods wagon.

"Probably. You would have to ask Mabel the question to

get an answer on that." She watched Mabel slowly moving about.

"Where did she get that fearsome looking gas mask?" Beech asked and Mr Grimble confirmed that it was his. "Can we get another one, Mr Grimble?" Beech asked. "Only the chaps who are coming from Scotland Yard will want to take fingerprints from all over the surfaces in both wagons."

Mr Grimble replied that he could certainly get hold of another one from the Assistant Station Manager and he bustled off on his quest.

Beech and Caroline removed themselves a little from the wagon and stood in silence for a moment, watching Mabel moving about the wagon. Then he screwed up his courage and asked, "How are you, Caro? I haven't had much opportunity to speak to you since Commander Todd wrote to you telling you he was being posted to Egypt."

Caroline looked momentarily sad and then took a deep breath and forced a smile. "I'll get over it," she said breezily, choosing not to look Beech in the face. "I'm not the first girl whose beau has been posted to some far-flung place and I won't be the last. Sorry…" she looked at Beech regretfully, "I didn't mean to be so cliched."

Beech put his arm round her shoulders and gave her a squeeze of reassurance. He really wanted to tell her that it didn't matter and that the man for her was actually standing next to her, but he lost courage as usual.

"The thing is, Peter," said Caroline in a sorrowful voice, "I have realised that whilst I absolutely adored spending time with William Todd – because he is so much fun – he's not really a man one would want to settle down with, you know. He's too addicted to excitement and adventure. He would be hopeless as a husband. He's probably a first-rate intelligence officer... well, you would know," she added, referring to Beech's adventure in Norway with Commander Todd. "But," she continued, "God knows how he will adjust to boring life as a civilian."

"He probably won't," said Beech, with a touch of envy in his voice, picturing the handsome, dynamic man they were both talking about. "I'm sure there will be plenty of skullduggery that Admiralty agents need to investigate in peacetime."

He was summoning up the courage to give her a consoling peck on the cheek, when Mabel emerged from the wagon and he hastily withdrew his arm from around Caroline's shoulders.

"Mabel! You look like Captain Nemo in his diving suit!" Caroline said, laughing.

Mabel pulled off the gas mask, took in several lungfuls of fresh air and looked puzzled.

"Captain who?"

"Nemo. You know...Jules Verne's Twenty Thousand Leagues Under the Sea? Illustrated by Eduoard Riou?"

"Ah, of course." Mabel stuck out her tongue and pulled a face whilst lifting the canvas strap over her head "Wearing one of these things is very uncomfortable and makes your mouth terribly dry. I'm gasping for a cup of tea!"

"Then you shall have one, immediately," said Beech, taking Mabel's basket and helping down the steps. "Have you done all that you need to do? Taken all the samples you need?"

Mabel nodded, taking her hat and hat pin from Caroline and affixing her hat back on her head. "Yes, I've been through the other wagon as well, where the footprints were. I did find some threads from a jacket, I think, caught in the wire mesh of the storage cage and I found several deposits of ash – from cigars rather than cigarettes, but I don't think there is any more to be gleaned from here."

Beech spotted that Gimble had hoved into view along the line and he seemed to be flanked by two uniformed policemen and two men carrying leather bags. "That will be the fingerprint men and escorts," observed Beech and he strode towards them to explain the need for the gas masks and to keep the doors to the wagons open at all times.

Once Mabel had advised the men that the mask was somewhat claustrophobic and to only wear it for fifteen minutes at a time, the trio of Caroline, Beech and Mabel set off to the nearest tea rooms in Borough High Street.

Beech and Caroline sat and watched Mabel drink at least three cups of tea before she announced that her mouth had "stopped feeling like the bottom of a bird cage." And she exhaled with pleasure.

"Apropos of that," she said briskly, "I found some feathers, which I'm certain belong to pigeons, and a label, which had obviously become detached from a pigeon basket."

She reached into her basket and produced a jar, which contained a label which stated:

> ## ON HIS MAJESTY'S SERVICE
>
> ### PIGEONS FOR COLLECTION FROM THE RAILWAY STATION MASTER
>
> To the Station Master at Waterloo Station
> upon receipt of these birds.
>
> Please immediately telephone the
> **Carrier Pigeon Service,**
> **Headquarters, Horse Guards, London**
> to arrange collection from the station.

"I propose that we go back to Maude's to consult with Tollman and Rigsby and have some lunch." Beech suggested. "I have to be at Scotland Yard for a meeting this afternoon and I'm sure you ladies have work also. We'll get Tollman to follow up on the pigeon mystery." The three of them drained the dregs of tea from their cups and Beech hailed a taxicab.

"I've suddenly realised that I am starving," announced Mabel.

"Do you think that it's caused by inhaling chloroform fumes?" asked Caroline.

"No," Mabel answered firmly, "I think it's caused by me forgetting to have any breakfast this morning."

Chapter Six

ARE THE PIGEONS IMPORTANT?

Tollman, Rigsby and Victoria were already tucking into some mackerel paté and toast, and Mary was ladling out some pea and ham soup, when Beech, Caroline and Mabel arrived.

Beech asked Tollman how the interview with the guard went, whilst Mabel, uncharacteristically, pounced on the food being offered. Tollman explained what little they had gleaned, and was about to expand on the matter, when the telephone rang in the hallway. Caroline leapt to answer it and then she called out "Mr Tollman, it's for you!" Tollman wiped his hands on his napkin and duly went out to the hallway. Everyone heard him say, "Yes…" then, "Did he now?" in an interested tone of voice, there was a long pause, punctuated by a few grunts, while he seemed to be listening, which was then followed by a "Thank you very much, Miss, much obliged."

Everyone around the table looked at Tollman expectantly, as he entered.

"That was a nurse at Guy's hospital, with a message from Durden, the train guard. Apparently, he had a little operation on his head this morning, after we had left, which required him to be knocked out, and when he came round he was agitated and told the nurse to ring me to say that he remembered the smell of chloroform, in the guard's wagon, before he was coshed on the head. He'd never had any sort of operation before, so he didn't know what the smell was, until it was administered to him this morning by an anaesthetist."

Caroline and Beech looked at Mabel, but her mouth was filled with toast, so Caroline said, "That's what Mabel found in the guard's wagon. A sponge soaked in chloroform. Mabel had to wear a gas mask," she added. Everyone looked at Mabel in surprise and she nodded, with a crumb-spattered half smile.

"What's this about a gas mask?" asked Lady Maud, as she entered, divesting herself of hat, coat and gloves and handing them to Mary.

"Mabel had to wear one – a prototype – to examine the crime scene this morning, because of the dangerous chloroform fumes," explained Beech.

"Was it very uncomfortable?" Maud asked and Mabel nodded, before swallowing, wiping her mouth and explaining that she wasn't able to wear it for more than fifteen minutes. "It's a very tight-fitting fitting rubber mask that grips the face," Mabel added, "and after while it gets very hot and breathing becomes a bit difficult."

"Oh, it sounds dreadfully claustrophobic!" explained Maud, sitting down at the table and looking dismayed. "I should never be able to put one on. How on earth will they get children to wear one?"

"The prototype which Mabel wore is, eventually, meant for front line troops, Maud," explained Beech. "It will be a very long time before the ordinary public get issued with them – if at all."

"But what if the Germans decide to drop canisters of poison gas, instead of bombs?" Maud was distraught.

"Mother, calm yourself," Victoria urged, putting a comforting hand on Lady Maud's arm. "Eat something. You'll feel better."

"Yes, you're right, dear. I've just had an upsetting journey home from my charity meeting. I passed one of my favourite milliner's, just off Bond Street. The windows had been smashed and hateful things painted on the door. Poor Madame Gisela! There was no sign of life in the shop. I do hope she hasn't been harmed in any way." Maud was visibly distressed.

"Well," said Tollman, whilst drinking his soup, "It's like I said this morning at breakfast, people in high places have been whipping up anti-German sentiment for a very long time. They should be ashamed of themselves."

Lady Maud temporarily forgot her distress and allowed her natural desire for a debate to take over. "Now, you did say something this morning, Mr Tollman, and I think you should expand upon it now. I am anxious to understand your stance on this issue." She began to spread a slice of toast with some paté.

"Well," Tollman's voice took on an impassioned tone, as he began to outline one of his favourite topics, "It seems to me that there has been a concerted campaign in Great Britain – long before this war ever started – to make the public constantly scared of German spies, invasion and evil plots. Look at all the novels that have been written about "the German Menace"! I must have read most of them. Er… *The Riddle of the Sands* by Erskine Childers, Hill's *The Spies of the Wight,* Tracy's *The Invaders* and Walter Wood's *The Enemy In Our Midst.* I've got all of those at home…"

Beech chipped in, "I've got two William Le Queux books, *The Invasion of 1910* and *Spies for the Kaiser.*"

Tollman nodded. "In the first year of the war, there were moving picture films about the *"German menace in our midst".*

Whilst you and Billy were at the front, Scotland Yard took all the detectives to a picture house in Victoria, near the station, where they showed us such films as *The German Spy Peril* and *The Kaiser's Spies*. The films were supposed to especially influence Special Branch but, unfortunately for Scotland Yard, there were no films about the problem of the Fenians in Ireland, so Special Branch weren't all that interested." He took another few mouthfuls of soup and then continued, "Then we have all the sensationalised stories in the newspapers about German atrocities. Granted, a lot of people died in France and Belgium as the Germans marched through but I don't believe, for a moment, that German soldiers bayoneted babies or chopped off children's hands."

Lady Maud thought for a moment and then she said, "A year ago, I might have agreed with you, Mr Tollman, as I am always inclined to think the best of people, wherever possible, but the last year of being bombed by German airships and our troops being bombarded with poison gas, has led me to revise that opinion. The Germans seem to have no regard for humanity at all."

Tollman nodded but then added, "I understand, your Ladyship, but we are in a very different war now. A mechanised, industrial war, on a giant scale. This is not like the cavalry wars of the last century, which took place in distant lands and never involved the civilian population of Britain at all. First of all, most of the fighting is right on our doorstep and wounded soldiers can be home by train in a day."

Both Beech and Billy murmured agreement. Caroline, Mabel and Victoria simply looked disconsolate. Tollman continued, "And more than that, there are a lot of people on both the German and Allied sides, who are making a lot of money out of this war. A lot of money. What is used on the battlefield and in the air is not dictated by the soldiers and airmen – it's dictated by the munitions manufacturers, scientists and politicians. War profiteering is the new racket and powerful men on both sides have a vested interest in keeping this war going as long as possible. And to that end, the propaganda gets more and more horrible in order to keep the likes of Mr Beech, and young Billy here, so outraged that they continue to volunteer to fight."

There was a silence as everyone digested Tollman's philosophy. Lady Maud stirred out of her reverie and said quietly, "My dear late husband always used to say, about the Boer War, that the men around the dinner table who pushed the hardest for war, were the ones who owned shares in the diamond and gold mines of Africa."

Tollman gave a grim smile. "Well, there you are, Lady Maud. Your husband was a very wise man."

Beech decided to draw a line under the discussion by saying, "If we have all finished lunch, shall we discuss our findings, because I am anxious that we should try and save these two poor abducted women as soon as possible."

"Quite right, Peter," agreed Victoria, eager to become involved in the investigation, if only by hearing a report of the morning's activities.

Maud rose to her feet, which prompted all the men to stand up, but she waved them down impatiently. "Well, I shall retire to my room and write a letter of condolence to Madame

Gisela, whilst you all go into the study to have your discussion. That will allow Mary to clear up in here." She swept out and delivered a parting shot over her shoulder, "I hope to see some of you at dinner tonight, for a less depressing discussion!"

* * *

The Assistant Station Master at Waterloo Station looked at the fairly substantial army Captain in front of him and shook his head. "I'm sorry Captain," he said firmly. "We've had no delivery of pigeons at all in the last week – let alone ones that were to be picked up by the Carrier Pigeon Service. If we had, someone would have telephoned Whitehall at once."

Captain Osman looked crestfallen. "Well, I just thought I would check. I was expecting a delivery this week and the last communication I had was that it was on its way."

"And where would this consignment of pigeons be coming from, Captain?" the Assistant Station Master asked.

"Well, I can't tell you the point of origin, that's restricted war information, but the pigeons would have been loaded on a train, in this country, at Southampton."

The Assistant Station Manager thought for a moment and then said in a confidential voice, "Captain Osman…I can't say too much about it…because it's now a police investigation…but we had an incident last night. I don't really know much about it but I think it would be best if you telephoned Scotland Yard and made enquiries of them. They may know the whereabouts of your pigeons."

Captain Osman realised, by the tone of the man's voice,

that he wasn't going to get any more information, so he thanked him and left hastily. He decided that he would go first to Headquarters at Horse Guards, to see if they had any knowledge of the missing pigeons, then he would go to the chief depot at Doughty Street, to see if they had had any word.

* * *

Eight year-old Eddie "Growler" Jones – so-called because his belly growled loudly when he was hungry, which was often – and his mate, Wally Tipton, spent their lives prowling around the back alleys of Southwark. They should have been at school – there were a variety of free, charitable or 'ragged' schools in Southwark and Lambeth but Growler's mother didn't hold with schooling and sent her son to scavenge what he could for their sustenance every day, and had done since Growler was six years old. Wally, who was nine years old, stuck to Growler like glue because Growler was the only boy who had never mocked his hare lip. Besides, Growler knew the best places to go and find free food and drink and Wally came from a home with an absent father (in prison) and mother (prostitute), so there was never anyone in the squalid one roomed slum where he lived, and certainly never any food.

Growler had decided that, after scrounging some two-day-old bread from a kind-hearted baker in Great Charlotte Street, they would work their way up to the wharves and warehouses on the river, either side of Blackfriars Bridge. Wally had filched an apple from a stall in the Blackfriars Road and the two of them took turns in taking a bite from the fruit as they strolled towards the river, eyes darting from side to side, looking for any opportunity to arise. Horses and carts, laden with goods picked up from the riverside warehouses, passed them frequently, going south to deliver their wares. Growler nudged Wally and pointed, "Tinned stuff," he said, as a cart went past laden with what looked like army-issue crates of tins. They could just make out the dull shine of metal tins in between the wooden slats of the crates. Neither of them could read, otherwise they would have known that the outside of the crates said "Boot Blacking – War Office Issue".

When they reached the southern end of Blackfriars Bridge, Growler decided that they would have a look around the goods station there, to see if any foodstuff had been dropped on the floor whilst unloading the trains. Since the outbreak of war, most of the work had been taken by women and most times they struggled with the heavy goods to be unloaded and had to use the mobile conveyor belt on the high sided open wagons. The motion of the conveyor belt sometimes caused sacks to split and the goods would dribble out on to the floor. Growler decided they would watch and see if they could seize a moment. Wally always carried an old canvas sack tied round his waist like a cummerbund. Growler carried a small knife, for slitting or prising open packaging. Both boys were always well prepared.

They snuck up the stairs to the track level and found a corner of piled up boxes to hide behind. There were several goods trains in the station – one on the main track and two in sidings. All were being unloaded. They watched patiently. The main train was unloading from a closed wagon and two women were heaving sacks of potatoes from the wagon on to a porter's trolley then wheeling them to a loading bay, where unseen hands were, presumably loading them on to a lorry or cart. A couple of potatoes escaped and the boys grinned at each other. But one large potato got inadvertently kicked by one of the women and it rolled off the platform and on to the track. They boys grimaced at each other. When one woman was inside the wagon and the other had pushed the trolley out of sight, Growler chose his moment and darted out from behind the boxes, grabbed the potato and darted back to the hiding place. The potato was almost bigger than his hand and he nodded in satisfaction. As neither of the boys lived in an abode that possessed an oven and mostly, not even a fire, they would find some amenable night watchman later and beg him to let them bake their potato in his brazier. It was close on three o'clock in the afternoon and the light was beginning to fade, as it usually did in October, and Growler knew that they would have to move on soon. Fortunately, a whistle blew, signalling a tea break, and all the women labourers straightened their aching backs and made their way gratefully towards the station building.

Growler nudged Wally and they nipped out from behind the boxes and began to move across the tracks and scour the ground like grubby birds of prey. Wally untied his sack and between them they gleaned more potatoes, a couple of bruised pears, a bashed-in tin of something (Wally shook it and it sounded like thick liquid), a large onion and, their prize of the day, a jar of jam that had rolled along the track and was not cracked or broken. Then they ran back to the platform, down the stairs and out into the street, laughing at their skill at scavenging.

Growler decided that they would now go and have a quick look at the jumble of warehouses and small wharves along the Commercial Road, to the west side of the goods station. They set off, Wally toting the precious sack over his shoulder and looking like some wizened Father Christmas. Today was already a success. Anything else they found would be a bonus.

There wasn't much activity on the various wharves – the first high tide and the frantic loading and unloading had already taken place early that morning and those ships that were not berthing overnight had beat a hasty retreat on the second high tide of the day to get to the estuary before they got deposited on the Thames mud at low tide. Most of the warehousing had been accomplished by the dockers before the light faded, so there were only a few stragglers taking inventory and locking up. Growler and Wally moved in and out of the deep shadows, keeping a lookout for watchmen, who might be prowling around with their lanterns, and, at the same time, the boys scanned the concrete beneath their feet for bounty. Wally found a split carton of much-prized sugar, which they wrapped in an old paper bag they found nearby. Growler said he would sell the sugar in small paper twists tomorrow, for a penny a twist. He laughed at their good fortune.

They scouted around the sizeable warehouses and found nothing else, apart from a few cigarette butts which Growler gathered up and put in his pocket. His mother would extract the tobacco and make one good smoke for herself and he would be in her good books for a few hours. So, they began to move back towards the goods station end of the dock area and the smaller alleyways which led on to Commercial Road. Around the second turning they came across two baskets up against a wall. Growler dragged them out into a pool of light from a house at the end of the alleyway.

"It's pigeons!" he said with surprise. He picked up one of the baskets and peered into it. "Dead, by the looks of it," he noted. As he was thinking about whether there was any way he could sell the dead pigeons to anyone, a watchman, carrying a lantern, came around the corner.

"Oy, you!" he shouted, causing Growler to drop the basket. "Get your thieving hands off whatever it is you've got there!"

"Scarper!" shouted Wally and the two boys ran as fast as they could in the opposite direction to the watchman's light.

The man advanced on the baskets and swung his lantern over them. He could also see that the birds were dead and then he spotted a tag, hanging off the handle of one of the baskets. He read it and shook his head. It was government business and now he would have to call the police in to deal with it. He sighed, retrieved a piece of chalk from his pocket and drew a big cross on the ground, then stacked the baskets of dead pigeons on top of one another to lift them up. As he rested his chin on the top basket, he wrinkled his nose slightly. There was a funny sweet smell – just a faint smell. He made his way slowly back to his cubby hole and decided that he would go into the goods station to use the telephone and alert the police.

* * *

Tollman was becoming obsessed with pigeons. When the team had started their meeting at two o'clock, he had discovered that the pigeons that the guard, Durden, had described, were now missing and that Mabel had found feathers in the guard's wagon. To Tollman, this had signalled that the pigeons, perhaps, were the key to the whole thing.

"I bet they were carrying vital messages and some German spies have nabbed them."

"But why would they also kidnap the women?" Victoria had asked. "It was pitch dark and the women wouldn't have seen the pigeon-kidnappers. There was no need to take them."

Tollman had been able to see the sense of this but he had still felt that the pigeons were the reason for everything.

"Do you know anything about carrier pigeons, Tollman?" Beech had enquired.

Tollman had shaken his head. "No, sir. But I know a man who does. Sergeant Stenton was a keen pigeon fancier before the war. He was heartbroken when he had to turn his pigeons over to the Admiralty at the outbreak of war."

"The Admiralty?" Billy had asked. "What's the Admiralty got to do with pigeons?"

"I have no idea, lad," had been Tollman's reply. "But I bet Horace Stenton knows."

It had then been agreed that Beech, Tollman and Rigsby would go back to Scotland Yard so that Tollman could talk to Sergeant Stenton whilst Beech telephoned the Carrier Pigeon Service in Whitehall. Mabel would go home and analyse her findings of the morning and Caroline would assist her.

Victoria had complained that, so far, she had not

contributed to any investigations at all and Beech decided that Victoria could stay in the house and use the telephone to try and find out if the kidnapped women had both boarded the train at Southampton and she could also telephone the Station Master at Waterloo Station to see if anyone had turned up, yesterday or today, looking to collect the pigeons.

"Then if you could report your findings, by telephone, to me, I would be most grateful," Beech had added.

Before they had all scattered to their respective assignments, Tollman had borrowed a couple of the feathers, which were placed in a separate glass jar by Mabel. "I know nothing about pigeons, as I said, but Horace might be able to tell something from the feathers – you never know," had been his parting shot.

* * *

"Horace, mate, I want to talk to you about pigeons!" Tollman said loudly as he came through the door, causing Sergeant Stenton to look up from his station at the front desk with a smile and the man talking to him to turn around to face Tollman with a sneer.

"That sounds like interesting work, Tollman," said the man, sporting a fading bruised cheekbone and a scar on his lip. "Got you rounding up pigeons in Trafalgar Square now, have they?"

Tollman, flanked by Billy, found himself confronted by the odious Detective Sergeant Carter. *A much thinner and paler Carter*, Tollman noted with some satisfaction, *and still bearing the marks of the beating he received at the hands of the two Irish military policemen.*

"Oh, Carter, we have missed you," Tollman said sarcastically and Billy sniggered. "Back at work now, are you? Gracing Scotland Yard with your quick mind and winsome personality?"

"No," interjected Sergeant Stenton. "D.S. Carter has been given another two weeks sick leave, on account of his broken ribs. I'm just preparing the paperwork."

"Oh dear," Tollman said with mock sorrow. "I can't imagine what sort of case you were mixed up in that caused such terrible injuries."

Carter's supercilious facial expression faded into his usual, what Tollman often referred to as, "his weasel face. Little shifty eyes and twitching mouth."

"It was a very difficult case and I am not allowed to talk about it, Tollman. It was a government matter and only certain detectives were privy to the case." Carter sounded defensive.

Tollman nodded and stared straight into Carter's eyes, which set the man starting to blink and, eventually, look at the floor. "Yes," said Tollman quietly and firmly, "I heard it was some murky business best not talked about." He very much hoped that he was giving Carter the message that he knew about his corrupt activities.

D.S. Carter swiftly turned and grabbed the papers out of Stenton's hand. "Right! I can't stand here all day, chatting." He pushed past Tollman and glared at Billy. "Good luck with rounding up those pigeons!" he called over his shoulder as he exited, "Don't forget to feed them!" and gave a mirthless laugh.

There was a moment's silence and then Stenton said, "Pigeons, Arthur? You wanted to talk about pigeons?"

Pulled back to reality, Tollman nodded. "Indeed, I do. Take a break, Horace, and sit down with me in an interview room, whilst Billy makes us all a mug of tea."

Once they were seated in the room, Tollman outlined the problem. Kidnapped pigeons from a train. The pigeons were government property and were to be collected from the Station Master at Waterloo Station.

"Collected?" asked Stenton, "Not *released* by the Station Master?"

"Collected," confirmed Tollman. "The guard swore they were to be collected and we found feathers and one of the labels."

"Have you got the feathers?" asked Stenton. Tollman duly produced the glass jar with two feathers inside. Stenton moved the jar around in his hands, looking at the feathers from all angles.

"These birds were sick," he pronounced, as Billy brought in the mugs of tea.

"How do you mean, sick? Anything catching?" Billy was slightly concerned.

"I doubt it, lad," Stenton said reassuringly. "See, the feathers are split. It's a sign of a pigeon being run-down, like. Needing some special care. You say there were two baskets of pigeons?" Tollman nodded. "Most likely they were being brought to the central pigeon loft in Doughty Street…"

"Doughty Street! Yes, the guard overheard one of the women say that!" Tollman had a gleam in his eye. Now he felt he was finally getting somewhere with this perplexing case.

Stenton continued. "Yes, they've got several pigeon lofts there. It's where they train some birds and look after the ones that are unwell. I don't know much more than that but I suspect that the birds that these feathers belonged to, were being repatriated from the Front in France or Belgium for some recuperation."

"They've got pigeons at the Front?" asked Billy in disbelief.

"Best and most reliable method of communication between the trenches and headquarters, son" explained Stenton. "And many of the pigeons, used by the Admiralty, fly three or four hundred miles with messages – from a ship in the North Sea to a receiving loft in northern England."

"And the messages are round one of their legs, yes?" asked Tollman.

"That's right. In code I would imagine. So, you see," Stenton explained, "There would have been no point in kidnapping these pigeons that were on that train. They wouldn't have been carrying messages. They were invalided out of service, most probably."

Just then, there was shout of "Tollman!" and all three men recognised Beech's voice and immediately stood up to investigate. Beech stood at the end of the corridor with a piece of paper in his hand.

"They've found the pigeons," he said urgently, "A night watchman found them at the docks near Waterloo and they've been taken to the police station in Borough High Street. But they're all dead, unfortunately."

"Oh, what a shame," Stenton muttered. "Poor little things."

Beech continued, "Various calls have been made and you and Rigsby are to meet a Captain Osman at the police station. I have to stay here, I'm afraid. Keep me posted."

Chapter Seven

"WHERE ARE THE WOMEN?"

Captain Osman was quivering with frustration. He had asked again and again if he could look at the birds, check the birds, to see if they really were dead, or whether any could be revived, but the police in the Borough Road Station flatly refused.

"We have strict instructions from Scotland Yard that nothing is to be touched until their people arrive. They say the birds are part of an ongoing crime. I'm sorry, Captain, but we have our orders." The Station Sergeant was polite but immovable on the subject.

Finally, Tollman and Rigsby arrived and a relieved Osman was, at last, able to look at the birds. Sadly, he confirmed that they were all dead and he slumped down in a chair whilst Tollman organised a strong cup of tea for the man, as he wanted him to be fortified for questioning.

"Now, Captain," said Tollman firmly, when Osman had drunk half of his tea. "Tell us about these birds and why you think some person or persons unknown would choose to abduct them, along with two women, and then leave them to die in an alleyway?"

Osman sighed. "I have absolutely no idea, Detective Sergeant. These birds were not carrying messages. They were being sent to England for medical treatment. They were hors de combat, so to speak."

"Being sent to England? From where?"

Osman hesitated, "I'm not sure that I can divulge that information. It is strictly forbidden for me to speak of such matters"

Tollman became impatient. "Captain Osman, there are two women's lives in danger, right now! We need as much information as we can get, and we need it quickly!"

Osman nodded. "I do understand, but I need permission to tell you any more. May I use the telephone?"

Tollman considered the request for a few seconds, then replied, "We can do better than that. You tell me who you would telephone for permission and I will get my boss to get his boss – the Commissioner of Police, Sir Edward Henry – to telephone the man in question and get the necessary permission. Would that suit?"

Osman nodded. "The man in charge of the Carrier Pigeon Service is Colonel Dixon. He's based at Horse Guards. If you can't get hold of him, his second in command, Lieutenant Romer might be able to help."

Tollman nodded. "Perhaps you might gently examine the birds, sir, while I make the call, so that we can ascertain cause of death?" Then he left the room to make a telephone call to Beech.

Billy watched as the Captain opened the first basket and tenderly lifted out bird after bird. At first, Billy thought the man was stroking the birds but then he realised that he was delicately feeling around their necks and down their backs. Osman sighed and closed the lid. Then he opened the second basket, simply surveyed the contents and closed that lid also.

Tollman returned and announced that telephone permissions were being sought and that Osman should be receiving a call from his Commanding Officer soon. "Meanwhile, Captain," Tollman continued, opening his notebook once more, "what can you tell us about the cause of death?"

"I have examined all the birds thoroughly, in the first basket, and their necks and spines are intact, so there has been no physical trauma involved."

"How do you mean?" Tollman asked by way of clarification.

"I mean that no one has broken their necks, which is the common way to euthanize a pigeon," Osman replied. "And, upon looking in the second basket..." he opened the lid to show the birds were all neatly huddled together, "there was obviously no explosion or trauma that caused them to open their wings in fright and start panicking."

Tollman and Rigsby looked at the birds and it was indeed a peaceful scene, as though they were all tucked up for the night.

"If I were to guess," Osman continued, "I would say that they were exposed to some kind of gas that, again, did not cause them to take fright but just depressed their respiratory systems."

Tollman nodded. "We know that chloroform was used in the abduction. So that would be the cause, I imagine?" Osman nodded.

Just then the Station Sergeant entered the room and said that a Colonel Dixon was on the telephone and asking to speak to Captain Osman urgently. Osman left to go to the front desk to take the call.

While he was absent, Tollman tutted and sighed, before saying to Billy, "I don't think the pigeons are as important as I thought but the location where they were found could lead us to the captive women. Go and have a chat to the Station Sergeant, find out exactly where the pigeons were found, then call Dr Allardyce and Miss Summersby and get them to meet you at that location. Tell them to bring all their stuff, in case we find the women and we need to examine the scene thoroughly. Oh! And tell them to bring Mrs Ellingham as well. She's razor sharp at spotting little clues and we need as many pairs of eyes as we can get." Billy nodded and recited all the instructions back to Tollman, before leaving and crossing over in the doorway with Captain Osman.

"Right, Captain…is everything sorted?" Tollman asked. "Now tell me where the pigeons came from and whether either of the missing women is known to the Carrier Pigeon Service?"

Osman explained that the pigeons were English homed. He pointed to the small metal rings on each bird's leg. "Every pigeon has a registration number, which tells us who owns and manages them. These registration numbers were given out by the police at the start of the war to those pigeon fanciers who decided to enlist in the service and offer their pigeon lofts for special training. *These* pigeons were owned by a man who lives near the South Coast but they were based in France for the purposes of sending messages back to him, I presume about important enemy movements in France. When one of his pigeons homed, with a message, he would transfer the message to one of *our* pigeons, who would home to Doughty Street, here in London. Then HQ would take it immediately to the relevant person in the War Office."

"But these pigeons *weren't* carrying messages you said?"

"No!" Osman sounded exasperated. "The birds were sick. There would be no value whatsoever in anyone taking them."

Tollman thought for a moment. "So where, in France, were the birds usually based?"

Osman shook his head. "I don't know that. Intelligence operations are compartmentalised. We are asked to organise the British part of the Pigeon Carrier Service. We set up the homing lofts – where the birds are received – we don't know who is operating the lofts outside of the British Isles. It could be intelligence operatives in France or Belgium, Royal Navy vessels at sea, Royal Flying Corps, Royal Naval Air Service… the only thing I can tell you for sure is that these birds were not kept at the Front."

"How do you know that?" Tollman was intrigued.

"Because pigeons used by the military, at the Front, are usually brought back to us by the military for treatment. They would come over on a troop ship and on a troop train – often on an ambulance train - and they are delivered to the Pigeon Carrier Service HQ. We don't usually have to pick them up."

Tollman sighed. "So, you wouldn't know who this foreign woman was who apparently brought the pigeons over with her?"

Osman shook his head. "And I never would have had the pleasure of meeting her. That's why the baskets were marked for collection. She would have left them in the guard's wagon, the guard would have taken them to the Station Master and the Station Master would have rung HQ."

"But you knew beforehand to expect them?"

Osman said yes. He explained that whatever loft housed

the birds in France or Belgium had sent a fit bird with a message to the homing loft keeper in the UK to say that two escorted baskets of birds in need of rehabilitation would be arriving yesterday and to be prepared for them. "That's all I knew," said Osman. "So, when I didn't get a call from the Station Master, I started to get worried. But I can assure you, Detective Sergeant, I do not know who brought the pigeons over from abroad. You will have to speak to the various intelligence departments for that."

* * *

Billy Rigsby stood in the gloom of a timber yard off Commercial Road, by the river, waiting for the ladies to turn up in a taxicab. The smell of rank river mud was in the air and the little wharves that punched spaces into the river front were nothing but beds of shining sludge and debris. Billy disliked the river - in fact he disliked flowing water in general. Travelling on boats made him feel nauseous and the murky depths of the River Thames made him shudder. When he had first joined the Metropolitan Police, all the new recruits had been taken on a tour of all the popular suicide spots in the centre of London. Waterloo Bridge was apparently the favourite. The training sergeant has joked, "Mind you, if they don't drown then they are just as likely to die from the filthy water they've swallowed." Billy didn't find the remark funny. A great deal of sewage emptied into the Thames, not to mention oil from boats, dead animals and other debris. No, the great River Thames was not the 'main artery' of London to Billy

Rigsby, it was more like its bowels, and the thought made him shudder.

A taxicab turned into the main road and Billy moved forward to meet it. The three women of the Mayfair team clambered out, carrying Mabel's usual paraphernalia for searching a crime scene. Billy moved forward to help them and, at that point he saw a police vehicle turn into the road. He could just make out Tollman's familiar face in the front passenger street and he waved. The vehicle drew to a halt as the taxi turned around and departed. Tollman stepped out, whilst the driver went round to the back and opened the doors. Eight policemen were disgorged and came to stand in a huddle around Tollman and the Mayfair 100 team.

"Gentlemen," Tollman began in a clear, loud voice. "We are searching for two women, abducted from a train during the night of the Zeppelin raid. Time is of the essence, men. We don't know what state the women may be in, when we find them. To that end, we have three ladies here – a doctor, a pharmacist and a nurse…" Billy smiled at Tollman's creative explanation of the presence of Caroline, Mabel and Victoria. Meanwhile the policemen all nodded in appreciation at the three women. "Now," Tollman continued. "All of us, thanks to Borough Police Station, have lanterns and torches, so we can search every nook and cranny of these warehouses and wharves." The driver of the police vehicle had assembled a small pile of lighting implements on the pavement and he began to dispense them to the gathered assembly. Before the policemen could move off, Tollman issued a word of warning, "If you find anything, do not enter or approach, as, firstly, there could be dangerous armed men on the scene. Do not blow your whistle, which may alert them, and do not enter the place where the women are being held, as you will disturb the scene and we need to get specialists down from Scotland Yard to examine it. So…proceed quietly." All the policemen nodded and the senior one amongst them began to direct them to start at different points along the river front. As they all moved away, Tollman came up to Billy and the ladies and murmured, "Right, there are a few lanterns left. Let's search in two groups, shall we? Billy, you escort Dr Allardyce and Miss Summersby and Mrs Ellingham can come with me." Billy nodded and his group moved towards the nearest group of warehouses, whilst Tollman and Victoria turned and went towards the wharves.

Unfortunately, because it was dark, the area was overrun with rats. Everywhere Billy shone his light, there were scurrying rodents making for the darkness. Caroline had emitted a small shriek when a rat ran over her shoe but, apart from that, both women made a supreme effort not to compromise the search by screaming. Mabel inwardly shuddered, now and then, but made no audible sound at all. Billy peered into the locked-up warehouses as best he could, pressing his nose against any gaps in the wooden slats and occasionally asking Mabel, who was carrying a torch, to direct her beam through a window, so he could see the interior more easily. But their search was proving fruitless. Caroline, meanwhile, kept scanning the ground, with her lantern, to see if she could spot any unusual signs or items.

Tollman and Victoria began to work their way westwards in and out of the basins and jetties that punctuated the riverfront. Occasionally, Tollman looked behind him and could see the lights of the police search shining above the warehouses and storage sheds, making a strange, moving display of light and dark, beams and shadows. Victoria was shining her torch into the basins, which were just pits of strange shadows, although the tide was beginning to come back in and trickle over the river mud. Her torch beam revealed so much debris that had been deposited on the beds of the basins by the tides. Driftwood, frayed and battered ropes, a distorted saucepan – even some wheels from a baby carriage. Strange shapes that emerged in the beam of light from her torch. Suddenly, she spotted something clinging to the wooden spars at the side of the basin. It looked...it looked like a woman's hat. She reasoned that her eyes might be playing tricks and she needed to be around the other side of the basin to see the object properly, because one of the wharf-side cranes was casting a shadow down and distorting the image. Victoria carefully picked her way across the concrete floor of the wharf towards Tollman, who was slowly moving his lantern, at head height, backwards and forwards in front of him to illuminate a jetty which stuck out into the river.

"Mr Tollman!" she said urgently but softly, as she approached. "I've spotted something that bears further investigation." Tollman turned with an expectant look on his face. He always had confidence in Victoria's sharp eyes. She had proved a valuable investigator on several occasions. He eagerly followed her as she led him back towards the basin. "It's over there," she shone her torch towards the far wall of the basin. "It looks to me like a woman's hat. But we need to go round the other side to get a better view." Tollman nodded and the pair of them picked their way around the end of the basin to end up standing almost below a crane that was bolted to a metal platform set into the concrete. Victoria shone her torch down the side of the wooden walls of the basin and they could both see, quite clearly, a wide-brimmed woman's hat, seemingly caught on the splintered wood of the basin wall.

"We need a ladder," said Tollman firmly and he told Victoria to stay put whilst he looked around. It was now approaching 9 'o'clock in the evening and Tollman knew that high tide would be at around midnight and the hat would be engulfed in over ten feet of water. He began a frantic search around the warehouses but it yielded nothing. Just then Billy, Caroline and Mabel came around a corner and Tollman motioned them over. He explained Victoria's 'find' and Billy wasted no time in volunteering to climb down to retrieve the hat.

Mabel remembered that they had just passed a pile of ropes and she bravely went back to face the rats and retrieve some.

Victoria was so intently watching the hat, that she jumped when Tollman tapped her on the shoulder.

"Billy's going to climb down there," he said and he began to tie one end of the rope around the base of the crane behind them. Once that was done, Billy stripped off his jacket and helmet and began his backwards descent down the basin wall. This was one of those occasions, he realised, where he needed to have a fully functional left hand which, of course, he did not, so he was relying heavily on his legs and his strong right hand to take his weight as he inched downwards. Fortunately, all three of the women were shining their lights down on to the basin, so he could easily see the possible footholds. A third of the way down the wall, was a horizontal metal beam, which held the wooden timbers in place. Billy was almost able to stand upright on this beam, which took the weight off his arms and shoulders, and he inched sideways until he was almost level with the hat. The best thing to do was, he decided, to put that hat on his head and then start his ascent.

By now the Borough Station police were beginning to trickle over to the lights that were pooled on the basin. They stood in a group and watched Billy struggle to ascend the rope with just one good hand. It was proving much more difficult for him than descending. One of the police went over to Tollman and suggested that they haul Billy up, as there were eight relatively fit and strong policemen and Tollman nodded. "Billy!" he yelled down into the basin, "The lads are going to pull you up. Can you tie the rope under your arms and round your chest?" Billy shouted back that he could. There was a silence whilst Billy accomplished this task and then he shouted "Give it a go now!" Nine policemen lined up and grabbed the rope, like a tug'o'war team, and heaved in unison, hand over hand, until the ludicrous sight of Billy's grinning face topped off with a lady's hat rose above the edge of the basin.

Once he was on dry ground, Billy insisted on shaking every policeman's hand, whilst Caroline plucked the hat off his head and shone a torch into its crown. Mabel and Victoria peered at the hat as well, hoping it might yield valuable information. It was Victoria's sharp eyes that found the answer.

"Look!" she said, pointing at a faded label, tucked under the reinforcing ribbon at the base of the crown.

Caroline peered closer. "Monsieur Pelseneer-Lambert, Bruxelles", she read slowly out loud.

"That's got to be our foreign woman," said Tollman hopefully.

Victoria took the hat from Caroline and turned it around in her hands. "The hat is not wet, maybe a little damp, but it hasn't been immersed in water. And it is not a new hat, judging by how faded the label is." She ran her fingers around and inside the exterior ribbon of the otherwise plain hat. Then she said triumphantly, "Eh voila!" Held between her finger and thumb was a very fine, wispy pale grey feather.

"Those bloody pigeons again," muttered Tollman. He turned to the gang of Borough policemen. " Did anyone find any trace of the two women?" The policemen shook their heads. Tollman turned back to Victoria. "I think the women were put on board a boat yesterday. A boat that was moored up here." He turned back to the policemen. "What's this place here called?" One of the policemen said "Letts Wharf, Detective Sargeant. It serves these eight warehouses here, from the Waterloo Corn Mill, that backs on to the bridge here…" He pointed behind him to the large building beside Waterloo bridge, "…to the long row of warehouses there, which take in all sorts of goods. Beyond those warehouses is Shot Tower Wharf, which only takes in stuff for the Lambeth Lead Works."

Tollman was impressed. He liked a copper with good local knowledge. "Right. I need your men to go to the nearest telephone and get hold of your station. Ask them to send the van back here to pick you lot up. Meanwhile, my group," he made a motion with his hand to include Billy and the ladies, "will be going in the other direction, across Waterloo Bridge, to have a little chat with the River Police. Thank you for your help this evening, lads. It has been much appreciated." He shook hands with all of them in turn and the two groups split apart to make for their different destinations.

"Let's hope that we're not too late," Tollman murmured, as he shepherded his team along the road to Waterloo Bridge. "If they loaded those women on to a boat last night and then the tide went out, I'm hoping the boat will have been moored in the middle of the Thames until the tide turns."

By now they were all up on the bridge and they looked out at the jumble of vessels at anchor on either side of the river and in the centre of the expanse of water. There was no sign of activity anywhere. All looked deceptively calm. Lights were shining through portholes on some of the vessels but most were in darkness, their crews having taken the opportunity to spend the night ashore and, possibly, sleep in one of the many seaman's missions along the river. Tollman muttered once more, "Let's hope we're not too late."

Chapter Eight

THE SEARCH ALONG THE RIVER

It was cold now. A stiff breeze was blowing down the river from the east and Tollman shivered. Billy took it upon himself to steady Caroline, Mabel and Victoria as they stepped down from the embankment on to the pier which held the floating police station and housed the Thames River Police (Waterloo Pier Section). The Pier was swaying gently in the wind and Billy gently guided each lady to hold on to the windowsill of the Station House whilst Tollman roused the station Sergeant from the comfort of his small cabin at the end.

When the Sergeant and his wife appeared, fresh from their bed it appeared, swathed in thick dressing gowns and her hair in rags, Tollman explained the situation and the Sergeant disappeared to get dressed.

"Would the ladies like to come indoors and have some tea whilst you're on the river?" asked the wife, noticing the three women clinging on to the Station House windowsill.

"Sadly for them, madam, they are needed to come with us." Tollman replied, "They are all medical personnel and we do not know in what state we might find these abducted women."

"Then I shall make you a big flask of tea to take with you," she responded. "Lord knows how long you might be searching and there's a cold wind on the river tonight."

Tollman doffed his hat in appreciation and she disappeared, just as her husband appeared in uniform and pulling on his waterproofs – preparing to take to the river.

"Henry Pritchett," he said, offering his hand in greeting and Tollman grasped it, replying "Arthur Tollman." Then he turned and pointed out his team, "Constable Billy Rigsby, Dr Allardyce, Miss Summersby and Mrs Ellingham. The ladies are our medical advisors," he added, by way of explanation. Pritchett shook each of their hands in turn, then he explained to them all that the Section's motor boat was due back to the pier very shortly. "It's on suicide patrol at the moment," he said with macabre cheerfulness, "Peak time for people throwing themselves off Waterloo Bridge is between 10 and 11 at night. We fished out three dead and two live ones yesterday night," he nodded and looked around at the stunned assembly. "And that was a quiet night!" he chuckled. "Anyway, whilst we wait for the boat to come back, let's go into the office and look at the paperwork for today's river traffic, shall we?" He opened a door in the main cabin and everyone tottered through as best they could, given the sudden movement of the pier from a particularly fierce surge of the water.

Pritchett opened a large box file containing a pile of papers and he began to leaf through them. "We never used to get involved in the paperwork of what the ships load and unload at the wharves along the river but since the war started it's become part of our job. We get regular inspections from the Ministry of War and, also, we have to pass on to them any suspicious activity or information that comes our way. Where exactly do you think these women were taken on board a vessel?"

"Letts Wharf," said Tollman firmly, "It probably would have been about this time, maybe a little earlier, yesterday."

Pritchett shook his head, "Not possible, DC Tollman. This time last night would have been low tide – just turning mind you. But a vessel wouldn't have been able to load in Letts Wharf until high tide…" Tollman looked crestfallen but Pritchett continued, "But, they could have had a rowboat tied up on the mud – a sizeable rowboat, mind, that could take half a dozen people and be rowed by more than one strong man. It takes a lot of muscle to row across the ebb and flow of the tide. All the vessels at anchor in midstream have rowboats so that their men can come and go. But…if your women were abducted last night and loaded into a rowboat and taken out to a vessel at midstream, they could have upped anchor and made it to the estuary when the tide came back in. So, I'd better look at movements…" He closed the box file in front of him, placed it up on a shelf and took down another box file. "This is the paperwork we keep in conjunction with the Port of London Authority, which is all about movements, rather than cargoes." He began to search through the sheaf of papers in the file.

Mrs Pritchett appeared with a canvas bag containing a very large flask of tea, a smaller flask of milk, a jam jar of sugar and a bag of currant buns. "The patrol is coming back in, Henry," she announced to her husband as she set everything down on a side table. Billy looked out of the window and he could see the lights of the motor yacht advancing on the pier and hear the rhythmic chugging of the engine.

"Ah! Thank you my dear," Pritchett responded without looking up and his wife nodded and took herself back to the warmth of her bed. Pritchett, made a last rummage through the papers and said "No, I have no evidence of a vessel leaving its berth yesterday apart from two. One was a coal barge, from Limehouse Docks, I know the crew that operate that one, and they went up river to Chiswick. The other was an empty ship just finished unloading lead on the morning tide at Shot Tower Wharf and decided to lay over midstream for the crew to go ashore, then left as soon as the tide turned. So," he said, closing the file, "your vessel should still be here, and we shall help you find it."

By then the patrol motor boat had docked and was being tied up and Pritchett went out to speak to the policemen. A sergeant called Langham came back in with him and introduced himself. "We just fished a dead person out of the river…"

"Is it a woman?" interrupted Caroline but Langham shook his head.

"No, madam. It's a man…elderly and, by the state of him, he has been in the water a while. Probably a drunken tramp that accidentally fell into the river and, due to being so bloated, has just popped up to the surface when the tide went out."

Billy found himself feeling grateful that he wasn't serving in the River Police. He had no love for the water and the thought of retrieving dead bodies from it made him shudder.

Pritchett picked up the canvas bag of refreshments and suggested that he take Tollman's team on board the patrol boat whilst his lads had some tea and a smoke. "Just give them fifteen minutes," he added, "and they'll take the boat out again."

Tollman, Billy and the ladies trooped out on to the pier and Pritchett assisted them all to board, then he insisted that they all wear lifejackets, which Victoria found to be rather heavy and wondered how on earth such things would keep her afloat in the water. Mabel was secretly delighted to be having a new experience and she insisted on examining every inch of the craft and asking Pritchett questions. How many times did the patrol boat go out? What speed was is capable of? How much weight could it carry? All of which Pritchett answered with good humour and with an expression of amusement on his face. Caroline managed to find a seat near the wheelhouse which, for the moment, offered some respite from the cold wind from the east.

Victoria joined her and huddled in close, murmuring, "Only Mabel could find a police motor boat fascinating." Caroline smiled and nodded.

Two of the river policemen boarded, the third, it was explained, had decided to stay behind, as Sergeant Pritchett was on board. Eight people onboard the vessel was enough. Besides, who knew how many people they would need to take onboard if they found the women and their abductors?

The stay-behind policeman came out of the office and began to unhitch the rubber dinghy they had been towing, which contained the dead body, in a canvas bag, that they had fished out the river, and he threw a line to Pritchett for a second, empty dinghy, which they would tow instead. Once that was completed, the policeman on the pier cast off the patrol boat and Pritchett started up the engine as they pulled away. Billy steadied himself and took in several lungfuls of cold night air, persuading himself that he would not be sick, under any circumstances.

The boat chugged out to the Fairway – the centre of the

river – and slowed to a crawl, as it shone its powerful searchlight on to the boats berthed in a line, waiting for the tide to turn. The spotlight brought several skippers out on their decks, wondering what the intrusion was for. These were obviously men known to the river police, judging by the good-natured exchanges that were shouted between all of them. None of them had seen a rowboat they day before – some of them had only recently arrived – and the police boat started its engine again and cruised a little further down the line of vessels, the searchlight sweeping all the time over them, from mast to waterline. There was a block of rowing boats and small canal boats, lashed together and tied to one large metal barge. Some of the large vessels were ranked in pairs and the police boat puttered down one side of the moorings and made a large arc in the water to come back up the other side. Pritchett revved the motor a little more, as they were now going against the tide and facing more resistance. The searchlight brought out other men from within the bowels of their vessels, and more queries were shouted and answered.

Suddenly, one of the men, on a big steel-hulled coal barge, nodded in response to the query about a rowboat containing some men and two women. He said he had seen such a thing, in the half light from the illuminations across the bridge. He noticed the two women were being propped up by one of the men and assumed that they were prostitutes and drunk. Two men had been rowing and the other man was propping up the women. He pointed out a sizeable fishing boat, rigged for sail but with a tall stack in the middle of the large wheelhouse that spoke of the use of steam. The police boat chugged alongside the vessel and played the searchlight over its length and depth. One of the policemen said "The rowboat's gone," and pointed at the empty davit system – its arms in the 'lowering down' position.

Pritchett nodded and began to manoeuvre his boat as close to the fishing vessel as possible, whilst one of his men, when close enough, threw a grappling iron across the bow. Pritchett cut the motor and said to Tollman, "My men will go in first and report on the situation…" Tollman was about to protest when Pritchett added, "You aren't allowed to arrest criminals on the water anyway, that's our job. But follow close behind my men. I'll stay here until the situation is known. Someone has to be in charge of the boat." Tollman nodded and signalled to Billy that they were about to move. The river policemen had put a short gangway up between their boat and the fishing vessel, so Tollman and Billy followed, gingerly across the planks, trying not to wobble as it moved from side to side under their feet and, in Billy's case, trying not to look down at the fast-moving black waters underneath.

"Try not to disturb the scene of the crime," called out Mabel, in vain, as they had disappeared down to the deck level of the other ship and the wind had carried her voice away in the night.

The two river police, carrying torches, entered the wheelhouse first, shouting a warning first to anyone who might be inside. Tollman and Billy hovered outside the door, ready for any trouble. One policeman swiftly returned and said, "Detective Sergeant, there is no sign of any men but there are two women here – sadly, both dead I would say." Tollman sighed and went to the rail of the vessel to address the ladies.

"We need to help you across!" he shouted, "It looks as though we have two dead women on this boat!"

There was a furious scramble by Victoria, Mabel and Caroline to pass baskets of equipment, plus Caroline's medical bag, over to Billy who was, reluctantly, standing on the makeshift gangway. He passed the baskets to Tollman, who then placed them on the deck outside the wheelhouse door. Then Billy took the hand of each of the ladies, in turn, and helped them across to the fishing vessel. Meanwhile, the two river policemen passed them, returning to their own boat, to get stretchers and body bags.

Tollman and Billy had taken over the torches of the two other policemen and were leading the way down into the wheelhouse and down the steep steps into the accommodation. Caroline, who was just behind the two men, gasped, when the torches illuminated the scene in front of them. Two women were tied to wooden chairs; arms behind the chairs, feet ties to the legs. They were blindfolded and gagged. One woman's head was slumped on her chest, the other woman's head was flung backwards and one side of it was covered in blood, where she had been shot in the head. Caroline heard Mabel behind her mutter, "Oh my God," and Victoria's hand flew to her mouth to stifle a cry.

Caroline pushed past Tollman and went straight to the woman who had not been shot. She took her gloves off and felt the woman's neck. "She's still alive!" she said urgently, "But only just! We must get her to hospital as quickly as possible!" Then she turned to the other woman and shook her head. "This one has been dead for several hours. She is quite cold and the blood has stopped flowing."

Mabel and Victoria moved out of the way to allow the river policemen in with their stretcher. "Forget the dead woman," urged Tollman. "This one is still alive. We need to get her to hospital as fast as possible."

Caroline had begun to untie the restraints around the woman's ankles and she noticed that the woman had emptied her bladder at some point, as her dress and stockings were damp and smelt of urine. Victoria had nipped around the various policemen and was untying the woman's hands. Caroline just caught the unconscious woman, as she slumped forward off the chair. The policemen took over and lifted her onto the stretcher and began to strap her in.

"Wait!" said Caroline sharply, and she prised open the woman's jaws and pulled her tongue forward in her mouth. "She'll have to be laid on her side," she commanded, "her breathing is depressed enough without her tongue falling back into her airway." The men nodded and turned the woman gently on to her side, strapping her in as best as they could.

Everyone had to clear out of the way in the cramped cabin, to allow the men to lift the stretcher up the stairs and out on to the deck, where they then proceeded to load her on to the police boat. Pritchett, under the watchful eye of Caroline, quickly covered the woman over with blankets to keep out the chill night air.

Meanwhile, Mabel examined the dead woman who had, she exclaimed to Tollman "been shot through the temple at close range with a pistol," and she pointed out the powder burns.

"Looks like a deliberate execution, to my mind," said Tollman grimly.

"There is also a smell of chloroform in this cabin," said Mabel firmly, "and I suggest that we remove ourselves before we pass out."

Everyone looked alarmed and swiftly moved up the stairs, through the wheelhouse and out into the bracing river air. "Breathe deeply," counselled Mabel, "get plenty of air into your system."

Pritchett appeared on deck. "We need to get this woman to the hospital as soon as possible, but we can't leave this vessel unattended, in case the men responsible come back. So I propose to leave both of my men here. I've issued them with guns – we keep them in the hold of our boat, in case of trouble. Once we've delivered the patient to the hospital, we will come back and tow the vessel back to our pier, so that it can be examined."

"Yes, I shall want to do that," said Mabel briskly. "So can you please lock up the cabin and hold and see that no-one disturbs anything. I will come back first thing tomorrow."

Pritchett nodded and looked at all her baskets of equipment. "You can leave those in our office until you return," he offered and Mabel nodded gratefully.

The two river policemen appeared, with rifles, and a case full of other equipment. Billy, Tollman and Victoria picked up Mabel's baskets and took them back to the police boat.

Pritchett removed the gangway and grappling hook, started the engine again and slowly turned the boat towards the River Police pier. Caroline kept a firm hand on the unconscious woman's head throughout the short journey and prayed that they would reach a hospital in time.

* * *

Beech had just finished speaking to Tollman on the telephone, when the Commissioner came through on the intercom, inviting him to come and visit for "a chin wag and a snifter", which was his way of requesting an update on their current case. Beech was pleased that, due to Tollman keeping him updated, he would be able to report some small measure of success.

So, settled in a leather armchair in Sir Edward Henry's office, whisky in hand, he related the information given to him over the telephone in the last half hour. "The surviving woman was first taken to Charing Cross Hospital," explained Beech, "it being the closest, but Dr Allardyce said it was absolutely bursting at the seams with wounded soldiers straight off the boat trains and she requested that the ambulance carry on to the Woman's Hospital, where she works, so that the woman could be given the best possible care."

Sir Edward nodded in appreciation and then turned to the topic that interested him the most – the examination of the place of the crime.

"Ah, yes," Beech smiled. "You can be sure that Miss Summersby has organised that as usual."

"Admirable woman," Sir Edward murmured.

"The vessel is under guard by the River Police and being towed to their pier, as we speak. Miss Summersby, apparently, gave strict instructions that they were to open as many windows and portholes as possible to try and dispel the lingering chloroform in the cabin. Then to lock up the cabin and no-one should enter, until she conducts a thorough investigation in the morning. All her equipment is in the River Police office and she says she will bring camera equipment tomorrow. Unfortunately," he added, his voice taking on a sad note, "it means that the unfortunate woman who has been murdered, must stay in place, until Miss Summersby has taken photographs."

"Will she require some assistance?" Sir Edward enquired, "Only I could dispatch some of the fingerprint specialists to help."

"I shouldn't think so, sir. Victoria Ellingham is going to assist, as Dr Allardyce wishes to stay with the unconscious woman at the hospital. As soon as Miss Summersby has finished, she will get the Station Sergeant at Waterloo Pier to telephone the morgue to come and collect the body and telephone me, then I will send in the fingerprint men."

"And we still have no idea who the two abducted women are, or who abducted them?" Sir Edward asked, pouring Beech another whisky.

"Not at the moment, sir," Beech shook his head. "We are hoping that the thorough investigation of the vessel in the morning might turn up some identification in the form of luggage, papers or something else. Meanwhile, DS Tollman and Constable Rigsby will be travelling down on a South Coast train to see if they can glean any more information about the women from the other guard who travelled with them from Southampton to Basingstoke, and also the ticket collector and station master at Southampton. We shan't waste any time, sir."

Sir Edward Henry drained his glass of the last dregs of whisky and gave a satisfied sigh. "Beech, you have an efficient little team working out of Mayfair. I am very glad you persuaded me to let you set it up. How is Lady Maud by the way?"

Beech grinned. "As formidable and energetic as always, Sir Edward. I don't know where we would be without her support."

"Well give her my best regards, Beech, and keep me fully informed of any developments."

Beech rose from his chair and said, with some satisfaction, "I shall, sir, I shall."

CHAPTER NINE

THE MYSTERY CORPSE

Growler and Wally had decided to spend the day 'mudlarking'. After their success the previous day in obtaining foodstuffs, Growler decided they should comb the muddy shores of the Thames for anything valuable that they might be able to sell. That meant waiting until low tide when the most lucrative stretch of mud, between Waterloo Bridge and Blackfriars Bridge – known as King's Reach, was exposed. It was the most prized area by mudlarkers because the Thames went into a dramatic curve at Waterloo and the outbound tide, rushing towards the sea, dragged many valuables with it from the more salubrious residences and activities taking place to the West of London. Waterloo Bridge being a favoured spot for suicides to leap into the river, some bodies washed up there too. Growler and Wally were not too squeamish about rifling through the pockets of bloated corpses, after all, as Growler stated "They're dead, ain't they? Why would they care what happens to their stuff?"

Mudlarking was an endeavour that the two urchins undertook, maybe once a month, mainly because it caused them to become covered in mud and because neither of them lived in dwellings that possessed a bath, they would have to go to a friendly scrap merchant's yard in Coin Street, where he would hose them down for free. This, of course, meant that they and their clothes would be wet for the rest of the day, so mudlarking was only an endeavour to be undertaken on reasonably warm and dry days. Wally, who was good at reading the weather, had pronounced that it was going to be dry all day so, they were sitting on the stone steps, sharing a stolen beef pasty and waiting for the tide to get to its lowest level.

They were oblivious to the young policeman who was standing on the other side of the embankment wall and watching them. Constable Fowler had been one of the gang of policemen from Borough Police Station who had been helping to search the wharves and warehouses the night before. He had decided to have another look around in daylight, as it was technically an area within his beat and, on his way into the warehouse complex, he had met the night watchman who had found and reported the baskets of pigeons.

"Those little bleeders who killed the pigeons are here again," the man had grumbled. He had been standing on his front doorstep, smoking a cigarette and looked as though he had just woken up.

PC Fowler had told him that the boys didn't kill the pigeons. A man from the government Pigeon Service had said that they had been gassed.

The night watchman had raised his eyebrows and verbally expressed surprise. "Well, I never! I would have sworn those boys had something to do with it."

Fowler had said no, but expressed an interest in the boys anyway.

"I see 'em strolling down towards Shot Tower Wharf," answered the man, and he had pointed eastwards along the Commercial Road. "God knows what villainy those two are up to," he grumbled. They're well known in this area as a couple of little thieving wasters. One of 'em's called Growler and I don't know the name of his mate but he's got a twisted lip."

Fowler had made a mental note of that and thanked the man for his help. That was how he found himself watching the two boys as they sat, eating, and waiting for the tide to expose the mud. It seemed to be a good hour before they actually made a move and Fowler observed them slowly squelching their way across the dank mud and bending now and then to pull something out of the soil. He smiled briefly when the taller of the two boys lost his boot in the mud and had to retrieve it and then he became alert with interest when one boy shouted to the other and they raced a few yards ahead to pick up some sizeable objects. It looked, from a distance, like they were retrieving some small bags. One of the boys appeared to be searching inside the bags and, whatever they found in there was enough to make them abandon their mudlarking and head for the stone steps back up to the wharf.

Fowler was lying in wait and, as the two urchins turned a corner, he grabbed both of them by the arm, holding them firmly against their angry struggles. He could see that they both seemed to have, in their other hands, what looked like women's bags – one small clutch bag and the other a sizeable handbag with two straps, one of which was broken.

"Right, my lads," he said firmly and loudly, "I'm marching you straight to my police station, so you behave, the pair of you."

"We ain't done nuffin!" yelled Growler, outraged to be 'arrested' when he hadn't done anything illegal. "We're allowed to mudlark! Everyone does it!"

"Not talking about you mudlarking. We're talking

about a load of valuable dead pigeons, that you were seen tampering with!"

"They was dead when we found 'em!" Growler protested, with an edge of fear in his voice. "Honest they was!"

PC Fowler smiled grimly. "Well then you won't have anything to worry about, will you, lad? Just answer the questions the Sergeant asks you and no cheek. You might even get a cup of tea out of it."

Growler considered this offer and decided it was a pleasant one.

"All right. We'll come quiet," was his sullen offer and allowed himself and his friend Wally to be marched towards the police station.

* * *

Mabel and Victoria were knocking on the Station Sergeant's door on the River Police Pier at 8 o'clock sharp and Pritchett's wife opened the door.

"Good morning, ladies," she said affably, "Henry is just finishing his breakfast. Would you like to come in and have a cup of tea, while you're waiting?"

The offer was gratefully accepted, as both women had left home without having anything to eat or drink, and they stepped inside the warmth of the cosy cabin. Pritchett's wife indicated that they were to sit at the table alongside her husband. "I'll make you a bit of toast as well," she said as she bustled into the small kitchen.

"Morning, ladies," Pritchett said, looking up from his

eggs and bacon and nodding. "Nothing has been touched on the vessel, which has been moored in front of the station office since midnight. It has all been locked up and guarded."

"Gave me the creeps last night," said Mrs Pritchett, setting down a fresh pot of tea, with cups and saucers, in front of Mabel and Victoria. "I kept thinking about that poor dead lady still on board and I barely slept a wink."

"Yes, it was unfortunate that we had to do that," Mabel answered, "But her dead body may yield up several clues as to the identity of her killers."

"If you don't mind me saying so, ladies," Sergeant Pritchett ventured, as he pushed his empty plate away, "this is very unsavoury work for such refined ladies." He looked at them questioningly.

Mabel looked at Victoria and appeared hesitant, so Victoria decided to explain. "It's part of our war effort, Sergeant," she replied smoothly. "The police, as I'm sure you know, have lost so many men to the front and so they are short of people to do the backroom stuff. Miss Summersby here is a scientist and has extensive knowledge of many matters pertaining to crimes, I, myself, am a trained lawyer and, as such, my skill is spotting any little thing that might be evidence for tracking down a criminal and bringing someone to a successful prosecution. Of course, we don't do any proper policework," she hastily added. "We simply make our reports and the police take it from there. Needs must in wartime, Sergeant!"

Before Sergeant Pritchett could answer, his wife placed a plate of hot, buttered, toast on the table and said, "Well I think you are very brave and public spirited. There aren't many women, from your station in life, who would volunteer for such work." Sergeant Pritchett nodded in agreement with his wife and, to Victoria's relief, the matter appeared to be settled.

Mabel suddenly thought of something and asked the Sergeant if she could use his telephone. Mrs Pritchett indicated where it was, in the corner of the room, and she rummaged in her handbag to find her rather battered address book. She asked the operator to put her through to a Belgravia number and when she was connected, and the number was answered, she said "Is that Sissy? It's Mabel Summersby here. Are you available to help with the examination of a body this morning?...Good. Can you get to us as soon as possible? We are at the River Police Pier on the embankment, north side of Waterloo Bridge...ah good, you know it. Victoria and I will be on board the vessel that is moored there...just ask for Station Sergeant Pritchett and he will show you where we are...see you soon."

Mabel sat down and began to tuck into the toast, then she realised that Sergeant and Mrs Pritchett were expecting an explanation. "I just telephoned another lady of our acquaintance, she used to lay out bodies for an undertaker and she is exceptionally skilled at noticing any clues regarding a person's manner of death."

"Fancy!" Mrs Pritchett was impressed and she nodded at her husband. "Leave it to the women to do all the unsavoury jobs, eh?" and she chuckled.

The toast had been gratefully despatched by Mabel and Victoria, as well as a couple of cups of tea each, and they were now ready for work. Sergeant Pritchett took them to the office, where they picked up Mabel's baskets of equipment, then he escorted them up the temporary gangplank and unlocked the wheelhouse door.

"All available windows and portholes have been left open all night, to allow any vapours to exit," he advised, "but it may still be hazardous down there. It's not always easy to ventilate ship's cabins."

Mabel nodded, "Don't worry, Sergeant, we will take regular breaks to come up on deck and get some fresh air." Then the two women descended into the depths of the boat.

* * *

PC Fowler had incurred the displeasure of his Station Sergeant at Borough Police Station by bringing in two smelly, scruffy urchins.

"They stink to high heaven, Fowler," the Sergeant had grumbled, but he had conceded that the boys might yield up some useful information for 'the lot at Scotland Yard', as he called Tollman and Rigsby. Just that morning, the Yard had sent over a photograph of one of the missing women who had been taken unconscious to hospital. The other woman was pronounced dead at the scene and there was no photograph of her at present. "The River Police and the Scotland Yard boys found them on board a vessel that was moored in the middle of the river near Waterloo Bridge." So, he gave Fowler the photograph to show the boys. "Those little tearaways are always round and about. They might have spotted something, you never know. They have eyes on everything, like magpies."

Fowler held up the objects he had confiscated from the boys. "They picked these up from the riverbank. Looks like women's handbags. Do you want to go through them, Sarge? They might belong to the two abducted women."

The Sergeant looked at the mud-caked objects with distaste. "Leave them there. I'll go and get a pair of gloves and a cloth and have a bit of a rummage."

Fowler went to the interview room, where he had left another policeman on guard, to make sure the slippery street urchins didn't escape. He had produced the promised cups of tea and now suggested to the boys that more tea plus biscuits might be on offer if they could give him any information. They looked at him warily as he displayed the photograph of the unconscious woman to them.

"Is she dead?" asked Growler with very little sympathy in his voice.

Fowler shook his head. "No. but another woman is. This one here…" he tapped the photograph, "is in hospital, still unconscious, and we don't know who she is…"

"We know her!" said Wally, without thinking and Growler glared at him.

"We *might* know her," Growler corrected his impetuous mate. "Depends what's in it for us."

Fowler marvelled at the street survival hardness of a young child. "How old are you, son?" he asked Growler, who scowled and replied, "I dunno. What's it to you, anyway?"

Fowler sighed. "Nothing to me at all. None of my business. Now, how about I get you those biscuits – give you a bag of biscuits to take away with you – and give you each sixpence. Would you tell me then who this woman is?"

Wally beamed but Growler's face took on a cynical look. "Make it a shilling each and we have a deal."

Fowler smiled and countered, "We'll give you a shilling each if you let us give you a wash."

The two boys erupted with sounds of disgust and noises of protest. Growler glared and countered with, "Ninepence each and *no wash*."

Fowler conceded defeat. "All right. Ninepence and no wash."

"And the bag of biscuits?" Wally was beside himself with glee.

"And the bag of biscuits, But information first. Now what do you know about this woman?"

Wally looked at Growler, who nodded, and Wally said, "We don't know her name or nothin' but she's a train cleaner at Waterloo."

Fowler was interested. "Is she now? And how do you know that?"

Growler took over the explanation, "We sometimes go there at night, when they're cleaning the trains, because they chuck out any food that people have left on the trains, like sandwiches and fruit and stuff. They put it all in these big bins and when they go for a tea break, we have a rummage."

Wally nodded. "She seen us once, that woman. But she was alright. She just said 'don't fall in the bin, lads' and she turned it on its side, so we could sort through stuff easier. She was alright," he repeated with a note of sorrow in his voice.

Growler nodded in agreement. "Yeah, she never reported us

or nuffin". The woman appeared to have been approved by them.

Fowler asked, "Do you know her name?"

Both boys shook their heads, then Wally had a rethink. "I think we heard her being called Thelma once but we can't be sure. Someone shouted it out and I saw her turn around but that doesn't mean it was her they were calling for."

Fowler told them to stay where they were and he would go and get the promised biscuits plus the money he had agreed. Both boys looked pleased with themselves. Out on the front desk the Sergeant was removing a pair of mud caked gloves and placing them in a bucket, along with a cloth he had used to wipe off the outside of the bags.

"Two women's handbags," the Sergeant pronounced, holding them up by the straps. "Both have railway travel warrants in them from the government. One of them has precious little in it apart from that and a few coins, the other has a load of foreign documents that bear further examination. So, I shall be passing these over to Tollman at the Yard. Any joy with those lads?"

Fowler explained that the good news was that they seemed to know the woman in the photograph and where she worked, the bad news was that it was going to cost the police a bag of biscuits and ninepence for each boy.

The Sergeant grinned. "You're too soft Fowler!" he commented. "I'm happy for that to come out of station funds, providing you write a report for this Detective Sergeant Tollman, to which I will add a bill for the biscuits and the 1 shilling and sixpence payment. As we're doing the Yard's work for them, they can cough up for the information." It seemed a fair deal.

* * *

Sissy had arrived and Mabel could now attend to the body. Up until her arrival, Mabel and Victoria had spent an hour carefully searching through the cabin and anything of interest was placed in paper bags. So far, they had found a crumpled wrapper from a sweet, which had a German name printed on it and they had also found an almost empty packet of pipe tobacco which came from a company in Vienna. "So Austrian then, rather than German?" Victoria had posed the question but Mabel pointed out that Viennese pipe tobacco could probably be purchased just as well in Berlin as it could in Vienna. They had also found some stubs of cigarettes, a comb with some grey hair in it and an empty bottle of chloroform. "A large bottle," Mabel had pointed out. "If they used all of the contents over a period of twenty-four hours, we will be very lucky if that woman we removed to hospital recovers at all."

Sissy and Mabel carefully untied the dead woman from the chair and laid her on a blanket on the floor. "Victoria," warned Mabel, "Although we are not going to perform an autopsy, you may find a naked dead body upsetting and wish to go outside for a while."

"Don't be silly!" Victoria retorted. "You forget that I have worked as a nurse. I have no intention of leaving."

Sissy and Mabel began to slowly undress the woman and hand the garments to Victoria for inspection. "You never know," Mabel commented, "whether a woman travelling alone across several countries, might not conceal valuables somewhere in her clothing." Victoria nodded and began a meticulous inspection of every garment as it was passed to her.

The entry wound of the bullet was quite obvious – in her left temple – but the exit wound was less obvious, as it was underneath her very thick hair. Sissy had raised the top half of the woman's body so that Mabel could remove the corset, and when she cradled the woman's head, she discovered a clump of hair stiffened by caked blood. Further investigation revealed an exit wound just behind the right ear.

"Victoria," Mabel commented, "if the bullet exited from the right side of the head, then it must be lodged in either the floor or the wall of the cabin over there," she pointed to a corner area. "Perhaps you could take one of the storm lamps and have a search?"

Victoria duly obliged and began to search whilst Mabel and Sissy continued. "Have you noticed anything about the body so far?" Mabel asked Sissy, because she knew that her powers of observation with regard to dead bodies were vastly superior to her own.

"Dehydration," said Sissy firmly. "I used to see it quite a lot in the elderly corpses I've dealt with – because they often forget to drink fluids. This woman's veins are enlarged on her arms – can you see? I was told once by a doctor that that means they are dehydrated."

Mabel thought for a moment and then said, "Victoria, I am so sorry to keep asking you to do things…"

Victoria laughed, "Goodness Mabel! Don't apologize! I'm only too glad to be of help! I felt, in the beginning, as though I didn't have anything to contribute to this investigation but you have made me feel very useful indeed. So, what can I do now? Any errand is gratefully accepted." she said brightly.

"I wondered if you could ring Caroline at the hospital and suggest a course of treatment for the surviving lady, based on what we have found here?"

Victoria grabbed a piece of paper and a pencil from one of Mabel's baskets and was poised to write.

Mabel continued, "Based on the fact that the dead woman is severely dehydrated, the survivor should be put on intravenous rehydration fluids, if she has not regained consciousness – but Caroline will probably have done that. Additionally, tell her that if she goes down to my pharmacy, in the rear left-hand cupboard, she will find an old Clover (as in the plant) oxygen therapy mask. I still think that design is the best for administering oxygen to a comatose patient, so I suggests she uses it. Tell her to ask Matron so supervise the oxygen administration, as she often assists me in anaesthesia and I would trust her to regulate the dosage. The amount of chloroform that may have been used on these women may, sadly, mean that the survivor may not recover, but we must give it our best shot."

"Got it." Victoria put her jacket back on and left the cabin to deal with the request. Sissy and Mabel continued to disrobe the corpse.

"The poor lady has some bruises on both cheeks, as though she had been slapped and, obviously, quite livid marks on her wrists and ankles from being tied up," Sissy noted.

"Yes," Mabel agreed, "It seems as though she was brutalised quite severely…and there are some strange marks here, around her waist," she pointed at one or two circular marks spaced at irregular intervals, like bruises made by buttons.

Sissy picked up the woman's skirt from the pile of clothes and felt around the waistband. "There are some, feels like metal…like coins, inside the waist of the skirt!" Sissy sounded surprised.

Mabel nodded in satisfaction. "Common trick of women when travelling. Sew some sovereigns, for emergencies, in their clothes. I used to do it myself when I visited the Continent. I'm willing to bet that we will find more than a few sovereigns in her clothes, eventually."

Victoria returned with the news that she had relayed Mabel's message and Caroline was most grateful, as the surviving woman was still unresponsive.

"We think that there are lots of things sewn into this woman's clothing," Mabel informed Victoria.

"Well, I think we should take her clothing back to Mayfair with us, so that we have several pairs of hands taking the clothing apart." Victoria suggested, "Meanwhile, I think I should continue to search for the bullet."

Everyone agreed and Sissy said that she would telephone her sister to meet them there. "Elsie's a dab hand at unpicking seams!" she laughed, "When I grew out of my clothes, she would unpick them and remake them into something for herself. Of course, she could, because she has always been at least two sizes smaller than me!"

Victoria resumed her inch-by-inch search in the corner while Mabel and Sissy turned the body over to note lividity. It was, as they expected in her bottom and the back of her legs, which showed that she had died sitting, tied up, in the chair where they, and the men of the River Police, had found her.

Suddenly Victoria said, triumphantly, "Found it!" and Mabel came over to the corner of the cabin, where a bullet was embedded in the floor.

"Well done!" Mabel commented. "See if you can find a knife in that cutlery draw over there, to try and prise it out of the wood. I'm willing to bet that Detective Sergeant Tollman knows someone in Scotland Yard who could tell us what sort of gun that bullet was fired from."

Mabel turned back to Sissy. "I have to take some photographs of the body, then I think we can wrap this lady up in the blanket now and get the River Police to take her to the mortuary, don't you?"

Mabel had brought along a Box Brownie camera for the job, as she had decided that bringing her big camera and tripod would be too much to handle on board a boat. She then directed Sissy to hold a light above the areas of the body that she wished to photograph. The wrists, the ankles, the marks on the waist, the face, the entry and exit wounds on the head were all recorded and Mabel pronounced that she was finished.

Sissy nodded and began to wrap the naked corpse in the blanket, then tie the blanket around her with some lengths of rope. The River Police had supplied them with an oilskin body bag and the two women managed to lift the corpse about six inches off the ground and move her into the bag.

Victoria, meanwhile, had been able to dig out the bullet and seal it up in a screw top jar.

"Ladies!" Mabel puffed, after the exertion of bagging the body, "I think we are done here. Let us go back to Lady

Maud's house and have some refreshment, before we set about our next tasks!"

Outside, the three women stood for a while as the bracing air whipped across their faces from the river and cleared their heads of the lingering traces of chloroform and their minds of the sadness of the tragic death of such a young woman.

Chapter Ten

THE SECRETS IN THE CLOTHES

Elsie Rigsby had left their guest, Mattie, in charge of the dog and had hurried over to Mayfair to assist the team. "Bring your sewing basket", Sissy had said on the telephone, so she did. Now, she was sitting with Victoria and Sissy in Lady Maud's dining room, with the dead woman's voluminous skirt spread across the dining table, so that they were all able to work on unpicking all the seams. Mabel had excused herself, after refreshments, as she needed to go home and develop the photographs and write up a report on their findings this morning.

"This is quite a fashionable ensemble," commented Victoria, looking at the skirt and jacket together. "I wonder if she bought it in Paris?"

Sissy and Elsie felt unable to venture an opinion, as neither were 'fashionable' women, having neither the money to buy the latest fashion, nor the time to make it at home. However, Sissy commented, "I suppose she must have been comfortably-off then, this poor woman, if she could afford the latest clothes."

Elsie gave a little gasp of surprise and said, "I should say she was well off! Look at this!" as the unpicked seam of the waistband had yielded up a gold coin. The other two women peered at it and smiled.

"It's not a British coin," Victoria commented as she turned it over in her fingers. "I think it's French." She examined it closely and said "It's a twenty-franc coin!" and she smiled.

Elsie triumphantly liberated another one, with her tiny, sharp, embroidery scissors. "I think there must be at least twenty of these in this waistband," she observed.

Sissy was carefully separating the lining of the skirt from the hem and she suddenly produced a slim wad of notes. "These are definitely foreign!" she said, brandishing them. "And they feel new, fresh off the printing press," she observed.

Victoria decided to involve Lady Maud. "Mother will love being treasurer for this hoard," she said, and left the room momentarily, returning with an excited Maud, thrilled at the prospect of being part of the team once again.

Once she had been shown the money, Maud pronounced the coin "A Marianne – after the head of the woman depicted on the coin". Then she examined the wad of notes and said "I am not sure, but I think they might be Romanian. I think that 1,000 Lei is Romanian but it could be Hungarian. We would have to consult a bank that had a foreign exchange department." Whatever the currency was, Maud was excited, and she sat and happily chatted to the ladies as they liberated yet more coins and notes from diverse currencies.

"Goodness me!" Maud exclaimed, as she sorted the various notes and coins into piles, according to denominations and countries of origin, "What a haul for her to be carrying around with her! Do you think that's why she was shot?"

Victoria thought for a moment and said "I doubt it. It would have been so simple to just strip her and do what we are doing, if they suspected she was carrying all this money."

Sissy suddenly produced what looked like a square of cream silk and she peered at it. "I think this might be what the murderers wanted," and she placed the silk in the middle of the table. Everyone gathered around to look at it.

"It just seems to be a lot of numbers and place names," said Victoria. She pointed at the top line and read it out, "5 Div. Transit Metz – Verdun...2 Br. Nam./Art...Cav.Div to Reims... " She stopped and said "I think this is Military Intelligence stuff that we shouldn't be reading. I think this woman was bringing information to someone."

* * *

Tollman was feeling relaxed after his train journey from Waterloo to Southampton. He and Billy had spoken to the Station Master at Waterloo about the possibility of speaking to the guard, Charlie Preston. The rota book had been summoned and it was discovered that Mr Preston was having a day off and would be at home in Southampton. So, furnished with his address and a couple of travel warrants, they had boarded the train and viewed it as a welcome break. They took tea in the dining car, played cards, Tollman took a nap whilst Billy read the paper, then they partook of a simple lunch in the dining car as the train passed through Winchester. Suitably refreshed by lamb cutlets, potatoes and peas, washed down with a couple of beers, they stepped off the train at Southampton with full stomachs but light hearts. Billy took in several lungfuls of sea air.

"It's nice to get away from the Old Smoke, once in a while, and breathe in some sea air, don't you think, Mr Tollman?" he commented, feeling relaxed and full of good cheer.

"I do indeed, lad," agreed Tollman, pulling his scarf tightly around his neck. "But, perhaps, not in October, eh?"

Billy laughed and followed Tollman obediently to the door marked "Station Master". Tollman knocked and, after a few seconds, the door opened. Tollman flashed his warrant card at the man, who looked surprised and motioned them in.

"What can I do for you, gentlemen?" The Station Master asked, having introduced himself as Ronald Cape.

"Well, Mr Cape," Tollman began and he then went on to describe the events of two nights ago, when the women were abducted and the pigeons were found dead. He had been furnished with a photograph of the surviving woman by Scotland Yard and he duly produced it. "Now, the two women apparently met up here, this is one of them here, along with two baskets of pigeons and then caught the London train. It probably would have been an early evening train, as it arrived just outside Waterloo during the Zeppelin raid, which would have been about 10 p.m. They both had government-issued travel warrants. One had come from London to meet the other one, the pigeon lady, who had come from abroad."

Cape thought hard, "I do remember a porter transporting pigeons on his trolley from the docks into the station and I remember a woman with a foreign accent fussing about where they were going to be kept. She said they were not well and must be kept in the warm and not in a draughty cargo shed. She said they belonged to the War Office and were valuable. So, I brought them in here. She said she would pick them up the next day and she was staying in the South Western Hotel overnight."

"When was this, sir?" asked Tollman, feeling hopeful.

"Three days ago," the Station Master answered confidently.

"Where had she travelled from, do you know?" Tollman persisted.

"Cherbourg, it would have been. Le Havre crossings are only troop ships at the moment."

"Right," Tollman shook Cape's hand. "Thank you for your help. We'll go over to the South Western Hotel and make some enquiries now." He could see the hotel through a station window and Billy and Tollman strode out towards it. Behind the hotel and surrounding the docks were formidable wood and corrugated iron walls, that had obviously been erected at the start of war, to shield troop activities from prying eyes. There were huge gates, flanked by the harbour police, and they noted that some of the railway tracks went under the huge doors and, presumably, the troop trains would disgorge their men at the dockside, away from sight. Tollman remembered that any elderly or female persons of German, Austrian or Hungarian heritage were not allowed to live anywhere near the docks or military facilities, so if anyone was spying on troop movements it would have to be a home-grown traitor.

At the South Western hotel, Tollman and Billy had no trouble finding staff who remembered the foreign woman who had stayed overnight. The young women who worked as chambermaids and waitresses were practically lining up to volunteer information, once they caught sight of Billy. One of them, a waitress named Freda, told them that the lady in question had had two male visitors on the morning after she arrived. The men were both dark and spoke with a foreign accent. She had served them coffee and cakes and one of them had complained about the taste of the coffee. They both looked very intimidating, she said. Unsmiling, big muscles like wrestlers. She also reported that when she cleared the cups away, she overheard the woman say, "No. I have to take the pigeons to Doughty Street, then I have to go to WL, then I will go to the Palace."

Tollman's eyebrows shot up at the mention of the word "Palace" and he asked Freda if she was absolutely sure she heard that correctly.

"Oh yes!" she replied. "I almost let out a little gasp because I realised that she must be a very important woman if she was going to the Palace. Anyway, the men left and she went back to her room. Then about an hour later a young woman wearing a brown two-piece came into the foyer and ordered some tea. She sat there, reading one of our newspapers, and when the foreign woman came downstairs again, they seemed to recognise each other and they hugged. Then they left together and I saw them walking over to the station. The woman in the brown two-piece waited outside and the foreign woman went in the station, then she came out with a porter, who had her luggage or something on a trolley. That was the last I saw of them."

"Do we have a name for this foreign woman?" asked Tollman.

Freda nodded. "She registered as Madame Etrangère."

Tollman pulled a face. He knew enough French to know that 'Etrangère' meant 'Stranger' and was obviously not the woman's real name.

Tollman thanked the girl and nudged Billy to do the

same, as he could see that Freda was waiting for the handsome young constable to speak to her. She blushed and giggled and scurried away.

"Thank God for nosey Freda," Tollman murmured. "Did you get all that down in your notes, Billy?" Rigsby nodded and grinned.

Tollman was pleased with their progress and said "Right! I think we have enough here, let's go and find this Charlie Preston and see if he knows any more."

* * *

Peter Beech was dealing with some paperwork in his office when Sergeant Stenton appeared, clutching what appeared to be two women's handbags and some paperwork.

"Just sent over from Borough Police Station, Chief Inspector," he said, as he deposited the items on Beech's desk. "Apparently, it's to do with a case that Tollman and Rigsby are working on and," he added, with a smile playing around his lips, "we appear to owe Borough Police Station 'a bag of biscuits and one shilling and sixpence for information supplied by informants' – they've sent an invoice."

"What?" Beech took the invoice from Stenton and scanned it. "So, it would appear! Good Lord. Would you organise that please, Sergeant Stenton? We can't have the chaps at Borough Police Station thinking we don't settle our debts!"

Stenton laughed and gave Beech a mock salute. "Yes, sir. At once, sir," and he turned on his heel, military-style and exited, still chuckling to himself about the petty bill from Borough.

Beech started to read the report compiled by Constable Fowler of his interview with Growler and Wally. "Extraordinary name...Growler..." Beech muttered to himself. Then, as he got further into the report, he realised that Constable Fowler had struck gold when interviewing the two street urchins. They now knew the first name of the surviving woman in hospital. His first action was to lift the telephone receiver and ask the Scotland Yard operator to put him through to the Women's Hospital. Once through he asked for Dr Allardyce and was rewarded by Caroline very quickly coming to the telephone.

"Is it important. Peter, Only I'm on my way out of the door," she said briskly.

"Yes, very important," he replied. "Don't ask me right now but I have discovered that the woman you rescued yesterday may be called Thelma. It might help her to regain consciousness if the nurses speak her name when they are tending to her, don't you think?"

"Yes!" Caroline sounded impressed. "Well done, Peter! Will you explain everything later at Maud's house?"

"Yes, I should be there about 6 o'clock. Tollman and Rigsby should be back by then as well. Can you round up the rest of the team for me?"

"Will do. See you later."

Beech felt a great deal of satisfaction that he had won Caroline's approval, even momentarily, and he then set about examining the contents of the handbags, being careful to put gloves on first – a practice that had been drummed into every policeman in Scotland Yard by the Commissioner, Sir Edward.

The first handbag, which was a slim bag with two

handles and a clasp, contained very little. Just a travel warrant and some coins. Beech felt carefully around the lining, in case there was anything concealed, but there appeared to be nothing, and he examined the one pocket, which yielded a lady's powder compact, which he could not work out how to open.

The second handbag was much more interesting. It also contained a travel warrant, some French travel documents and, surprisingly, a Romanian passport in the name of Marie Radu. "So, not French or Belgian," he murmured to himself. "How interesting."

* * *

Charlie Preston was digging over his compost heap in his small back garden when his wife escorted Tollman and Rigsby through her scullery and out into the vegetable plot.

"Man after my own heart," said Tollman affably, extending his hand. "I always trust a man who tends a garden."

Preston smiled uncertainly as he shook Tollman's hand and his wife hovered, looking anxious, and casting glances at Billy, who took his helmet off to make himself less daunting.

"Nothing to worry about, Mr Preston," Tollman reassured him. "We just want to ask you a few questions about two women who were abducted from the guard's wagon of the train you were working on."

A look of relief came across Preston's face as he suggested that they should all go inside, in the warm, and his wife would make them all some tea. "Let me scrub my hands in the scullery, detective, and then I'll help you as best I can."

They all sat in the front parlour, Mrs Preston included,

whilst tea was poured and homemade biscuits handed round.

Preston started off the conversation. "I heard about the crime from the relief guard who took over from William Durden. Have you seen him? How is he?"

"He is as well as can be expected, with a whacking great lump on the back of his head," Tollman answered and Mrs Preston tutted.

"That could have been you, Charlie," she murmured anxiously.

"Thankfully it wasn't, Mrs Preston," replied Tollman. "Now, Mr Preston, we know that these two women boarded the train, with two baskets of pigeons, at Southampton," Preston nodded and Tollman continued, "Did they sit in the guard's wagon right from the start of the journey?"

"Yes. The foreign woman insisted on staying with the pigeons. She said they were unwell and she wanted to keep an eye on them. Her and the other woman just sat on two seats near the door and chatted. Well, whispered more like. I think they didn't want me to hear their conversation…but I wasn't really listening anyway, I was checking all the stuff that was loaded at Southampton and making sure that it was all correct on the paperwork."

Tollman then asked, "Did you notice anyone watching the women, or loitering around to be near them?"

Preston thought for a moment and then said, "Well there was one bloke, very tall, a bit like your constable there. He was standing around smoking a cigarette in the good's wagon, next to the guard's wagon, when I went to check on the stuff that had been loaded into the cage. While I was in the cage, checking off the boxes that were due to be dropped off at Basingstoke, he started looking into the guard's wagon and I told him he couldn't go in there. He moved off sharpish, when I told him and went back to the first passenger carriage. I think he was with some other blokes – I couldn't really see."

"Was he foreign? I mean did he speak to you at all?"

Preston shook his head. "He didn't speak to me. Just nodded and moved away. He didn't look particularly foreign."

"Describe what he looked like – apart from being very tall."

"He was blonde…fair haired…like my wife," Everyone looked at Mrs Preston and Tollman noted that her hair was what he would call 'sandy-coloured'. Preston continued, "He had a beard, close cropped, same colour as his hair but with a bit of grey in it. Sort of blue-grey eyes. Face was a bit tanned and lined. I would have put him in his 40s. I can't tell you about the blokes he was with. I saw him sitting opposite two of them and they had hats on, so I couldn't tell the colour of their hair and they had their backs to me."

"Nothing else eventful happen?" Tollman asked hopefully.

Charlie Preston shook his head. "No. Eventually I went back into the guard's wagon and did a crossword in my newspaper. The two women had their eyes closed and were resting against the wall, trying to have a nap. Then we got to Basingstoke and I had to supervise the unloading of the cargo, hand over to Will Durden and he supervised the loading of fresh cargo while I went off-shift to go and have a mug of tea."

Tollman nodded, wrote the last bit of information down and closed his notebook. "Well thank you, Mr Preston, you've been most helpful. If you think of anything else – anything at all, please ring me at Scotland Yard."

Preston nodded and promised that he would have a good think about whether there was anything else he may have seen or heard and had momentarily forgotten.

On their way back to the station, Tollman said to Billy, "I think we have learned quite a lot about the foreign woman today, don't you, lad?"

Billy agreed. "A bit rum though, her saying she was going to go to the Palace. Perhaps she was some foreign princess that was abducted for a ransom and it went wrong and she was killed. Although she could be the one that's in the hospital and may yet be saved."

Tollman laughed. "Billy, lad, you have got to stop going to the picture house and watching all that romantic twaddle. You're beginning to sound like my daughters. They think every man is a prince or a count, in disguise! Which means they are eternally disappointed when some poor bloke says he's just a butcher or a clerk. I'm never going to marry them off if they keep believing all these American films!"

* * *

The whole Mayfair team stood in silence as they surveyed the amount of money that Lady Maud had piled up on the dining table. From the clothing, underwear included, of the woman who had been shot, they had extracted gold sovereigns, several wads of Romanian lei banknotes, even more wads of Russian rouble banknotes and gold French coins. It was quite a haul.

"What, in God's name, did she need all this money for?" asked Beech, not expecting an answer from anyone.

"Then there is the question of this piece of silk we found, which has all kinds of letters and figures on it" Victoria pointed out. "I think it's probably something that should be shown to Special Branch or Military Intelligence."

"You may be right, Victoria," Beech responded. "Although I should like to take the advice of the Commissioner on this one." He gazed for a moment at the piece of silk and then snapped out of his reverie, saying briskly, "Well! Time is pressing and we need to progress with this case. Everyone, take a seat and let's hear what you have discovered. Tollman, you go first."

Everyone sat whilst Tollman spoke about his visit to Southampton with Rigsby. "We gathered quite a bit of information about the foreign woman. She had arrived the day before she travelled up to London and stayed the night at the Southwestern Hotel by the station. She had travelled from Cherbourg, with the baskets of pigeons, which she had entrusted to the Station Master at Southampton overnight. She booked into the hotel under an assumed name, Madame Etrangère…" Most of the assembled team gave wry smiles. Tollman continued "…and she was visited by two, described as, 'burly, dark-haired, unsmiling, foreign men'. She was overheard by the serving waitress to say, 'No. I have to take the pigeons to Doughty Street, then I have to go to WL, then I will go to the Palace.' " Everyone in the room made sounds of shock or surprise. "Then later that day, the other woman, came to meet her…according to the same nosey waitress…they seemed to know each other and embraced as friends. Then the foreign woman checked out of the hotel and the two women went off to the station."

Beech interrupted. "Before you carry on, I can add to that information. I received a report from Borough police station today and it was accompanied by two ladies' handbags." Beech produced the handbags from a canvas holdall. They were grimy and dusty. "They have been through the fingerprinting process, but due to the fact that they were in the water and then caked with river mud, there has been no luck with any fingerprints. Anyway, a search of the contents revealed that our foreign woman is Romanian and her name is Marie Radu."

"Ah! That explains the Romanian money!" exclaimed Lady Maud.

"Yes." Beech continued, "And, sadly, it appears that she is the one who was shot. Borough police inform us that the two street urchins who recovered the bags from the Thames at low tide, recognised the photograph of the woman in hospital. They said she cleans trains at Waterloo and her name is Thelma. We don't have a surname. Caroline?" Beech looked at her expectantly, "Any change in the lady's health.?"

Caroline shook her head, "I'm afraid not. She is being given oxygen at regular intervals and a small amount of liquid nourishment via a throat tube but, as yet, there is no change."

Mabel sighed and commented that overdoses of chloroform can be extremely damaging to the nervous system and it was possible that the woman would never fully recover.

There was a moment's silence as they all reflected on

the fate of the two women and then Beech said, "Please continue, Tollman. Apologies for the interruption."

Tollman nodded and then looked at his notes again. "We then went to interview the train guard, Charlie Preston, who had been on the first leg of the train journey from Southampton to Basingstoke. He confirmed that the two women had sat in the guard's wagon right from the start. He also noticed a man, loitering around in the adjoining good's wagon, having a smoke. He said the man was as tall as Constable Rigsby, sandy coloured hair and a close-cropped beard. He had a tanned and lined face and he estimated he was in his 40s. He seemed to be with two men because the guard saw him go into the passenger section and sit and talk to them. They had their backs to him and wore hats, so he didn't really know what they looked like."

Beech turned to Mabel and asked her if she would like to make a report. Mabel took a sheaf of notes out of her bag and began to read. "The guard's description of a very tall man in the good's wagon would tally with the thirteen-inch boot prints I found there. The two other sets of prints – ten inches and nine and a half inches long – would probably belong to men of around average height, say, five foot six or seven? One has a jagged hole in the front right-hand sole of the boot. I found several cigarette ends and obviously pigeon feathers – the little baby feathers that just float in the air. Did the fingerprint people find anything in the goods wagon?"

Beech shook his head. "Well, I am informed that they found a great many fingerprints – too many to separate – and I suspect that with all the unloading and loading that goes on, in and out of those wagons, a great many people put their fingerprints all over the walls and door. However, I have been informed also that they found one complete hand print – on the wall by the entrance to the guard's wagon. They could tell me nothing remarkable about it, really, except that there appeared to be a thick gold ring on the third finger."

"Left hand print?" asked Mabel. Beech nodded. "So, a married man," she surmised then she continued referring to her notes. "So, when we undertook the examination on the boat – Victoria, Sissy and I – we found a sweet wrapper and a packet of pipe tobacco that came from Vienna, more cigarette ends and a brush with some blonde – one might say sandy, Mr Tollman, – hair in it. We found a large empty bottle of chloroform but no rags or cotton wool. I suppose they could have thrown those overboard. I am surprised that the men themselves weren't overcome by the fumes of the chloroform but they may have ventilated the cabin and spent quite a bit of time on deck. The women were small. The murdered woman was only 5 feet and 2 inches. They were tied up and would have had the chloroform applied directly to their mouths and noses. The murdered woman had been shot through the right temple. Sissy found the exit wound in the right side of the head and Victoria found the bullet in the wooden floor. That would suggest that she was shot at quite an extreme angle by a tall person. I have the bullet here and would be interested to know if there is anyone in Scotland Yard who could tell us what sort of gun fired it." She held up a glass jar with the bullet in and Tollman peered at it.

"Well, it's not squashed with the impact," he observed, "so I reckon Sergeant Thurlow in the Firearms Department might be able to tell us. I'll take it in first thing tomorrow."

Mabel handed over the bullet, then spread out some photographs on the dining table and everyone crowded around. There was a shocked silence as Mabel explained the various bruises on the corpse's wrists, ankles and face. "These marks around her waist were made by the gold coins sewn into her waistband. The gaps in the line of coin impressions were because of her corset stays. The bruises on her face were probably from her being struck around the face. Sissy noticed that she was dehydrated because the veins on her body were prominent. They had obviously kept the women captive without giving them any water."

Billy had flushed and Tollman muttered "Barbaric."

Caroline chipped in at that point. "I have not seen any marks on the woman in hospital, other than her wrists and ankles. There is no bruising around the face. We haven't examined her clothes. They are just wrapped up in a bag in the cupboard by her bed. Shall I bring them back with me tomorrow?"

"We might as well have a look at them," Beech replied, "but it is looking increasingly like the Romanian woman was the target for the kidnappers. She was the one who was brutalised and then shot."

"There is something important that we haven't addressed," Victoria suddenly said firmly, and everyone looked at her. "The men who abducted the women obviously had the boat ready for the captives. They abducted them in the middle of a blackout from a mostly unused station in Blackfriars Road and they must have had a vehicle waiting by that station to transport them to the wharf where the rowboat was moored. Therefore, it would suggest to me that they knew, or it had been arranged, for a Zeppelin raid to take place that night, to enable their activities to take place."

"Good God, you're right, Victoria," Beech exclaimed. "We are now in the realms of high-level espionage. Other people will *have* to be involved. I need to speak to the Commissioner first thing tomorrow."

The telephone rang in in the hallway and they heard the maid, Mary, answer. She then popped her head around the door and said, "Begging your pardon but the operator is asking if Detective Sergeant Tollman is willing to take a call from a Captain Osman in Doughty Street?"

"He most certainly is," said Tollman firmly and he hastened out of the door. Everyone waited, with interest, for him to return.

"Who is Captain Osman, Constable Rigsby?" asked Lady Maud, unable to contain her curiosity,

"In charge of the military's Carrier Pigeon Service, your ladyship," answered Billy helpfully.

"The pigeons! Of course! I'd quite forgotten them!" said Maud, jovially.

Tollman came back in the room with a strange smile on his face. "I knew those pigeons were important," he said, almost congratulating himself. "The captain was about to bury the dead pigeons this afternoon, when he noticed that one of the velveteen pads in the baskets was heavier than the other. He opened it up and found a load of documents in a foreign language and a Romanian passport for some elderly man."

"So, that's why Marie Radu was so anxious for the welfare of the pigeons!" exclaimed Beech.

"So many secrets," said Elsie. "Seems like our two ladies were spies."

"It's looking increasingly likely, Mrs Rigsby. In fact, it's looking highly probable." Beech replied.

CHAPTER ELEVEN

WHO IS WL?

Beech and Tollman stayed up until almost midnight preparing a full report for the Commissioner. They wrote it between them and Tollman laboriously typed it up. It was a slow business, as Tollman was a poor typist, at the best of times, employing only his two index fingers, but he felt that he had to take special care with this report, as it contained such important details. He was also a bit concerned about Beech's plan to ask Elsie and Sissy to take temporary train cleaning jobs, in an effort to find out more about the unconscious woman 'Thelma', still in hospital.

He was very fond of both ladies, especially, of course, Sissy, and it seemed to him that the men involved in the abduction and murder obviously had no morality at all and Billy's mother and aunt could be in extreme danger.

* * *

Billy had been dispatched to collect the documents and passport that had been hidden in the pigeon basket. He was walking up from Holborn to Doughty Street and thinking about Mattie. He was thinking about taking her to the cinema, maybe tomorrow, if he wasn't working. He realised that it was a very long time since he had been on a proper outing with a girlfriend and he smiled happily to himself. A real relationship with someone of the opposite sex would be just the ticket, now that he no longer had to worry about fighting at the Front. Before the war, he had not been ready for a settled relationship. He had been, in his mother's words, "a proper Jack the Lad, with no thought for anyone but himself." Then, when the war started, no one wanted to seriously start courting because of the fear of being killed at any moment. Now it was different. Billy felt different. He felt he was ready for an attachment and he hoped that Mattie would feel the same.

Captain Osman answered the door instantly, when Billy knocked. He was almost quivering with anxiety about the documents he had found.

"I've never encountered such a flagrant misuse of our rules in the Carrier Pigeon Service," he said firmly, as he hung Billy's greatcoat up and offered him a mug of tea. "These were valuable birds, performing a sterling service for the country and, once they had been rested and tended, would have gone on to give yet more service. To use the baskets as a hiding place for illicit documents is something I have never encountered before."

Billy tried to be sympathetic but realised that he would never understand the passion Captain Osman felt about pigeons. To Billy, born and bred in London, pigeons were just like rats – always around and regarded as vermin. He appreciated, of course, that these racing pigeons were not the same as London pigeons but, nevertheless, they were birds and to him, not especially loveable.

"Would it be possible to look at the item that these documents were concealed in, sir?" Billy asked.

"Yes, of course." Osman opened up the basket and retrieved a pad of fabric that lay in the bottom. "It's just a soft pad of fabric that protects the bird's feet and keeps them warm during transit." He opened up another basket and took another pad out. "This is what is should be like," he explained, handing one to Billy, "and this is the one that concealed the documents."

Billy took the other pad, noting that it was bulkier and heavier than the first. Osman had ripped the seam open and, amongst the cotton wadding, was a sheaf of documents and a passport, showing a picture of an elderly man with white hair. Billy kept the documents and handed the pad back. "And no one had tampered with the pad that you have opened?" he asked.

Osman shook his head. "No, it was quite tightly sewn up." He vented his anger again. "I shouldn't be surprised if that's why the pigeons were killed! Disgraceful."

"Why would anyone kill the pigeons and then not take the documents, if that's what they were after, Captain Osman?" reasoned Billy, "And, besides, I was there when you opened up the baskets in Borough Police Station, and all the birds were nestled together, like they were sleeping. They didn't look as though they had been manhandled at all."

Osman had to concede that this was true. "But why gas them?" he asked plaintively.

Billy chose his words carefully. "We now think, due to evidence that has come to light, that the death of the pigeons was accidental. The women who were kidnapped were knocked out with chloroform and the pigeons, being, I imagine, sensitive little things, were just overcome by that as well."

Osman nodded and seem to accept that explanation. Billy thanked him for the tea and explained that he needed to get the documents back to Scotland Yard as quickly as possible. As he was leaving, another thought occurred to him. "Captain

Osman, these pigeons were supposed to be picked up by you from Waterloo Station, were they not?" Osman nodded. "So, I wonder when the woman was going to retrieve these documents?" Billy really didn't expect an answer to his question from the aggrieved Captain Osman.

Tollman had almost finished his typing by the time Billy got back to Scotland Yard with the documents. Beech looked them over and added them to the other items he needed to show the Commissioner – Mabel's report and photographs, the women's handbags, all the money, documents and passport, and, most importantly, the silk square imprinted with all the mysterious numbers and place names.

"Well, it's quite an impressive haul of evidence," Beech stated, as Tollman appeared with the finished report. "I shall now go and place the whole thing on Sir Edward's desk, with a covering note and await to be summoned in the morning, when he has read everything."

"Sir, can I just voice my concern about something?" Tollman decided to speak up.

"Of course, Tollman," Beech replied.

"Given the brutal nature of this crime and it's seeming involvement with, possibly, our government and foreign governments...I am a bit concerned that Sissy and Elsie might be placed in danger..."

"What's this?!" Billy was alarmed, as this was the first time he had heard about his mother and aunt being 'placed in danger'.

Beech held up his hands to stop any wild speculation. "I do understand your concerns, Tollman...and your alarm,

Rigsby… but, *if* the Commissioner agrees, and I emphasise *if*, I would insist on both of you being undercover bodyguards for the ladies. Pretending to be porters or some other occupation, in order to watch over them."

Tollman was relieved. "Yes, sir, of course. That would set my mind at rest."

"Would someone please tell me what, exactly, we are talking about?" Billy was insistent that someone should explain.

"Yes, of course, Rigsby." Beech apologised and then explained. "It has been proposed, by me, that your aunt and mother do a stint as train cleaners to see if they can find anything out about the woman, Thelma. And, quite rightly, D.S. Tollman was concerned for their safety."

Billy grunted and nodded. "Yes sir…understood, sir."

"Right," said Beech, picking up all the evidence and the report. "If you two would escort me to the Commissioner's Office and open all the doors for me, I think we can then go home to our beds, don't you?"

* * *

The next morning was tense. The whole team was waiting for the verdict of the Commissioner on how their investigation might proceed.

Billy had taken the opportunity of the pause in proceedings to run a few errands for other departments, which gave him an excuse to pop into the house in Belgravia to see his mother, aunt and Mattie. Nothing was more pleasurable, he decided, than sitting around the table in a warm kitchen, drinking tea and eating cake with the three women he cared about the most in the world. And he had decided that he did care for Mattie, very much. He sat watching her smile and chat with Elsie and Sissy as though she had known them all her life. She was animated and her bruises were beginning to fade. He could see that she was relaxed, probably because she felt safe and she wasn't alone anymore. *Yes*, he thought to himself as he listened to the three women chatting and laughing, *Mattie could just be the one for me.*

He decided not to tell Sissy and Elsie that they might be called upon to do more in the current investigation. Firstly, he reasoned, it might not happen. The Commissioner could read the report and decide that everything should be handed over to Special Branch immediately. Secondly, he wasn't happy discussing the team's private work in front of Mattie, until he knew her better. He wasn't, of course, aware that his mother and aunt had already told her about the work that they did.

Billy stood up and said "Well, I'm sorry to love you and leave you, ladies, but I must get back to work." There was a general noise of disappointment amongst the ladies, then he said, "Mattie…could I have a word?" Mattie nodded and walked to the door with Billy. Sissy winked at Elsie and they pretended to be oblivious of the two young people.

"If I'm not working tonight, would you like to come to the picture house with me? There's a Charlie Chaplin film on, amongst others."

Mattie beamed and said, "I'd love to!"

Billy smiled with relief. "I'll pick you up about 6.30. We

can get a fish supper to bring back here, if you like." Mattie nodded happily. Then Billy looked serious. "I hope I'm not working but if I am, I'll telephone here and let you know."

"I hope you're not working too," she said, "but if you are, it doesn't matter. We'll go another night."

Billy smiled at her gratefully and then kissed her on the cheek. "I hope I see you later," he said as he walked out of the door.

Sissy and Elsie immediately chorused "Ooooh!" in unison and made Mattie blush.

"There was a lot of 'hope' in that conversation!" commented Sissy.

"Not that we were listening or anything," said Elsie, with a laugh.

"Do you think Billy really likes me?" asked Mattie, "Or do you think he just feels sorry for me?"

With cries of "Don't be silly!" and "Of course he really likes you!" Sissy and Elsie took Mattie into their respective embraces of reassurance.

* * *

The call to Peter Beech to attend upon the Commissioner came at about noon. Sergeant Stenton appeared and said that the Commissioner was about to go out for a short meeting but would Chief Inspector Beech like to meet him at his club for lunch at 1 o'clock? It was an instruction, rather than a request and Beech simply nodded. Stenton disappeared to relay the acceptance message to the Commissioner before he left the building.

At about 12.30 Beech decided to catch the omnibus from Scotland Yard up to Trafalgar Square. Then he would walk from there to Pall Mall and the Athenaeum Club. It wasn't far but Beech had felt, in the last few days, that his damaged leg was not functioning as well as it could and he wanted to exercise it. He still limped slightly and, as he passed several bright and attractive young women, out of their offices, presumably, on their lunch break, he attempted to smile at them, but then regretted it when he fancied that he saw one of the girls give him a look of pity. He conceded that it may have been his imagination but, nevertheless, it made him feel less of a man.

He reached the Athenaeum Club in a darkening mood and it was made no better by being told that Sir Edward was in a private dining room on the second floor and, therefore, his aching leg was going to have to be cajoled up the vast marble staircase.

After several pauses on the way up, Beech arrived at the room to find that the Commissioner was not alone. A thin man with a moustache, dressed in military uniform, rose as Sir Edward introduced him, "Beech this is Lieutenant Colonel Vernon Kell…Kell this is Chief Inspector Peter Beech." The two men shook hands and took their seats. A waiter appeared with a tray of three whiskies and the menus. Normal conversation ceased whilst they chose their meals, then, once the waiter left with their orders, Beech was able to ask what government department Kell worked for.

Vernon Kell chuckled and said, "I head up the little-known Security Service called MI5(g). We deal with any security threats within Great Britain. Sir Edward, here, knows me because my department often works in tandem with Basil Johnson and his Special Branch mob."

Beech was impressed, primarily because Kell's department was so shadowy that he was not particularly aware of its existence.

Sir Edward took up the baton next. "The thing is, Beech, it is obvious that what you and your team have uncovered, beyond the initial crime, strays into the areas of national security and foreign diplomacy, and so we must determine the best course of action for everyone's benefit."

Beech felt, with dismay, that it meant that the Mayfair team was going to be bounced off the case but, to his surprise, Kell said, "So you would be doing my department a great favour if you would continue with this case, with perhaps one of my men to assist you."

Beech smiled in relief. "We would be very happy to do that, Colonel Kell."

Kell went on to explain that his department, and Special Branch, were overburdened at the moment. "We have our work cut out at the moment dealing with Indian revolutionaries who are aiding the Germans in spying in this country and the other half has just been given the onerous task of tracking down every Bulgarian in the country because Bulgaria has just entered the war on the German side. So, we potentially have spies everywhere and not enough manpower to cope!"

Sir Edward explained that he had decided that all the money and documentation from the investigation of the Romanian woman would have to be dealt with in conjunction with the Foreign Office. "I have been in touch with Lord Robert Cecil – he is the Under Secretary of State for the Foreign Office – who appears to be dealing with all sorts of things at the moment because the Foreign Secretary is unwell. He has suggested that he will endeavour to make an appointment with the Romanian Ambassador this afternoon and that you and I will attend this appointment as well. To that end, Lord Robert is suggesting that we call into his office at 3 o'clock and we will travel to the Romanian Embassy together."

At that point the food arrived, and all three men said nothing, except expressing admiration for the food laid out in front of them and how hungry they were. Once all the napkins were placed on laps and the wine was poured, the two waiters left the men to their eating, drinking and conversation.

As they fell into a companionable silence, expressing only their admiration for the cuisine, Beech silently acknowledged how much he admired Sir Edward for his ability to get things done in Scotland Yard. The man commanded great respect amongst all of the police force and his sharp mind meant that he had accumulated a great deal of knowledge about the workings of government and the people involved in decision-making. No other Commissioner had been able to take such swift decisions and move events along so quickly.

"By the way," Kell interrupted everyone's absorption in their food, "I had a look through all the evidence that your team produced – quite remarkable by the way – and I can help you with one small part of it. Where you reported that the Romanian woman said she had to go to Doughty Street then to see WL… I'm pretty sure that she is referring to another little known – in fact fairly obscure – department supported by the War Office which deals with train spotters." He reached into his uniform breast pocket and produced a piece of paper. "I've written the address down for you."

"Train spotters?" Beech looked puzzled as he took the piece of paper.

Kell laughed. "I know it sounds bizarre but this Major, his name's Ernest Wallinger…he lost a leg at Aisne in 1914 and got invalided out of the war…because he used to work, before the war, with some European railway bureau, he set up a network of French and Belgium train watchers. He very quickly established a valuable information source. These people are in the German occupied zones and they watch all the troop and armament movements by train and report back to Major Wallinger. I understand that Military Intelligence has had many valuable insights from them. I don't know any more than that. You'll have to pay Wallinger a visit and find out how this woman might fit into his organisation."

Sir Edward opened his briefcase and handed Beech an envelope. Inside was the imprinted piece of silk that Sissy had found in Marie Radu's clothing. "I suggest that you seal the envelope and mark it for Detective Sergeant Tollman to collect from the office downstairs here. You can leave it with the porter on our way out and telephone Tollman to come and retrieve it before he goes to see Major Wallinger."

Sir Edward had thought of everything and Beech's admiration for the Commissioner just continued to grow. Business had been concluded and the men settled once more into the enjoyment of splendid food, good company and camaraderie, all matters of work and wartime abandoned for a time.

* * *

Tollman put down the telephone and went to search for Billy, who was just returning from Belgravia and was chatting to Sergeant Stenton at the front desk.

"Billy!" Tollman said briskly, "Leave Horace alone, he'll only lead you astray! We have work to do, order of Mr Beech."

Billy and Horace Stenton grinned. "Where are we off to then?" asked Billy, as he put his helmet back on and followed Tollman out of the building.

"First the Athenaeum Club to pick up a package and then to Knightsbridge to meet some Major who organises train spotters."

"Well, aren't we having a posh afternoon then, Mr Tollman?" said Billy jauntily, then he stopped. "Did you say train spotters?"

"I certainly did," replied Tollman. "It appears that the security of our realm depends upon pigeon fanciers and train spotters...the ingenuity of the British, eh?"

CHAPTER TWELVE

DIPLOMATIC INTRIGUES

*L*ord *Robert Cecil is an avuncular man*, thought Beech as he took a seat in the Under-Secretary's office. He seemed uniquely suited to a diplomatic role whereas he gathered from the murmured conversation between Cecil and the Commissioner that his superior, Sir Edward Grey, was not similarly suited. Cecil murmured something about the Foreign Secretary "suffering with his nerves again" and the Commissioner nodded sympathetically.

"So," Sir Robert said briskly, smiling at Beech, "this remarkable case certainly requires further investigation. The money and the documents will have to be returned to the Romanian Embassy, of course, and to that end I have been able to secure an appointment for us at 4 p.m. The ambassador, Nicolae Mişu, has been in place since 1912 and is a fairly decent fellow. The government is anxious for us to be very nice to the Romanians, because they want them to enter the war on our side. The old king was firmly pro-Austrian but the new king – Ferdinand – is married to our King's cousin, Marie – has been persuaded, by his wife and others, to be pro- British."

"Forgive my ignorance, sir," Beech boldly spoke, "But why is Romania's entry into the war so important – it is a relatively small country, with a small army, I would imagine."

"Oil," answered Lord Robert. "Pure and simple. If you look out of any London window, you will see that the world is becoming more mechanised, day by day. The war itself has become highly mechanised. Trucks and ambulances – no longer horses and carts but engine-driven vehicles. The Germans are even more mechanised than we are. And for that, everyone needs petroleum. Not many people in the world know that Romania was the first country to produce oil, in the modern sense, to refine it and to export it. Until last year, they were the third largest oil producer in the world, with an annual production of 2 million barrels. The French and the Americans have invested heavily in the Romanian oil fields and the Germans want them. Also, the Romanians are sitting on a huge amount of gas, which all of Europe needs to light its homes and streets. The Austrians have already taken the gas fields over in the disputed area of Transylvania. Romania is very valuable to everyone and their ambassadors know it. Throughout Europe they are taking a tough line with the Allies. They want a signed agreement that, if they come into the war, we will guarantee that, if the Allies win the war, we will give back to the Romanians the Principality of Transylvania and several other provinces that currently belong to the Austro-Hungarian Empire. So, Chief Inspector Beech, as you can imagine, Romania has suddenly become of great interest to every country in Europe. And, what you have uncovered in your investigations may have great relevance to all of our ongoing negotiations. The woman who was killed was, possibly, one of their agents and was involved in some business that warranted her losing her life."

"Would it be possible that the Allies kidnapped this woman and killed her?" Sir Edward asked in a subdued voice.

Cecil frowned. "I can't answer that, in all honesty. It wasn't Vernon Kell's department or he would have asked you to back off. We can make enquiries of the branch of military intelligence that deals with overseas espionage and is run by Mansfield Cumming. Our agents do not have permission to torture and kill people. I can't speak for the French or the Belgians, who may have pursued this woman from the Continent. But I think it is more likely that it was either the Germans, Austrians or Hungarians that killed her because she was involved with several branches of our intelligence services. You mentioned earlier, the Pigeon Service and the Train Watchers?"

Sir Edward nodded. "Two of Beech's men are pursuing the Train Watcher's lead as we speak."

Sir Robert nodded and, at that point his private secretary knocked and entered. "Sir Robert, the automobile has been brought round to take you to the Romanian Embassy," the woman reminded him.

"We must go, gentlemen," Sir Robert advised and they all stood up. "I shall leave it to you to explain everything about the case to Ambassador Mişu. I shall only intervene if the talk turns to matters of diplomacy."

✳ ✳ ✳

As Tollman and Rigsby exited from Knightsbridge tube station, they reflected upon how rarely they got to visit this part of London.

"I don't think I've actually been around here since the present King's coronation in 1911. That was just before I retired," said Tollman, reminiscing about his first career in the police force. "We were all on policing the crowds around Buckingham Palace – undercover like. There was some worry that Fenians might try and throw a bomb at the royal coach, in the name of Irish independence, so we were all on edge trying to spot anyone with suspicious packages. I remember one bloke got arrested for carrying a bag with a dodgy object in it. Turned out to be a large swede he was taking home for his dinner.! I mean who takes their shopping with them to watch the coronation? Bloody idiot! Anyway, afterwards, when the whole coronation was over and the main crowds had dispersed, we all strolled off into Knightsbridge and ended up in the Grenadier pub…"

"I know it well!" Billy interrupted.

"Well, you would, being a former Grenadier guardsman," Tollman said affably. "I just remember getting being totally hemmed in by uniformed soldiers, all wearing those great bearskin hats of theirs. They seemed to be about a foot taller than me, very loud and very thirsty…as you would be when you've been standing to attention along the coronation route all day. I can't say as I've ever been back to Knightsbridge ever since, particularly as I don't have the sort of money to spend in shops like Harrods and other establishments."

"Oh, I've spent many a happy hour in the Grenadier Pub," said Billy with a smile and then his face took on a reflective look. "But I haven't been in there since I left the army."

Tollman wasn't prepared to let his young companion become maudlin. "You're better off, lad. That pub takes advantage of being in Knightsbridge and charges all the soldiers more for a pint of beer than a decent pub south of the river."

Billy's smile returned. "True. I hadn't thought of that."

They had arrived at the address Beech had given them. Lincoln House, Basil Street, SW3. Tollman surveyed the block of flats with concern. "Strange place for a department of government intelligence to be," he muttered in disapproval.

Billy agreed but then pointed out that maybe that was to throw foreign spies off the scent. Tollman considered his point but reserved his judgement until later. They entered the building and climbed the stairs to find Apartment 5. It was on the fourth floor. Just a normal apartment. They knocked and a woman answered.

"Is Major Ernest Wallinger in, by any chance?" Tollman asked as he flashed his warrant card.

"Yes, yes. Come in," she beckoned and took them down the hallway to a study where an unassuming man, dressed an a tweed suit was sitting in a room where the walls were covered in maps, the bookshelves were stuffed with what looked like train timetables, and his desk was covered in pieces of paper.

"Two policemen from Scotland Yard," the woman announced to the man seated at the desk and he immediately stood and turned round, the stiffness of one leg betraying that it was an artificial one.

"Gentlemen!" he cried, extending his hand, which they both shook. "Find yourselves a chair and tell me why you are visiting me."

There was a general clearing off of one chair in the study

and the woman disappeared and reappeared with a dining chair.

"Ah, thank you, Phyllis," Major Wallinger said gratefully, "Could you organise some tea, please?" Phyllis nodded and Tollman looked relieved. He was parched and had missed his regular afternoon mug of tea.

"I understand, sir, that you are the head of an intelligence unit that gathers information on trains?" Tollman asked hesitantly.

"Yes, that's right," Wallinger confirmed. "We're quite new really. I just started it up in April of this year but, already, we are reaping the rewards of our agents in occupied France and Belgium giving us valuable information on enemy troop and equipment movements by train. These pieces of information are relayed to us by couriers and the Pigeon Carrier Service, and help our military gauge whether the enemy is massing for an attack, for example."

"Ah," said Tollman, understanding now why the dead woman was involved with pigeons. Until now, he had not been able to make the connection. He paused as the tea arrived and the next few moments were taken up by the serving of tea, milk and sugar. Once all that was settled and Phyllis had left the room, Tollman resumed. "Do you know of a woman called Marie Radu?"

Wallinger's face fell and he said hollowly, "Yes, I'm afraid I do. She is one of our couriers. Why do you ask?" Tollman could see that Wallinger was fearing the worst.

"I'm sorry to have to tell you sir, but Miss Radu was abducted and killed three nights ago."

Wallinger put his head in his hands and groaned, "No, no, no," under his breath. He looked distraught. "How was she killed?" he asked in a voice filled with anguish and despair.

"Bullet to the head, I'm afraid. But we think she was… tortured…before that." Tollman reluctantly informed him.

"I'm sorry but I need a whisky," Wallinger muttered and moved a pile of books to get at a whisky decanter and glasses. "Can I offer you a drink, gentlemen?"

Tollman and Rigsby shook their heads. "Not on duty, sir," said Tollman.

"Of course," Walinger poured himself a glass and downed it in one.

"We did, however, find this item, sewn into the lady's clothing," Tollman said and he held up the brown envelope. Wallinger seized it hastily and prised it open, then withdrew the silk.

"Oh my God!" he gasped, "Marie Radu, you are an angel!"

Literally, thought Tollman and then, because his curiosity got the better of him, he asked, "Is it information meant for you, sir?"

The Major nodded. "It is the details of many and significant enemy troop movements on the railway lines that go in and out of Germany and Luxembourg to major railway junctions in Belgium and Northern France. I would have to analyse this material in detail but it looks, upon first glance, to be massive troop movements down towards the Ardennes, which could mean the enemy is planning a major assault down there. Gentlemen, I must press on with analysing this information at once."

"There is just one other matter, sir, if I may. Miss Radu was overheard to say…" Tollman consulted his notes, " that she was going to Doughty Street, seeing WL, which is you, and then she would go to the Palace."

"Good Lord!" Wallinger seemed surprised.

"Would the lady have had any reason to go to Buckingham Palace, that you know of, sir?"

Wallinger almost laughed. "Marie? No. She would have been more likely to visit the Palace Theatre of Varieties than Buckingham Palace. She was a performer in the Theatre de Vaudeville in Paris!"

Tollman looked as though a gas lamp had been turned on in his head. "Thank you very much, sir, you have been most helpful."

When he and Billy were outside in the street, Tollman said, "Billy, I think we have been looking for the wrong Palace. We need to consider all the theatres with that name, cinemas, restaurants…take your pick. Let's get back to the Yard and start looking through all the Directories in the library."

* * *

Ambassador Mişu was pleasant but inscrutable, Beech had decided. The Romanian Embassy was a modest affair but quietly impressive. The Ambassador was obviously intrigued as to why he was suddenly being visited by the Commissioner of the Metropolitan Police and the Under Secretary of State for the Foreign Office. Until it was explained to him, he had a wary look about him, as though he feared that something was about to be exposed. When he was informed about the death of Marie Radu, he looked deeply shocked and his eyes seemed to fill with tears, which he hurriedly brushed away, before saying, "I am distraught that Marie has been killed. She was a great patriot and gave tremendous service to our country. How did it happen?"

Sir Edward nodded at Beech to explain. "She was abducted three nights ago, with another woman, from a train, during a Zeppelin raid. I am sad to report, Mr Ambassador, that Marie Radu appears to have been tortured and then shot through the head. We found her body on board a vessel that was moored in the Thames. The other woman survived but is still unconscious."

The Ambassador stared at Beech but said nothing. He did not seem moved to ask if Marie Radu had been carrying anything, so Beech continued.

"Sewn into her clothing," Beech paused as the Ambassador leaned forward in anticipation, "were the following items," Beech nodded at Sir Edward, who opened his briefcase and deposited a canvas evidence bag on the Ambassador's desk. "A great deal of money in various denominations…" The Ambassador allowed a small smile to creep across his face. "…documents in, we assume Romanian, and her passport," The Ambassador started emptying the contents of the bag on to the table and the last thing he retrieved were the documents that Rigsby had brought back from Doughty Street. An old man's Romanian passport and other documents. "…and that," Beech said, pointing at those very documents. For a moment, he thought he saw a flicker of panic cross the Ambassador's face, but it was quickly gone and to have been so ephemeral as to leave Beech doubting that he had actually seen anything. There was a moment's silence whilst the Ambassador sat back in his chair and surveyed the items on his desk. "Marie Radu was, as I said before, a great patriot and she frequently used to collect money from Romanians in France and Belgium to bring to us here at the embassy in London."

Sir Robert Cecil felt moved to speak and asked, "And what, Mr Ambassador, do you do with that money?"

Mişu turned a benign smile onto Lord Robert and said smoothly, "Why we get the best rate of exchange for it all in Britain and the money is used to buy equipment for our army back in Romania. Surely it is in your country's interest, Lord Robert, that the Romanian army is as well equipped as possible? Especially as you want us to fight on your side." The last comment was barbed – calculated to make Cecil react, who wisely said nothing.

"And the documents, Ambassador," Beech asked. "What relevance do they have?"

"Do any of you read Romanian?" the Ambassador asked blithely, knowing very well that there would be no affirmative answers. He picked over the documents and said, "These are various letters of authority signed by different government officials in Romania, giving Marie Radu permission to collect money from expatriate Romanians to assist our country…"

"What about the passport for the elderly man?" Beech was intrigued. He was beginning to feel that the Ambassador was hiding something and he was very skilful at talking his way out of difficult situations.

"Ah. Well, this will interest you as well, Lord Robert,"

Mişu turned to Cecil with a look of amusement. "We have a great many Romanian nationals who once lived in the Principality of Transylvania which, as Lord Robert knows, belongs to the Austro-Hungarian Empire at the moment. Now, these Romanian nationals live in Britain but they have been rounded up in and interned by the British as enemy aliens – because of their Hungarian passports. Whenever possible, we put out a call for assistance to our homeland and our civil servants manage to unearth someone's birth certificate, showing that they were actually born in Romania and we can then issue them with a Romanian passport and get them out of an internment camp. Because the postal services are so unreliable, we prefer to use couriers for these documents, and Marie Radu was one such courier."

It was a glib response, which didn't quite pass muster with the Commissioner, who said, "Mr Ambassador, Miss Radu chose to hide this man's passport and other documents in the bottom of a basket of pigeons. Can you explain that?"

There was a moment's pause and then the Ambassador said, "Miss Radu was an experienced courier and, I believe you call them, intelligence agent. She must have had her reasons and I couldn't possibly guess at those." Mişu gave a polite smile and, again turned to make a point to Lord Robert, "Once we have Transylvania back as part of Romania again, such efforts to liberate our countrymen will become totally unnecessary, I'm sure you agree?" Lord Robert gave a small smile and one brief nod of acknowledgement.

The Ambassador then made his excuses for having to cut the meeting short, shook each man's hand in turn and told his assistant show his visitors back to their waiting automobile.

"Hmm," said Lord Robert, as they sped back to the Foreign Office. "That's about as slippery a set of explanations as I've heard in my long career of dealing with foreign diplomats. I think we need MI5(g) to keep an eye on him for a while, if they can spare the time. Meanwhile, I suggest, Sir Edward, that your people continue with this investigation and see how far they can get with it. Marie Radu seems to have been far more important than you all thought."

* * *

"This is a 21 millimetre cartridge from a Pistol Parabellum, more commonly known as a Luger," pronounced Sergeant Thurlow of the Firearms Department of Scotland Yard, holding up the jar that Tollman had just given him. "Standard service pistol of the German Army and Navy: Switzerland; Portugal; the Low Countries; Brazil; Bolivia; and..er...Bulgaria." There wasn't anything that Thurlow didn't know about guns. Tollman patted him on the back.

"Would you find any of these on the streets in London?" asked Tollman.

Thurlow shook his head. "I doubt it", he replied. "Too difficult to get them. Your average crook would more easily get hold of a gun made in Britain or the Empire. Or even a Ruby pistol that the French Army uses. But not a Luger. Apart from not being able to get hold of the guns, you would have a lot of trouble getting hold of the cartridges. I mean, as guns go, the Luger is relatively new. It's only been used by the German military since 1908. I suppose you might be able to get one in Switzerland but how many London crooks do you know who would travel over to Switzerland to get some guns? Especially since the war started. No, there are much easier guns to lay your hands on."

After they had left the basement dwelling of the Firearms Department, Tollman said to Billy, "It's looking increasingly, to me, like the men who shot the Romanian women were enemy spies."

"If that's so, Mr Tollman, how are they going to get out of the country again?" Billy pointed out.

"That is something that we need to give some consideration to, Billy, but not until we have been through the directories and made a list of all possible Palaces that the Romanian woman might have wanted to visit."

Billy pulled a face. "Will it take long, Mr Tollman, only…I've got a date with a young lady tonight."

Tollman grinned. "Have you now? Well, if you treat me nicely and go and make me a cup of tea, I'll let you off at six o'clock and you can go and make this young lady happy."

✳ ✳ ✳

Mattei said that she had laughed so much, in the picture house, that her stomach muscles hurt. Billy agreed that it had been a long time since he had had so much fun. The film had been Charlie Chaplin's *Shanghaied* and the audiences had laughed loud and long at the antics of the 'little tramp'. In part, it had been a reaction to the British Pathé newsreel beforehand, which had showed a piece about the Irish Fusiliers in trenches in Gallipoli, braving the gales, flooding and cold, then British troops being transferred from Gallipoli to Greek Macedonia to shore up the failed Serbian campaign. The sight of the trenches and the men huddled in misery, but smiling for the camera, made Billy's chest constrict and his breathing became more rapid. Mattie had sensed that Billy was quietly struggling and she had slipped her hand into his injured hand and squeezed it. Startled, he had looked at her suddenly, and she had smiled encouragingly, breaking him out of his anxiety and he had relaxed. When he had turned his face back to the screen, the images had gone and they had entered the world of a Charlie Chaplin comedy.

"The pianist was good," commented Billy, as they were coming out of the cinema. Mattie agreed, and she took his arm as they strolled along the pavement.

"You look nice out of uniform, Billy," she said admiringly. "I like that suit," and she stroked his sleeve. They turned the corner and Billy realised that he had not once thought about the scar on his face for the whole evening. He looked at Mattie and smiled.

"What?" she asked softly, thinking he was going to say something.

"Nothing" he replied. "Just happy." *She doesn't notice the scar,* he realised, and he smiled again, just to himself.

"Edna Purviance is such a beautiful actress," said Mattie suddenly, as they were queuing for fish and chips.

Billy shook his head. "Nah. All that make up. Makes women look like pandas! Besides, she isn't as beautiful as you." He blushed when he said it and Mattie blushed too, but neither of them looked at each other..

As they walked back to the house in Belgravia, they talked about other Charlie Chaplin films they had seen. Mattie had seen far more than Billy but he realised that she had spent a good part of her time going to the cinema alone.

"Don't you have mates…girlfriends…to go to the picture houses with?" he asked.

"I used to have," she said quietly. "Lots of girls I went to school with in Whitechapel. But when war broke out, they didn't want to know me anymore. I stopped being their friend Mattie and I became the 'German girl' whose Pa was interned as an enemy alien."

Billy was outraged. "Well, you don't need fair weather friends like that!" he said sharply.

As they went down the steps and into the kitchen area of the Belgravia house, Billy could see Arthur Tollman sitting at the table with his mother and aunt and he felt a bit peeved, as he had hoped for a quiet meal, just with Mattie.

"I'm just leaving, Billy!" declared Tollman, retrieving his hat off the table and making for the door. "I was giving Elsie and Sissy their orders for tomorrow."

"We're going to be cleaning trains at Waterloo," Elsie pronounced, "and finding out what we can about this poor girl who's in hospital at death's door."

"The oven's warm," said Sissy as she took the paper parcel of fish and chips out of Billy's hands, "I'll pop these in there and you can have a cup of tea with us before we make ourselves scarce and you can eat." She winked at Billy and made him laugh as he accepted two mugs of tea from her.

"Right, I'm off," said Tollman putting his hat on. "Billy, no staying up late. You and I are on guard duty for the womenfolk tomorrow. That means out of uniform, looking a bit scruffy, and at Waterloo sidings at six in the morning."

"Six!" Billy was dismayed.

"Oh, so you don't think that protecting your old mum is worth getting up early for?" Elsie said, teasing him.

Billy rolled his eyes at her and said to Mattie, "The things I have to put up with…"

Mattie laughed and she went to help Sissy butter bread. Billy watched her smiling and chatting to his aunt and suspected that she had probably been quite lonely over the last year. No mum, no relatives and shunned by her friends, before her dad was taken away and interned, leaving her utterly alone. They locked eyes as she passed him a plate and Billy felt a great urge to protect her. Sissy caught the look and she winked at Arthur Tollman.

"Go on, Arthur, be off with you. We've all got to be up early in the morning," and she kissed him on the cheek before ushering him out of the door. "Right, you two," she said to Billy and Mattie, "That food will be nice and warm now, so get on and eat. Your mother and I are going to take our cups of tea into our bedroom and leave you be."

Elsie and Sissy kissed Billy and Mattie on their foreheads. "And we're only in the next room, Billy Rigsby," said Elsie with mock sternness, "so no getting up to any hanky panky."

"Behave, mother," said Billy, with a grin, waving her away.

Mattie went to the oven and retrieved their food – dishing it out on to the plates – while Billy fetched the salt, pepper and vinegar. Then they settled down to a companionable meal, in between whispered conversation and stifled giggles.

CHAPTER THIRTEEN

THELMA'S SECRETS

"Show me your hands, please, ladies," said Mrs Fallon, the Cleaning Superintendent. Elsie and Sissy duly obliged and Mrs Fallon pronounced them satisfactory. "I can always tell if someone is going to be a thorough cleaner, if their own hands and nails are clean." She looked them up and down – they had both dressed in serviceable clothes and aprons – and shook her head. "I'm sorry, ladies, but you will have to wear trousers, all our ladies do. Come with me and we'll see what we can find." Mrs Fallon led the way to a series of wooden sheds which lay back a little way from the sidings. She opened the door of the third shed to reveal a dressing room, where the women all changed into dungarees or trousers and left their ordinary clothes hanging on pegs. She started to rummage about in a large wicker basket and came up with one pair of trousers and one pair of dungarees. She held each of them up, in turn, against Sissy and Elsie and said "I think these should do. Now, after your shift, you must take them home and wash them, put a name label in them, and bring them back for your next shift. Understood?" They both nodded their heads. "Right, well I'll leave you to get changed, then come and find me in shed one and I'll take you to your work stations." With that she left.

Sissy and Elsie looked at each other.

"I feel about ten years old and being ticked off by the headmistress," observed Sissy.

"I've never worn trousers in my life," said Elsie and she began to get undressed and pull on the hated garments.

"It's alright for you," Sissy retorted, "I'm going to look like a sack of spuds in these dungarees."

Outside, in the sidings, Tollman and Billy were loitering around in scruffy dress themselves. Tollman had, what he called, his gardening clothes on and Billy a pair of old trousers, a collarless shirt, waistcoat and a neckerchief. They were sitting outside a tea hut, which appeared to be for everyone but, at the moment, was mostly men who were either train drivers, stokers, apprentices, or goods porters. These were the unseen face of the railway – those who did the back-breaking and dirty work. No one was in a railway uniform. From where Tollman and Billy were sitting, having a mug of tea, they had a perfect view of the teams of women cleaning the trains and they had spotted Elsie and Sissy being taken into one of the huts. When the two women came out, attired suitably for their temporary cleaning job, Billy sunk his head in his hands as Tollman said, "Oh my God, look at the sight of them!" Sissy seemed to be walking very awkwardly, almost with her legs apart, like a sailor, as she tried to get used to wearing the dungarees. Elsie, on the other hand, was pausing every ten steps to hoist up the waistband of her trousers, which were slightly too large, and she feared that they were slipping down.

The two women knocked on the door of Hut Number One and Mrs Fallon came out. Tollman could see that there was a bit of a discussion, then the Cleaning Superintendent disappeared and swiftly re-appeared with a piece of string and Elsie began to thread it through the waistband of the trousers as a makeshift belt. Then, off they went to one of the stationery trains, already swarming with women, washing and scrubbing.

"We'll start you off on one of the passenger trains," said Mrs Fallon, "they get a lot less filthy than the goods trains. Daisy!" she bawled at the top of her voice, and a young woman stuck her head out of one of the carriage windows, "Two new ones for your team!" Daisy nodded, and climbed down out of the train. She seemed a pleasant girl, as she smiled and shook Sissy and Elsie's hands. Mrs Fallon continued, "As they are new, Daisy, put them both on interiors. And, in view of their age… "(Sissy raised her eyebrows) "don't put them on roof or undercarriage cleaning." Daisy nodded and Mrs Fallon departed.

"Don't mind her," said Daisy cheerfully, "her bark's worse than her bite. She's quite fair when you get to know her. So, what's your names?"

"I'm Elsie and this is my sister, Sissy."

"Elsie and Sissy, right. So, I'm going to take you to the inside of this train in a minute. There are just a few rules I need to tell you. First, any money you find under the seats or down the side of the seats, goes into a central kitty, which we all share out once a month. So, basically give it to me and I put it in a special box. Second, if you find any valuables, like cigarette cases, watches, jewellery and the like, they have to be handed in to the Lost Property Office on the main station. Finally, whatever gossip or information someone tells you, stays in the station. Because the railways are now part of the military war effort, we have to keep our mouths shut about anything we hear. Understand?"

Both Elsie and Sissy nodded and Daisy looked satisfied. They were then led down the platform to the second passenger carriage. Daisy opened the door and shouted, "Edith! Got two new cleaners for you!" A woman, with some black marks on her cheek, where she had wiped her hair out of her eyes with dirty hands, popped her head around one of the passenger seats and smiled. "This is Elsie and Sissy," said Daisy, as she ushered them into the carriage. You show them the ropes, whilst I go and get some tools." Then she disappeared.

"Tools?" asked a puzzled Sissy.

"Oh, that's just what we call dustpans and brushes, mops and buckets and the like," explained Edith. "See everything needs cleaning in a different way. I'll show you." She demonstrated that the ashtrays, set into the doors, had to be cleaned out first, then the upholstered seats had to be brushed, so that dust and debris coming off them on to the floor could be mopped up with a damp mop. "Damp mind, not wet," she emphasised. "We don't want a lot of water sloshing around on the floor, 'cos it won't dry in time for the train going back out into service." She then explained what they used to get sticky stuff off the seats, "Little bit of white spirit on a rag,". Then she explained that they had to poke a piece of rag down the sides of the upholstered seats with a thin stick and move it along, to try and get the dirt and fluff out that collected down the sides. "Now, Daisy will bring some bottles of white vinegar. We use that, on a cloth to get the cigarette, pipe and cigar smoke stains off the ceiling and we do that before we polish any of the brass on the luggage racks and the doors."

Sissy and Elsie felt that it was no different from the cleaning they might do at home and so they were quite happy. Just then Daisy arrived, rattling metal buckets outside for them to open the door. "Here you go ladies!" she said as she dumped everything on the floor. "Edith will show you where to get water and where to throw away your dirty water and so on. If you need to go to the toilet, they are in Shed Four – don't use the ones in the train. A whistle will blow when it's time for a break and then Edith will show you where we all go for a brew and some bread and jam."

It was time for some serious cleaning.

※ ※ ※

Constable Fowler, from Borough Police Station, was on a mission in the streets around the old Blackfriars Road station. His Sergeant had told him that Scotland Yard suspected that a vehicle must have been waiting for the men who abducted the women on the night of the Zeppelin raid.

"It could have been a horse and cart, a lorry, or a delivery van…or even a taxicab or horse drawn cab. They don't know. And, seeing as you fancy yourself as a detective, PC Fowler, I'm giving you the job of wasting your time trying to find this vehicle. Don't say I don't do you any favours."

So, Fowler was standing at a tea stall, drinking the first of many cups of tea during the day and reflecting upon the fact that his station Sergeant was not wrong – he did fancy himself as a detective and, one day, he intended to be one. Then he turned his thoughts to what sort of vehicle he might be looking for. He ruled out any of the, now becoming old-fashioned, horse drawn cabs.

There was not enough room in one of those for three men, two semi-conscious women and two baskets of pigeons.

Even the vehicular taxis were on the small side. Also, he felt that the kidnappers would want to be screened from view, so that ruled out a horse and cart without a canopy. Again, a delivery van was too small and many of them had built in shelves or racks for produce or bottles. *No, he reasoned, it would have to be a lorry.* The trouble was that around the Waterloo Station area, and the docks, wharves and jetties there were many companies of hauliers and also many companies that used lorries for delivery of their products. Tea finished, Fowler decided to walk his beat and see what he could spot.

He started going south from the old Blackfriars Road station and began a slow, rhythmic walk down past the Methodist Chapel, the Library and the Post Office, making a deviation into Pocock Street where there were some industrial units. He stood at the gates of a yard that serviced a pottery and watched the wooden crates being packed with vases and straw and nailed down, before being loaded into the side of a 30cwt lorry. It was a smart-looking vehicle. The front had a cab, like a car and the rear was a good size, separate metal compartment, with canvas sides. Fowler could imagine two women being lifted into the lorry. The sides were just hip-height for the average man – a considerably easier height than loading into the back of a bigger lorry. He noted the name of the company… The Dutch Pottery Works…and he moved on, before his presence aroused suspicion.

Fowler carried on his perambulations down the east side of the main street until he reached St. George's Circus, then he crossed the road, opposite the Surrey Theatre and started to walk northwards. He passed a couple of haulage companies but they only had large, open lorries, which did not fit the bill. He turned left into Weber Street, where there was an iron foundry but all their vehicles were large dump trucks, currently disgorging mountains of coke onto the concrete yard. Fowler decided that all those vehicles were too large and too dirty for the job that Scotland Yard described.

Fowler wandered around the back streets and noted many vehicles, used by many companies, which were either uncovered, too large or were kitted out inside with racks or shelves. He made his way back to the main road again. He made a mental note of the large Salvation Army shelter set back off the street. Fowler always found vagrants a good source of information, when they were sober. He might pay the shelter a visit later and see if anyone could remember anything from that night.

The last place he investigated, before he would pause for lunch, was a printing works in Boundary Row. As he walked into the yard of the works, all he could see was row upon row of army vehicles and soldiers loading pallets of books. He walked up to one of the teams of soldiers and casually asked about the books. A corporal laughed and said, "Very important books, Constable." He pointed at some small books with blue covers, *The British Soldier's Pocket Book of Prayers and Hymns*," he said, with some irony. "But," he added, "While you're praying and singing hymns, you definitely need to refer to this one!" He pointed again, to a brown-coloured leather wallet with the title *Machine Gunner's Pocket Book*.

Fowler nodded. "Is that all that this printing works

produces?" he asked, as he watched the soldiers efficiently loading up.

The corporal nodded. "Well, these and loads of other Army and Navy manuals. When they think we've all got time to read these, I don't know. Let alone just how many pockets they think the average soldier has got in his uniform to store them all."

The stowing away of pallets of books in the truck was done and the corporal shouted "Finished!" and banged the side of the truck, which then began to pull away. Fowler watched it leave, with interest, bade good day to the corporal and set off to find some lunch.

*** *** ***

Edith was proving to be quite chatty. Elsie and Sissy had already found out about most of the family lives of the women who cleaned trains at Waterloo and when she asked them how they got the job, Sissy had the bright idea of saying that they had met this woman called Thelma, but they couldn't remember her surname, who had put in a word for them.

Edith didn't seem surprised. "Oh well, you move in exalted circles then," she said cheerfully. "No one seems to have more sway than Thelma Barnes." Elsie nodded. They now had a surname to give to Tollman.

"What makes this Thelma so special, then?" asked Sissy.

"Don't get me wrong," Edith said hastily, "I like Thelma and she's a good worker. She goes up on the top of the trains 'cos she has no fear of heights and, when she's here, she always volunteers to scrub the locomotives – that's a mucky job! All that coal dust and chimney smoke. That's a real elbow-grease job, that is!"

"You said, 'when she's here'. Does that mean she's not a regular worker?" Elsie wanted clarification from Edith.

"Well, that's the thing…" Edith lowered her voice. "She's got some funny arrangement with the bosses. She's down as full time on the books, but she goes missing quite a lot – you know, the odd day, here and there – so it can't be sickness. Daisy asked Mrs Fallon once, about Thelma's unreliability, but Mrs Fallon gave her short shrift and told her it was none of her business." Edith was in her stride now. "Course all the girls thought perhaps she was the boss's girlfriend, but nobody really gave that any serious consideration. I mean Thelma's quite a nice-looking woman and the boss…well, have you seen him? He looks like Buster Keaton!" All the women laughed heartily at the comparison with the famous star of the silent films. "Anyway, I should think that Thelma holds herself more highly than that."

"Is she posh, then, this Thelma? We thought, when we spoke to her, she was a bit posh," lied Sissy.

"Yes, I would say so," answered Edith, after a moment's reflection. "Not posh, posh, but probably stayed on at school longer than the rest of us. She can quote bits of poems and seems to know quite a bit about a lot of things. I think her father's probably posh. She mentions him in her conversations. He's in the Army, that much I know, and he's an officer, but I don't know any more than that." Then Edith had a moment's reflection and she said, "Come to think of it, this is the longest

Thelma's ever been absent from work. Must be three days now."

Sissy looked at Elsie and she nodded imperceptibly. This was information they needed to pass on to Tollman. Just then, a train whistle blew, and Edith put down her mop and said gleefully, "Time for a break, ladies! I'm gasping for a cuppa, aren't you?"

* * *

PC Fowler was rested and replete with beef pie, chips and mushy peas from a local cafe, when he made his way back out on to the street, and he carried on his way northwards, beyond the Blackfriars Road station, towards the river. In between the running of the trams, which somewhat blocked his view, he noted the many types of commercial vehicles that were going up and down the road, to and from the docks and wharves along the river. None of them struck him as the type of vehicle he was looking for. He decided that, as he turned left and passed into the dock area, he would knock on the door of the watchman he had spoken to yesterday. The man appeared and immediately invited P.C. Fowler in, but the young policeman declined and said he had to press on.

"I just wanted to ask you a question about motorised vehicles, on the night *before* you found the dead pigeons," Fowler asked.

"What? The night of the Zeppelin raid?" the watchman asked.

Fowler nodded and continued. "Just before you went on duty, did you notice any vehicles coming down to the wharves – or even, leaving the wharves? Anything at all?"

The watchman thought long and hard, pulled a face and slowly shook his head. Then, something came to him and he said, "Hold up! There was a small lorry came down, very late. Everyone else was gone and I was just starting out on my rounds. That was the night of the Zeppelin raid and it was dark, no lights at all, in the street or on the vehicles. I saw that the omnibuses had stopped up on the main road, put all their lights out and I could just make out that some of their passengers were getting off. Trying to go down the tube station, I expect, to shelter from the bombs. I was going up towards the main road and this small lorry was coming the other way. It can't have been delivering to a boat, because the tide was out, but it could have been delivering to a warehouse, except it came out of the riverside area quite quickly – within five minutes – and I remember thinking that it had probably just taken a wrong turning. It was pitch black because there was no moon…but there was light in the sky from the fires from the bombing. I could just about make out that there was only one bloke driving and that company usually has two in the front, for unloading."

"You know the company the lorry came from?" asked Fowler.

"Oh, yes," the watchman said, confidently. "It was from that Dutch Pottery Company up the road. They come in and out of here quite a lot and their lorries have the company name in white lettering on the canvas sides of the lorry. They've got three of those little Guy Motors' lorries."

Fowler thanked the watchman and decided to go back to telephone Scotland Yard with the interesting information.

* * *

Beech had just returned from a meeting with Basil Johnson, the head of Special Branch, which had become a little heated as Johnson had received a communication from MI5(g) to say that Beech's men were going to investigate a possible espionage case which had arisen out of a murder case. Johnson had made Beech feel young and inexperienced, simply because he was annoyed at having to admit that Special Branch was overstretched.

"Don't expect this to be a permanent arrangement," he had muttered at Beech in irritation. "I shall be having a word with Vernon Kell to make sure that this doesn't happen again. We can't have unqualified bobbies doing the work of specialists."

"Oh really!" Beech had uttered in exasperation. "Your department has had no more training in detection than any other department and, now that the whole nation is at war, I think that the various sections of the Metropolitan Police should pull together."

Basil Johnson's faux smile had been icy and he had said, patronisingly, "Oh do you, young Mr Beech? Some of us earned our status through hard slog in the ranks. We were not fortunate enough to be the son of a baronet and, therefore, elevated to a senior position in record time."

That comment had stung and Beech knew that his face was flushing with anger and all he could think to say, which had worsened the situation was, "Well, some of us got our experience fighting for King and Country – I think that counts for something, don't you?" which caused Basil Johnson's face to darken with anger. Beech felt he had scored a point.

Johnson's final word had been, "Colonel Kell wants me to allocate a man to assist you but, sadly, as he points out in his letter, Special Branch is overstretched and I doubt whether we can accede to his request."

Beech had simply said, "Fine. I quite understand," and had walked out. He had felt foolish and inadequate and, he reflected that he felt like that in so many areas of his life, and he was cross that these feelings were now impinging on his professional life.

Sitting at his desk and about to sink into one of his bottomless depressions, he was startled by the internal telephone system trilling into life. It was Sergeant Stenton, who was speaking very quietly on the end of the telephone.

"Chief Inspector, there is a lady...a *Countess*...who has arrived at my desk and is insisting that she needs to see you."

"A Countess?" Beech was momentarily confused. "I will be right down."

He hurried down the corridor and two flights of stairs, to see a woman seated in the receiving area, her head bowed and her magnificent hat obscuring her features.

"Er...Countess...?" Beech said enquiringly, as he reached the bottom of the steps and the woman raised her head. He found himself looking into the most beautiful face he had ever seen. In the fading light from the street, her skin appeared to have a golden sheen. She had lustrous amber hair piled up underneath her hat. Her green eyes were cat-like and the lashes long and dark. But the mouth...Beech was staring at her full, red lips, which parted into a smile over even, white teeth. *She has a face like Botticelli's Venus,* he thought with admiration.

The countess raised her right hand to be kissed and, fortunately, Beech had the presence of mind to galvanise himself into action. He took the gloved hand, bent over it, brushed it with his lips and smelt her heady floral perfume. He looked straight into the unblinking green eyes as she said, in a slightly husky foreign-accented voice, "I am Helena, Countess of Covasna. You are Chief Inspector Beech?"

Beech reluctantly straightened up and said, "I am, Countess. How can I help you?"

The countess looked at Sergeant Stenton and said quietly, to Beech, "Is there somewhere we could discuss a delicate matter?"

"Of course," Beech offered his arm, "May I escort you to my office? It's upstairs."

The countess gave a small smile and linked her arm through Beech's, lifting the front of her skirt with her other hand, for ease of walking up the stairs. They said nothing as they ascended. Beech was feeling a slight constriction in his chest and he occasionally darted a sideways look at the countess but she was concentrating on each step up the staircase. Once they came to the corridor leading to his room, she showed no inclination to disengage her arm from his and Beech felt a little self-conscious as they continued to walk arm in arm towards his office door. He swiftly removed his support as he opened the door and ushered her in and to a seat. Once he was behind his desk, he could, once again, marvel at the sheer beauty of the countess and he found himself gazing at her breathtaking eyes which boldly stared unwaveringly at his. *She is not young,* he assessed, *but nevertheless, she is ageless.*

He was hopeless at assessing women's ages but he guessed that she was probably older than he and this only made him feel more inadequate.

"Tell me how I can help you, countess," he asked.

To his astonishment, the magnificent eyes glistened and one small tear escaped down her cheek. She immediately produced a lace handkerchief and captured the tear before it trickled any further. "The Romanian Ambassador told me that my cousin has been killed...Marie Radu. I should like to claim the body and take her back to her homeland for burial."

Beech finally understood what had brought this magnificent creature into his orbit. He answered, "Dear Countess, your cousin's...er...body is undergoing a post mortem today and, providing the findings do not deviate from the evidence we have already, we should be able to release the body after the weekend. But we will, I'm afraid, have to keep the clothes she was wearing."

The countess smiled and nodded. "That will be perfect," she said. "I leave for Romania next Wednesday. Marie's coffin will accompany me and I shall dress her in the finest clothes for her burial." She stood and Beech stood, hastily.

"Let me escort you back downstairs," he offered and she bowed her head in agreement. Again, she linked her arm with his. He felt her warmth and the full power of her perfume.

She suddenly stopped walking, turned to him and said, "You are limping. You have a wound?"

Beech blushed and explained that he had been wounded in the war. "I apologise for my disability," he said, flustered.

She raised her eyebrows in astonishment. "You British

are strange," she said simply. "In my country, for a man to possess battle scars – even if he loses a limb – women consider it a sign of great virility." She gave a little, suggestive, smile and Beech found himself suddenly a little short of breath.

"Are you married, Chief Inspector Beech?" she suddenly asked boldly.

"No."

"Fiancé? Mistress? Paramour?"

Beech was shocked and yet excited to be questioned so frankly. "No, countess, I have no woman in my life."

The countess gave a small smile of satisfaction. "My ambassador, Nicolae Mişu, is coming to dinner at my residence tonight, with his wife. They are such a kind couple - but boring. Please come to dinner and…relieve my…boredom." Her voice had dropped to almost a whisper and her face betrayed nothing other than a direct vitality that was beginning to make Beech feel as though he were drunk.

"I would be honoured, countess," he said, unable to control a small croak in his voice.

"Good. Eight o'clock. Here is my address," and she produced a small, embossed card from her handbag. "Now you can escort me to my automobile."

Beech, in a daze, took her arm again, whilst she scooped up the front of her dress, and they descended the stairs and out into the street. An elegant, highly polished Swift vehicle was parked in the courtyard of Scotland Yard and a burly, dark-haired man in a chauffeur's uniform was standing to attention. He opened the door and assisted the countess to step into the rear of the automobile. The countess leant out of the window and said, "I shall expect you tonight at eight. Until later." She turned on her dazzling smile and Beech could only nod his head as the chauffeur drove away.

He came back into the building and noted the time on the wall clock. It was 5 'o'clock. If he was going to get ready for this dinner with the intriguing countess, Beech decided he needed to go back to his flat in Albany and prepare. A bath and fortifying brandy – he might even stop off at his barbers first for a haircut, a shave and cologne. He was so distracted that he did not hear Sergeant Stenton telling him that Tollman had rung.

Two and a half hours later, an anxious Peter Beech stepped into a taxicab and asked to be driven to Kensington. He realised that his hands were trembling slightly as he paid the driver and he took several deep breaths before he knocked at the countess' door. A maid answered and ushered him through to a parlour with low lighting. She took his coat and scarf and left him there. For a moment he felt the urge to feign illness, perhaps, and make his excuses…to make a bolt for it and not face up to the fact that he found the countess eminently attractive…but then she entered, the eyes, the hair, the face and the perfume overwhelmed him as he bowed over her outstretched hand.

"Sadly," she murmured, "the Ambassador's wife is unwell and they will not be joining us. Which means that I get you…all…to…myself." She grasped his hand and refused to let it go, pulling him towards her, slowly, until their faces were within an inch of each other. "I mean to get to know you, very well," she whispered as her mouth closed on his and Beech was able to feel nothing at all except overwhelming desire.

CHAPTER FOURTEEN

MISSING IN ACTION

"What do you mean you can't get hold of him?" Tollman said on the telephone in irritation.

"Look," Sergeant Stenton was trying to be patient. "All I know is that I told him that you called, at about five o'clock, but he was in a bit of a daze."

"Daze? What was wrong with him?"

"A woman…"

"A woman!!?" Tollman interrupted. "What do you mean…a woman?"

Stenton sighed. "If you would just let me explain, Arthur, it will all become clear."

"Go on," Tollman said grudgingly.

"Right," Stenton began. "This Countess turns up at the Yard…"

"Countess?"

Stenton sighed again. "Are you going to let me explain?"

"Yes, sorry, carry on." Tollman was not the most patient of men.

Stenton continued. "This Countess turns up and…how can I describe her? Probably, the most beautiful woman I've ever seen. Better than an actress in the films. Exquisite the woman was. Anyway, she had come to see Beech. Well, when he comes down, I can tell he's smitten…has it really bad…you know. Blushes, stutters, looks all hot and bothered," at this point Stenton chuckled.

"Chief Inspector Beech? Smitten?" Tollman asked

incredulously. Tollman had passed that point in life, sadly.

"Oh yes. So, he takes her upstairs and it turns out, according to a note he left me, that she is the cousin of the woman who was shot. The Romanian woman. And we are to release the body to her so she can take it back to Romania. Anyway, when Beech escorts the lady out to her fancy chauffeur-driven car he looks like someone has addled his wits, and he comes back in and rushes up the stairs like a madman. Then he rushes out again, ten minutes later, and leaves me a note to ring you. The note says stuff about the Romanian corpse and then it says 'Tell Tollman I won't be at the meeting this evening and to carry on without me. I trust his judgement.' That's it."

There was a moment's silence from Tollman, whilst he digested all this information. Then he asked, "That's it, is it? Nothing about tomorrow or what me and Billy are supposed to do?"

"No. Just, he trusts your judgement. If I were you, Arthur," Stenton counselled, "I would proceed on the assumption that Chief Inspector Beech has lost his mind and you won't see hide nor hair of him until he's pulled himself together."

"Don't be daft," Tollman responded briskly. "Sensible men like Mr Beech don't go insane over some woman. Thanks for telephoning, Horace."

Tollman put down the handset and went back into the parlour, where the rest of the Mayfair team were assembled. They all looked at him expectantly.

"It appears we are to proceed without Mr Beech, this

evening." He said, somewhat tetchily, resenting the situation.

"Oh? And where is Peter?" asked Caroline, with a curious note in her voice.

Tollman looked embarrassed. "Apparently, involved with some woman...I don't know...Sergeant Stenton reckons Mr Beech has gone insane."

"WHAT?!!!" There was a chorus of astonishment from every woman in the room. Billy's face broke out in a wide grin.

"What did your Sergeant Stenton actually say, Mr Tollman?" asked Lady Maud, determined to get to the bottom of this.

Tollman reluctantly relayed everything that Stenton had told him about the incredibly beautiful Countess appearing at Scotland Yard and Beech apparently being deeply affected.

Billy was laughing. "When I was in the Guards, we once went on a training exercise in Wales and this lonely widow took a fancy to my mate, Donald. Well, he quite liked her too, and he disappeared into her house and didn't re-appear for a week. When he did, he'd lost almost half a stone in weight and he was starving hungry."

"You're making that up!" said Tollman, his voice managing to convey outrage, envy and disbelief in one sentence.

"No, honestly, Mr Tollman," Billy answered. "I don't know what she did to him but I've never seen a man eat like he did, when he reappeared." Billy winked at Lady Maud and she stifled a giggle with her handkerchief.

Tollman decided enough was enough. "I suggest we abandon this salacious topic and discuss today's investigations." Sissy rolled her eyes at Tollman's pomposity.

Billy noticed that both Victoria and Caroline were very quiet and Victoria, particularly was looking uncomfortable and slightly flushed. *Jealousy?* he wondered.

Elsie Rigsby spoke first, explaining what they had found out about Thelma Barnes. Her mysterious absences, which seemed to be tolerated by the railway management and the fact that her father was, it was thought, an army officer. But that was all they had found out, at the moment.

Caroline added that Thelma was showing some response to stimuli, but not enough for her to be able to say that the woman would definitely recover.

Then the telephone rang again and Tollman left the room to answer it. It was Sergeant Stenton once more.

"I'm nothing but a messaging service for you, Arthur," Stenton joked.

"Mr Beech re-appeared, has he?" asked Tollman hopefully.

"No, it's a message from a PC Fowler at Borough Police Station. He thinks he may have a lead on the vehicle that could have been waiting to transport the kidnapped women and could you telephone him tomorrow?"

"Thank you, Horace. Will do."

Tollman went back into the parlour and reported the latest piece of news. "This needs investigating," he said, "So I will go to Borough tomorrow and Billy, you will have to be on solo guard duty for Elsie and Sissy in the morning, until I come back. Although," he paused, as he had had another thought, "I probably, also need to talk to the Station Manager at Waterloo about these regular mysterious absences of Thelma Barnes."

"Can't I do that?" asked Mabel, suddenly. "I'm off duty tomorrow and the Station Master knows me from when I did the examination of the guard's wagon."

"I can't come with you, Mabel, I'm operating tomorrow," Caroline said, regretfully.

"Could I go with Mabel?" Victoria suddenly asked. "I'm anxious to help. I could take notes of the meeting."

Tollman looked uncertain. "I don't know. Mr Beech has strict orders that you ladies are not to appear to be doing police detective work."

"Well, Mr Beech isn't here, is he?" Victoria said acidly. "He appears to be off enjoying himself."

"We don't know that, Victoria!" said Caroline in sharp rebuke. Billy raised his eyebrows at Tollman. He sensed an atmosphere between the two women.

Tollman raised his hands to ask for moderation. "Alright, ladies, I understand. Let me think." He looked at Billy and rolled his eyes in exasperation.

"May I make a suggestion?" Mabel suddenly said. "Why don't we use the public health story that we used in our case at the munitions factory?"

"How do you mean?" Tollman asked hopefully.

"Well, if Victoria and I go to see the Station Master and I explain that I found traces of tuberculosis in some sputum in the goods wagon and I am enquiring about the health of the workers and that I understand that one of their workers is frequently away and ask whether that is because of her health… something like that?" Mabel offered a reasonable solution.

"I could put my nurse's uniform on again!" added Victoria brightly.

Tollman nodded and pronounced that a splendid notion. "So, now we all have our assignments for tomorrow. Elsie and Sissy, once more on the train cleaning, and see if you can find out more about Thelma Barnes. Billy - you are to look after the ladies. I am off to Borough Police Station and Miss Summersby and Mrs Ellingham will go to Waterloo to see the Station Master. I suggest we reconvene here late afternoon to relay our findings."

The ladies got up to leave and Lady Maud congratulated Tollman. "You see, Mr Tollman, you managed perfectly well without Peter!" Tollman thanked her for her encouragement. "The trouble is, your Ladyship, we are a bit short of manpower, with Mr Beech missing. We still, for example, have a list of establishments with the name 'Palace' in them to check out, haven't we Billy?" Rigsby made a face and nodded.

"You should draft in an ordinary constable to do that job, Mr Tollman. I'm sure you'll find someone," she said breezily as she wafted out of the room.

That set Tollman thinking and his face took on the 'dog with a bone' look, as Billy liked to call it. "I think I may know just the man," he murmured.

* * *

When Bill, Elsie and Sissy got home, they found that Mattie had made some dinner for them. Not only that, she had walked and fed Timmy and cleaned the kitchen floor until it shone.

"What a luxury!" exclaimed Sissy, "to get home to a cooked meal!"

"It's only a chicken pie," said Mattie. "Besides, it's quite nice to be able to cook for someone again. I've missed that, since my Pa got interned."

Everyone sat down and tucked in to the hearty meal she had prepared and pronounced it lovely.

"I couldn't have made better myself," said Elsie, which Billy knew was high praise indeed.

"I was wondering if you would all be able to come with me, when I visited my Pa on Sunday?" Mattie asked hesitantly, "Only I wrote to him about where I'm staying and he wrote back today to say that he's glad I'm safe and he would like to meet you all. I understand if you have important work to do…" she trailed off apologetically.

"Of course we'll come!" Sissy said happily, helping herself to some more peas. "We should be finished on the job we're doing by tomorrow and Billy usually has Sundays off, unless it's an emergency." Everyone nodded and Mattie smiled happily.

Conversation then turned to Mattie's shop and how she felt that next week she should get back and takeover the business again. It became quite obvious that Billy wasn't at all happy with that idea. He remembered, only too well, how they had first met – when Mattie had been attacked by local people in a German-hating frenzy.

"I think you should get rid of that business and stay here permanently…" he pronounced, before remembering that it wasn't in his gift to give Mattie a permanent bed in the house his mother and aunt were looking after. "Sorry...I know it's not up to me," he mumbled.

Sissy and Elsie looked at each other and Sissy nodded.

"Look, we'd be more than happy for you to stay here with us forever," said Elsie, "but we need to sort some things out first. To start with, you need to talk to your Pa about closing the business. After all, it's his business as well, isn't it?" Mattie nodded. "Then, if he says yes, then you need to decide whether you want to set up shop somewhere safer than Whitechapel, or you want to do something entirely different..."

"I'd like to do something important, like you do." Mattie answered, with an urgency in her voice. "I don't want to be stuck behind a shop counter when there's a war on."

"We understand – we really do," said Sissy, "So, first things first, you have a chat with your Pa on Sunday and then we'll see what's what, eh?" Mattie nodded happily and looked at Billy with a smile.

"I made an apple crumble for pudding," she said, "and custard."

* * *

Tollman was bright and early at Borough Police Station, having got the omnibus from his house in Clapham. He was in a good mood, as his daughter Daphne had been able to source some bacon. The butcher had put some aside for her, as he appeared to like Daphne. Tollman had casually quizzed his eldest daughter about the butcher and judged that, from her blushes and attempts to be offhand about it, she quite liked him too.

Thus, fortified by a bacon sandwich, buoyed up by the thought that at least one of his daughters might be courting and cheered by the ability to read a newspaper during his bus journey, Tollman felt that all was right with the world. He smiled one of his rare smiles at the female bus conductor as he gave her his fare and, when he stepped off the omnibus, near the police station, he acknowledged the fact that it was a bright, sunny day, if a little chilly.

The Station Sergeant sent for PC Fowler, as soon as Tollman arrived, and the young policeman explained his findings, yesterday, regarding vehicles. He told Tollman how most of the businesses he visited had what he regarded as unsuitable vehicles. They were either too small, too large or too open for a clandestine operation. "I tried to imagine myself lifting an unconscious woman into a vehicle and some of them were just too high off the ground for even the strongest man to manage such a feat," Fowler added.

Tollman was impressed. "Thinking like a detective," he said and PC Fowler smiled, then he continued with his evidence, detailing what the night watchman had said about the vehicle from the Dutch Pottery Company coming in and out of the wharf area on the night of the Zeppelin raid.

"So," Tollman continued, "I think that you and I should have a quiet look at this Dutch company but then I need to get the 'funny boys' involved from military intelligence. I wouldn't want to be responsible for frightening off some German spy because I didn't know what I was doing! Have you got some civilian clothes, Fowler?"

P.C. Fowler answered, "Yes, sir. In the locker room

downstairs." Hopeful that he might be given another assignment.

"Well, you go and get changed, lad, and I'll wait here. I'm sure your Sergeant here will make me a mug of tea while I'm waiting." Tollman winked at the Station Sergeant.

"You'll be giving PC Fowler ideas above his station," grumbled the Sergeant, as he went off to make some tea.

Fowler re-appeared just as Tollman was finishing his tea and they took a leisurely stroll down towards Blackfriars Road Station and the Dutch Pottery Company. Once there, they loitered by the gate – Tollman lifting his leg up, pressing his boot into the wall, whilst pretending to do up his bootlaces. He registered the number of vehicles parked in the yard. There were three of the type described by Fowler and one large lorry, which appeared to be visiting, unloading sacks of powdered clay.

A dark-haired man, supervising the unloading, gave Fowler and Tollman a suspicious look, which caused them both to move on, past the pottery.

"Mm. I didn't really form any opinion about anything," said Tollman, "but that doesn't mean to say that the place isn't a hot bed of intrigue." He agreed with Fowler, though, about the smaller canvas-sided lorries being suitable for the transportation of the abducted women.

"I think I shall have to get the intelligence boys involved. So, you keep an eye on this place and let me know if it shuts up shop or anything drastic. I doubt that I will be able to get anyone down here before Monday, but I'll do my best." Again, Tollman felt a little irritable because of the unavailability of Beech. *It's useful to have a 'high-up' smoothing the way with other departments and government organisations,* he thought to himself and then decided that if he hadn't heard from Beech by tomorrow, he would have to get the Commissioner involved.

*   *   *

The Station Master at Waterloo, Mr Grimble, looked slightly alarmed when Mabel Summersby turned up with a nurse in tow and asking to speak to him about a public health matter. He felt that life as a Station Master of one of the largest and busiest stations in London was quite difficult enough without 'public health' problems.

He ushered the women into his office and order his secretary to bring some tea. Then he anxiously asked Mabel to outline the problem.

"Mr Grimble," she began confidently, "whilst examining the goods wagon and guards wagon the other day, I unfortunately found some sputum which, upon microscope analysis, contained tuberculosis bacterium. Now, it could belong to a man or a woman, I have no way of knowing..."

Mr Grimble looked horrified and interrupted her to point out that the railways frowned upon people spitting on their trains. He opened up a drawer in his desk and produced a poster, which read: ―――――――――

NOTICE:
DO NOT SPIT.
The practice is OFFENSIVE and DANGEROUS.
It favours the spread of CONSUMPTION
through the scattering of the germs of the disease.

"Very commendable, "Mabel commented, "But, the police think now that the woman who was abducted, but survived, was one of your workers – a Thelma Barnes…" Mabel noted that Mr Grimble suddenly looked extremely shocked but she continued, "and we are aware that she is known to have frequent days off from her work. Could it be that she is ill?"

Mr Grimble shook his head vigorously. "No, not at all. Thelma has never been ill a day in her life. Miss Summersby, I cannot tell you why Thelma Barnes is allowed several absences from work, without getting authorisation from a government department. I suspect that, even if I get that authorisation, I would only be allowed to speak to your Chief Inspector – or higher – as it would be a matter of wartime security."

Mabel could see that she would get no further information from Mr Grimble, who then asked, "May I ask, Miss Summersby, which hospital the woman you believe to be Thelma Barnes is being cared for?"

"The Women's Hospital in Edgeware Road. I understand that anyone who wishes to visit her may only do so with the express permission of Dr Caroline Allardyce and Scotland Yard."

Mr Grimble nodded and replied, "I will make certain telephone calls and I will apprise you of the situation. Do you have a number at which I can reach you?"

Mabel gave him the options of three numbers. Her own number at her home, the number at the hospital, and Mayfair 100.

* * *

Tollman had persuaded the Station Sergeant at Borough Police Station to allow PC Fowler to be 'on loan' to Scotland Yard on Monday, so that he could trawl around the various establishments in London that boasted the name 'Palace' - and there were quite a few of them. Tomorrow, Sunday, everyone would have a day off, Tollman had decided. *If Mr Beech can go absent without leave, then we can all have one day off from this difficult case,* Tollman thought to himself. He then said that he would send a Scotland Yard messenger to Borough Police station with the list of establishments and a photograph of the dead woman. Fowler was to undertake the task in uniform, not plain clothes, but would have no powers of arrest. If he needed assistance, he should telephone Tollman. Needless to say, Fowler was thrilled to be given such a task.

When Tollman arrived at Waterloo station, Billy looked relieved, as he had consumed three mugs of tea during the morning and his bladder urgently needed emptying. There was nothing to report, he said, as he hightailed it to the nearest conveniences.

Tollman bought himself some tea and a currant bun, from the stall, and sat down to watch the activity of the women cleaning the trains. He couldn't see Elsie and Sissy but he assumed that they were working inside the carriages, so he wasn't unduly worried.

The ladies were, indeed, cleaning inside the second train in the sidings, along with their new friend, Edith. Unfortunately, they had started on the toilets in the train and, as Edith remarked, "They don't pay us enough, really, to do jobs like this." Elsie and Sissy agreed. Fortunately, between the three of them, they got the job done quickly and were able to move on to the passenger carriage.

"Ooh! A lucky day today!" Edith exclaimed, as she scooped up a shilling and two farthings from the side of a seat. "That will go towards my Christmas fund," she said, as she put them in her pocket.

"What's your Christmas fund?" asked Elsie.

"Well, Daisy, who's our team leader, puts all the findings in a box and we share it out each month," explained Edith. "I put mine in a Post Office savings account and, by Christmas, I'll have over ten shillings! Comes in handy when buying the essentials, I can tell you!"

Just then, Daisy climbed up into the carriage, looking serious. "Just to tell you, ladies, there's a man who is going around the trains asking if anyone knows where Thelma Barnes is. If he comes in here, don't tell him anything, understand?"

"That won't be difficult, 'cos I don't know anything about Thelma," said Edith, as she handed over the 'findings' to Daisy. "And these two ladies have only met Thelma once."

Daisy nodded, "Well, I'm just telling you, that's all. Orders from Mrs Fallon." Then Daisy left.

Sissy gave Elsie a nod and suddenly said, "Ooh, I've forgotten my liver pills. I've left them in my cardigan. Excuse me ladies while I go and fetch them. If I don't take one now, I shall have acid indigestion all day." Then she climbed down out of the train and went to find Tollman and Billy.

"There's apparently a man roaming around the trains asking for Thelma Barnes," she muttered as she stopped by their table and pretended to fiddle with her shoelaces.

"Gotcha," said Tollman and he made a sign to Billy, who was returning from the gents. The pair of them moved off and began to search along the sidings and around the trains – opening doors to carriages and getting a frown or a sharp word from the women intent on cleaning.

Billy saw a woman up on top of one train, hosing the roof, and shouted up to her "We're police. Have you seen a man asking after Thelma Barnes?" The woman shook her head and carried on with her task.

Tollman went down into the pit of the sidings, where a group of women were cleaning under the train and showed them his warrant card. "Have you seen a man who is asking after Thelma Barnes?" One of the women nodded and said he had spoken to them not two minutes before and then gone off down the track. She pointed to indicate the direction and Tollman sped off. He somehow managed to meet up with Billy and they moved quickly towards a second train at the very moment a middle-aged man descended from one of the carriages.

"Stop! Police!" shouted Tollman and Billy gathered speed to apprehend the man, before he decided to run for it. Curiously, the man showed no inclination to bolt and stood perfectly still. Billy reached him and immediately turned him round and handcuffed him. Again, the man offered no resistance.

Tollman reached them and said, "We understand that you have been asking about Thelma Barnes? May we ask why you are interested in the lady?" Tollman's voice was sharp. When the man didn't answer, Billy pulled on the handcuffs and said aggressively, "Answer the Detective Sergeant, sir!"

The man furrowed his brow and looked anxious. "I have every right to be interested in Thelma. I'm her father."

Chapter Fifteen

TOO MANY FINGERS IN THIS PIE!

The man claiming to be Thelma Barnes' father sat calmly in an interview room at Scotland Yard and said nothing. In fact, from the moment Tollman and Rigsby had arrested him, he had not spoken a word. The Station Manager had been summoned but was unable to identify the man as he had never met Thelma's father. All through the wait for a police vehicle, the journey to Scotland Yard and the signing in at the front desk, the man remained silent. In fact, he was eerily unperturbed by the whole procedure. Tollman was curious as to why this was so, and his curiosity was about to be answered.

"Now, sir," Tollman said firmly, as he put a mug of tea and an ashtray in front of the man. "If you would just give us your full name, please?" He nodded at Billy, who was poised to take notes.

The man replied, "Major Henry A. Barnes, Royal Engineers," in a matter-of-fact tone of voice.

"And you allege that Thelma Barnes is your daughter?"

"I do. And I want to know where she is and if she is alright." The man spoke calmly but firmly.

"Is there anyone who can vouch for you and confirm that you are, indeed, the father of Miss Barnes?"

The man sighed. "I believe that you would have to telephone the War Office and ask for Major General Donop, who is the Master General of the Ordnance. I liaise with him mostly, or you could ring my own superior officer in the Royal Engineers, but he is in Didcot, near Oxford, at the RE Depot."

Billy raised his eyebrows and pursed his lips at this mention of such exalted ranks in the War Office. Tollman sighed and rolled his eyes. "Constable Rigsby, please guard the prisoner whilst I go and speak to the Commissioner." Then he left the room.

Major Barnes casually looked over Billy, as he was standing to attention, noted the scarred face and said, "Been in the Army yourself, son?"

"Yes, sir. Grenadier Guards, sir."

Major Barnes nodded. "Well, you've done your bit for King and Country, now. My compliments." He said it without looking at Billy and in a tone of voice which sounded bitter and Billy shot him a puzzled sideways glance.

"I don't suppose you can tell me where my daughter is?" Barnes ventured.

"No sir, I'm sorry, sir," Billy said firmly. "Detective Sergeant Tollman will tell you everything when he gets back." Barnes grunted and said no more.

It was a good fifteen minutes before Tollman returned. "My apologies for the delay, Major, but I had to get my commissioner to ring Major General Donop. May I look at your left arm, please, sir?"

Barnes gave a sardonic smile, stood up and took his overcoat off, rolled up his sweater sleeve and revealed an old, but still livid, burn mark which covered the inside of his arm from the wrist to the elbow. "An engine blew up whilst I was working on it," Barnes explained, "I was damn lucky that I escaped with just a burnt arm."

"Thank you, sir," Tollman sounded a little more respectful now that he had established the identity of the man before him. "Can you tell me, please, why you were looking for your daughter? Did you feel that she was missing, in some way?"

"Thelma was supposed to visit me at...down in Kent," Barnes began and Tollman noted that the man corrected himself mid-sentence, as though he had nearly given away a location in Kent and had stopped himself in time.

"When was this, sir?" Tollman asked.

"Two days ago."

"You live down in Kent?"

Again, there was a hesitation, then Barnes said "Yes, in a way. I work and live down there. I'm afraid I can't say more than that Detective Sergeant. War work, you understand."

"Did your daughter visit you often?" Tollman persisted with his line of questioning.

"Usually once a week, or thereabouts. Look, Detective Sergeant..." Barnes' patience was beginning to fray, "You have proved my identity, would you please tell me where my daughter is?!"

Tollman decided to come clean. "I'm afraid your daughter was kidnapped, with another woman, three nights ago..."

"Good God! Where is she now?" Barnes was suddenly jolted out of his calm demeanour. "You must tell me!"

Tollman held up his hand. "Calm yourself, sir. We found her and she is safe, but she is very poorly, in hospital. The other lady, however, was not so lucky. She was tortured and killed before we found them. Your daughter is getting the best care."

Barnes sunk his head in his hands and muttered, "I told her, time and time again, not to get involved in this business..."

"What business would that be, Major?" Tollman's sharp ears had picked up the man's words.

"I can't tell you!" was the anguished cry, "Now, for God's sake, man, take me to see my daughter!"

* * *

Ernest and Lily King had had a difficult time running Mattie Grunwald's shop in Whitechapel. On the first day, Lily manned the shop, whilst Ernest borrowed some ladders from a neighbouring establishment and set about painting out the name above the window with the dark green paint he had purchased. Then he had decided that the black paint, that had been used to scrawl "German Pigs" on the brickwork below the shop window, would not come off with turpentine, so he had painted that as well. The resulting effect was, in Lily's words, "funereal".

"Dark green paint, top and bottom. It looks like an undertaker's!" Lily had said crossly. "Now I shall have to fill the window with brightly coloured fabrics to make it look more cheerful."

Ernest had sloped off to return the ladders, muttering "There's no pleasing some people," under his breath. But he had felt that his wife was secretly happy to have something to do, as business had been sorely lacking all morning. There had been a few youths who had turned up outside the shop, Ernest assumed they were there to cause trouble again, because they looked disappointed to see that the shop front was altered and slunk away fairly quickly. There had been one ugly incident where a man had stood in front of the shop and shouted "Huns should leave Britain!". He had repeated it several times until Ernest had appeared, brandishing his cosh and looking mean, then he had scarpered.

"Gutless bullies, these people," Ernest had said, when he came back in the shop and Lily had agreed.

The next day, with the shop freshly painted and the window display a blaze of colour, customers had decided to come back. However, Lily then had to endure a stream of women making snide remarks about 'the previous owner' and saying terrible things like "Thank God we don't have to buy our necessaries from that little German slut." Lily had been quite sharp with some of them. Ernest had been quite proud of her. Especially when she had told one woman off.

"I haven't met the previous owner myself," she had said haughtily, "but I understand she was a kind young girl who was trying to run a business all by herself and she was struggling. Perhaps if people round here had been a bit more neighbourly, they would have considered that before they smashed up her shop and tried to harm her person." The customer had left with a flea in her ear and Lily had commented to Ernest that she had probably ruined the shop's trade forever, by losing her temper. Ernest had replied that he was proud of her for making a stand for Mattie and to hell with the shop trade.

"In fact," he had said, "I think that girl would be mad to come back here, when she could run a nice little shop near us in Clapham – you know – an altogether better neighbourhood."

Lily had smiled at the remark and was secretly pleased that Ernest was progressing nicely along the route she was marking out for him. She was even more pleased when, on the third day, trade having been brisk and without any incident of an unpleasant nature, Ernest had said after dinner, in the evening, "Do you know, Lil, you're rather good at this shop lark. I've been quite impressed today."

"Thank you, Ernest. That's very kind of you," she said simply, gave him a kiss on the forehead and then she hummed a tune to herself as she did the washing up.

* * *

When Tollman, Billy and Major Barnes walked into the reception area of the Women's Hospital, Caroline was, by chance, there, writing up some notes. She looked up in surprise and said, "Mr Tollman! I was just about to ring you! Thelma Barnes has revived."

"Thank God!" the Major said loudly and Caroline looked quizzical.

"This is Thelma's father…Major Barnes," Tollman explained as the Major strode forward to shake Caroline's hand in gratitude.

"Wonderful!" Caroline said happily, "I'm sure she will make a full recovery now that you are here. We had put her in a private room, for her safety, and to make it easier for Matron to give her regular oxygen therapy. A nurse has been with her constantly and no-one has been allowed in the room, other than medical staff. Let me show you the way." She strode out towards the staircase and the men followed her up to the second floor, where she took them to a small side room. Thelma was asleep but Caroline gently woke her, so that she could take her pulse.

As soon as Thelma caught sight of her father, she said, in a croaky voice, "Dad!"

"It's alright, dearest, I'm here now. I've been so worried about you." He drew up a chair and took her hand.

Thelma's eyes filled with tears and she said, "I didn't tell them anything, Dad. I promise."

Major Barnes shook his head and said "Shush, dear. Of course you didn't."

"I am going to need to talk to Miss Barnes, I'm afraid," Tollman said quietly.

Caroline looked doubtful. "Her pulse is still erratic. I don't want her upset as it could put a strain on her heart."

"But we need to know about the men who abducted them. It's urgent, Dr Allardyce!" Tollman was insistent. Then he turned to Major Barnes, who was stroking his daughter's hair, trying to soothe her. "You must understand, sir, that we desperately need to find and apprehend the men who kidnapped your daughter and murdered the other woman."

"Is Marie dead then?" Thelma asked tremulously.

"I'm afraid so, Miss. And we need your help to get the men who did this."

Thelma looked at her father and said, "What can I tell them, Dad?"

Major Barnes sighed and said, "Just tell them what they need to know about the criminals and I will tell them the rest."

Tollman and Billy looked at each other, intrigued as to what secrets were going to be revealed by father and daughter.

"First of all, Miss Barnes," Tollman began, "tell us about the abduction."

Thelma slowly recounted the fact that she, and the other woman, Marie Radu, had been sitting in the guard's wagon and, having exhausted all conversation, had lapsed into silence and were both nodding off, with the rhythm of the train. Then the bombs had started – in the distance at first – but as they neared the centre of London, the blasts had become quite severe. The guard told them that the train was pulling into a nearby station, extinguishing all its lights and everything went dark. Thelma then smelt an odd odour which made her feel a little nauseous and quite dizzy. She heard Marie give a little cough and a groan, then she heard the guard being hit and he crashed to the floor. The next thing she knew, she had passed out, but not before she had felt herself being lifted off the floor and slung over a man's shoulder, with her head hung downwards and her face pressed into his back.

She had then passed out again but was in some strange twilight world where she could hear some things and feel some sensations. She fancied that she heard water splashing and she felt as though she was being rocked from side to side. When she briefly came around later, she was tied hand and foot to a chair, her mouth was gagged and her eyes were blindfolded. What made her come to was the sound of Marie screaming and a man shouting. Thelma had struggled and made a noise and then she smelt the sickly odour again and sank into oblivion.

The second time she woke up was when she heard a loud bang or crack. She thought she heard footsteps and a door slam and she lapsed back into unconsciousness. She remembered nothing after that, until she awoke in her bed in the hospital.

"There were two things that were important, to my mind," she said to Tollman. "One is that I remember that the men spoke German to each other. I mean I heard more than one man's voice and the second thing is that they weren't interested in me. They never asked me anything, they really didn't pay much attention to me, except to keep me drugged with whatever it was. It was Marie they were interested in." She turned to her father and said, "So, you see, Dad. I didn't tell them anything – because they never asked me…"

* * *

Billy had been sent home and Tollman found himself sitting, along with the secretive Major Barnes, in the Commissioner's office. He was wondering what was going to be revealed.

"I have telephoned your superiors at the War Office, Major Barnes," said Sir Edward, "and, in the light of this being a murder investigation, you are authorised to tell us exactly what your work is and how your daughter is involved."

Major Barnes took a breath and began. "As you know, I am a major in the Royal Engineers. For the last four months, my unit has been working on building a new railway line and port, down in Richborough in Kent. The line is linked to the main line that feeds up to Waterloo. The port is being designed so that it can accommodate the straight transfer of railway wagons to ship, which makes it unique, and the port will be specifically for taking heavy artillery, other munitions, railway locomotives, mechanised vehicles, horses and fuel over to the

Front. It is hope to have it operational by the middle of 1916. None of the existing ports are able to deal with this traffic. Dover is devoted to ferrying casualties back from the front, Folkestone is used for fresh troops being deployed overseas, as is Southampton, to a lesser degree."

"And how is your daughter involved?" Tollman asked.

"The new port under construction is a top-secret project and we have had problems with telephone line interception before, so it was deemed best by the War Office that information and messages should be sent backwards and forwards by courier. My daughter already worked for Military Intelligence, as a courier and escort for various personnel coming over from the Continent. It seemed sensible to use her. What is more natural that a father and daughter should meet up once a week? When she didn't turn up at the appointed time, I naturally became worried."

Sir Edward contributed to the explanation by saying, "As you might appreciate, Tollman, if word of this secret project were to filter out, it could become a target for aerial bombardment or sabotage by land. So, you understand the need for secrecy."

Tollman nodded but then felt he had to say his piece. "I do understand, Major Barnes, the need for all this cloak and dagger behaviour, however, let me say something that you may find unpalatable. Your daughter was very lucky. The men who abducted her appeared to only be interested in the Romanian woman, who had information they wanted - and for that she was beaten and shot. They appear not to have been interested in your daughter or have been aware that she had any information that they would find useful. Make no mistake, Major, your daughter almost died. If we had not got to her when we did, and if we had not had a doctor with us, she would, most certainly, have died. I understand that young women want to do their bit for King and country but there comes a point where these things are just too dangerous. For all we know, your daughter may have lasting health problems from this episode. It is time for you to persuade her to stop this work."

Major Barnes looked miserable and Tollman's lecture certainly appeared to have hit home. He thanked Sir Edward, shook Tollman's hand and then he left to get back to his daughter in hospital.

"Whisky, Tollman?" Sir Edward offered, as he got up to walk to his drink's cabinet.

"I don't mind if I do, sir. It's been a long day." Tollman gratefully accepted a glass of whisky.

"Are you managing, Tollman? Without Mr Beech, I mean?" Sir Edward enquired lightly.

"Yes, sir…managing would be the right word. However, I do miss Mr Beech on a case like this, as I am not of sufficient rank within the police force to be able to speak with all these Johnnies in the War Office, Military Intelligence or whatever. So, I miss Mr Beech being able to smooth the path, as it were. There are just too many fingers in the pie on this one!" His response, he was aware, sounded a touch exasperated.

Sir Edward thought for a moment and said, "I understand. But you will be surprised to know that Mr Beech isn't always successful in 'smoothing the path'. He wrote me a letter, which arrived this afternoon, to say that he had received short shrift from Special Branch over providing an extra pair of hands…"

"Special Branch!" muttered Tollman, managing to convey all the disgust he felt about that section of the police service, in two words.

"Yes, quite," murmured the Commissioner. "I shall be letting them know of my displeasure on Monday morning. Meanwhile, I have spoken to Lieutenant Colonel Kell of MI5 (g) and he has assured me that he will provide a man to assist you. His name is Thomas Brockhurst and he will pay you a visit tomorrow afternoon, at your home, if that is convenient. Apologies for assuming that you would be free on a Sunday, Tollman, but I felt you needed to discuss your next moves on this case, as soon as possible, with this agent."

"Yes, sir, that will be quite convenient," Tollman wasn't sure if it was the whisky or the thought of support that was making him feel more cheerful. Then he decided to ask about Beech. "Is Mr Beech unwell, Sir Edward?"

The Commissioner gave a small twitch of his mouth, perhaps supressing a smile, as he doled out another dram of whisky into Tollman's glass. "Mr Beech…is not himself," he said tactfully. "He has, for some time now, been mentally, as well as physically affected by his experience in the trenches. I have been aware that he was sliding into a depression…that the dynamic and energetic young man who persuaded me to set up your valuable team, had disappeared. I am hoping that this… entanglement…with this 'beautiful Countess', to quote Sergeant Stenton, who waxed eloquent to me about the lady, will prove of some benefit to Beech, and he will return to us, restored in health and vigour and in an altogether better frame of mind."

Tollman was suspicious. "Do we know anything about this Romanian Countess? How do we know that she won't do Mr Beech some harm?"

Sir Edward was having trouble restraining a smile but his eyes held a mischievous twinkle. "I am ahead of you, Tollman. I straight away telephoned the Romanian embassy and the ambassador gave the lady a glowing reference. She is, in his words, 'a valued member of Romanian high society, a confidante of the Queen of Romania, a founder of a children's charity, a tireless patriot, as well as being a great beauty and… ahem…passionate' in all her endeavours."

"Blimey!" said Tollman, "Let's hope Mr Beech survives!"

Chapter Sixteen

NEW FRIENDS

Sissy awoke to the most wonderful smell. *Was it gingerbread? It couldn't be?* She put on her dressing gown and shuffled out to the kitchen to find Mattie taking a cake out of the oven and putting another one in.

"Well, the smell of gingerbread is not a bad way to wake up!" said Sissy, smiling.

Mattie looked flustered. "I'm so sorry to disturb you. I hope you don't mind. I wanted to make some cake for my Pa and I made the fire up in the oven early. I haven't used any of your store cupboard, I promise!" she added anxiously, "I bought all the ingredients myself."

Sissy put her arm around the girl and reassured her that no one was cross. "If you'd have mentioned it to us, we would have gladly helped you! In fact, I'm sure there are things in the pantry that we can add to your lovely cakes." She went to have a rummage in the large, cold room that led off the kitchen, where they kept all the food, and she came back, smiling, with a jar of blackberry jam, an apple pie, cheese and two bottles of beer. "Elsie and I were going to make some sandwiches for us all to take with us today," she said, "So we'll make sure that we make extra for your Pa."

Mattie's eyes were glistening as she was determined not to cry. She simply said, "Thank you. You are all so kind."

By this time, Elsie and Timmy were up as well. Timmy sat expectantly by the oven, hoping that whatever was in it would be shared with him as well. Mattie cut Elsie and Sissy a piece of the gingerbread she had already baked. It was warm and very soft. Sissy made them all some tea and they sat down together and planned the morning.

"How long will it take us to get there…to see your Pa?" asked Sissy.

Mattie thought and said, "The omnibus from Victoria station takes about two hours. Of course, it used to take me less time from Whitechapel."

"And what time to we want to get there?" asked Elsie, as she gave Timmy a small piece of her gingerbread to stop him looking at her with pleading eyes.

"We're not allowed to visit until after lunch – about half past one they start letting people in."

Sissy reckoned that they should leave at about eleven. "Billy's turning up about ten, so you and he can take Timmy for a nice long walk, so we can settle him down before we go, whilst Else and I make the sandwiches."

Plans made and gingerbread eaten, Sissy and Elsie disappeared whilst Mattie let Timmy out into the garden to do his business, then she returned to the oven to supervise the second lot of gingerbread.

* * *

Conrad Grunwald was watching the sudden departure of one of his fellow internees, Georgi Hofer, who had been visited this morning by two formidable looking men, and who were now supervising him as he packed all his meagre possessions.

"Are you being moved to another camp?" asked the man

– a concerned Hungarian, who slept in the bed next to Hofer.

"No!" Hofer answered with glee, "They have finally proved that I am not Hungarian – I am Romanian. These men brought my papers from the Romanian embassy. I am free!"

There were shouts of "Well done!", "Good for you!" and "Lucky man!" from the internees who overheard the conversation.

Conrad did not really know Hofer, as they all tended to socialise within their ethnic groups (it was easier if they all spoke the same language) and with the men who slept in surrounding beds, in the vast dormitory where they were all corralled. However, Conrad had heard stories about Hofer's previous career as a criminal, and he wondered why the Romanian embassy would go to such trouble for a man with such a poor record. *Still*, he reasoned, *it's nothing to do with me and Hofer is an old man now. Good luck to him.*

Hofer was finally leaving, and stopping off to speak to various individuals on his way out of the great hall. There were lots of handshakes and smiles, but the two men who had come to escort him remained unsmiling and watchful. *Perhaps they are criminals too,* thought Conrad, *they certainly look the part.* But then he reasoned that they could, just as easily, be policemen as he watched them grasp Hofer firmly by each arm and propel him out of the door.

Conrad was certainly envious. It had been a great shock to him when he had been interned and he had despaired, not for himself, but for his daughter Mattie, being left alone to run the haberdashery shop in Whitechapel. In his worst moments of despair, he would have to take himself off to walk around the beautiful grounds that surrounded his prison. Then, in private, he was able to cry and, eventually, he would return from the depths of his sorrow and be able to interact with his fellow inmates again.

When he had received Mattie's letter, telling him that she had been attacked and the shop vandalised, he had felt that his world had completely shattered. Fortunately, the letter had continued with the story of her rescue by the police and the kindness of a young policeman and his family. For a while Conrad had felt relieved and optimistic – there is benevolence in the world, he had thought. But, in the small hours, when he lay in his narrow camp bed, listening to the other internees snoring, moaning, whispering and breathing, he would despair again. Supposing this family that had taken his Mattie under their wing, were not what they seemed? Supposing they were taking advantage of her? She could be in danger!

When daylight broke, he would feel more positive and, today, he was excited but nervous, because Mattie had written to him to say that she was coming to visit and was bringing the young policeman that she spoke so highly of, and his mother and aunt. Today, Conrad would be able to judge whether they were genuine people and were truly caring for his dear daughter.

✳ ✳ ✳

Tollman's Sunday morning had been spent in trying to coerce his daughters to clean and tidy the downstairs of the house and to make themselves look respectable for his afternoon visitor. This, he decided, was like trying to herd cats, and he eventually gave up. The eldest, Daphne, had co-operated somewhat – at least she was dressed and looking relatively smart. The other two girls refused, as Sunday was their only day off from working at the department store and they preferred to spend their day, still in their nightgowns, laying on their beds, reading magazines. Daphne, however, was only properly dressed because she had an afternoon tea appointment with the young butcher who fancied her. Because of this event, she had declined to cook the usual Sunday roast dinner, saying that she "didn't want to smell of beef dripping" when she met her young man. So, the beef had been cooked the night before and Tollman would have to make do with cold cuts and pickles, she had announced.

This denial of a proper Sunday lunch had not gone down well with Tollman, who was already in a bad mood, having woken up with a headache, probably caused by imbibing two generous glasses of the Commissioner's expensive scotch the night before. Added to which, he was not looking forward to the visit of Mr Thomas Brockhurst from MI5(g) who, he had already decided, would probably be an upper-class, public school educated twit of the type that seemed to infest the corridors of the civil service. So, he was somewhat surprised when, at 12.30, he opened the door to a well-built youngish man, dressed in slightly scruffy clothes and a flat cap, who said, in a distinctly lower-class voice, "Detective Sergeant Tollman? Tommy Brockhurst, mate. How do you do?" He showed Tollman his identification papers.

"Come in, come in." Tollman ushered him inside. "I wasn't expecting you so early. We're a little bit untidy, son."

"Oh, sorry," Tommy said affably. "But I thought that we probably had a lot to discuss and we should get to it, as it were."

Tollman agreed and then said, "Fancy a beer?"

"Don't mind if I do, Arthur. It is Arthur, isn't it?" Tollman said it was, indeed.

"Have you had any lunch, Tommy?" The young man shook his head and Tollman added "It's only cold meat and pickles."

"That's champion, Arthur."

So, the two men settled down, each clutching a bottle of beer, and began to discuss the task in hand.

* * *

The omnibus journey had been long, but not uneventful, for Billy, Mattie, Sissy and Elsie. They had eaten sandwiches, drunk tea, gossiped, laughed and even got the conductress to join in a song with them.

"Looking forward to this," said Sissy, towards the end of the journey, "I haven't been to Ally Pally since…ooh… 1912! Went to see a pantomime. No, I tell a lie, I did go back there in 1913, to the park. The grounds are beautiful." She turned to Mattie and said "If the government was going to lock you up as an enemy alien there are worse places you could be." Just as she said that, the omnibus rounded the corner and the full glory of Alexandra Palace came into their vision – the endless windows, the central church-like building and the turrets and domes and also, to Sissy's dismay, a long, long wooden fence topped with barbed wire. Suddenly, their good humour evaporated and the reality of alien internment hit them. So, it was a slightly sombre group that got off the omnibus and joined the long queue of, mostly, women and children waiting to visit their loved ones.

After they had passed through the checkpoint and Billy, just for extra effect, had flashed his warrant card, their bags and baskets were searched.

"Planning on feeding the whole camp?" enquired a guard cheekily, as he looked at the contents of Sissy's basket. She gave him a raised eyebrow and one of her sardonic looks, which was enough to wipe the smile of his face.

Mattie had raced ahead and was already hopping between the ranks of neatly made beds to cry "Pa!" and fling her arms around a tall, distinguished-looking grey-haired man. Billy nervously followed her, unsure of what sort of reception he would get from Mattie's father, but the man immediately shook his hand warmly and said, "You must be Constable Rigsby – thank you, thank you for all you have done for my daughter." Billy instantly relaxed and smiled, saying that it was entirely his pleasure and privilege to look after Mattie.

Billy introduced his aunt, Sissy, and she was rewarded with a hug from Conrad, then Elsie brought up the rear and Conrad's face softened and he took her hand, bowed and kissed it. Sissy's face took on a "here we go again" look and she made a mocking face at her sister. Elsie knew that she would never hear the end of it, when they got home, that Mattie's Pa had kissed her hand and not Sissy's.

The magnificent hall, with its vaulted ceiling and a stage at one end, complete with wood panelling and huge pipe organ, was filled with the noise of adults talking loudly, children crying and men shouting.

"Pa" said Mattie loudly, "Put your coat and scarf on and we'll go out into the gardens. It's bedlam in here!"

They filed out into the autumn sunshine and found a quiet spot, with a bench, to sit down and have a talk. Mattie showed Conrad all the food they had brought him and he was almost overwhelmed. "Beer! And gingerbread!" he exclaimed, "It's like Christmas!"

First, Sissy, Elsie and Billy decided to go for a stroll round the gardens and leave Mattie some time alone with her Pa. Looking back, Billy could see that they were both deep in conversation and he hoped that he had made a favourable impression on Conrad.

He needn't have worried. Mattie's Pa was singularly impressed with the whole family. "They seem like very kind people," he said to his daughter, "And, after twenty years as a shopkeeper, I feel I can recognise genuine people when I see them."

"Pa...about the shop..." Mattie began and Conrad interrupted her.

"Oh, Mattie, you must leave it! I insist! The thought of you being alone there and subject to violence is giving me nightmares. Find another shop in a better neighbourhood – but if you do set up somewhere else, don't put our surname on the shop front."

Mattie felt relieved but she said, "Pa, would you mind very much if we gave up the shop altogether? I don't want to spend the war behind a shop counter. I want to do something more useful." Her voice was passionate and her eyes pleading.

"Like what?" Conrad was surprised.

Mattie shook her head. "I don't know yet but I will let you know when I find something." She hugged him again. "I'll put all our stuff in storage for a while. Billy's mum and aunt said that I can stay with them as long as I need to."

"If that is what you want, Mattie," Conrad reassured her, then he gently quizzed her about Billy and he realised, when he saw his daughter's face light up, that she was very fond, indeed, of the tall young policeman. So, when Billy, Sissy and Elsie came back, Conrad began gently coaxing Billy's life story from him. He was astonished that Billy had been a professional soldier, like his father before him, and a professional boxer. "Obviously a very good boxer," Conrad commented, "as your face is still handsome and you don't have a broken nose," and he made a face at him, whilst pushing his own nose to one side. Billy laughed and thought, *Like father like daughter. He hasn't commented on my scar at all.*

"What do you do to pass the time in here?" asked Billy, curiously. Conrad went on to describe the wonderful orchestra and string quartet that had been formed amongst the internees "Mostly amongst Austrians and Hungarians – they are wonderful violinists, you know. We Germans love our music but we are better at playing marching music rather than romantic melodies!" Then he turned to Mattie and said, "Oh, I forgot to tell you! Peter came, from the Society of Friends and paid us for the baskets we made. The Friends are selling them for us! Look!" Conrad took six shillings out of his pocket to show her, and then he counted the coins into her open hand.

"You make baskets?" asked Sissy, quite impressed by such skill.

Conrad shook his head. "No, other men do. I cut and make up the linings and sew them into the baskets."

"Pa used to be a tailor, when he was young," explained Mattie.

"So, I get a whole shilling for every lining I do." He said happily. "It gives me money to give to Mattie to help with her expenses. I don't need anything in here."

Sissy and Elsie began to ask Conrad questions about life in the Alexandra Palace internment camp and Conrad described what it was like…the lack of privacy, the noise, the chill at night, the cramped sleeping quarters and so on. "But," he added, "the food is good – even if there isn't enough of it – because the kitchens are run by internees who used to be chefs in London restaurants, and German chefs at that!"

"Has anybody ever escaped?" said Billy, looking at the barbed wire on top of the fence.

Conrad shook his head. "Sometimes people get transferred to worse camps – I hear such tales of awful conditions elsewhere – and, this morning, a man was actually released because it was proved that he was Romanian and not Hungarian!"

Billy's stomach suddenly did a flip over at Conrad's statement. Carefully he asked, with mounting excitement, "Did someone come to take him home then?"

Conrad shrugged. "Not exactly. He was escorted by two serious-looking men, who behaved as though they were policemen and they were taking him into custody. Mind you, Georgi Hofer was, reputedly, a talented criminal." he added conspiratorially.

"That was his name…Georgi Hofer?" Billy thought he recognised the name, "And what sort of criminal was he?"

Conrad smiled, "Well he's an old man now, but I hear from others that he was a top safecracker."

Billy decided he had to make a telephone call, so he excused himself and left everyone to carry on chatting.

* * *

Tollman and Brockhurst had had a splendid lunch, eating their cold cuts and pickles, with plenty of fresh bread and a bit of cheese, all the while swapping humorous tales about life in the police force and the theatre, because it turned out that Tommy Brockhurst's previous job had been as an actor, on the West End stage, and he could put on any accent, in any sort of voice, and disguise himself to appear be any age. Military Intelligence stumbled across him and decided he would be useful – particularly as he spoke German and Turkish – having been raised by a German mother and a Turkish father.

Tommy's boss, Lieutenant Colonel Kell, had filled him in on Tollman's current case, up to the point where he had met Beech and Sir Edward for lunch. Tollman told him what progression they had made since then – Thelma Barnes waking up, her father appearing, and PC Fowler finding a possible source of the 'getaway vehicle' at the Dutch Pottery Company.

Tommy's ears pricked up at this point and he said firmly, "We know about that Dutch company…or we think we do. It gets some stock of materials from Rotterdam, which is a neutral port and absolutely infested with German and Austrian spies.

The company here also sends completed pottery back to Rotterdam every so often. It actually charters a whole ship for that purpose – not a big ship – and probably only once every three months. It just so happens that they have a ship being loaded at Tilbury this coming week and we have put a man down there to keep an eye on it. What we really need is to get someone into the company here."

Suddenly, the telephone rang in the hallway and it was swiftly answered by Daphne, about to go out to meet her young man. She popped her head, adorned with her finest hat, round the door and said, "Dad! The operator says that Billy is on the telephone!" then she disappeared. Tollman looked surprised and got up to take the call.

"Yes, I'll take the call, put him on please," he said to the operator and Billy came on the line. "What is it, lad?" Tollman enquired.

"Mr Tollman," said Billy urgently, "we forgot about Alexandra Palace!"

"Eh?" Tollman was confused.

"What was the name of the bloke on that Romanian passport?" Billy asked.

"Er…George something beginning with an H, I'd have to have it in front of me to be sure."

Billy said. "Yes! It was Georgi Hofer," he pronounced it just like Conrad has pronounced it, "and this morning, two foreign-looking men arrived at Alexandra Palace and got him released because they had a passport that proved he was Romanian and not Hungarian. I reckon they came to get him because the Romanian lady who was going to go the palace, couldn't, because she was dead. Alexandra Palace is the 'palace' we were looking for. The waitress in the hotel in Southampton heard her say she was going to go to Doughty Street, which she would have done, if she'd been alive, to retrieve the passport and other papers, then she was going to WL, obviously with the secret train movements information, then to 'the palace', which was probably to Alexandra Palace with the passport to get the Romanian man released. Don't you think?"

"Yes, Billy, I do. Well done, lad for thinking like a detective. Tell everyone to meet up at Lady Maud's tomorrow morning at nine sharp. Well done again."

CHAPTER SEVENTEEN

MATTIE GETS HER WISH

The team was assembled at Lady Maud's house – all except Peter Beech of course, who was still missing – and they were dipping in and out of the breakfast buffet. Billy was in a cheerful mood, after the successful visit to see Mattie's father at Alexandra Palace, and was happily tucking into a full breakfast of eggs, sausages, mushrooms and fried bread. Tollman was on tea and toast, Sissy and Elsie had already eaten, whilst the rest of them just picked at their food. Victoria had looked sombre from the moment that Tollman had announced that Mr Beech would not be joining them. Billy had noted that Caroline had flushed slightly at the news and was now watching Victoria pushing some scrambled eggs around her plate. Mabel was oblivious to any emotional tension and was reading a newspaper whilst spreading butter on her toast and managing to get grease marks all over the newspaper at the same time. Lady Maud was starting her day in the usual way, by commenting loudly on the war news in the paper and hoping that someone around the table would respond. Fortunately, Arthur Tollman was always up for a debate on the issues of the day.

"I see that the Bulgarians have attacked Serbia," she began, "and Serbia has asked for help from Greece and Romania – both of whom have refused! Disgraceful! However, the French have gone to aid Serbia and are attacking the Bulgarians in Macedonia. Britain and Montenegro have officially declared war on Bulgaria and, it says in the Times, that Britain has begun to set up a naval blockade in the Aegean off the coast of Bulgaria." Maud announced.

Tollman pursed his lips in distaste. "Yes, Lady Maud. More and more countries are coming into this war but, sadly, for the wrong reasons."

"The wrong reasons? How so, Mr Tollman?"

Tollman took another swallow of tea and answered, "I feel that it is more for gain in territory or assets, than principle. For example, I read a Foreign Office Bulletin to Scotland Yard the other day. They send us these bulletins to warn us if they think any of their policies might stir up trouble in the populace and we should be prepared," he said by way of explanation. "This particular bulletin warned us that the British government had decided to offer the island of Cyprus to Greece, in order to persuade them to come into the war. We had a few disturbances amongst Cypriots in London when we annexed Cyprus last year because, understandably, people were concerned that what the British government did was illegal but, also, they didn't want to be annexed by the Turks who had partnered up with Germany to declare war on us. So, suddenly, we're offering to give away an island, that we don't technically own, to Greece, just to get them to provide more manpower is this ever-enlarging war that is getting out of control!"

"That's fascinating, Mr Tollman. I had no idea about Cyprus." Lady Maud smiled at this extra nugget of news.

"I wouldn't worry about it, Lady Maud, because the Greeks, sensibly, turned down the offer, preferring to not send their men to be slaughtered, and we promptly got another missive from the Foreign Office saying "It's all off, ignore our last message." Tollman decided that it was time for business and said "If you will excuse me, your Ladyship, I think it is time for us to start our meeting, as I have someone new arriving this morning."

Victoria looked up from her reveries and asked, sharply, "Is this 'someone' a replacement for Mr Beech? If so, I think we should have all been consulted!"

Tollman was about to respond when Caroline asked Victoria, "What difference does it make, Victoria? Peter is entitled to some time off."

Victoria glared at her, mumbled some excuse and fled the room. Everyone looked at Caroline and she, in turn, looked at Maud.

"I apologise, Maud, for upsetting Victoria."

Lady Maud shrugged. "Think nothing of it, my dear. You and I are both in the doghouse with Victoria because I already said to her this morning that as she has made it perfectly clear that she doesn't want a romantic involvement with Peter, much to my regret I may add, then she isn't entitled to sulk if he has found someone else."

Sissy and Elsie raised their eyebrows at each other and Tollman looked astonished. Mabel and Billy just carried on eating.

Tollman cleared his throat. "Yes, well, to return to business…a gentleman will be arriving very soon, who is from military intelligence. His name is Tommy Brockhurst, he's a bit of a Jack the Lad, used to be an actor. He is a very clever man and I was most impressed with him yesterday. He came to my house yesterday and discussed the whole case. He's here to help us out, temporarily, as this case has, so far, involved us with two intelligence agencies and one military department and Brockhurst can liaise with all of them, if necessary."

Everyone heard the doorbell ring and Mary put her head around the door to announce Mr Brockhurst.

"Show him into the drawing room, Mary," said Lady Maud, "and we will join him immediately. Oh, and ask him if he would like some tea, make some fresh if he does and bring it in to him."

"Right!" Tollman was anxious to get started, "Let's all have a meeting, shall we?"

* * *

Lily King was opening up the shop, when she saw a young woman looking in the shop window and smiling. "I'm open now, if you want anything!" she called out of the doorway and the woman turned around, still smiling and held out her hand.

"Hello…Mrs King? I'm Mattie Grunwald. Thank you so much for looking after the shop for me."

Lily was startled and chose to hug Mattie, rather than shake hands. "You poor thing!" she said with feeling. "Come in, come in. We'll have a natter upstairs. I don't need to open the shop yet. No-one ever comes at this hour anyway!" Then she laughed in embarrassment, "Listen to me, telling you what you already know!"

Lily locked up the shop again and the two women went upstairs. "My husband is out at the moment," she said, "so it's a perfect time for us to have a chat. There are so many things I want to ask you!" She was very pleased by this opportunity.

Over tea and biscuits, Mattie explained that she had consulted her father and he had agreed that she could close the shop and find other employment. He was worried for her safety, running a shop all by herself. Lily could hardly contain her excitement as she explained her plans to open up a haberdashery shop of her own, but in an area of Clapham that would be more profitable and would be a home for her and her husband as well. Mattie looked pleased and then they spoke about the stock. Most of it was paid for, so Lily asked if she could purchase it from Mattie and transport it to Clapham. Mattie said she could and praised Lily for the beautiful window display she had created.

"I think your heart is much more into running a haberdashery shop than mine ever was," confessed Mattie. "My Ma and Pa set the shop up, just after they were married, because he was a tailor and she used to be a seamstress. Sewing was their passion, whereas me…I mean I can sew, but I'm not really interested in it. But I saw in the window, downstairs, that you had made some really lovely bags and doll's clothes for the display, and I realised that you had the same passion as my parents."

Lily nodded. "Yes, I love making things. I was even thinking of creating my own patterns and having them printed, to sell in the shop, and selling things by post as well, to people who don't live in London…ooh, I have so many ideas!"

Then Lily explained that she had not yet broached the subject with Ernest and she wondered if Mattie could come back, later in the day, when Lily would have an answer. "Just so that Ernest can ask you any questions, for reassurance you understand."

Mattie agreed to come back after lunch, as she wanted to go and see a storage place in Victoria and then she would go back to Belgravia and walk the dog, before coming back to Whitechapel. The two women hugged each other, as they parted in the street and Mattie waved as she walked away towards the underground station. It wasn't a cold day but she huddled into her coat as though she felt a chill and preferred to look at the ground, rather than catch the eye of anyone she might know, passing by. She would never forget how they had turned on her and wanted to harm her, because of her name. Mattie felt relieved to be leaving Whitechapel and she would not regret her choice for one minute.

✳ ✳ ✳

Tommy Brockhurst was warmly received by the team – especially the ladies – as his cheerful and informal personality won them all over within minutes. Once it was known that he had been an actor before the war, Sissy whispered to Elsie, "I fancy that I've seen him once on stage at the Princes' Theatre in Shaftesbury Lane." He made Caroline chuckle with some comment about her being too young and attractive to be a surgeon and he made them all smile with an observation that whilst Tollman was supposed to be the head of the team he suspected that it was really Lady Maud who whipped them into shape. In short, he was utterly charming, but Tollman knew that, underneath it all, Brockhurst was also completely ruthless when unpalatable things needed to be organised and done.

Tollman explained to everyone the progress that had been made. He told them about he and Rigsby visiting the Train Watcher's organisation with the piece of silk covered in names and numbers and that it was, indeed, valuable information about enemy troop movements. Then he told them about all he had learned from the Commissioner about the visit to the Romanian ambassador with the Under-Secretary for the Foreign Office and Mr Beech. When he got the part about Thelma Barnes being awake, he said nothing about her father and just said that "Thelma appears to have been some kind of courier and escort for foreign intelligence agents," but it appeared that the Germans were not interested in her, only the Romanian woman. Then he detailed the thorough search that Constable Fowler had done to try and find the vehicle that had been waiting for the kidnappers and their abductees outside the station. Tollman and Fowler had had another look at the company that Fowler had identified and Mr Brockhurst had confirmed that it was 'a place of interest' to the intelligence services. Finally, he asked Billy to speak about his discovery yesterday.

"When we were visiting Mattie Grunwald's father in Alexandra Palace," Billy explained, "he was telling us about an internee called Georgi Hofer, who was released earlier in the day because the Romanian embassy had furnished a birth certificate and passport, proving that he was not Hungarian, and I suddenly realised that that must be the 'Palace' that Marie Radu was going to visit, after the Train Watchers, but because she died, two men from the embassy had to take the papers to the 'Palace' instead." Lady Maud loudly congratulated Billy.

"Did Mr Grunwald happen to mention what these two men looked like? And what this Georgi Hofer's profession was?" Brockhurst suddenly asked, looking thoughtful.

"He said they were two serious-looking men who, he thought, were policemen because Georgi Hofer, when he was younger, was a top safecracker." Billy explained.

Brockhurst gave a half smile and said, "I suspect those men were Siguranţa…the Romanian Secret Intelligence Service. And they won't have gone to the trouble of springing an expert safecracker from an internment camp unless they have a special job for him. The question is…what? Could be bank robbery, could be anything. Word is that the Romanians are looking for something in London…but we can't concern ourselves with that now. We have German psychopaths to catch, before they leave the country. Which brings me to this,"

Brockhurst took a piece of paper out of his pocket. "This morning, I visited two Labour Exchanges in Southwark, within striking distance of the Dutch Pottery Company. In my capacity as a 'special' government employee, I was able to extract the information that the company is in the market for several workers, and I think that we should endeavour to fill those vacancies today. I have arranged for the job listings to be 'filed away' temporarily, so we should be the only people applying for these openings. Firstly, it will be easy enough for Constable Rigsby and I to fulfil the roles of labourers. We are big and strong and young – well, in my case, youngish – but we really need someone, a lady, who speaks and reads German, to fill the very important vacancy of a clerk inside the company's office."

"Well, that would be me," said Mabel, "But, unfortunately, I cannot get any time off work this week, not even if I were sick. Every afternoon, for the next five days, the hospital, the pharmacy and the staff are being inspected by the dreaded Board of Health."

"Oh gosh, yes! I'd forgotten that!" Caroline looked flustered. "Good job you reminded me, Mabel."

"I'm afraid I only have very rudimentary German," offered Lady Maud.

Brockhurst smiled. "Somehow I can't picture you, Lady Maud, as a credible office clerk."

Maud pretended to be offended. "I'm quite a good actress, you know – but point taken."

Sissy spoke up. "We know someone who speaks German like a native…"

"NO!" Billy almost shouted at Sissy, which made her jump. "Mattie is not to be involved in this!"

Elsie said firmly, "Billy, I know you want to protect her, but she has already said that she wants to contribute to the war effort in some way…well, what better way than to help track down the murdering swine that killed the Romanian lady?"

"Because it's dangerous!" said Billy stubbornly.

"Hold up! Hold up!" Tollman decided to intervene. "Without wishing to sound like a hypocrite, as I have just given Mr Barnes a lecture about his daughter doing a very dangerous job, Mattie won't be in danger if you and Tommy are working in the yard and are armed. You will be armed, won't you?" Brockhurst nodded and patted his left chest to indicate that he had a gun, in a shoulder holster. Billy still looked uncertain.

"Are there any jobs at that place for us?" asked Sissy hopefully.

Brockhurst looked at the sheet. "Well, maybe one of you. They want a woman in the packing shed."

"Right, well that will be me, then," she said firmly. "Else can stay home and look after the dog." She turned to Billy, "So, you see, Billy Rigsby, if you two are in the yard, armed to the teeth, and I'm inside the building, with my famous right hook – Mattie will be perfectly safe." As she said it, she brandished her fist at him and everyone laughed.

"I suggest you leave the final decision to the girl herself," observed Maud wisely and everyone agreed.

* * *

Mattie had just returned from finalising matters with Lily and Ernest King about the closure of the shop, when Elsie and Sissy came home, flanked by Billy, Tollman and a man she'd never seen before.

"How did you get on today, love?" asked Elsie, as she picked up Timmy and cuddled him.

"Perfect!" was Mattie's response and she briefly recounted her successful discussions today with Lily and her husband. Tollman chuckled and he explained that Lily had told him of her plans to open her own shop, the moment she had stepped into Mattie's shop.

"Old Ernest didn't stand a chance," he observed, "with you and Lily mounting a pincer attack on him. He would have had to surrender." Tollman then introduced Tommy Brockhurst by saying, "This man here, Mattie, wants to recruit you for an undercover job. You'll be helping us catch some enemy spies."

Billy was about to tell her that she didn't have to do it, but he saw her face light up and her eyes were shining with excitement. "Me?!!" she almost shrieked.

"Let's sit down and have some tea, while Tommy here explains everything to you," suggested Tollman. Billy made sure to sit opposite Mattie, so that she could see him clearly if he shook his head in disapproval.

Brockhurst explained the job. She would be, according to the job description, a clerk in the office of the Dutch Pottery Company, doing a little secretarial work, a little typewriting, some accounts and filing and answering the telephone. He also explained the importance of speaking German but that no-one in the company should know that she could speak and read the language.

"We have suspected this company for some time as working for the German intelligence service but we need proof. Anything that you can discover, from the accounts books, receipts or files, that can help us locate these men who are probably in hiding, waiting for transport back to Germany via Rotterdam, would be most helpful. We know that the Dutch Pottery Company have a planned shipment of goods leaving Tilbury next week, but we don't know which vessel, or whether it is more than one vessel. This you should be able to find out from their order books."

Brockhurst went on to explain that, hopefully, he and Billy would be working as labourers in the yard of the company, they would be carrying concealed firearms, and Sissy would be working in the packing shed. This was all for Mattie's protection. Billy was poised to give her a speech about the danger of it all, to remind her that a woman, not much older than her, had been brutally tortured and killed, but Brockhurst began to caution Mattie about the very same hazards. It made no difference to her. Billy could see that she was determined to do this assignment.

"I can read Dutch too," she said, "but not speak it." She explained that her father had a close friend who lived in Holland and they used to write to each other regularly, in Flemish. Mattie would often read the letters. Brockhurst was impressed and Billy realised that there was no argument he could make, now, that would dissuade her from doing this job and he resigned himself to protecting her as best as he could.

Brockhurst was anxious that they should all present themselves, at slightly different times, during the afternoon, to apply for the jobs, as time was of the essence. So Elsie and Mattie set about making a quick lunch of sandwiches and cake for everyone before they started their new assignment.

Over lunch, Tollman suddenly said "Oh my God!" and clapped his hand to his forehead. He realised that he had completely forgotten to telephone Constable Fowler who, by now, would be trawling around the West End of London, armed with a photograph of Marie Radu, looking for any establishment with the word "Palace" in it that she may have visited. Billy tutted and grinned at the thought of the poor beat copper fruitlessly pounding the streets and said "Never mind, Mr Tollman, you'll have to write him a letter of commendation and take him for a drink. Just tell him that, although he didn't get any results, his efforts were extremely useful to the investigation anyway…or something equally as flattering."

Tollman looked at Billy with surprise. "That's an excellent idea, Billy. Do you know, sometimes you astonish me with your capacity for management. You'll be a Sergeant before you are thirty, mark my words."

* * *

PC Fowler was actually enjoying his task of visiting theatres and restaurants in the West End. There weren't that many 'Palaces' on the list and he had started with the Palace Theatre in Cambridge Circus, where they were showcasing a revue. Pictures of scantily-clad girls were posted outside the theatre, which was attracting the attention of several men and boys. Fowler ignored them and walked round to the stage door entrance at the side and spoke to the elderly stage door manager, seated in a cubby hole to the side. He showed the picture of the Romanian woman to him and asked if she had visited the theatre at all. The man shook his head but said he would ask the proprietor, if Fowler would wait. Then he disappeared up some stairs to an office, returning fairly quickly with a shake of his head and a negative answer. Various artistes, rushing through the stage door for rehearsals were asked if they had seen the woman and they all said "No." So Fowler deemed it time to move on.

He walked through Covent Garden, picking his way through the fruit and vegetable detritus on the cobbles, left over from the early morning wholesale market, and made his way towards Drury Lane. The large theatre there was not his intended destination but a Chinese restaurant opposite, called *The Heavenly Palace*. As he turned into Drury Lane, he noted that there was a small protest taking place. It appeared to be a group that was an amalgamation of the Suffragette Movement and the Anti-Slavery League. They were handing out leaflets and he took one. It said:

> D.W GRIFFITH'S *"BIRTH OF A NATION"*
>
> This scurrilous American moving picture
> should not be shown in Britain as it
> demeans our Commonwealth cousins
> in its portrayal of the negro.
>
> BOYCOTT DRURY LANE THEATRE

P.C. Fowler looked up in interest at the theatre, which was displaying banners announcing the forthcoming showings of the moving picture in question. He wondered if the local police in Bow Street were going to have their work cut out on the opening night. As he turned, he also noticed a dark well-built man, wearing a mackintosh and a brown Homburg hat, was loitering at the end of Drury Lane, looking in a tobacconist's shop window. Fowler frowned. He was aware now that this man had been shadowing him since he boarded the bus south of the river. He hadn't given it much thought at first but, now, he was conscious of the man's persistent presence. He resolved to mention it to Detective Sergeant Tollman tomorrow, when they met up. He redirected his gaze to *The Heavenly Palace* restaurant opposite and had already decided that it was not the place that the murdered woman was likely to have visited but, nevertheless, he liked to do a job properly, so over the road he went.

CHAPTER EIGHTEEN

THE WATCHERS ARE WATCHED

Tollman had left after lunch, as he was of no value to the team undertaking the operation at the Dutch Pottery Company. He simply kissed Sissy and murmured to her to "take care" and left Brockhurst to mastermind everything. In any event, he felt he needed to be at Borough Police station to, firstly, apologise to Constable Fowler, when he returned from his fruitless trawl of the restaurants, theatres and picture houses of the West End and to, secondly, be on hand if there was trouble at the pottery. Borough would be the nearest police station to be mobilised if arrests needed to be made.

It had been agreed that Mattie would give her name as Mathilda Greenwood, which was, after all, the English version of her real name, Sissy would use her real name, whilst Billy Rigsby and Tommy Brockhurst would become Billy Jones and Tommy Meadows.

"Always keep your real Christian name," counselled Brockhurst, "so that you react to it, if it is shouted out in an emergency."

Brockhurst decided that they would go in to the Dutch Pottery Company in dribs and drabs. Billy and Tommy would go first, pretending to be out-of-work mates, Sissy would follow half an hour later and Mattie would appear about fifteen minutes after Sissy.

Knowing it would cause some resistance, Brockhurst nevertheless said to Billy that if there was only one vacancy for a labourer going, Billy must defer to Brockhurst and let it go to him. "I know you are a big, strong lad," Tommy said quietly to Billy, "but, believe me, if anything should kick off and Mattie needs protection, she needs me in there, more than you. I've been trained in every dirty trick going and I know what I'm looking for and how to sense trouble before it's even got its boots on." Billy wasn't convinced but he realised that it was sensible and he nodded unhappily.

"Now, let's get you tooled up," Brockhurst said, as he produced a small gun. Billy's large right hand almost covered the gun and he was just about able to get his finger through the trigger. "I know that you know about guns, Billy, I've read your police notes…"

"You have, have you?" Billy said, in a voice that signalled he was not sure whether he approved.

Brockhurst smiled, "Well I like to know who I'm working with. Helps me know how you might react in a tricky situation. Anyway, this gun is a Beretta, Italian Army issue. Semi-automatic. This is a new model, which stores eight cartridges instead of seven." He pointed at the various parts of the gun. "This is where the magazine loads, at the bottom of the grip. This is where the used cartridge ejects and, with this gun, it tends to fly upwards, so never fire it near your face or you'll lose an eye. The thing that I like about the Beretta is that it is nice and flat and lightweight, which is good for concealment. If you put that in a side trouser pocket, with your wallet in front of it, no one will know that you are carrying a gun. You have a spare magazine here, so you will have 16 bullets in total, which I hope you won't use. If we get into a shooting match, then we're in trouble. The safety device is here."

Billy expertly, by balancing the gun on his rigid left hand, removed and checked the magazine and re-inserted it. He practised a few times, lock and unlocking the safety catch and then practised inserting it in his trouser pocket and quickly removing it. Brockhurst nodded in approval. "Well done, mate," he said and patted Billy on the back.

Elsie, meanwhile, had been applying make-up to Mattie's face, to hide the bruise on her cheekbone, which was disappearing, but not quite fast enough. "There, that should do it," she said, dabbing a last bit of powder on Mattie's skin. "Just remember not to rub your eye or face, or it will all come off."

Sissy had dressed in her most drab clothes, "Does this make me look respectable but poor?" she asked Elsie.

Unable to resist, Elsie said quickly, "Sis, you've never been respectable, but it will do." Sissy laughed and made a show of being about to slap Elsie. It was a bright spot of humour which made the tense group of individuals relax.

Brockhurst gave everyone a last pep-talk. "The point of this exercise is to find out information – not to engage in any dangerous behaviour. Be calm, be careful, be watchful. Mattie and Sissy, if you are, at any time, concerned about the atmosphere in the place, feel that someone is watching you, feel you might have made a mistake, don't panic, come out to the yard and find me. Pretend to tell me off for swearing, or something and I will know you are in trouble."

Everyone nodded. Elsie kissed Billy, Mattie and Sissy and said to Brockhurst, in a stern voice, "Now you look after them, Mr Brockhurst, I'm relying on you." Tommy grinned and promised he would and they all left to scatter to use different transport to take them to Southwark and the Dutch Pottery Company.

Tommy Brockhurst was very good at his job. He was sharp and observant and could fight his way out of any trouble but, on this afternoon, he failed to notice the well-muscled, dark-haired man, dressed like a labourer, who was sitting on a bench in the garden square opposite the house and who got up and began to follow Tommy and Billy, at a distance. Elsie noticed him, however, because she had decided to take Timmy for a walk and she passed the man just after he had deposited the newspaper he was reading into a public bin in the square. As she watched him go along the pavement, in the same direction as Tommy and Billy, she felt a pang of anxiety, not really knowing why. He disappeared around the corner and Elsie decided to look in the bin at the entrance to the garden square, and fish out the newspaper the man had been reading. It was foreign but she couldn't make out what language it was in. She decided to keep it, until the team got back this evening. So, she tucked it under her arm whilst she walked around with Timmy.

She felt a knot tighten in the pit of her stomach. *Perhaps they are being watched,* she thought to herself as she let the dog off his lead so that he could happily snuffle in and out of the shrubs. But she had no way of warning them and she thought that she could just be imagining things anyway. *All this spy business gives me the willies*, she decided and she wondered how she was going to take her mind off things until they all came back safely this evening.

* * *

Billy and Tommy were fortunate in that the Dutch Pottery Company were preparing to load a great many crates on to one lorry bound for the port at Tilbury and were, also, expecting a delivery from up north of a large quantity of clay. So, both were hired on the spot, no questions asked. The manager just saw the bulk and height of the two young men and that was enough for him. He was just showing them the requirements of the job – which were quite simple really, they had to be gentle with the loading of the crates and fast at shovelling the powdered clay under cover, in case it rained – when another well-built man sauntered in asking for a labourer's job. He had a foreign accent and he was dark-eyed and dark haired. When asked by the manager what nationality he was, he answered "Greek." Brockhurst was immediately suspicious.

Anyway, all three of them and the one labourer who was already employed, called Harold, set to, gently loading the heavy crates, full of completed pottery, on to the waiting lorry. It seemed like a never-ending task, as every time they took a crate from the stack, it would be replaced with another one, brought out from the pottery by two women. It was the strength required by these women that got Sissy her job, when she appeared some ten minutes later. The manager looked at her hands and noted that they were not rough and calloused, he asked her if she had ever done 'delicate' work and she swiftly invented a story of her hobby, when she could afford it, was doing intricate embroidery. Then he asked her if she was strong, asked she answered firmly "yes". He seemed satisfied and told her that she had the job and he took her through to the packing shed, where there were shelves from floor to ceiling, packed with rows and rows of beautifully painted and glazed pottery vases, teapots, sugar bowls, larger bowls and decorative plates. He introduced her to another woman, called Alice, who then showed her how they carefully inspected the pieces, then packed the items in straw, in the crates. Once the crate was full, it was inspected by Alice, then sealed, and two women would carry it out to the labourers, who would load it on the lorry.

"It's a simple job but you must be very careful not to damage anything," added Alice. Sissy assured her that she understood. She was shown where to hang her coat and hat, and where the ladies' facilities were, and she had just started packing her first crate when she saw Mattie walking across the yard.

Billy was shocked when Tommy suddenly gave a wolf-whistle as Mattie walked past but then realised he was playing a part and grinned. Mattie blushed suitably and hurried her steps as a natural reaction to unwanted male attention. Brockhurst was silently appreciative of how well things were playing out and winked at Billy.

The manager looked both surprised and gratified that all his employment needs appeared to being fulfilled in one afternoon. He stood and shook Mattie's hand and introduced himself as Mr Steen. She noted that his very slight pronounciation of the S of his name as 'Sch' betrayed the fact that he was not British but, otherwise, his English was impeccable. He asked Mattie various questions and, as instructed by Brockhurst, Mattie answered that her name was Mathilda Greenwood, otherwise known as Mattie. She had run a shop for her father, but he had died and so she was forced to give up the shop. She had bookkeeping, secretarial and typewriting skills and really needed a job urgently, "to keep the wolf from the door, as it were, Mr Steen." He nodded and said he perfectly well understood. He explained the salary he was offering – a very generous twelve shillings a week, payable every Friday – and he said that "providing her hand was good" (meaning her writing), the job was hers. "On a week's trial," he said and he immediately set her to work typing up some handwritten invoices, furnishing her with all the necessary stationery. Billy could see, from the yard, that Mattie was sitting in front of a typewriter and he indicated so to Brockhurst with a sideways inclination of his head. Brockhurst wiped his brow and winked again at Billy. So far, so good.

* * *

Beech awoke in the perfumed vastness of his lover's bed and wondered what time and day of the week it was. For the past however-many days, he had existed only within the formidable countess' arms. They had occasionally broken off from their lovemaking, talking and sleeping to eat from a tray left outside the room but, mostly, they had ignored the food, preferring to stay in the intimacy of the great bed and each other's bodies.

Bit by bit she had told him her life story – virtually from beautiful peasant girl to marriage to a middle-aged count, who had died within a few years of their marriage, leaving her a very rich widow. Beech privately wondered whether she had killed the count with her physical appetite, for she truly seemed, at times, to be insatiable, and he smiled. *So far*, he thought, with a sense of pride, *I have not failed when she has made demands of me.* She called him "My Warrior". Whispered it in his ear, whilst tugging on his ear lobe with her teeth. He called her "Beloved", yet he knew that he did not love her. He had not told her his life story, realising that it was so boring that it would not entrance her. She knew that he was the son of a Baronet, which impressed her, and he had been a soldier. That was enough for her to weave, in her own mind, a picture of an aristocratic military hero and that stimulated her.

She would tell him about Romania...the mountains, the wild scenery, the horses that she loved to ride, the Court of the Royal Family, "I am pledged, with all my soul, to work for the monarchy of Romania," she had said fervently, but then had added, "but the present Queen, once a British Princess, is foolish and makes rash decisions which others have to repair." She had pronounced the Romanian Court as "very stuffy, since the old king died." The late King Carol had been, apparently, at some point, one of her lovers, briefly. Beech suspected that her lovers did not last very long. They either did not match up to her demands or she grew bored with them for other reasons.

Now, he was a very different Peter Beech from the man who trembled with indecision at the thought of his desire for her...the man who would have made an excuse and fled from her, when he had first arrived in her house. Not only had she taught him the art of lovemaking, in its many variations, but she had proved to him that he was an attractive and virile man. Far from turning away from the long, jagged scar on his leg, her lips had traced its length in a ribbon of kisses and filled him with astonishment. She was utterly passionate about everything but he suspected that her passions frequently burnt themselves out. For the moment, she was enchanted with him, with his youth and his initial timidity. He suspected that it gave her a thrill to be able to take the rough clay of a man and mould him into something magnificent. She had certainly done that to him. He now felt invincible, powerful, charismatic and confident. He was totally her creation and he was grateful for it.

Beech smiled and turned over to sleep some more.

The countess, meanwhile, had slipped from the bed to write a brief note to her 'chauffeur', to leave on the tray outside the door. It said, simply, in Romanian:

> Both deeds must be done tonight.
> We leave with the coffin on Wednesday.

* * *

Mattie had proved that her writing was clear and precise, so Mr Steen gave her the accounts book and a pile of bills. "Put them in date order and enter them into the accounts book," he had asked and he had given her a few examples of what bill would be entered in what column. "Ask me, if you are unsure," he said, and left her to it. She had been given a briefing by Tollman and Brockhurst what to look out for. "Anything about a vessel called the *Ariadne*." Tollman had said. "That was the boat where we found the kidnapped women. Someone must have chartered that vessel for the men. I doubt they would have done it themselves." Brockhurst had urged her to note the addresses of any room rentals. "These Germans must be hiding somewhere near to the docks. I suspect someone arranged for them to have lodgings for a few days. They could all be lodging together or separately, so it could be more than one bill for accommodation." There had been a note of hope in his voice, although he wasn't altogether sure such details would manifest themselves. "Also," he had added, "any correspondence in German, which you must memorise, if you can." Billy had looked for some sign that Mattie was overwhelmed, and he could step in and call it all off, but her face had just radiated happiness at being included in this great adventure.

As she was sorting all the miscellaneous bills into date order, to enter into the book, she found the very name that Tollman had mentioned, the m.v. *Ariadne*. The bill was for two weeks' charter, the vessel to be collected at Tilbury and taken up the river Thames to Letts Wharf, South Bank. The start of the charter period was two days before the women had been abducted. Mattie made a mental note. Eventually, she came across a bill for the charter of another vessel – a Dutch barge named m.v. *Winhaven* - berthed at Gravesend – and finally a bill for charter of the vessel named on all the crates out in the yard – the HMS *Eendracht*, to be loaded at Tilbury today and tomorrow and to set sail on Wednesday. She decided, as Mr Steen had been called urgently into the packing shed, to make a note of all the vessels and put the note in her coat pocket. She kept darting looks out of the window in front of her, to make sure that Mr Steen was not approaching. Her eyes were so fixed on the door to the packing shed that she neglected to see that the Greek labourer was watching her intently. Her task completed, she stood up and put the piece of paper in the pocket of her coat and then sat down again quickly. Pleased with herself, she started entering the amounts of the bills into the accounts book.

Sissy was enjoying herself packing up the pottery. It was an easy enough job, if you were careful, and everyone seemed quite friendly. The only bit of excitement was when a girl screamed, which nearly made Sissy drop the teapot she was packing. The girl had stuck her hand in one of the barrels of straw and been bitten by an angry mouse that had taken up residence. Mr Steen had been called and Alice had lodged a complaint. The girl who had been bitten was now crying and was claiming that she was going to 'die of plague, or some such thing!' Mr Steen had shouted for Mattie, after trying to reason with the girl, and Mattie had abandoned her accounts to go over to the packing shed. Mr Steen then asked Mattie to put her coat on and run round to the pharmacy in the next road, to purchase some iodine. "Here's a shilling," he said, taking it from his own pocket. "It shouldn't be more than that."

So, she ran back to the office to fetch her coat. The Greek labourer was coming out of the office with his hand wrapped up, as though he had hurt it and he grunted at her, in his thick accent, "Wash cut in sink," then disappeared back out to the yard.

Mattie put her coat on, walked across the yard and called loudly to Mr Steen, so that everyone in the yard could hear, "I'm off to the pharmacy then, Mr Steen – won't be long!" She looked at Billy and he gave the briefest of nods, then she left. When she got to the pharmacy, she asked for the iodine, paid for it and put the change in her pocket. That was when she realised that her note about the chartered vessels had gone. In a panic she ran back to the pottery and looked around for the Greek labourer, because he was the only one who had been in the office whilst she and Mr Steen were absent – but he was nowhere to be seen.

"Where is the Greek man who had cut his hand?" she said loudly, and the three remaining men came off the lorry and looked around.

"He must have gone, Miss," said Harold, "but I didn't see him go…did either of you?" he asked Billy and Tommy. They both shook their heads and Tommy looked annoyed. He was a man who didn't like to admit that he had taken his eye off everyone briefly. "Did you want him, Miss?" asked Harold.

Mattie held up the bottle of iodine and said "Mr Steen sent me to buy this and I just thought he might like me to put some on his hand, that was all. He was in the office before I left, washing his hand, and he said he'd cut it." She was looking at Tommy and hoping that he would get her message that the Greek man had been up to no good.

Tommy bit his lip in irritation and said, "He was grumbling about the work earlier, he was probably looking for an excuse to skive off."

"Was he grumbling?" Harold looked puzzled as he hadn't heard the Greek man say anything.

"Of course he was!" Tommy said firmly, "but it was in Greek! I know a Greek swear word when I hear one. I used to work on the ships in Battersea Reach. That's where they unload all the wine and raisins. Place is crawling with Greek seamen down there."

"Oh," said Harold, losing interest. "Well, he's done an

afternoon's work for no pay. More fool him." He shrugged.

Mattie ran into the packing shed with the iodine and the change for Mr Steen and Alice began to administer the orange liquid to the bite whilst the girl in question cried a bit more with pain. Then Alice demanded that Mr Steen get rid of the barrel that contained the rodent and Mattie took her opportunity to run back to the office and write down, again, the names of the chartered vessels and their locations. This time she removed her clean handkerchief from where it was tucked up her sleeve, wrapped it round the piece of paper and pushed it back up her sleeve. She wouldn't make the same mistake again of putting it in an easily accessible pocket.

The rest of the afternoon was uneventful, although there was not much left of the day, and Billy could see that Brockhurst was impatient to get away from the pottery and get back to Belgravia. He had realised that Mattie was trying to tell him something and he wanted to find out what it was. When the lorry had finished loading and had departed for Tilbury, Mr Steen gathered everyone together and praised them for a good day's work. He made particular mention of Mathilda, as he called her, and said that she appeared to be a valuable addition to the workforce. Mattie almost felt sorry for him, as she thought it was probable that none of them would be turning up tomorrow and Mr Steen would be in a bind.

They slowly left the premises, in ones and twos, and Mattie was expecting to be returning to Belgravia on the omnibus alone, but she found Billy and Tommy waiting for her, around the corner, near the bus stop. Billy wrapped his arms round her at once, grateful that the day was over and Tommy anxiously asked her what had caused the mysterious disappearance of the 'Greek'.

"Who wasn't Greek, by the way," he said with great authority. "I speak a little Greek and I tried to have a conversation with him at one point. His Greek was bad and he had a definite Balkan accent – maybe Serbia or Bulgaria – I don't know."

Mattie told him about her discoveries, and then explained that she had written them down on a piece of paper and put it in her coat pocket. Then she got called to the packing shed and when she came back, the Greek had been coming out of the office, with his hand wrapped up. When she bought the iodine from the pharmacy, she realised that the paper was no longer in her pocket. "But I managed to make another copy," she added, which made Brockhurst's eyes light up, and she retrieved the piece of paper from her sleeve and gave it to him. He hurriedly read it and exclaimed "Of course! They are keeping the kidnappers on a barge in Gravesend. I should have realised. No enemy aliens are allowed to live within five miles of any port or military area, and no landlord, no matter how sympathetic to the German cause, is going to risk giving bed and board to a foreigner, in case they are reported. But in a barge on the river? Any foreign men can come and go, without arousing any suspicion. People assume they are merchant sailors from allied countries." He then looked worried. "It seems our 'Greek' friend may get to them before we do. Perhaps to warn them. There is no time to lose. Billy, can you get hold of Tollman? He'll want to be in on this." Billy said that he was at Borough Police Station and he could go and fetch him. Brockhurst agreed but told him to tell Tollman to meet him at Scotland Yard. "I'm going to hail a taxicab and go there straight away. I need to get my department to organise the River Police at Blackwall. Time is of the essence."

CHAPTER NINETEEN

A TWO-PRONGED ATTACK

Tollman was adamant, when he telephoned Brockhurst at Scotland Yard. He wanted to arrest the manager of the Dutch Pottery Company, whilst Brockhurst went after the Germans hiding in the barge on the river.

"After all the work we have done, I'm not handing over this case to Special Branch so that they can waltz in and take the glory," he said firmly. "Anyway, you don't need Billy and me when you've got a bunch of armed River Police to back you up." Brockhurst could see the sense in this. They agreed that Tollman would mobilise Borough Police station to get warrants for the search of the Dutch Pottery Company and the arrest of the manager, Mr Steen. Brockhurst had already set in motion what was needed at his end, and they would liaise later at Elsie and Sissy's place, or tomorrow in Mayfair.

Tollman put the telephone down and turned to the Station Sergeant. "I need you to get hold of your tame Justice of the Peace to sign a couple of warrants. Tell him it's a matter of national security and he must move quickly. We'll type up the warrants and send PC Fowler round with them, to get his signature." The Sergeant nodded and began to dial on the telephone. Tollman then turned to Billy and Mattie and said, "Right, you two will come with us because I need Mattie to identify the documents in question and, probably, go through any other paperwork in the place, which might be in Dutch or German, that could be relevant. I'm going to type up the warrants now, so Billy, you telephone your mum and explain briefly what is happening and tell her that we will be round after it's all done and dusted."

Just then, P.C. Fowler appeared, in his plain clothes, about to clock off his shift. Tollman said loudly, "Constable Fowler! Go and put your uniform back on, lad! You are about to run an important errand!" and he winked at the Station Sergeant. Tollman was in a good mood. He liked making arrests. It was a satisfactory conclusion to a case.

* * *

When Sissy got home, she found Elsie sitting, furiously knitting what looked like a 'cabbie's chest protector' – a garment which was, basically, a scarf but with a square piece tacked on the front that went over a gentleman's chest and tucked in his waistcoat.

"Oh! Thank God you're home in one piece!" Elsie cried dramatically, as she flung down her knitting and hugged her sister.

Sissy was astonished. "I've only been packing teapots for an afternoon," she said with a laugh, "not packing munitions." But her smile disappeared when Elsie told her about the man who had been watching the house and had followed Tommy and Billy. She showed Sissy the foreign newspaper he had been reading.

"I had no way of letting you all know!" Elsie said, "I've been so worried."

Sissy asked her if she could remember what the man looked like and, when Elsie described him, Sissy realised that the 'Greek' labourer who disappeared and the man who was watching the house, were the same individual.

"Well, he didn't harm anyone," Sissy explained, "It was a bit odd, really. He just disappeared before the end of the day. Didn't collect any wages, or anything."

"Oh! I am relieved," Elsie moved to the sink to fill up the kettle. "So, what was the job like?"

"Not bad at all," Sissy answered. "In fact, if I was in the market for a job, I could quite take to that one. Much better than cleaning railway trains! And I got a teapot at the end of it!" She produced a beautiful blue teapot from her bag that was painted with charming spring flowers.

"Oh, it's lovely! Did you steal it?"

"Elsie Rigsby, what do you take me for?!" Sissy was outraged. "The supervisor gave it to me. It's only 'seconds',"

Just then the telephone rang and the operator put Billy through. He explained to his mother that he and Mattie would be some time, as they were about to participate in the arrest of the Manager of the Dutch Pottery Company. When Elsie relayed this to Sissy, she pulled a regretful face. "I quite liked Mr Steen," she commented, "I never would have taken him for a wrong 'un. Now all those poor ladies will be out of a job."

Elsie commiserated with her sister and decided to christen Sissy's new teapot. So, she poured some boiled water into the pot to warm it up. Immediately, it began to leak from where the spout was attached to the body of the pot.

"Now we know why it was 'seconds'," she shrieked, as she rushed towards the sink to allow the hot water to safely discharge.

Sissy sighed. "Never mind. It will make a pretty ornament."

* * *

Brockhurst and two men from MI5(g) were on a Royal Navy motor launch, which had come from Greenwich to pick them up at Westminster Pier, and they were now speeding, at a rate of 15 knots, down river towards Blackwall. The river was very choppy and the military intelligence men were being thrown off their legs occasionally by the wind whipping off the estuary. Once they reached the Blackwall pier of the river police, they took on a waiting team of six policemen – all armed. Then the launch moved off towards Tilbury Docks, where they would swing out into the upriver current and turn to find the barge, the *Winhaven*, moored at Gravesend, on the opposite bank of the Thames to Tilbury. Brockhurst was very tense. He had a gnawing feeling that whoever the 'Greek' had reported to was at least an hour or more ahead of them.

Very large commercial vessels were now littering the river. Those that could not get into Tilbury port, were at anchor in various positions across the river, loading into lighters. The motor launch slowed down in order to begin manoeuvring around the big ships and across the Thames to be facing upstream and approach the shoreline of Gravesend. Added to the volume of moored vessels and general river traffic, there was also the newly erected Tilbury section of a pontoon bridge to negotiate around. The bridge, made of wooden lengths of walkway, supported by flat-bottomed lighters, normally stretched for around half a mile between Tilbury and Gravesend but sections of it could be moved to allow for shipping traffic to pass through. The residents of both towns had no idea why it had been constructed, and they rarely used it, preferring the age-old provision of the regular Gravesend to Tilbury ferry, but Brockhurst, being privy to some military secrets, knew that the purpose was a military one. It had been built to allow fast access for troops to get from one side of the river to the other in the case of invasion.

The river was so littered with vessels, all queuing for the port or unloading that the captain of the motor launch was forced to go almost as far as Canvey Island, where it broadened out into the estuary, in order to turn and head back along the southern bank of the river.

Finally, the captain pointed out the lights of Gravesend in the distance. It was quite dark now and the launch was cautiously making its way towards its destination but being wary of the great expanse of the North Kent marshes on the port side. "The river gets very shallow and there are lots of small inlets," the captain explained to Brockhurst. "We don't want to run aground."

Finally, the lights strung along the 80-yard-long remaining section of the Gravesend part of the pontoon bridge came into view, next to a large hotel, which stood grandly overlooking the river. There were a couple of piers after that – one obviously used by the Gravesend to Tilbury Ferry, as it was docking as they passed – but the captain of the launch was heading for Northfleet Dockyard, where he was expecting to be met by an officer of the artillery regiment currently based at the barracks in Gravesend. The Royal Navy, before picking up Brockhurst at Westminster had organised a discreet search for the *Winhaven* barge by the Gravesend military. "After all," the captain had explained to Tommy, as the MI5(g) men had embarked, "It's going to take us almost two hours to get to Gravesend. We don't want to waste that time." The military were under strict orders to 'identify and observe only'. The pleasure of arrest would be for Brockhurst's men and the armed River Police only.

The waiting artillery captain informed Brockhurst that they had found the barge, there were lamps lit inside the vessel, and it was moored on the river near Gravesend West Station. They would have to approach on foot. So, the three military intelligence men, of which Brockhurst was one, and the six River Police, set out, led by the artillery Captain and three of his armed men, picked up along the way. The route along the riverside was quiet, it being the hour when most people were indoors and eating their evening meal. There were some noises from pubs along the way and the occasional vessel still unloading. As they passed the station, there was the grinding and screeching sound of a train engine being turned around on a turntable and various men shouting instructions. Beyond the station, all was quiet. There, by the waterside was the m.v. *Winhaven*, tied up both ends to cleats on a wooden pontoon and gently moving her squat metal frame backwards and forwards with the ebb and flow of the water. There was the gentle flickering of lamp light in two of the windows.

Brockhurst nodded to the leader of the River Police, a sergeant, who, in turn, motioned his men and, in their rubber boots, they slowly and noiselessly boarded the vessel, guns at the ready. Brockhurst indicated to the artillery captain, that his men should wait on the pontoon, in case any of the Germans managed to exit the boat on the landside. The River Police would fish any escapees out of the river, if they jumped out of the barge that way. They were used to entering the water to retrieve people – dead or alive.

Brockhurst gave a 'thumbs-up' to the police and then, from the gangplank he shouted as loudly as he could in German:

"Come out! We are all armed! You are being arrested under the Defence of the Realm Act!"

There was no response. No sound of feet scrambling inside the boat. No shouted replies. Nothing.

"Dammit, they're not there!" Brockhurst muttered under his breath. Then he shouted, "Right! Gain entry!"

The River Police, shouting more warnings, opened the door down to the cabin, It was unlocked. Brockhurst and his men followed them in a scramble down four steps into a wide -open cabin. Then, there was silence from all of them as they surveyed the bodies of the three Germans, laying in pools of blood, their throats having been cut from ear to ear. On the bare wall of the cabin was written in blood:

Răzbunare pentru Marie Radu

"The Romanians," said Brockhurst, with a short sardonic laugh. "The bloody Romanians got here first."

"What does it mean, Mr Brockhurst? The writing on the wall?" asked the River Police Sergeant.

"Well, my Romanian is a bit patchy," Brockhurst answered, "but I'm pretty sure it means 'Vengeance for Marie Radu', who is the Romanian woman that they killed."

* * *

"My darling Warrior," the countess breathed into Beech's ear, as he lay sleeping again, after an earlier, particularly energetic, bout of lovemaking. "I have been summoned by the Ambassador but I will return in an hour or so. If you want anything, just ring the bell, and my maid will bring you food, drink or anything else." He noted that she was fully dressed.

Beech murmured assent and, as she kissed him once more, he mumbled "Hurry back."

Once she had departed, he waited for a few minutes and then left the bed to pad over to the window that overlooked the street. He watched from the darkness of the room as the countess, escorted by two heavy-set men, got into a waiting automobile in front of the building. Someone was waiting in the car for her, he saw a hand reach out and assist her into the car. *The Ambassador?* Beech wondered, then the vehicle drew away.

He realised that he was now cold and so he wrapped himself in a blanket. He was also a little light-headed, having spent so much time laying in bed and not enough time standing up. He turned the lights on in the room and made his way into the adjoining bathroom, to drink some tap water, as he felt dehydrated as well. The bathroom was full of expensive crystal bottles of perfumes, pots of creams, vials of lotions and more. *Mm, the dark arts of remaining so beautiful in middle age,* Beech thought as he peered into pot after pot.

He decided to run a bath and, while it was filling, he pottered around the countess' bedroom, looking at the bits and pieces on her writing desk. There was a large brown file, which he opened, and it contained a great many photographs of Queen Marie of Romania. Beech would never have had any idea who the aristocratic lady, if it were not for the fact that there were also some magazine articles about her – some British, some French and an American magazine. They had all been written before the war, showing the Queen of Romania in various exotic evening dresses and, in every picture, she was festooned with jewellery and different tiaras. Finally, there was a sheet of typed paper, which seemed to be an inventory of the jewellery. Beech put back the file where he had found it and shrugged. *Perhaps the countess is jealous of the Queen's jewellery*, he thought. *Perhaps she covets those baubles.* His bath was ready and he thought no more about it as he sank into the hot water and winced slightly. There were certain parts of his body that were…a little sore.

* * *

Tollman, Billy, Constable Fowler and three other policemen from Borough Police Station, with Mattie waiting at a safe distance, issued warning shouts and, upon no response, broke into the office of the Dutch Pottery Company. There was no-one there, so Mattie was summoned and she began to go through the invoices, to pull out the ones that related to the charters of the three vessels. Then, because there could be more evidence to incriminate Mr Steen, it was decided that Mattie, guarded by two of the Borough policemen, who had been issued with firearms, would continue to search through all the paperwork to try and find more evidence of espionage involvement, whilst the rest of them went to Mr Steen's home to arrest him.

Tollman had been furnished with the address by the Station Sergeant at Borough who, like all good Station Sergeants, kept the list of local companies' proprietors up to date, so that the police could contact them in case of fire or burglary at their place of work. So, Tollman, and three armed policemen turned up at the residence of Mr Steen, just as he was sitting down to his evening meal. Tollman pounded on the door and a frightened woman opened it. "Madam! We have a warrant for the arrest of one, Diederik Jacob Steen, on charges of espionage and aiding the enemy in time of war." The woman screamed and Steen came running out into the hallway, his napkin still tucked into his short collar.

"What is this? What is this?" Steen was angry and frightened at the same time. Billy grabbed him and handcuffed him whilst Tollman recited chapter and verse of his crimes that they could, so far prove, with the distinct possibility that their search of the company premises at this very moment, would yield up more evidence to incriminate him. Steen protested in the strongest terms, lapsing into Dutch as he became ever-more worried.

Tollman held up his hand. "Save it, Mr Steen. Although I am arresting you, and taking you to Scotland Yard, where we will record this arrest, we will then be handing you over to military intelligence. God help you from then on. I don't know what rules they play by and I don't want to know." Steen had gone very quiet and pale. "Is this your wife?" Tollman asked and Steen nodded. Regretfully, Tollman then said, "Constable Fowler, put your handcuffs on the lady and bring her along."

"She has done nothing!" Steen insisted and then he spoke to his wife in Dutch. It didn't seem to Tollman that he was trying to comfort the sobbing woman but rather issuing harsh instructions for her to keep her mouth shut. She was too distressed to respond and Tollman barked at Billy to "remove this piece of dirt before I lose my temper." So, Billy dragged him out to the waiting vehicle.

Tollman shouted, "I'll ring the Yard to send another vehicle, so you go ahead with Steen. We will follow, with the wife, after we have sealed the place for MI5(g) to go through everything." Then he turned to Fowler. "You can come with me to the Yard, with this lady in your custody, whilst you, son," he turned to the remaining Borough constable, "can go back to your station and tell your sergeant that you need another vehicle to take Miss Mattie, and all her evidence, to Scotland Yard."

When Tollman arrived at the Yard, female prisoner in tow, Sergeant Stenton was just finishing logging in Mr Steen and locking him in one of the cells. "A Mr Brockhurst, from military intelligence, telephoned from Blackwall River Police Station for you, Tollman."

"Oh, yes?" Tollman smiled, expecting to hear good news. "What did he have to say?"

Stenton consulted his notes. "He said he's on his way back but they were too late. The Germans were all dead when they got there."

"Oh!" Tollman sounded surprised. "Well, I suppose it saves the Scots Guards having to put together a firing squad at the Tower of London...'cos that's where they would have ended up."

"True," agreed Stenton as he turned his attention to P.C. Fowler and his sobbing prisoner. "So, lad. Who do we have here?"

"Another German spy," said Fowler.

"Cor Blimey!" exclaimed Stenton. "They're coming out of the woodwork tonight!"

* * *

It was very late when they were all finished. Billy had waited for Mattie, who had arrived at Scotland Yard with armfuls of documents, which all had to be entered into the evidence file and only Mattie could explain what each document was, as they were all in Dutch or German. There were copies of cryptic telegrams to addresses in Rotterdam. There were letters written to foreign individuals in Britain, which had nothing to do with the pottery business. Steen had obviously kept copies of everything, perhaps for his own security? That was for the military intelligence men to find out.

By the time Tommy Brockhurst pitched up at Scotland Yard, Mattie, with the assistance of Sergeant Stenton, had almost finished and there was a nice fat file of incriminating evidence to take to MI5(g). To Brockhurst, this just about compensated for the loss of the German assassins in Gravesend but he had understood why the Romanians did what they did.

"They're not in the war...yet," he said to Tollman, "So they weren't interested in the value of those German men to

British intelligence. They just wanted revenge for the murder of Marie Radu. They're a passionate lot, Romanians. You wouldn't want to cross them." With that, he gathered up Mattie's file of documents and signed for them, as he would be taking them to MI5(g) headquarters. "I'll pop round to Lady Maud's house for a debriefing in the morning," was his parting shot to Tollman, and to Mattie he said, "Well done, young lady. I can see that you have a great future in espionage."

Mattie smiled but Billy said, "Oh no, she doesn't. I don't want her ending up like Thelma Barnes and Marie Radu."

Brockhurst looked at Billy's concerned face and Mattie's dismay. He paused and thought for a moment. "What if I told you that there was the perfect...and safe...job for Mattie...and one that was vital to the war effort. Would that be acceptable to you, Billy Rigsby?"

Billy nodded but Mattie said firmly, "Mr Brockhurst, it's *my* choice whether I take a job or not. No one else's," and she gave Billy a defiant look, which made him flush.

"Mattie," Brockhurst said softly, "Of course it's your choice, but be grateful that someone cares enough about you to want to protect you. I know that I would be." With that parting shot, he left.

Billy said softly, "Sorry, I didn't mean to interfere. It is your choice, of course. It's just, if you had seen those two kidnapped women when we found them, you would understand my fears. But I'm sorry..." he couldn't think of anything else to say and he just trailed off.

Mattie nodded, then she kissed his cheek. "I forgive you. I know you're only looking out for me." She wrapped her arms around him and laid her head on his chest. "Poor Mr Brockhurst. I think he is very lonely, you know."

Billy nodded and stroked her hair. "Yes. I don't imagine that being in his job allows for him to form relationships with people. No-one like him can hope for any companionship until this war finishes."

* * *

It was almost two o'clock in the morning when the countess returned from her 'meeting with the Ambassador' and Beech was awoken by her stroking his face.

"My darling," she said softly, "This is to be our last night together, I'm afraid. I have to leave for Romania on the boat train tomorrow night at midnight."

Beech turned on the light and looked at the clock on the wall, "You mean tonight, don't you? I have lost track of time a little but I think that it is probably the early hours of Wednesday morning."

The countess said, "You are right, of course. So, we have only a few hours to say our goodbyes."

Beech smiled, if a little wearily, then he sat up in bed and kissed her passionately, whilst beginning to undress his lover.

"My Warrior..." she murmured, in a haze of passion, "who has become a mighty Warrior..."

Then all verbal communication between them ceased.

CHAPTER TWENTY

A GOVERNMENT CRISIS

The whole team, plus Mattie but, minus, at the moment, Tommy Brockhurst, was gathered at Lady Maud's for breakfast. Billy, Mattie and Tollman were tired, having been up until nearly midnight, processing documents and locking up spies at Scotland Yard. Sergeant Stenton had telephoned Tollman at almost the point he had arrived at the Mayfair house, to report that the night sergeant had released the two prisoners into the custody of military intelligence at two o'clock in the morning, and he had Lieutenant Colonel Vernon Kell's signature on the release papers. "So that's that, Arthur," said Stenton cheerfully. "Another case completed." Tollman had grunted in agreement and put the receiver down to go and find some reviving tea.

They were all sitting in relative silence. Mattie had been overawed by Lady Maud, Victoria, Caroline and Mabel. "Such important and well-educated ladies," she would say to Elsie and Sissy later and they would tell her not to be silly. In fact, as they all gathered some breakfast from the buffet, Mattie watched in wonderment as everyone chatted easily to Lady Maud, who seemed to Mattie to be almost one step down from the Queen. There was a gentle hum of conversation between various groups of two or three, as they sat down around the vast dining table. It was a tranquil scene.

Then suddenly, like a blast of energy coming through the door, Peter Beech was in the room, brimming with life, vitality and confidence. "Morning everyone!" he said cheerily as he took Maud's hand and planted a kiss upon it. Nine pairs of eyebrows shot up at this unaccustomed gesture by Beech.

"Peter! You look as though you have lost weight," commented Maud mischievously, "Have you been unwell?"

"Never felt better in my life," he answered breezily and advanced on the display of food on the sideboard. "Absolutely starving though," he announced, piling eggs, bacon, sausage and bread on his plate. Billy nearly choked on his tea trying to suppress a laugh and Tollman glared at him. Mattie, who had never met Chief Inspector Beech before, just stared at him and almost fell out of her chair when he grinned and winked at her. All the other women recoiled slightly with shock. Caroline, who had known Beech since childhood found herself thinking, *I don't know that I have ever seen Peter wink at a woman,* ***ever****!*

Beech, in between mouthfuls, said that he had spoken to the Commissioner about the case that they had just completed and he conveyed to them Sir Edward's admiration for the work they had done.

"We missed your guiding hand, sir," said Tollman, determined not to let his boss off scot-free.

"Ah yes, apologies for my absence," he said blithely, scooping up another portion of bacon. "I was engaged on diplomatic work." A smile played around Lady Maud's mouth, which she tried desperately to control. "Anyway," Beech continued, getting up to help himself to more bread, "I hear that you did splendidly without me. MI5(g) are full of praise." As Beech turned back to his seat, Tommy Brockhurst entered, looking tired. Spotting Beech, he went up to him, hand extended, and said, "I presume you are Chief Inspector Beech?

I'm Tommy Brockhurst from military intelligence, by the way."

"I am honoured to meet you!" Beech leapt to his feet and pumped Brockurst's hand enthusiastically. "Sir Edward was singing your praises this morning. Thank you for guiding my team so effectively."

"Pleasure," said Tommy, looking around the table. "It's quite a team you've got here, I have to say, Beech. Vernon Kell says it was all your idea." Beech nodded and smiled. Caroline noted that, BTC (Before The Countess, as she had decided to call it), Peter would have been all embarrassment and evasiveness when he was complimented, almost as if he felt he didn't deserve the attention. The new Peter was confident and accepting of praise. *It will take some getting used to,* she thought.

"I've just come to wrap things up, as it were," explained Brockhurst. "About what happened last night."

"Absolutely!" Beech agreed and he swept his empty plate up off the table. "Sit here, at the head, and then everyone can see you. I'll go and sit next to Tollman. Would you like some tea or coffee, Brockhurst?" Tommy nodded, asked for coffee, then took his coat off and sat in the chair Beech had vacated. Beech placed a cup of coffee in front of him and sat down with Tollman, patting the Detective Sergeant on the back, and disconcerting him again. Tollman wasn't used to Mr Beech being over-familiar. Like Caroline, he felt it would take some getting used to. Meanwhile he gave him a watery smile and nodded.

All eyes were on Brockhurst whilst he explained about his dash down the river Thames to Gravesend, in the hope of capturing the German assassins, but was sadly foiled by the Siguranţa – the Romanian Secret Intelligence Service. "I could kick myself, really," he said. "I should have suspected the phoney Greek labourer earlier – the one who stole information from Mattie's pocket and disappeared..."

Elsie interrupted to tell him about the man she had seen follow them, when they had left to go to the pottery yesterday afternoon. She showed Brockhurst the newspaper she had retrieved and said, "I was beside myself with worry but I couldn't think of a way of warning you."

"No, of course you couldn't, Mrs Rigsby." Brockhurst assured her. "We were just lucky that the phoney Greek wasn't hightailing it to Gravesend to *warn* the Germans and help them get away. I should have liked to extract some information from them but I suppose it is enough that the Romanians killed them for their brutality towards Marie Radu."

"There is one question that I have," said Caroline, raising her hand tentatively. Brockhurst nodded in encouragement. "How could they be so sure that the Zeppelin bombing would happen at the right time and cause the train to stop at that virtually disued station at Blackfriars Road?"

Brockhurst smiled. "A German Zeppelin commander can be utterly precise in how long it will take his ship to get to London from its docking point, by measuring wind speed, the weight of his vessel fully loaded with bombs etc. Also, I suspect that the kidnappers would have had some plan in place to stop the train in the event of unforeseen circumstances. Plus, we have to factor in the utter reliability of our railways during wartime. They have never been so efficient and, at the moment, run like clockwork and one can guarantee that they will be in a certain spot at a certain time. However, Mr Steen, who was waiting for them in the pottery company lorry, had been told to wait for several hours, just to be sure. Anyway, we also had our own good luck with Deitrick Steen and his wife, thanks to you and, most importantly, Mattie here..."

Everyone, led by Beech, broke into a spontaneous round of applause, which made Mattie turn bright red with embarrassment.

"Steen is looking at a life sentence, rather than execution, because of the amount of information he voluntarily gave us..."

"Voluntarily?" said Tollman suspiciously.

Brockhurst gave a sardonic laugh. "Yes, Tollman. We didn't lay a finger on him! After we had described what we *might* do to him and the fact that he was facing execution by a firing squad, Mr Steen couldn't tell us chapter and verse fast enough! His wife was merely a postbox and had no real involvement in any of it, other than knowing vaguely what her husband was up to. It is down to the judge whether she is imprisoned or deported. So..." Brockhurst stood up and started to put his coat on again. "I have been assigned to another job and shall leave you to your next case...oh! Except for this..." he drew a letter from his pocket and gave it to Mattie. "It's a letter of recommendation from Kell, Head of MI5(g) to the War Office Postal Control Department, recommending you, as a German speaker, who has already undertaken secret work for military intelligence, for a job in the Post Office Censorship Department. You are to report to a Mrs Waldheim at this address at 9 a.m. tomorrow and start training immediately."

Mattie gasped and clasped her hands to her face. Brockhurst looked at Billy and smiled. Then he said, "Mattie, you will be doing nothing more dangerous than reading and examining hundreds of letters written by Germans and Austrians to other Germans and Austrians, either resident in Britain or abroad. It's an important job. We have caught many German agents through this channel. So, do you think it might suit you?"

Mattie nodded and couldn't hold back the tears. Sissy hugged her and said, "There now. You got what you wanted. A proper job that contributes to the war effort."

"I can't thank you enough, Mr Brockhurst," said Mattie.

"My pleasure." Then Brockhurst went round and shook everyone's hand. Before he left, he said one final thing. "If you should see me in the street sometime, don't acknowledge me. I may be working undercover and cannot break from character. I apologise in advance but this is the game I'm in. It's harsh, I know." Then he left.

There was a silence of appreciation around the room which was suddenly broken by the telephone in the hallway ringing. Mary answered it, stuck her head around the door and said, "The Commissioner for Mr Beech, m'lady."

Beech looked curious and went into the hallway. After a brief conversation, he came back into the room and said, cheerfully, "We have another case. It's a burglary, which sounds rather odd. It's shrouded in mystery and only myself, Tollman and Rigsby are needed, for the moment."

"Well, if you want an examination of the scene done,"

observed Mabel, "Caroline and I are only available until midday, then we have a hospital inspection. But we could do something after 5 o'clock. As long as you seal off the scene of the crime and don't allow it to be disturbed."

Victoria said nothing. Caroline noted that she had been flushed and subdued ever since Beech had appeared this morning. Lady Maud announced she had letters to write anyway and Sissy and Elsie were simply grateful for a day off, after the train cleaning and drama of the last few days. Mattie was still on cloud nine, clutching her introduction letter to her chest like it was a missive from the King.

Somehow, a burglary seemed rather a low-key case for the Mayfair team.

* * *

Tollman, Rigsby and Beech stood in the Commissioner's office whilst an unusually irritated Sir Edward explained that there had been a crime...and yet there had *not* been a crime.

"In other words," he added, "a crime has been committed but it is not anything that we can prosecute or really investigate, but we must be seen to be doing something."

Tollman was confused. Ever the man who liked clean instructions about criminal behaviour, he was becoming almost as irritated as Sir Edward.

Finally, the Commissioner said, "It is a diplomatic matter and it involves a member of the government."

Finally, the penny dropped. "Ah" said Tollman knowledgeably. He had been a policeman for long enough to know that it was almost impossible to prosecute a member of the government. Parliament and the political parties would close ranks and the matter would be 'made to disappear.'

"So, what is it that you want us to actually do, sir?" asked a bemused Beech.

Sir Edward thought for a moment. "I dislike the Metropolitan Police used in this way but we must be seen to do something. There has been a robbery at the London Silver Vaults in Chancery Lane. A strongroom, which is registered to a member of the aristocracy who is also a member of the War Cabinet, has been expertly broken into, and a large quantity of valuables have been stolen. The thing is..." he paused as he tried to frame the delicate matter as best he could, "the valuables did not belong to the person to whom the strongroom was registered..." he trailed off, unable to find the words to describe such a peculiar situation.

Tollman needed clarification, so he said, "Excuse me sir, but, if I have this straight, someone stole some valuables from this toff, who, himself, had stolen them from someone else?"

Sir Edward seemed uncomfortable with the description and all he could say was, "Possibly."

Beech, Tollman and Rigsby looked at each other in confusion.

"So how, exactly, can we assist with this strange case, sir?" Beech asked.

"Right...yes, of course," the Commissioner said awkwardly. "Well, it may seem a bit of a fruitless task, men, but Tollman and Rigsby must go and arrest a man called Georgi Hofer..."

"Bloody hell!" Tollman couldn't help his outburst and

he immediately said, "I do beg your pardon, Commissioner."

Sir Edward raised an eyebrow and continued, "...recently released from Alexandra Palace internment camp under a Romanian passport and currently residing at this address...so I'm told." He passed a piece of paper to Tollman.

"Yes, we know of this man. Constable Rigsby happened to be at Alexandra Palace the day that this Hofer was released. Expert safe cracker we understand." Tollman explained.

Sir Edward nodded. "He may, of course, have left the country, but we have to try. Here is a warrant for his arrest." He passed another piece of paper to Tollman. "If you find him, just bring him in for questioning. I suspect that we will be unable to prove anything."

Tollman nodded and indicated to Billy that they should go. All three men turned to leave but Sir Edward said, "Chief Inspector Beech, please stay. You and I need to go to the Foreign Office."

Once Tollman and Rigsby had left, Sir Edward said, "We have to visit Lord Robert Cecil once more, for an explanation of what, exactly, has happened. At the moment, you know as much as I do. Very unsatisfactory, the whole thing."

＊ ＊ ＊

Tollman and Rigsby were on their way to West Kensington, to the address given to them by the Commissioner.

"I hate doing things like this," muttered Tollman. "Being used as errand boys in a case that involves the aristocracy. If we find this bloke and arrest him, he'll get a nice cup of tea at Scotland Yard and then some embassy functionary will appear and claim that he's got diplomatic immunity...you mark my words."

"It's very odd that this Georgi Hofer is implicated in this business," observed Billy. "Do you think he was sprung from the internment camp to specifically do this job?"

Tollman thought about it and decided that it was a reasonable supposition. "Brockhurst mentioned that the word was that the Romanians were looking for something. I shouldn't be at all surprised."

"But the Silver Vaults has a military guard," said Billy, "I know someone who did a stint there. I wonder how they overcame them and pulled off a robbery?"

"I think that the blokes who got to Gravesend ahead of our intelligence services and cut the throats of a bunch of Germans, can probably pull off anything, don't you?" Tollman said sarcastically.

They reached the designated address, only to be told by the landlady that "Mr Hofer – a very nice man - left early this morning for Romania," Tollman nodded and thanked the woman.

"Wild goose chase, of course." He said to Billy matter-of-factly. "The commissioner knew it would be. But, of course, we have to now go back to the Yard and fill in a report, so that he has something to show the powers-that-be when they ask what the police did to pursue the case. But," he said, as they walked towards the station, "there is a very nice pub round the corner. As we are not technically on duty, I suggest we have a pint of beer before we go back and do the blasted paperwork."

Billy grinned and Tollman led the way to the warmth and companionship of the pub.

* * *

Beech and Sir Edward sat opposite Lord Robert Cecil who was not his usual amiable self. In fact, he was simmering with rage and frustration.

"Years of diplomatic negotiations ruined by one egocentric member of the House of Lords!" he thundered.

Then he calmed down, poured himself and his two visitors a large scotch each and explained that Queen Marie of Romania, being a British Princess by birth, and the cousin of King George V, had unwisely, but in good faith, sent all her large and very valuable jewel collection to King George for safekeeping, in case the Hungarians invaded Romania. This was a private matter between the King and his relative, that the government knew nothing about, at the time. The War Cabinet, of course, were very anxious that Romania, with all its oilfields, should not fall into the hands of the enemy and had been using all its powers to persuade Romania to enter the war on the Allied side, so that Britain would have a valid excuse to send troops in to Romania to protect its assets.

"This member of the British aristocracy, whom I am forbidden to name," thundered Lord Robert, "took it upon himself to persuade the King, with whom he is great friends, to hand over the Romanian jewel collection to the safekeeping of the government. By which he meant himself – for he, most certainly, did not speak for the government - and none of us knew anything about it. He then bypassed the usual diplomatic channels and intimated to the Romanian Ambassador that the jewels would be sold to the highest bidder if Romania did not agree to declare war on Austria-Hungary. In other words, this man tried to blackmail the Romanians."

The words were spoken bitterly and an awkward silence hung in the air.

Lord Robert continued. "This man came to me this morning, in a state of high anxiety, and confessed all. His strong room at the London Silver Vaults had been stripped bare – all except for this," and he held up one large pearl and diamond teardrop earring. "The Romanian Ambassador is refusing to see me," Lord Robert said with a note of despair in his voice. "However, he has agreed to see Chief Inspector Beech."

Beech looked surprised. "Me? Why me? I've only met the man once!"

"Apparently, it is due to the intervention of the Countess of Covasna. She assured the Ambassador that you are an honourable man and can be trusted."

Beech flushed slightly and Sir Edward looked amused.

"What do you want me to say?" Beech asked.

"I have written down a formal apology in this letter," said Lord Robert, and he handed over an envelope bearing an official wax seal. "It has been signed by the Prime Minister and myself. It assures the Romanians that the British government knew nothing of the jewel collection; considers the jewel collection to be Romanian property and no further action will be taken over the unorthodox way in which the jewels were reclaimed. The member of the aristocracy who has disgraced the British government will be dealt with discreetly but the Ambassador should be assured that the man will be punished. And you can give this earring to the countess, to complete the collection."

Lord Robert looked relieved when Beech answered that he would, of course, undertake the assignment.

"Good. Thank you, Beech. The government is most appreciative, I can assure you, and the Ambassador is expecting you at one this afternoon."

* * *

Ambassador Mişu broke open the seal of the letter and read it in silence. Then he looked up at Beech and nodded grimly.

"You can tell Lord Robert, Mr Beech, that I accept his and his government's apology. However, I should like you to take a message to him for me." Beech waited respectfully as the Ambassador gathered his thoughts. "You can tell him that Romania is a proud, as well as rich, country. We know that the Allies want to stop our assets from being used by the other side and that they also want us to act as a bulwark for Russia. They want our soldiers to give their lives to save the Russian front line. But we will not be bullied, threatened, bribed or tricked into a decision. We will make it in our own time – on *our* terms. I think the British have had a demonstration of what we will do to achieve our aims. We will not allow *our* women to be indiscriminately killed by Germans and we will not allow *our* property to be used to blackmail us. Soon, our King and Queen will make a decision about our part in the war. Tell Lord Robert he must be patient."

Beech confirmed that he would deliver the message.

"Now," said the Ambassador, "if you will follow me, please, the Countess of Covasna would like to say her goodbyes."

Beech followed the Ambassador down a corridor, to a door which was flanked by two grim-faced men – one of whom he recognised as the countesses' 'chauffeur'. The Ambassador gave a sign and the two men opened the doors and Beech was waved into the embassy's private chapel, where he found himself alone with the countess, who was praying.

She stood and threw her arms around him, murmuring words of endearment in his ear. He stroked her hair and asked, "This is our real goodbye, then?" She said it was, and a small tear trickled down her beautiful face.

Beech produced the pearl and diamond earring and the countess smiled. "Come," she said, "I will make Marie complete."

Beech had been so absorbed with the countess, that he had failed to register the open coffin laid on a trestle table in front of the small altar. As they approached, the countess made the sign of the cross. Beech stared at the contents of the coffin. There was the cold, lifeless body of Marie Radu and every inch of her corpse was covered in glittering jewels. She was wearing a magnificent tiara on her brow; around her neck were diamonds and ropes of pearls. Every finger, on the hands crossed over her breasts, wore huge diamond, sapphire and ruby rings; her arms were girdled by sparkling bracelets and bangles; and in her ears, one pearl and diamond drop earring. The countess bent over the body, kissed the dead woman's forehead and applied the earring Beech had given her, to Marie's naked ear.

"Marie Radu will make her last journey as a courier," the countess said, brushing away another tear, "and it is fitting that she should look like a Queen for her final return to Romania."

"Was she really your cousin?" asked Beech.

The countess shook her head. "No, that was a lie. But she was like a sister to me. We were both women who would undertake any task for our country."

"Was I one of your 'tasks'?" asked Beech.

"No!" the countess was horrified that he should ask such a thing and came round the coffin to fling her arms around him once more. "You were...are...my genuine passion. A wonderful encounter that made my life perfect for a short while."

They kissed again and Beech felt a pang of sorrow that they were actually parting forever.

"Never forget me," she whispered, "but you must marry one day...and when you do...Peter Beech...make sure you marry a woman with fire in her soul, or you will become weak and fearful again. Stay as a warrior, my love." Then she turned and left through a side door, leaving him with the bejewelled corpse of Marie Radu.

EPILOGUE

Mattie Grunwald was thrilled with her new job at the Post Office Censorship Department. After her first day she had come home to Belgravia and told them about all the things she had learned about searching for secret messages in letters and postcards. She told them how she and another girl had carefully prised apart postcards and photographs with razor blades to see if there were any messages in between the layers of card. Then she told them about ironing handwritten letters with a warm iron to reveal messages written in invisible ink in the margins, which would be shown up as soon as the paper was heated.

Elsie, Sissy and Billy had hung on her every word and marvelled at the espionage tricks that she told them in confidence.

However, the smile had been wiped off Billy's face when Mattie told them that she had accepted a place in the women's hostel attached to the Censorship Department. He had hoped that she would lodge with his family and he would have constant access to her. Elsie had laid her hand on Billy's arm and given him a warning glance.

"This is Mattie's chance, son, to make friends amongst the other women and to not be judged because of her name, because they are all in the same boat," she had said wisely. Billy could see the sense of this but it had irked him, nonetheless.

Elsie and Sissy had purposefully left the two young people alone for a while, to sort out this little problem. Mattie had kissed Billy's check and assured him that nothing would affect their relationship. "We can see each other every evening, if we want, like regular boyfriend and girlfriend – it won't make any difference, I promise." She stroked his face lovingly.

Billy had sulked a little and had found it difficult to see why Mattie wanted to live with a bunch of women that she saw all day. She, for her part, had said that she refused to be dominated. Billy should trust her and be glad that she was making friends. "I can't restrict my world to this house and you," she had said firmly. "I want to be independent and if you can't accept that, then I don't see a future for us, Billy Rigsby."

Billy said he would think about it but, in his heart, he knew that she was right. He would have to adjust to a different kind of relationship with Mattie – even if it meant that eventually he might lose her.

* * *

Tollman was exhausted from helping Lily and Ernest King move into their new premises in Battersea. Lily was almost hoarse from shrieking instructions to the two men to "mind you don't trail that fabric roll on the floor!"; "Watch what you are doing with that box of china!" and other such admonishments.

Finally, when Arthur and Ernest had moved the entire stock of Mattie's old shop to Lily's new shop; supervised the removal to storage of the personal effects of Mattie and her father; and emptied Ernest and Lily's house in Clapham into the new flat above the new shop – both men were ready to drop. This was exacerbated by the arrival of Tollman's daughters, fresh from their day's work at the department store at Clapham Junction. They had promised Lily they would help get everything straight and the noise level, comprising of shrieks of approval, laughter and arguing, had gone through the roof.

Arthur and Ernest wisely decided to take themselves off to the nearest pub.

"Women," said a weary Ernest as he supped his pint of beer. "They always get their way and make plenty of noise about it while they are doing it."

"Huh!" retorted Tollman, "Don't expect me to sympathise, Ernest. You only have one daughter – and she's married and off your hands. I've got three of them at home, constantly squabbling, constantly giving me cheek and constantly ignoring any of my requests. If you lived in my house, you would consider the Western Front a peaceful rest."

Ernest considered this for a moment and just said with feeling, "You poor bugger."

The two men drank their beer in blissful silence, which was only interrupted by the quiet murmur of other men who had, probably, also escaped the tyranny of their womenfolk.

* * *

Beech had stopped by Maud's house after a dinner engagement, looking very dapper in evening dress, and he found Caroline and Maud still up, drinking tea and quietly chatting.

"No Victoria?" he idly enquired, helping himself to a cup of tea.

"No, I've sent her away to my sister in Cheshire." Maud said firmly. "Her moodiness was getting on my nerves and I felt she needed some bracing countryside walks and a good dose of my sister's lack of patience with modern women." She allowed herself a chuckle at the thought of her daughter being given a lesson in life from her thoroughly no-nonsense aunt.

"Ah, I see," responded Beech, with a meagre amount of interest. "And how are you, Caro?" he asked, with genuine solicitation.

"I'm fine!" Caroline said brightly. "Mabel and I survived the Board of Health inspections. Matron and the Hospital Administrator nearly had nervous breakdowns but we pulled through!" she laughed and Beech smiled warmly.

"Well, if you'll excuse me, young people," Maud announced, "I am going to take myself off to bed. I've had a whole day of charity committee work and I feel as though my brains are scrambled." She kissed both of them on the cheek and left the drawing room. Beech wandered over to the window and gazed out at the square opposite the house. He fancied it was beginning to rain.

"And how are *you*, Peter?" asked Caroline softly from just behind him. He turned and gave her a quizzical look.

"Never better," he said affably.

"You know that you have changed a great deal, don't you? More confident, you've bought yourself some new suits, there is even a little swagger in your step..." Caroline observed.

Beech laughed and a little of his old shyness peeped through for a moment. "Yes, I know I've changed, Caro. For the better, I hope."

Caroline shrugged and said, "Time will tell, Peter. We all have to get used to the 'new' you." Then she boldly asked, "Did you love her very much...the beautiful countess?"

Beech smiled ruefully and shook his head. "No. I loved her for what she did for me as a man. In a few days, with her passion and formidable energy, she taught me to value myself more highly. I will always be in her debt for that. But I didn't love her in the true sense of the word."

Caroline digested this piece of information and wasn't sure how to respond. She could feel herself blushing a little and wondering what to say next. She decided she had lost courage and mumbled that she should go to bed and gave Beech a kiss on the cheek. There was a moment when Beech brushed her face with his hand, then it was over, and she hastily left the room.

Beech turned back to the window and murmured to himself, "Doctor Caroline Allardyce, I wonder, do you have fire in your soul?"

THE END

BOOKS BY THE SAME AUTHOR

IRIS BOOKS

THE MAYFAIR 100 SERIES

COMPELLING CRIME DRAMAS SET IN WW1

Women are flooding into
London to do men's work
and a different team of
detectives is needed.

www.irisbooks.co.uk

Available from www.irisbooks.co.uk. Also from Amazon (in Kindle too),
and can be ordered from your local bookshop.

FOR YOUNG AND NOT-SO-YOUNG ADULTS

THE NATHAN FOX SERIES

ELIZABETHAN ESPIONAGE, BLOODY BATTLES, CODE-BREAKING AND SORCERY...

The Nathan Fox Trilogy

what more could you want?

www.irisbooks.co.uk

IRIS BOOKS

HISTORICAL NON FICTION TO ENJOY

Can you cook as well as a 10 year old girl in 1900?

Practical Cookery classes were just beginning to be taught in primary schools then, and this book is a compilation of the little text books that were handed out to pupils at the start of the 20th Century.

THE 100 YEAR OLD SCHOOL COOKBOOK

A compilation of British domestic science textbooks from 1900 to 1920

With over 130 pages of recipes from a bygone age, this book is a nostalgic treat!

IRIS BOOKS

Available from www.irisbooks.co.uk, other online outlets, and the book can be ordered through your local UK bookshop. We can ship worldwide.

HISTORICAL NON FICTION TO ENJOY

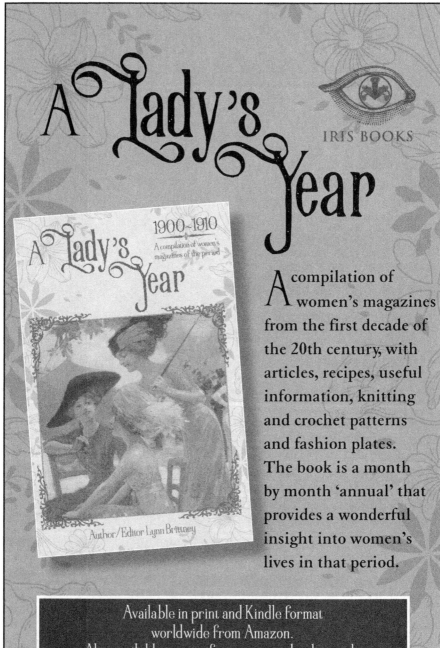

A Lady's Year

IRIS BOOKS

1900~1910
A compilation of women's magazines of the period

A Lady's Year

Author/Editor Lynn Brittney

A compilation of women's magazines from the first decade of the 20th century, with articles, recipes, useful information, knitting and crochet patterns and fashion plates. The book is a month by month 'annual' that provides a wonderful insight into women's lives in that period.

Available in print and Kindle format worldwide from Amazon.
Also available in print from www.irisbooks.co.uk.